Janny Wurts is the author of several successful fantasy novels including the Cycle of Fire trilogy (*Stormwarden*, *The Keeper of the Keys* and *Shadowfane*). She is co-author, with Raymond E. Feist, of the bestselling Empire series (*Daughter of the Empire*, *Servant of the Empire* and *Mistress of the Empire*).

Her next work is the remarkable series, *The Wars of Light and Shadow*.

She is also a talented and successful illustrator.

Also by Janny Wurts

Sorcerer's Legacy
Stormwarden
Keeper of the Keys
Shadowfane

With Raymond E. Feist

Daughter of the Empire
Servant of the Empire
Mistress of the Empire

JANNY WURTS

The Master of Whitestorm

Grafton
An Imprint of HarperCollins*Publishers*

Grafton
An Imprint of HarperCollins*Publishers*
77–85 Fulham Palace Road,
Hammersmith, London W6 8JB

Special overseas edition 1992
This edition published by Grafton 1992
9 8 7 6 5 4 3 2

First published in Great Britain by
HarperCollins*Publishers*

Copyright © Janny Wurts 1992

The Author asserts the moral right to
be identified as the author of this work

ISBN 0 586 21068 7

Set in Century Old Style

Printed in Great Britain by
HarperCollinsManufacturing Glasgow

This book is for three behind-the-scenes
who make of their work in publishing
much more than a job:

Elaine Chubb
Jonathan Matson
Peter Schneider

ACKNOWLEDGMENTS

My warmest personal thanks to these folks
who have made my life as an author possible:

Dot Gerke, my former landlady,
for the roof under which to make dreams

Topher Wurts, for keeping the apple alive

Don Maitz, for asking, "Is it done yet?"

The Eleven Kingdoms
of
Aerith

0   40   60 70 75 77.5

scale in leagues

I. The Galleys of Mhurga

Jostled from sleep by the bang of a fist against the beechwood oar which pillowed his head, Haldeth started upright, muscles tensed reflexively. But the command he expected never came; no guttural shout followed to transform the night into a misery of hardship, rowing against endless ranks of sea swells. By the dim fall of moonlight through the aft oarports, Haldeth surveyed the lower deck of the galley *Nallga*. Every slave remained hunched and still over his loom, but one. The blow which roused him had not arisen from his Mhurgai masters, but from his own benchmate, in a useless fit of rage.

Annoyed himself, Haldeth forgot tact. "Mind your temper!" he whispered urgently.

The man at his side looked up. Confronted by gray eyes and a face which held no trace of laughter or compassion, Haldeth felt his breath catch in his throat. Gooseflesh chilled his skin. Although the air was tropical and mild, he shivered and glanced aside, reminded of the first night his benchmate had been dragged on board. As a battered, soot-streaked captive not yet past his seventeenth summer, that savage look had been with him then, graven upon young features by the atrocities of the Mhurgai who routinely pillaged and burned towns on the shores of Illantyr. But who he was, and what family he had owned before he was chained for the oar, Haldeth never knew. The boy had grown to manhood in stony silence.

The Mhurgai called him *Darjir*, sullen one, for the flat, unflinching glare he returned when anyone addressed him. No man heard him speak, even through three years of abuse on *Nallga's* lower deck. Haldeth believed him insane.

The cruelty of the Mhurgai could drive the strongest

mind to madness, Haldeth well knew. Soured by bitter memories, he shifted a foot cramped by the bite of the galley's floorboards. Even now, he suffered nightmares of his wife and two daughters; they had been butchered before his eyes the day his own freedom was lost. Daily he cursed the smith's constitution which bound him to life and health, for other than hair turned prematurely white, seven years as a galley slave had changed him little. Haldeth envied Darjir's witlessness. Better to feel nothing than to endure the ache of grief and hatred, helplessly chained.

Sleep alone afforded respite. Determined to take full advantage of the hours *Nallga* would remain at anchor, Haldeth leaned once more across the oar and settled his head on crossed wrists. Darjir's eyes followed him restlessly, luminous as coins in the moonlight.

"Neth Everlasting!" Haldeth lifted a resentful fist to emphasize his meaning since words were wasted effort on a man never heard to utter an intelligent sound. "Bother somebody else, will you? *I've had enough.*"

Darjir flexed callused fingers against the oar. Then he lifted his head and spoke with sudden, startling clarity. "I'm going to get off this hulk." His tone cut like the wind's edge in winter.

Haldeth gasped. Shocked, he took a moment to react. *No man escaped the bench of a Mhurgai galley alive.* Attempts earned agonizing punishment, and since by custom the fate of the offender would be shared by the slaves surrounding him, a man dared not trust his fellows. Through three centuries of marauding, the Mhurgai held no record of slave mutiny; *Nallga* made an unlikely choice for exception. Caught by an involuntary shudder, Haldeth shook his head. "Be still!"

Darjir moved his ankle. A dissonant rattle of chain destroyed the night silence. "*I've* had enough."

"Quiet, fool!" Haldeth felt fear, cold as the touch of bare steel against his neck. "The forward oarsman will kick in your ribs if he wakes and hears you."

"I was named Korendir. And I'm getting off." The words left no chink for argument.

Haldeth abandoned the attempt. Nervously, he surveyed the forms of the surrounding slaves for any trace of movement. But the lower deck remained peacefully undisturbed, quiet but for the lap of water against the hull. Prompted by reckless impulse, Haldeth met Korendir's gaze.

"I'm with you." The steadiness of his voice amazed him. "I'd prefer the knife found me guilty."

Korendir's bearded features split into a slow, ill-practiced smile which left the flint in his eyes unsoftened. "I thought you might."

Haldeth bent once more over his oar, but sleep would not come. Years of suffering had inured him to his fate; he knew in his heart that Korendir's proposition was nothing but desperate folly. Sweat sprang along his naked back. No mercy would be shown should their plot be discovered; and even if they managed to escape their chains, the Mhurgai collared their slaves with iron. The sea made an infallible warden. Reminded by the ceaseless slap of waves against the hull, Haldeth hoped the water would claim his life. The knives of a Mhurga seaman never killed. They crippled.

"*Bhaka! Bhaka!*" *Nallga*'s mate shouted the call to rise from the companionway ladder.

Haldeth roused from an unpleasant dream and knuckled gummed eyelids. Dawn purpled the calm of the harbor beyond the oarport; in the half-light of the lower deck, the unkempt complement of *Nallga*'s slaves stirred and stretched. The mate strode aft, thick hands striking the back of any man slow to lift his head. Swarthy, round-shouldered, and short, the officer wore no shirt. Scarlet pantaloons were bound at his waist with gemstudded, woven gold; a whip and a cutlass hung in shoulder scabbards from crossbelts on his chest, companioned by a brace of throwing knives and a chased dagger.

Haldeth shifted uneasily. Mhurgai sported weapons like women wore jewelry, even to the four-inch skewers which decorated their earlobes. Conscious of damp palms and a hollow stomach, the ex-smith cursed his impetuous pact with Korendir the night before. Surely as steel would rust, the plan could only lead to grief.

The mate strutted like a fighting cock down the gangway and glowered over the double rows of captives. "Out oars!"

Haldeth moved at his order, one with a hundred men

who unshipped fifty oars counterweighted with lead and held them poised over the sea. A deep rumble sounded overhead, and shadow striped the oarports as the upper-deck slaves followed suit.

"Forward, stroke!"

With a drumbeat to set the speed the shafts dipped, shearing *Nallga* ahead against the tide. Chain rattled in the hawse as the deck crew raised anchor, but whether the galley left port for plunder or commerce, Haldeth could not guess. He bent his back to the oar, flawlessly coordinated with the man at his side. Korendir's face remained as expressionless as ever beneath his tangled bronze hair. Except for the memory of his given name, the plot and the promise exchanged in the night might have been hallucination caused by too many years of confinement.

By noon the air below decks became humid and close. Sweat traced the bodies of the rowers, and the waterboy made rounds with bucket, mug, and a sack of dry biscuit. Haldeth chewed his portion, resentfully watching the mate dine on salt pork, beer, fresh bread, and grapes, provisioned at *Nallga*'s last port. Though the man's eye-lids drooped, his ear remained tuned to the oar stroke; not even the lethargy of a full stomach would lighten his whiphand if he caught a lagging slave.

Korendir paid the mate little mind. He pulled his end of the oar one-handed and flicked weevils from his biscuit with a cracked thumbnail. Though bugs invariably infested the entire lump of hardtack, he never over-looked one. Haldeth endured the extra weight of the loom without complaint. Bored to the edge of contempt by Korendir's fussy habit, he nearly missed the discrepancy even as it happened: his benchmate passed up an obvious cluster of insects and raised the biscuit to his mouth.

Korendir tasted the mistake the moment he bit down. He choked, and with a swift, thoughtless gesture, thrust his face through the oarport to spit over the gunwale.

Haldeth tightened his grip on the loom. Should a wave dislodge the oar from its rowlock, Korendir risked his neck and head to a hundred and twenty pounds of leaded beech shoved by water with an eight-yard mechanical advantage. Haldeth cursed and leaned anxiously into the next stroke. More than once he had seen slaves killed by such carelessness.

Korendir ignored the danger. He emptied his mouth with unhurried calm, then executed a pitched imitation of the captain's gruff voice. "Alhar!" Deflected by water, the shout seemed to issue from above decks. "Get topside, thou son of a lice-ridden camel tender!"

The mate flinched. His sallow features suffused with rage, and weapons, mustache, and tasseled pigtail quivered as he sprang to his feet and stamped the length of the gangway. Haldeth felt his heart pound within his breast. But the mate passed without glancing aside, even as Korendir withdrew from the oarport, stupidly intent upon his biscuit.

"Great Neth," murmured Haldeth. Perspiration threaded his temples. The Mhurgai language was not a tongue readily mastered by foreigners; Korendir's ruse indicated painstaking forethought. Yet however well planned his intentions, Haldeth perceived no advantage to be gained through a trick upon the mate. The man was notoriously bad tempered; his unpleasant mood would shortly be vented upon the hapless backs of the slaves.

Korendir finished his meal. He licked his fingers and returned his hand to the oar, apparently unruffled by the raised voices abovedecks. Between strokes, Haldeth caught fragments of the mate's protest, clipped short by a bitten phrase of denial; the captain had summoned no one on deck, far less attached insult to such an order. He dismissed the mate amid startled laughter from the crew. Since gossip thrived on shipboard as nowhere else, the unfortunate officer immediately became the butt of spirited chaffing. Haldeth knew even the waterboy would smile at the mate's idiocy before the incident was forgotten.

Shortly, the red-faced and furious mate stamped down the companionway. Braced for trouble, Haldeth glanced at his benchmate. Korendir never flicked a muscle. His mouth described as grim a line as ever in the past, even when the mate ordered double speed from the rowers with vengeful disregard for the heat.

The drumbeat quickened. *Nallga*'s oars slashed into

the water. Waves creamed into spray beneath her dragon
figurehead as the full complement of her two hundred
slaves bent to increase stroke. Faster paces were normally maintained only to keep the slaves in battle trim;
today, the drill extended unreasonably long. Soon the
most seasoned palms split, blistered and raw, and each
stroke became a separate labor of endurance. Blood
pounded in Haldeth's ears, cut periodically by the crack
of the lash as the mate laid his whip across some unfortunate laggard's back. With lungs aching and eyes stung
blind with sweat, he reflected that Korendir's fellow captives would pound the life from his body should they
discover him responsible for the mate's ugly mood. Yet
the man himself bore the agonies of exertion with impassive lack of regret.

The mate's fury did not abate until the waterboy arrived with evening rations. Sensible enough to recall that
unfed slaves made slow passage, the officer restored his
whip to his belt and at last slackened the pace. Beaten
with exhaustion, Haldeth dropped his head on crossed
wrists. Since the evening meal was more lavish than that
served at midday, the slaves ate in shifts, permitted use
of both hands. But like Haldeth, most of the men were
far too winded to eat. Still irritable, the mate paced the
gangway, urging them to haste with his whipstock until
the night officer reported for duty. Soon after he called
the order for rest, heavy sleep claimed the entire lower
deck.

Nallga held course under reduced speed, driven by her
upper oars. Midnight would bring a reversal, the lower
oarsmen resuming work while the slaves above slept until
dawn. The wind blew steadily off the starboard quarter,
and the galley's single, square sail curved against a zenith
bright with tropical constellations. Mhurga's fleet plied
south in winter, to avoid the cold, storm-ridden waters
of their native latitude. In expectation of mild seas and
fair sky, the captain retired below, which left the quartermaster the only officer awake on deck. Phosphorescence
plumed like smoke beneath the galley's keel. The lisp of
her wake astern described a rare interval of peace between the frailty of wood and sinew, and the ruthless
demands of the ocean.

"*Bhaka*! Out oars! Reverse stroke!" The shout disrupted the night like a warcry, its bitten, authoritative tones unmistakably the mate's.

The lower deck oars ran out with a rumble. Dry blades lapped into water, muscled by a hundred rudely wakened slaves. Entrenched in the long established rhythm of forward stroke, the exhausted upperdeck rowers adapted sluggishly to the change. Chaos resulted.

Slammed by the conflicting thrust of her oars, *Nallga* slewed. Crewmen crashed like puppets against bulkhead and rail. The sail backwinded with a bang which tore through boltrope and sheet. Canvas thundered untamed aloft while the oars crossed and snarled, slapped aside by the swell. Leaded beech punched the ribcages of some rowers with bone-snapping force, and a barrage of agonized screams arose from the benches.

"Oars in! Quartermaster, hard aport!"

Nallga's captain pounded up the companionway, still naked from his berth. His hand clutched a bleeding shoulder, and his face was purpled with outrage above his broad chest.

"Send the mate on deck!" he bellowed to the nearest seaman. While the galley rounded to windward, he turned on the quartermaster and shouted over the crack of wind-whipped canvas. "What in Zhaird's blackest pit provoked that nullard's act of stupidity?"

The quartermaster had no answer. *Nallga* rocked gently, her bow pointed to windward. A stricken groan from the benches recalled the captain to his responsibilities. He issued rapid orders. Hands ran aloft to subdue the mainsail and assess damage. Escorted by the heavily armed bulk of the ship's marshal, the healer made rounds of the slave benches to tend the injured. His task took the better part of the night.

The mate spent an unpleasant interval in the captain's cabin. He insisted he had been asleep in his hammock at the time the shout disrupted *Nallga*'s course, but repeated denials only made him look silly.

"Thou hast made a fool of thyself." The captain gestured crossly. "No crew respects an officer whose behavior lacks logic. Thou art relieved of duty for the next watch. Perhaps rest will restore thy reason. Zhaird's hells, it had better. This vessel cannot afford another of thy mistakes."

Nallga resumed headway at daybreak. Crewmen labored over her sail with rigging knives and needles, and the oar banks stood gapped where injuries laid up several rowers. Seven looms had snapped off at the rowlock; replacements were fitted from a store of spares, and the broken ends stacked behind the lower deck companionway, their lead-spliced handles saved for salvage. Slowly the galley regained her trim, while fore and aft, her crewmen whispered that the mate had lost his honor. Perhaps, they said, he had been cursed with madness, and their thoughts strayed often from their work.

Haldeth bent to the rhythm of the oar and furtively studied the emotionless man by his side. Last night's call for reverse stroke had roused him from deep sleep. With reflexes ingrained through years of obedience, he had run the loom half out before his benchmate stopped it with his fists.

"Wait." Korendir fumbled his end of the oar and seemingly by chance the blade splashed short of its full sweep. In the following second, the reverse stroke of the lower deck tangled with the entrenched beat of the upper, with disastrous results. The mate had issued no order, Haldeth perceived at once. The voice and words had been delivered with diabolical skill by the one man who would least be suspected: the Darjir named by the Mhurgai never spoke, far less rendered pitched imitations of his masters. Now, Haldeth watched the same oar rise, dripping from the sea. He concluded his thought grimly. If a man sought to undermine the mate's authority, no method could be better. Except Korendir's wayward performance had left two slaves dead from punctured lungs; six others gained multiple broken ribs, and their moans of pain could be heard as the day wore on.

"The dead no longer suffer," Korendir whispered in reply to Haldeth's silence. "And shattered bones are a small price to pay for freedom."

His words held a ringing arrogance which allowed no grace for reply. Haldeth did not try. Either Korendir was a madman with a taste for cruelty, or he knew explicitly what he was doing; his implied intent was to release every slave on *Nallga*'s benches. Haldeth splashed the oar into the swell with bitter anger. More likely his benchmate would earn them all the cold taste of the knife.

*   *   *

Nallga entered the tiny harbor of Kahille Island late that afternoon. Mhurgai ships often anchored there, for springs flowed like silver down the islet's mountain slopes. Most southern archipelagoes relied on rain cisterns for fresh water; controlled by a water-broker, the price came dear. But Kahillans were too unsophisticated to levy a fee, and free water made their harbor a popular port.

Nallga moored inside the barrier reef, and instantly became the target of a flotilla of native vendors in dugouts. Reduced swell offset their nuisance; casks made awkward handling, and the captain wished the loading accomplished as smoothly as possible. The Kahillans did not concern him. A culture without knowledge of metal could traffic no weapons with the slaves, and any guard spared for security left one less man for work.

On the lower deck, Haldeth lounged at ease, grateful for the respite. An unfamiliar deckhand stood watch. Seated on the gangway enjoying a basket of fruit, the man was tolerant of contact between the slaves and the Kahillan merchants. One bold wretch had managed to wheedle himself a bunch of grapes, but the officer was too busy eating to intervene.

Korendir leaned across the shaft of his oar with his head cradled on folded arms. To an inboard eye, he appeared asleep. Haldeth knew he was not. A Kahillan dugout drifted close to the galley's side, all but moored beneath his oarport. The occupants sat with upturned faces watching a humorous mime as Korendir pretended to hunt lice in his beard. By periodic stretching, Haldeth caught the gist of the performance. The sham puzzled him until he noticed the Kahillan men were clean-shaven. For a people without knives or steel, the fact was a telling oddity.

Evidently Korendir intended to exploit the implications if he could. A final, furious round of scratching raised applause from his audience. The men in the dugout pushed off. Chattering and laughing as if they shared a fine joke, they unshipped paddles and executed a graceful stroke. As the canoe slipped out of sight beneath *Nallga*'s counter, Korendir shut his eyes and drowsed in earnest. Presently, Haldeth did likewise.

"Baja!" cried a smiling native in accented imitation of the Mhurgai call to rise.

Haldeth opened his eyes in time to see Korendir lift his head and peer cautiously through the oarport. Balanced precariously on tip-toe in the stern of his dugout, a Kahillan man stood with his paddle extended above his head. Lashed to the end was a small wooden box. Korendir squeezed both shoulders through the oarport to reach it. Untying the knots on the waving blade took him an imprudent amount of time.

Haldeth cast a nervous glance at the watch and observed that the sight of a slave straining through an open oarport did not pass unnoticed. The officer spat grapeskins onto the deck and shouted a guttural warning.

Korendir ignored him. With an irritable frown, the deckhand rose and unslung his whip.

Haldeth kicked his benchmate's ankle, imploring prudence. But with the final knot nearly undone, Korendir refused to relinquish his prize. The string fell loose, just as the deckhand strode the length of the gangway and uncoiled his lash. Korendir started to unwedge his shoulders from the oarport, but the deckhand moved first. Seven supple feet of braid struck, splitting through muscled flesh.

Korendir recoiled and skinned his collarbone on the oarport. Silent and sullen, he straightened. Gripping his oar with both hands, he lifted gray eyes and glared at the deckhand. The insolence earned him the whip-butt across the face in a blow that left him reeling.

"Mind thy manners," snapped the officer. But the slave's cold gaze left him strangely unsettled. He blotted sweat from his lip and sauntered back to his seat.

The instant the officer's back was turned, Haldeth caught his friend's shoulder and whispered. "Was that necessary?"

Korendir shifted his hand, surreptitiously exposing the corner of a small wooden box. Kahillan shaving tools were bound to be inside, and if his brief act of defiance had distracted the deckhand from noticing, Korendir considered the price worthwhile. One bruised eyelid dipped into a wink as he tucked his prize under his loincloth. Curled once more over his oarshaft, he ignored the flies which lit upon his opened back with impressive single-mindedness, and presently fell asleep.

In the dark, still hours after midnight, Korendir examined his contraband. Haldeth craned his neck to see over his companion's shoulder as the box fell open. The contents were immediately disappointing. By the wan light through the oarport, Haldeth discovered that Kahillans removed their beards with slivers of sharpened shell, each imbedded in a layer of pitch to preserve their fragile edges. A slot to one side contained a well-used whetstone.

"Neth," said Haldeth. Disgust blunted his habitual caution. "Those things are worthless."

Korendir lifted his head. "They're precisely what I expected," he said mildly.

But Haldeth remained too irritable to demand any explanation. Angered that he had permitted himself any hope at all, he hunched at the far end of the oar shaft and sleeplessly waited for dawn.

The dishonored mate resumed duty the following day. His jaw was clenched, and his strut more pronounced as he relieved the officer on the gangway. Interpreting the signs as fishermen read weather, Haldeth knew the man's temper would be short. No slave needed Korendir's crusted back to remind how readily the Mhurgai whip might fall. All orders on the lower deck were obeyed as though the rowers sat balanced on eggshells.

Nallga cleared the barrier reef just after sunrise. Driven by both banks of oars, she thrust through the swells under a stiff breeze, her forward slaves drenched in spray.

Accustomed to the shudder of planking against heavy waves, Haldeth rowed, preoccupied by thought. Korendir's exchange with the Kahillan natives had been outright recklessness. Certain the mate would discover the contraband, Haldeth worried. Sharpened shells were no match for Mhurgai steel. Korendir was crazy to believe in them.

Scarcely an hour beyond the barrier reef, Haldeth noticed cold water wetting his feet. He glanced downward, immediately suspicious of a leak. *Nallga* was clinker built, her strakes lashed through eyes on the ribs with tarred cord; one of the lines had given way, and seawater welled between the floorboards with each roll of the hull.

Haldeth swore. Korendir surely had been at work with his shells; the line showed no trace of chafing previously. And with the mate's competency questioned by the entire crew, now was the worst time to discover hull failure. Yet Haldeth had no choice. Refusal to report a leak carried worse penalty than the whip. Reluctantly he raised his voice.

"Zhaird's hells," snapped the mate. "How did that happen?" Surly and impatient, he rang the brass bell to summon the ship's marshal since no Mhurga seaman ever walked among slaves without an armed escort to cover his back.

The mate strode down the gangway to Haldeth's bench. Even where he stood he saw the water sluicing through the floorboards. The cause was certainly minor, and in his present vicious mood, the protocol which demanded he wait for assistance rankled. The moment the marshal's weaponed bulk loomed above the companionway, the mate barked orders to hold stroke. Then he stepped down between the slave benches.

Haldeth relinquished his oar and moved clear. Left to tend the loom alone, Korendir stared through the oarport as if unaware that an officer had arrived to inspect the leak.

The mate muttered an insult and added a curt gesture for Darjir to move his feet. Korendir complied without haste. He fixed intent gray eyes upon the mate and appeared not to notice the foam-laced swell which rose beneath the poised blade of his oar. The sucking smack of impact tore the shaft free of his grip. The high end of the loom rose in a neat arc and struck the mate in the side of the head.

Haldeth cried out in alarm as pounds of leaded beech thumped into skull. The officer toppled like a felled tree. His weapons clattered over the wood of slave bench, rib, and floorboard. Korendir controlled the shaft with a one-handed motion and swiftly bent over the fallen body of the mate.

Haldeth trembled uncontrollably. A man four years at the oar could never have misjudged the swell; Korendir's act surely was deliberate. The marshal had witnessed its entirety, and his muscled, gut-round figure now pounded the length of the gangway. Both huge fists contained knives.

Fear closed Haldeth's throat and sealed the breath within his lungs. Only divine intervention would spare him from hamstringing, and as he knew the Mhurgai, he would be lucky to escape that lightly. He remembered the mate's knife too late; the marshal's lumbering charge had already carried him aft. Haldeth found himself throttled by a hairy wrist, while ten inches of bare steel pricked his exposed neck.

"Get back!" commanded the marshal. He spoke past Haldeth.

Instantly obedient, Korendir straightened. He withdrew his hands, which surprisingly held no weapon, but instead had supported the mate's shoulder to hold him clear of the bilge. Salt water welled beneath the floorboards, lifting plumes of blood from the man's split scalp. His tasseled braid was already sodden scarlet and his body lay ominously still.

Korendir shrugged, artfully emphasizing empty hands. The marshal snorted in disgust, but his death grip on Haldeth relaxed slightly.

"Zhaird's own fool, thou art, to have made such a move," he muttered at the unconscious mate. Then he fixed unfriendly eyes on Korendir. "Ship that oar, slave, and make certain it causes no further mischief."

The marshal raised his voice and summoned *Nallga*'s healer. The man arrived, accompanied by a brace of deckhands who removed the mate from the bilge under the vigilant eyes of the marshal. After a brief examination, the healer stood up and pronounced the mate dead. He accompanied his prognosis with a clipped gesture toward Haldeth and Korendir.

"Those slaves should both suffer punishment."

The marshal crossed his arms over his belted chest and spat on the deck. "I think not," he said. "Why ruin two fine strong backs? The mate's own carelessness earned his death. I saw. No hand held the oar which struck Alhar down. Any fool who thinks himself clever enough to walk alone on a slave deck well deserves a split skull."

"The captain must decide," retorted the healer. "I doubt the injury to Alhar was an accident."

The marshal shrugged. He extended a hand for the healer's satchel and helped the man back onto the gangway. A crewman arrived to replace the departed mate, and both officers retired abovedecks.

Interrupted at breakfast by news of Alhar's misfortune, the captain heard the marshal's account through without comment. But when the healer insisted the slaves be tortured in retribution, *Nallga's* commander spared no patience for tact.

"Zhaird's hells, I'm well rid of that incompetent excuse of a mate!"

The healer frowned. "That's a dishonorable way to account for an officer who was murdered in thy service."

The captain's face went white. "Alhar's weapons were not touched." He qualified with menacing clarity. "Slaves who kill usually have courage enough afterward to strike a blow in self defense. We're short-oared enough without wasting the morning carving sheep."

The captain sized the healer up in a manner that withered the reply in the man's throat.

"Get thee gone from here," he finished. "Quickly, or I'll teach thee the meaning of insubordination with a rope on the end of a yardarm."

The healer backed through the doorway, his satchel forgotten in his haste. The captain booted it out of the cabin with such violence that medicine flasks shattered within. With no pause for apology, he rounded on the marshal.

"Clear that oar and get the joiner to work on the leak. Lock the slaves in the sail room, and don't trouble me again concerning the matter."

Confined in the semidarkness of the sailroom, Haldeth shivered as the sweat chilled his body. The stroke of the upper deck oars rumbled through the bulkhead at his back, and he breathed air thickened with the smell of mildewed canvas. The new location held nothing by way of advantage. Stout chain secured him to the ring set in the hatch grating, and a guard stood watch beyond the companionway. The man would not sleep at his post; every sailhand down to the waterboy had suffered repercussions from the captain's foul mood. Haldeth found no comfort knowing that blame rested on the slaves whose oar had caused Alhar's death.

As though sensing his companion's thoughts, Korendir whispered from the shadow. "I never promised there wouldn't be risk."

Haldeth's temper flared. "What have you gained us but misery? You've seen what happens to those who earn the disfavor of the Mhurgai. How long do you think it will take you to break, when they strip your back raw because you moved to swat a fly?"

"Be still!" snapped Korendir. "I never act without purpose."

Haldeth felt his wrist gripped, and a warm object pressed against his palm. He raised it toward the dull streak of daylight which fell through a crack in the hatch grating, clued by the pungent scent of pine before his eyes confirmed. Korendir had passed him the pitch which once had lined the Kahillan box. Deeply pressed in the surface was an impression of the leg-iron key, surely purloined from the ring at the mate's belt during the confused moment while the marshal had raced the length of the gangway.

Sobered into reflection, Haldeth returned the pitch. Over the stroke of *Nallga*'s oars, he heard the whispered scrape of a whetstone grinding shell and in darkness, Korendir's slow smile could almost be felt.

"I'll have you a copy," he said softly. "Wooden, but good enough, since the marshal so kindly oiled the locks."

Haldeth suppressed a mad urge to laugh. Under normal conditions, the leg-irons were frozen with rust. But the marshal had nearly bent his key while unlocking the slaves for transfer to the sail room. In an irritable fit of efficiency, he had commanded a deckhand to work the slide bars with oil, then inspected the job personally to ascertain the work was done well. The locks now operated with a minimum of friction. For the first time, Haldeth entertained belief that escape might be possible.

He touched his companion's arm. "Let me help. I can sharpen while you carve."

Korendir passed the whetstone and the duller of his two shells, then resumed work in silence. The joiner would repair the leak in under an hour, and the duplicate key must be complete before the marshal returned to fetch them back to the oar.

II. Southengard

A scant hour later, Korendir tested his finished creation on the leg irons. His own fell open with a gratifying click, but Haldeth's proved too stiff for the wood the Kahillans used to fashion boxes. The makeshift key slivered in the lock and snapped off.

"Neth," murmured Korendir, keen disappointment in his tone.

Haldeth felt sweat spring along his spine. Caught with one leg iron opened, and the other crammed with splinters, nothing shy of miracle could spare them retribution from their Mhurgai masters.

But Korendir wasted no time brooding over consequences. "I'll not be stopped," he whispered. With quick, fierce motions, he twisted off a bit of pitch and used the sticky substance to bind his own lock shut.

"Listen carefully," he said to Haldeth. "Until we reach the bench, the Mhurgai won't know the locks have been tampered. Before then, we have them off guard. Keep your wits and wait for my move."

Hardened by terrible resolve, Haldeth steadied his shaken nerves. He had no choice now but see the matter through. Relieved that their plot could hold no more surprises, Haldeth reviewed the steps his captors would take to return them to the lower deck. A desperate man could perhaps find an opening which might be turned to advantage.

In the past Haldeth had observed slaves removed for punishment often enough to guess the procedure. The Mhurgai would unlock their chains at the hatch grating, then attach them to rings on the belt of the officer-appointed mate in Alhar's stead. He and Korendir would then walk the length of the upperdeck gangway, followed by the mate and the marshal. Since Mhurgai invariably adhered to custom, Haldeth assumed the marshal would move to the lead at the head of the companionway ladder, for no officer ever risked descent with an unguarded slave at his back.

"The lower deck companionway," Haldeth murmured softly. Loose, Korendir could drop from above and kick the marshal off balance. And piled behind the ladder lay the leaded handles of seven broken oars, ready weapons against Mhurgai taken by surprise.

"A likely choice," Korendir agreed. "However, if better opportunity presents itself, don't expect me to wait."

The light through the grating reddened and slowly turned gray as sunset faded into twilight. The Mhurgai seemed in no hurry to fetch the slaves who had caused Alhar's death. With a prolonged rumble of sound, the upperdeck oars ran in for the evening meal, heralding the close of the watch. The sailroom became oppressively quiet despite the beat of the lowerdeck oars which maintained *Nallga*'s headway. Even whispered conversation became too risky. Haldeth clenched damp fingers against his forearms. Should the wait last very much longer, he felt as if he must shout to relieve the pressure. Taut and unsettled, he glanced at his companion.

Stretched full length against a roll of spare canvas, Korendir seemed asleep. Haldeth strove to match his patience. Presently the reverse in the oar shift signalled the fact that the lower deck received supper without them. Scant minutes later, the marshal and the mate wrenched open the sail room door. Both wore their full regalia of weapons. The marshal stepped briskly inside. He bent with a grunt and unfastened the bolt ring from the hatch grating.

"Come along," he said impatiently. "Lively, unless thee fancy an empty stomach."

Korendir sprang to his feet. The lightest jerk would part the pitch which bound his leg iron, and he could ill afford to have his freedom exposed untimely.

The marshal's huge lips spread into a grin. "This wretch wants his dinner, I believe." He snapped the ring into the lock at the mate's belt, and his grin widened into a leer. "Let him be first. We'll take bets to see whether he can swallow fast enough to beat the call to oars.''

Haldeth blotted sweating hands on his loincloth and feigned unconcern. The marshal pulled his own chain from the grating, then yanked him forward and secured the end to the officer's belt. Shoved toward the companionway, Haldeth stumbled. The mate cursed the wrench at his balance which resulted, and viciously retaliated with a kick. Haldeth crashed to his knees, but managed to grab the doorframe before he fell full length. Resolved to take his revenge, he stepped through with an exaggerated limp. Yet his eyes fixed hungrily on the back of the mate, and his ear remained tuned to the tread of the marshal on his heels.

Sandwiched between their Mhurgai escort, Haldeth and Korendir began their walk down the upper deck gangway. On either side, row upon row of slaves bent muscled backs in unison over the sweeps; a few grimaced in hatred as the detested marshal passed by. Sunk in animal misery, most showed no emotion at all. When Haldeth and his benchmate reached the companionway to the lower deck, the upperdeck mate caressed his whipstock and spat on the boards at Korendir's feet. The insult drew no reaction. Korendir stepped squarely on the patch of spittle and stood with witless subservience while his Mhurgai overlords rearranged themselves for the descent.

The inhuman quality of Korendir's acting left Haldeth chilled. He forced a deep breath to steady himself as the marshal stepped around him and lowered his bulk onto the ladder. Korendir followed. His palms left wet marks on the top rung; except for that small betrayal, he might have been born nerveless so little emotion did he display. Haldeth felt a quiver invade his knees.

The mate seemed not to notice. Encumbered by the slave chains, he lowered himself awkwardly, head tipped back to watch Haldeth. "Step on my fingers, thou, and I'll draw blood."

With a silent vow to break the man's knuckles, Haldeth set his weight on the ladder. That moment, Korendir snapped his heel upward. His leg iron cracked into the marshal's chin. The man overbalanced and tumbled backward with a bellow of surprise. The mate twisted on the rungs and snapped savagely at Korendir's chain. The pitch binding the lock parted instantly. Korendir launched himself from the ladder, dropped like a stone toward the deck. He struck the marshal's chest with both feet. Bone splintered, accompanied by a hideous scream.

The mate jerked back in horror. Before he could reach for weapons, Haldeth stamped down and pinned his knuckles to the rungs. Helpless, the officer cried out as Korendir closed his fists over the leg iron now which dangled empty from his belt. Haldeth jumped upward, caught the companionway latch and banged the hatch closed overhead, just as Korendir set his weight to the fetter and yanked.

Bruised fingers wrenched loose; the mate toppled, yelling, from the ladder. The lowerdeck guard charged down the gangway to the rescue. He dared not throw his knife for fear of striking the wrong man. His concern proved a waste of effort. Haldeth leapt the full height of the ladder and landed squarely on the mate's skull. He bent, plundered keys to his freedom and weapons before the corpse had stopped shuddering.

Bloodied to the wrists over the body of the marshal, Korendir straightened, sword and knife in hand. He met the guard's rush with a stop thrust and skewered the man through the chest. Korendir ripped the ring from the officer's belt and dangled the keys before the stupefied lowerdeck slaves.

"You all stand condemned," he shouted. "Who among you would fight?"

A crack punctuated his words. The companionway hatch swung open, and the upperdeck mate dropped through, screaming a Mhurga battle cry. Newly released from his chains, Haldeth met the attack with seventy pounds of leaded oar wielded like a quarterstaff. The officer crumpled like a burst grain sack.

A shout from the benches hailed his fall. A pair of hands shot up. Korendir tossed the keys. Haldeth flung himself up the ladder and once again slammed the hatch. He clung to the grating, holding it closed with his weight while slaves frantically unlocked shackles. Feet pounded overhead, counterpointed by staccato strings of orders. *Nallga* drifted uneasily on the sea, her orderly stroke abandoned.

Men leapt from the benches and joined the rebellion
beneath the companionway. Soon the bodies of the fallen
were stripped of weapons; other men brandished the
sheared ends of their oars. A yelling horde waited to
receive any Mhurga who dared attempt the companionway by the time Haldeth's strength yielded to the prying
tool applied from above.

The smith dropped clear. Caught by a dozen pairs of
hands, he was shoved aside by men crazed with hatred
through years of Mhurgai oppression. Slaves forced
themselves at the ladder. Bodies swayed and battered
upward, struggling to reach the open hatch. Their rush
was messily stopped by a stand of Mhurgai dartmen. The
slaves who survived fanned in an angry ring around their
dying companions and screamed threats. Others sought
longer lengths of oar to bludgeon any dartman foolish
enough to show his face.

"Stalemate," Korendir said softly in Haldeth's ear.
"We'll have to end it quickly. Choose six steady men
and follow."

The smith complied without question. He picked his
men swiftly and met Korendir and a second party on the
gangway amidships.

"Out," Korendir ordered. "Through the oarports and
climb the strakes. Take the quarterdeck, and *Nallga* is
ours."

The men needed no urging. They footed their way over
benches vacant and inhabited. Others joined them as the
keys circulated into fresh hands. The squeeze through
the oarport left each man vulnerable for a moment, but
with the companionway the focal point of the mutiny, no
crewman thought to guard the rail. A brief, bloody struggle saw captain, quartermaster, and three sail hands dead
on the deck. Armed with their weapons, a shark gaff,
and several marlinspikes, the slaves resolved the dispute
over the lowerdeck hatch with vengeful dispatch. At the
end no Mhurga remained alive.

Haldeth stripped the scarlet salamander device from
the masthead and pitched it over the rail. Laughing like
a drunk, he pronounced *Nallga* a free vessel. The keys
of her murdered crewmen circulated quickly, and the top
deck became packed with rejoicing humanity. Men rifled
the captain's coffers for gold, then broached the rum

stores to sounds of tumultuous cheering. Fruit nets and perishables shortly littered the planking of the quarter-deck. Lifting two brimming tankards from the cask, Haldeth sought amid the chaos for Korendir and did not immediately find him.

Worry dampened his exuberance. Fate had a malevolent touch if Korendir proved to be one of the handful of fallen. Haldeth shoved his way aft. Inquiries after Darjir drew a string of blank faces. Openly distressed, the smith thrust his tankards into the startled hands of a stranger, then extended his search beyond the laughing crowd of the living.

Twilight had long since faded into night. Stars hung poised over the yardarm, cold after the orange glow of the lanterns. Oppressed by rising hopelessness, Haldeth almost missed the slim shadow bent over the lashing which secured *Nallga's* cutter to its davits.

His relief found release in anger. "What in Neth's almighty image are you doing now? We're free men. Isn't that worth a celebration?"

Korendir paused. Wind flapped the folds of the officer's cloak draped over his shoulders. "Free?" His breath hissed through his teeth. "How long will that last, in waters infested with the entire Mhurgai fleet?"

Haldeth perched himself on the rail. "There's talk of sailing north."

Korendir interrupted. "Also talk of sailing south." His tone turned icy. "South, Mhurgai vengeance will finish us off. North, unless someone browbeats this crew into sealing the oarports against the weather, winter storms will make a quicker end. The first gale would see us awash to the quarterdeck, and that scrap of a sail won't draw to weather."

"What in Aerith do you propose instead?" Haldeth clenched his fists on his knees, unhappily aware his companion had spoken nothing but fact.

Korendir shrugged. "I don't intend to spoil my chances by waiting to see if this lot of drunken revellers can reach agreement." He jerked his head at the cutter. "She's provisioned already. I'll sail for the coast of Southengard."

Haldeth stared, openmouthed. "What then?"

Korendir's expression could not be read in the close,

tropical night, but his hand moved to his belt and
emerged cradling a pair of rubies pried from the eyes of
Nallga's figurehead. "I'll build myself a holdfast," he said
carefully. "The defenses will become the death of any
man who tries to break in."

"That's well beyond price of your gems," Haldeth
pointed out.

Korendir rattled the stones like dice in his palm.
"These should buy me a horse and a good sword. I've
heard any man who lifts the Blight of Torresdyr will inherit a wizard's treasure. Perhaps there is enough wealth
to quarry the stone."

Haldeth felt a qualm pervade his middle. "That quest
is impossible! Every man who attempted it ended up buried without a marker in the King's tiltyard. *Are you
mad?*"

Korendir turned back to the lashing. "Impossible tasks
pay best," he said simply. "Don't look to me for
patience."

Haldeth resisted a sudden urge to grab the man's
shoulders and shake him. "Would you sail alone, then?"

Korendir's fingers hesitated on the knots. A strangely
mirthless laugh convulsed his throat. He tossed one of
the rubies to Haldeth. "Help yourself to Alhar's other
cloak and a rigging knife. I need a second man to launch
and crew this cockle shell anyway. All along I meant to
remind you of that."

Emarrcek, southernmost peninsula of Southengard, lay
one hundred and fifty leagues to the north, a long, tortuous sail in an open boat, even for men seasoned to the
hardship of the oar. Yet the first days of freedom passed
pleasantly. Warm, southern winds pressed the cutter on
a steady course, and dolphins danced in the swells. Haldeth scratched the scabbed-over sores left from the chafe
of his leg irons. He spoke in wistful remembrance of
two daughters and a wife, murdered by Mhurgai on the
morning his village was raided.

"They must have landed to reprovision. Neth knows,
we had nothing of worth to merit a sacking, and the
boats they used for landing carried water casks. I was in
the forge, heating stock to make horseshoes, when the
shouting drew me out. Costermongers were being cut

down in the market as they protested thefts from their stalls. Lindey and my girls were at the well. I ran there with no other weapon than the iron stock I had in my hand." Immersed in the grip of ugly memories, Haldeth failed to notice: Korendir was no longer quietly listening, but had turned his back. His fists were clenched white on the rail, and the tension in his shoulders had little to do with keeping balance against the wave-driven pitch of the boat.

Haldeth bent his head, knuckles pressed to his temples. "You know," he said bitterly, "they never screamed. They had no time. The Murgai with their butchering swords were that fast. Lindey first, and then the girls, all three were beheaded in a heartbeat. Just because they happened to be in the way. I was behind the hedgerow, close enough to strike, but Neth! For the one murdering animal I might have laid out, five others would have instantly skewered me." The retelling broke off as Haldeth heaved in a tight breath. "I still remember how the blood plumed in the water of the filled buckets. When the pressgang came and set chains on me, I was too dazed with horror to even care."

Haldeth spasmed in a violent shiver, and as if the shrug that followed held power to throw off past horrors, he forced a dry practicality. "I could not have saved my family. Any who resisted were killed. But each day I wake up wondering why I was left to survive. I have no home to return to. The people I cared for are dead." His eyes turned, searching, toward Korendir. "What about you?"

No answer came back. The only movement about the braced figure at the rail was the slap of black cloak in the gusts.

Pressed by loneliness and the need for shared catharsis, Haldeth at length asked outright: "Did anyone you love escape slaughter?"

That caused Korendir to turn around. His face showed no expression. The glare which had unsettled his late Mhurgai masters focused for long minutes on Haldeth. With no more recognition than if the smith were a total stranger, the eyes stayed bereft of human warmth, while the hand clenched on the haft of the boat's only rigging knife could at a stroke turn to violence. Unnerved afresh by the ruthless slaughter that had overcome *Nallga*'s crew, Haldeth offered diffident apology. He moved and spoke cautiously in his companion's presence after that. But relations between them stayed edgy. Korendir perversely remained aloof. Sounds and sudden motions startled him to his feet, muscles braced taut against threats only he could perceive.

The weather turned cold, gray, and forbidding. In alternate shifts the two men slept and stood watch at the helm. If the demands of the winter ocean forestalled moments for idle companionship, the boat was too cramped for avoidance. Korendir kept to himself. During meals and off hours he maintained a brooding solitude, speaking only when necessary.

A fortnight later, the wind shifted and blew furiously from the north. Spray shot like needles of ice over the bow, drenching the boat and everything within. Korendir was forced to fall off on a northwest course lest both of them perish from exposure. Haldeth shook his fist at the sky, but the weather did not relent. The tiny craft drove haplessly through the Inlanic ocean, past Emarrcek and the haven of the south coast.

The days turned bitter, and the nights black and miserable, with the wind a tireless moan through the stays. Whipped by sleet, then snow, the boat pounded closehauled through the northern latitudes, graced only fitfully by cloud-bleared glimmers of sun. Rimed with salt and ice crystals, Korendir's beard whitened to match his companion's. Unkempt as a fur trapper, Haldeth slapped raw knuckles on his knees and swore he would never again venture upon the sea.

The boat reached Karjir Head in the depths of a midwinter freeze. By then, the sail streamed in tatters, and water leaked through every seam in the hull. Both men were bone thin and exhausted from days of constant bailing, and landfall went badly. Wallowing and sluggish under a water-laden bilge, *Nallga*'s boat slewed in the surf. A rock punched through her starboard planking.

"Praise Neth for a favor," gasped Haldeth. Still infected with sardonic humor, he leapt the gunwale and splashed into a churning moil of foam. Korendir dove for the forward locker. He managed to salvage the rigging knife before the craft rolled and tossed him headlong into the sea. He surfaced, swimming strongly. The refugees from Mhurgai captivity dragged themselves ashore, soaked, starved, and bleeding. The land which greeted them was untenanted; a wilderness of dark forest which stretched to the far horizon.

Korendir stood shivering on the sand, seemingly absorbed by the breakers that chewed their boat into splinters. "Do you know how to snare rabbits?" He sounded unconcerned, as if he offered conversation in a tap room.

"What?" Haldeth shook his wet hair like a dog, his earlier levity stripped by the bite of cruel wind. "No."

Korendir managed a mangled smile. "You'll cook, then."

Haldeth whirled, one fist clenched to strike. His knuckles raked air as Korendir dodged and vanished into the brush beyond the dunes. Belatedly Haldeth recalled that they possessed no flints to make fire. The rabbits, if Korendir caught any, could hardly be eaten raw, and were they to have any warmth, the spark must be made by friction.

Four days later, in the coastal town of Dun Point a gemsetter cleared his throat. Before him, two square-cut stones splashed highlights like blood across the white linen covering on his countertop.

"Rubies, you say?" He straightened with a depreciative sigh. "The 'stones' you brought are glass. Common cut glass." He blinked myopically, and noticed his clients' appearance for the first time.

Clad in filthy, ill-smelling rags, the ruffians exchanged a long glance. Starved as beggars, both were heavily muscled through the chest and shoulders; their skins were chapped from exposure to salt wind and weather. The gemsetter did not care to imagine what circumstance had brought them into his shop in Dun Point. Afraid that his word might be taken badly, he wished only for these strangers to depart.

"Glass," he repeated. He poked the stones with chubby fingers. "Only glass. I'm sorry."

The men exchanged no word, but acted with perfect timing. The white-bearded giant seized the gemsetter's wrists, while his bronze-haired companion vaulted the counter and locked the stunned merchant in a wrestler's grip from behind. The move was accomplished with such speed the victim caught no glimpse of drawn steel. Before he could think to react, he found himself pinioned with a dagger pressed to his throat. The hand which held the blade bore down with steady and merciless pressure.

"They're glass, you insist," an equally cold voice said in the merchant's ear.

The gemsetter quivered in helpless outrage. "My trade is honest, unlike yours, thief. Take what you will and go. And may your neck get stretched in the hangman's noose for your crime."

A breath of air tickled the merchant's collar; the chill of the knife disappeared. The bronze-haired man stepped back, and his white-haired companion opened his fists. Freed, the gemsetter spun to face the attacker with the dagger. He met eyes disturbingly gray.

"Who are you?" he demanded.

"Not a thief." The barbarian's accent was cultured, strangely in contrast to his dress and manners, and the coloring of his hair was something not seen among mortals. He sheathed his blade with a leopard's easy grace. "Have you any market for glass jewels?"

The gemsetter rubbed bruised wrists, a shaken expression on his face. "Travelling players sometimes want baubles for costume pieces. And of course, the east quarter trollops own chests of them. I'll give four silvers. You won't get a better offer."

"Done," said the bronze-haired man. No smile touched his lips as he extended a grimy hand.

The gemsetter shivered and counted coins into a palm welted with calluses. Silly with relief over the fact he had not been robbed, he stood and trembled as his strange clients left the shop.

The red glass remained, a bright glitter against the linen. Odd, the gemsetter thought as he scooped up the ornaments and wrapped them away in tissue. He had seen such a pair only once, glued to the eyes of a figurehead on board a Mhurga galley. He paused, one hand on the lock of his strongbox, then shook his head. Impossible; in all the Eleven Kingdoms no thief existed who could steal from the Mhurgai and survive.

*   *   *

Haldeth stopped squarely in the center of Craftsman's Alley. "You're mad as a dogfox!" Sea wind whipped his hair against reddened cheeks as heatedly, he continued. "Two silvers won't buy passage as far as the next crossroads, and you claim you're going to lift the Blight of Torresdyr! Neth! Tell me, with what? That quest has killed the best heeled men-at-arms in all the Eleven Kingdoms."

"Watch me," Korendir said. In a gesture unthinkingly casual, he tossed one of his silvers to a beggar who shivered in the gutter.

Haldeth shook his head. "I'd rather get drunk. Daft, that's what you are. Escape the Mhurgai, and you think of nothing but risking your neck. Torresdyr lies *a hundred and sixty leagues* from here, over mountains, don't forget. Be reasonable and wait till spring. I'll find work at a smithy. If you're still this keen when the weather breaks, I'll go with you."

"No." Korendir met Haldeth's glare with an expression as final as death.

A wagon rumbled into the alley. The carter cursed and brandished his whip at the two men blocking the roadway. Even then Korendir refused to relent.

"Go alone then!" shouted Haldeth. Out of patience, he whirled and jumped clear as the harness team jogged past. Iron-rimmed wheels rang over dirt rutted like stone by winter ice. By the time the wagon passed, Haldeth had disappeared into the tavern across the street. The signboard swung in the gusts, invitingly torchlit, its promise of warmth and comfort depicted in gilt letters and a brightly painted bullfrog with a tankard.

Alone in the windy alley, Korendir stood for a long moment, his face expressionless beneath tangled copper hair. Presently, he grimaced, turned his back on the lighted inn windows, and continued on his way. His last silver bought him worn but serviceable clothing. With the change, he acquired a tired black gelding with ruined lungs; but he had to include his rigging knife to complete the bargain.

The horse trader stroked the fine, Mhurgai steel and spat through broken teeth. "You'll be getting no bridle with the nag, now."

The gelding nibbled at the salty wool of his owner's

cloak, and received a mild slap on the muzzle. "I need none," said Korendir.

On his way to the town gate, he begged a length of twine from a wagonmaster and braided it into a hackamore. Then, penniless, weaponless, and saddleless, he vaulted astride his sorry mount and turned north.

The horse made no speed on the road. Any gait beyond a walk made its flanks heave pitifully as it labored to draw air into scarred tissues. Resigned, Korendir named the animal Snail. Winter warmed into spring, and spring passed, turning the fields rich green at high summer. Korendir made his way across two kingdoms, working at farmsteads to earn lodging and meals; in the wilds between settlements, he hunted and slept in the open. From dusty, travel-worn boots to tangled hair, his appearance grew as unkempt as his mount. Yet no stranger dared refuse him passage. The stern set of his features silenced any ridicule; directions to Northengard were forthrightly given to speed him on his way.

But as his mount shambled out of earshot, heads shook, and laughter flourished. What could an honorless, nameless unknown on a broken-winded hack achieve that had not already been tried, and by heroes well sung into fame? Even the White Circle enchanters would not trifle with the Blight of Torresdyr, and they held more power than any mortal born.

Summer mellowed into autumn, and nights grew brisk with frost. Oak leaves crackled in drifts under the gelding's hooves as Korendir climbed the passes which marked the far border of Northengard. Beyond lay the misted acres of Torresdyr, barren since blight had withered the land.

Korendir journeyed through hills smothered under pallid banks of fog. Thickets sheltered no wildlife. The vegetation hung sere and brown, as if ravaged by early winter. In the valleys, unmended fences bordered fields left fallow, and pastures grew snarls of nettle and thorn. Those few travelers who ventured on the roads turned unfriendly faces upon the stranger and his tired gelding; his coming and his quest offered no cause for hope.

Korendir continued undaunted. Seven nights before

equinox, he drew rein beneath moss-caked arches in the courtyard of the royal palace.

The king granted the stranger's request for audience, saddened by renewed despair. Torresdyr embraced poverty and ill luck indeed, if a rag-tag nobody dared shoulder the burden that had ruined the finest armsmen in the Eleven Kingdoms.

"Let the wretched man in," the king said to his sniggering chamber steward. "We're beggars ourselves, and have nothing to lose but pride."

The royal words were no understatement. In what had once been the richest land in Aerith, the visitor waited in a damp, unheated antechamber, and the servant who admitted him was gaunt beneath threadbare robes of state. Taken to the throne room, Korendir walked past a thousand sockets where gemstones had been pried out of fretwork and furnishings to fund a starving court. The carpet he knelt on was mildewed, and the king he saluted was toothless and hunched with ill health.

Korendir straightened. Quietly he spoke. "Your Royal Grace, I request leave to recover the Wardstone of Torresdyr from the witch Anthei. Your land is dying of curse, and I have need of her riches."

"Anthei murdered every man to challenge her." The king did not bother to suppress contempt. Korendir was every bit as nondescript as the steward described, from creased black cloak to cracked leather boots. Except for the rare combination of bronze hair and gray eyes, he looked like a street thief. "Who are you to demand burial with the bravest blood of the Eleven Kingdoms when Anthei returns your remains?"

In pointed disregard of the insult, Korendir chose his words like a miser spending coin. "I was robbed, once, of everything I valued. That day I swore to hold nothing dear until I possessed means to hold it secure. Should I die, you may feed my flesh to your hunting hawks if you please. I ask only that you tell how the blight was set against you, and give your blessing on my departure."

The king tugged the worn tassels which adorned his throne of state. "There's no virtue left in my blessing. And any beggar in the square would tell of the Blight for a half copper. Why trouble me?"

"Because from you I would hear the simple truth." Korendir shrugged. "That might make a difference."

"How could it?" snapped the king. "My last hawk was slaughtered for the table many a long year past, and my subjects need not be burdened with the task of digging your grave. Be gone from here. I have nothing to offer and even less left to lose."

"I know." Korendir returned a queerly reluctant smile. "In that, Your Grace, we are very much alike."

The ruffian retired from the royal presence. His final bow was offered with a respect reminiscent of better days; the king noticed, surprisingly touched by regret. Once, the royal consent to an adventurer's challenge included great lists of obligations. Torresdyr's treasury had been exhausted serving up weapons, horses and mercenaries to back each separate attempt. Yet Korendir came knowing the vaults were empty. He had asked without demanding so much as a pin, and even ridicule had not driven him to discourtesy. Ashamed for his mean hospitality, the king rose painfully to his feet.

He shuffled from his dais and unlatched the casement. The mullioned frame opened, pattering flakes of gilt into the weeds beneath the sill. Alone in the dusty courtyard, Korendir turned toward the sound. His hand paused on the string which served his mount as hackamore.

"Your Grace?" He waited, watching with stony gray eyes.

The king felt suddenly uneasy. "The guard at the gate will tell you the tale of the Blight. Then go with the royal blessing." Speaking no further word, Korendir vaulted astride and reined across the courtyard. He passed beneath the far archway, unaccompanied and unremarked by fanfares. Left to his despair, the king wiped rheumy eyes and addressed his chamber steward.

"That man hasn't so much as a penknife on him, Neth take his foolish soul. Find a brace of pages. Have them dig a grave, and don't let me see that man's corpse when Anthei sends him back."

III. The Blight of Torresdyr

The gatekeeper of the king's palace leaned against the lichened stone of the barbican. He squinted up at the stranger on the tired gelding and spoke in a voice gone rusty as the hinges he tended. "So, ye would hear the story of the Blight? Why ask here? Any man in the city could tell you."

Unmoved by the sarcasm, Korendir said, "I want the truth, not tales told in taverns by the tap." He paused, aware haste would earn nothing but the gatekeeper's contempt.

At last the old man kicked at the weeds underfoot and gestured toward crumbled stone walls. "Torresdyr was a fair land once. But the old king committed an injustice. Now lord and farmsteader suffer alike." Then, irritation intensified, he accused, "Why care? Ye look to be poor as the rest of us."

Korendir's hand stayed quiet on the rein and his eyes remained expectant.

Discomfortable under that steady gaze, the old man shrugged; in plain phrases he described how the fairest of the Eleven Kingdoms became cursed.

A generation past, when the current king's sire ruled the land, Torresdyr employed a court wizard to provide fashionable wonders for the revels. Iraz of Idmire last held that post. Though his face and one eye had been grotesquely scarred by a miscast spell, he was without dispute the finest master of lesser magic in the Eleven Kingdoms. Not all his spells were illusions. Iraz could make roses bloom at wintertide, and pears grow from thorn branches. His skills became the envy of rival courtiers, and he rose quickly to fame and favor. Quartered like a lord in the palace, he fell in love with the king's second daughter and got her with child.

The king's rage knew no bounds. Rather than grant

consent for his daughter to wed a man who was scarred, landless, and untitled, he ordered Iraz imprisoned. The princess was sent to a distant keep to bear her wizard's bastard in shame. On the eve she went into labor, the king's wardens discovered Iraz's cell empty, the steel lock a misshapen ruin. Left in runes on the dungeon wall was a threat that the wizard would marry the princess, else curse all the land to misfortune.

The king mustered his men-at-arms, yet before they could march, the princess died in childbed. Inflamed with grief, Iraz of Idmire claimed both her surviving daughter and the tower for his own.

His walls were defended with sorcery, and weapons in the hands of soldiers could not breach his spells. Fearing Iraz's threat of vengeance, the king appealed to the White Circle, the mightiest enchanters on Aerith and as far beyond the powers of mortal wizards as sunlight above plain clay. To aid the king's cause, the White Circle created a wardstone of tallix crystal. The completed gem was round as a man's fist, each of two thousand two hundred and forty facets angled to deflect one aspect of ill fortune.

"Guard it well," warned the Archmaster when he gave the talisman to the king. "There shall not be another."

Iraz labored seventeen years on his curse against the king. Its final consummation claimed his life, but his illegitimate daughter Anthei survived him. Grieving alone in her tower, she saw a land unspoiled under sunlight. Angered that her father's death had achieved no vengeance, she swore to see his work complete.

On the old king's death, Anthei made her way to court. There, with her beauty and knowledge of Iraz's arts, she beguiled the distraught prince and stole the wardstone away. Secure within her tower, she worked foul sorcery upon the White Circle's defenses and at last limited their virtues to the gardens surrounding her keep.

The Blight of Iraz fell in full measure upon Torresdyr. Crops withered, and starvation shriveled the livestock in pasture and barn. Children sickened with fever, cloth mildewed upon the loom; the sun vanished behind a mantle of mist and did not reappear. Country folk fled over the mountains to Northengard, but the Blight traveled with them, and their farmsteads did not prosper.

Torresdyr's young king issued a proclamation challenging any man of courage to regain the wardstone, great wealth to be awarded the one who succeeded. Seventy-four tried only to fail. Anthei delighted in returning their corpses. Hopelessness and poverty overran the court of Torresdyr and adventurers ceased to appear at the royal gates. The king grew old. Ruined by apathy and misfortune, he offered his crown for recovery of the wardstone, but no man came forward to risk his life for the rule of a desolate land.

"You're the first to answer that challenge in many a weary year," the gatekeeper finished. He spat in the dust. "But don't you know? You ride for a hopeless cause. The king bartered his crown to the traders for cloth. Men say Anthei's tower holds treasure, but wizard's gold carries a bane. Only a fool would chance death for such stakes."

"I'm going anyway." Calm to the point of obsession, Korendir asked questions until the gatekeeper tired of giving answers. Words had no power to unravel Anthei's sorceries; the old man gave vent to annoyance. He turned his back and set his hands to the winches. Chain clanked. The gates which guarded the royal palace began ponderously to close. Yet before the rusted portals completed their groaning descent, Korendir passed through and turned his gelding's wheezing nose northwest. He would persist on his fool's errand to pursue Torresdyr's lost wardstone and no man's argument would deter him.

Anthei's tower rose above the flats on the Jardine Sea. There shone the only sunlight in Torresdyr since the wardstone spared her grounds alone from the Blight. Although blue sky showed intermittently over the surrounding acres, Korendir covered the final league upon roads overgrown with brown bracken; the farmsteads on either side stood abandoned. The gatekeeper claimed children had died of poisoning after tasting the fruit which ripened on the trees near Anthei's walls. Other folk whispered in dread of the guardians that protected her gates.

Korendir rounded the final bend in the hills near sunset. Ahead he saw a great stone keep silhouetted against the gray breakers of the shoreline. Walled round with the famed white agate of Torresdyr, Anthei's gardens were a marvel in the midst of a wasteland. With cold eyes, Korendir studied the beauty of rare blossoms and exotic trees. The wind filled his nostrils with the perfume of flowering vines and the sour smell of salt off the sea; a third scent intermingled with these, a sharp tang of woodsmoke which did not fit.

Korendir drew rein. As his gelding halted, he noticed one other in Torresdyr who had disregarded rumor's warning; a white-haired man crouched over a fire toasting barley cakes almost within the shadow of Anthei's walls. Korendir's frown lifted. He set his heels to the gelding's sides and called out in a rare display of pleasure.

"Haldeth!"

The man by the fire glanced up and shaded seamed features with one hand. Then he stood and grinned until the gelding's walk brought its rider within earshot. "I guessed you'd be along. Hadn't we promised to see this through together?"

Korendir dismounted. He closed the remaining distance with impatience, but when he reached Haldeth's side, his face showed nothing of his earlier welcome. "What changed your mind?"

Caught in that critical gaze, Haldeth felt suddenly exposed. "I hope you like barley cakes," he said evasively. He took the gelding's hackamore and motioned toward the camp. "Eat. I'll tend your animal."

"He's called Snail." Even more spare with words than usual, Korendir sat on a log by the fire. "Let him go. He never strays."

Haldeth slipped the hackamore over the gelding's ears and watched it snuffle the grass and begin to graze. Presently he chose a seat beside his friend. Yet after the surprise of reunion, awkwardness settled between the two men. Haldeth knew better than to press with questions. Instead, he prepared a mix of barley dough and told of a gamble on a card game that had won him employment at a forge. On impulse, he had bought back the fake rubies from the Mhurga galley's figurehead. One he wore set in silver as a belt buckle; the other he kept loose with his coins.

"I wanted the things to remind me." The smith's hands stilled over the flour sack, and his eyes lost focus into distance. "Something by which to recall that the cost of survival came dear."

If Korendir also thought of loved ones left barbarously slaughtered, he ventured nothing in comment. Since time had not blunted his reserve, Haldeth most wisely kept silent.

Perched beside a lancet window beneath the tower's upper battlement, the witch Anthei leaned across the sill and braided a clothyard length of pale gold hair. Intent as a cat, she studied the man recently arrived; this one she knew had come with the king's blessing, his intent to destroy her father's vengeance against the court of Torresdyr. Very soon he would be dead. Anthei had savored the challenge, even toyed with the lives of seventy-four of his predecessors; but this time she did not smile with her customary anticipation. Never before had a man approached her tower unarmed. Now, one had dared. The precedence disturbed her.

Korendir, she heard the white-haired smith call him. The word did not harbor any resonance of power. Yet names could be misleading. Shabby clothing and cracked boots could not hide the bronze hair and cold light eyes, coloring unknown on Aerith except among the blood of White Circle enchanters. Anthei knotted her braid with slender fingers and fretfully started another.

In the campsite, Korendir leaned forward and burned his fingers on a barley cake. He swore mildly, sat back, and blew on his blistered thumb with the chagrin of a common vagabond. Assured now of his mortality, Anthei eliminated the fear that the White Circle had sent an initiate against her. She pulled a blood-red ribbon from her lap and bound it into her hair with langorous enjoyment. She had been left to herself for a very long time. Sage or fool, this man's struggles would amuse her well before he died; the corpse she returned to the King of Torresdyr would hereafter deter even the most destitute adventurer from fouling her garden air with cooking smoke.

While twilight settled ghostly gray over her tower, Anthei leaned on her elbows and began very softly to sing. Intent on their supper, the mortals below never noticed

Korendir's gelding raise its gaunt head, ears pricked taut with attention.

Night fell. The dunes muffled the boom of the surf and the snap of burning logs seemed brittle, almost crushed by the weight of a greater silence. When the gelding sucked a sudden, sharp breath into its damaged lungs, the sound parted the air like the rip of a knife through cloth.

"Snail!" Korendir leaped to his feet. A barley cake fell from loosened fingers as he ran, but his action came too late. The gelding gathered itself on bony haunches and launched itself over Anthei's garden wall.

The horse's forehooves flung a spray of gravel as it landed on the pathway beyond. Its form became hidden in darkness, but a quavering scream betrayed its suffering. Haldeth surged to his feet. He seized a brand from the fire and raced for Anthei's front gate.

Korendir checked, whirled, and saw the streaming sparks thrown off by the torch. Guessing Haldeth's intent, he shouted. "Don't touch the latch!" But his warning was masked by the gelding's dying convulsions. The smith rushed heedlessly onward.

Running also, Korendir tore the belt from his tunic. The buckle was plain wrought metal, next to worthless. But earlier he had noticed Anthei's gates were forged entirely of bronze; perhaps, like an earth witch, she could not make a spell which ruled cold iron.

The horse's cries shuddered into silence. Korendir reached the wall, unslung belt in hand. Again he shouted, but not before Haldeth raised the outer bar. Utterly deaf to his peril, the smith flung wide the gate.

Torchlight grazed flickering highlights across bronze as the heavy grille swung inward. The white expanse of a footpath glimmered through the gloom beyond. At first glance it appeared deserted, but a closer look showed a red-cheeked country matron with a bucket; two pretty, dark-eyed daughters clung to her gray wool skirts. The sight of Haldeth lit their faces with radiant welcome. The girls called to their father and joyously skipped toward the gate.

Haldeth gasped in hoarse disbelief. "Lindey!" He surged forward.

"No!" Korendir jerked his friend cruelly back. "Lindey's dead, slaughtered by Mhurgai along with both of your children."

Haldeth twisted around in rebuttal. He lifted his torch in a vicious swing straight at his companion's head.

Korendir ducked, showered by sparks. "Lindey's dead! Anthei's conjured her image to trap you."

Haldeth wrenched free. The child in the lead had nearly reached his outstretched hand. Left no space for finesse, Korendir spun the smith away and chopped his hold free of the latch. Next he whipped his belt in a wide arc before him. The buckle passed clean through the cheek of the running little girl. Her face crumpled, marred like a reflection on ruffled water. Briefly Korendir glimpsed spread claws and a ravening beast's mouth before Anthei's illusion restored the innocent features of a child. Without break in motion, he hooked his belt on a wrought bronze spike and dragged the gate panel shut. The bar fell with a clank. Korendir stepped back. Narrowly spared from one threat, he had no thought for another. The fist that slammed his shoulder from behind caught him utterly unprepared.

Korendir staggered sideways in a half-spin. Blinded by flamelight as Haldeth jabbed the torch at his face, he blocked the attack with his forearm. Fire licked his sleeve. Seared by pain, he shouted again. "Lindey's dead!"

Crazed by Anthei's sorceries, Haldeth charged in for another blow. Korendir lashed back with the belt, then launched shoulder first into his companion's stomach. Haldeth clawed for balance and fell. He dropped the torch. Fire laced through dried grass and lit the hellish struggles of the men.

Locked in conflict, Korendir and Haldeth rolled across the ground. Crushed against a shoulder corded with muscle from the forge, Korendir counterstruck with precision. Haldeth jerked once. He released his hold on a grunt of agony, and the fight raged on in unchecked, primordial ferocity. The grass fire spread by the torch became quenched by tumbling bodies.

Trapped in a second hold, Korendir fought to suck air past the knuckles which ground at his windpipe. Dizzied to the edge of consciousness, he banged his belt buckle edgewise on the side of Haldeth's skull. The smith's head snapped back, a nasty gash opened above the ear; his arms went mercifully limp. Korendir shook off his friend's unconscious bulk and swore with expressive vehemence. After a pause to assess his own damages, he arose and searched with bleeding fingers among the grass until he hooked the cord of Snail's hackamore. He used the reins to bind Haldeth hand and foot. Then, after a lingering glance toward Anthei's darkened tower, he fetched the pan used to mix barley dough and stumbled through the dunes to fetch seawater.

Haldeth groaned as Korendir knelt to cleanse the cut on his scalp. The sting of salt water roused him back to consciousness, and the first words he uttered framed a ritual malediction that would have shaken a seasoned man-at-arms. Korendir continued his ministrations without twitching a muscle. He rinsed the blood from Haldeth's hair, emptied the fouled pan over a tuft of smouldering grass, then returned and looped his belt securely around the smith's neck. Haldeth's curses continued as he tethered the end to a log by the fire. After testing the knots, Korendir climbed into a tree overlooking Anthei's garden. There he remained, though Haldeth screamed abuse at him for the remainder of the night.

Silence returned with the sunrise. Beyond the wall, where the gelding had leaped, the new morning revealed shrubbery festooned with gobbets of flesh. The path was splattered scarlet for yards in each direction, and not so much as a sliver of bone remained of the equine victim of the carnage. Korendir removed a gaze cold as ice from the garden. He lowered himself to the ground and guardedly approached the ash of last night's fire.

Haldeth lay asleep. Torn earth at his hands and feet told of exhaustive struggles to free himself. Korendir bent to check the frayed cord at his wrists, and roused by that slight movement, Haldeth stirred. He attempted to rise and gagged, jerked up short by the belt.

The smith let his head fall back. "Great Neth," he murmured. Lucid at last, and afflicted with a misery of aches, he focused on his companion. Beneath the soot which smudged cheek and forehead, Korendir's skin was raw with burns; absent was the grim expression, replaced by an intense compassion. Haldeth caught his breath, and as if startled by that slight sound, Korendir turned sharply away.

Unsure whether the moment's revelation had been supplied by his own imagination, Haldeth spoke gruffly. "Neth, lad, you're a sight to make a young maid faint. You'll scar badly unless you tend those cuts."

"Stay clear of Anthei's gates, and I'll try." Korendir yanked the stake from the ground. All businesslike efficiency, he loosened the belt and set his hands to the knots restraining Haldeth's wrists. "Have you any more barley flour?"

Still prone, Haldeth gestured at the satchel left beside the dead embers of the fire. While Korendir tossed away the hackamore string and busied himself with the contents, Haldeth worked the bindings from his feet.

The smith sat up. Wincing from stiffened muscles, he accepted barley gruel from fingers as marked as his own and said, "What do you plan to do?"

Korendir never looked up. "Avenge Snail." The words left no space for compromise. Finished with eating, he vanished beyond the dunes, and later reappeared with a clean face. For an interval after that he stared at Anthei's tower, the agate walls now innocently mellowed under sunlight. At length he retrieved his belt.

"I have a task for you," he said to Haldeth as he cinched the buckle at his waist. "Half a league back lies an abandoned forge. Would you go there and make a fire hot enough for tinker's work?"

Affronted, Haldeth set his bowl aside. "Better you asked whether any tools remain for my use."

"The Blight will have warped them, I expect." Korendir bent and adjusted his boots. "I'll come at noon. Wait for me, and try not to crush your great thumbs under any hammers."

Haldeth took a swipe at him. Korendir ducked clear and with maddening purpose strode off into trackless bracken. His companion stared after, and only then realized he had neglected to ask what Korendir wished him to forge.

"Arrogant get of a sow!" Haldeth yelled. "What idiocy are you about?"

But Korendir had vanished beyond earshot into the scrub behind the dunes.

*   *   *

Shivering beneath mouldering thatch, Haldeth bent over the firepit in the abandoned smithy and coaxed damp kindling into coals. He cursed steadily in monologue, and did not see Korendir enter, laden with rusted ironware. Looted without discrimination from the surrounding farmsteads, the collection included anything from chipped axe blades to punctured buckets. Warned by a metallic clank, Haldeth looked up in time to cringe; Korendir unburdened his load with an ear-jarring crash just beyond the threshold. He ignored the smith's yelp of annoyance, but moved to the canted work table and laid out his other acquisitions: a dusty lump of tallow, the haftless remains of a kitchen knife, and several soggy grouse feathers.

"Have you ever cut fletching?" he inquired of Haldeth.

"No." The smith swung around and gave free rein to irritation. "Nor will I. If you plan to make paste with my barley flour, take it from your dinner ration."

Korendir smoothed one of the feathers against his forearm. "You can forge a score of arrowheads, surely?"

"Out of *iron?*" Haldeth laughed, incredulous.

Korendir paused, a quill poised between long fingers. "They needn't be pretty to look upon."

"Pretty!" Haldeth kicked the nearest corroded pot and bashed a hole through its base. He dared not say what he felt, that arrows could never breach Anthei's fortress; Korendir would be killed. Too distressed to stay silent, he threw up his hands in disgust. "Neth, man, the Blight afflicts everything in this Kingdom, even the building of fires. Broadheads forged in this place will hold no edge, and anything iron will rust to nithering bits."

Now dangerously still, Korendir said, "I don't intend to keep them." He selected a stick from the kindling pile and deliberately began to strip the bark. Left no option but to work, Haldeth stalked over to the junk pile by the door and rummaged for suitable scrap.

By sundown, the two men had completed a crude sheaf of arrows. They returned to the campsite, where Korendir put the finishing twist on a bowstring fashioned from Snail's hackamore cord.

Haldeth looked on with a frown. "Those arrows would barely dent the skin of a pumpkin. No doubt Anthei is laughing at you."

"Let her." Korendir set the bow aside, dumped tallow into the cookpot and waited while it melted over the fire. He used the softened wax to stop his ears, then muffled his head under the hood of his cloak. "Shout at me."

Haldeth complied, splitting the evening stillness with an epithet.

Korendir nodded, oblivious, and shouldered his arrows and bow. He climbed the tree beside Anthei's garden. There, straddling a limb, he scratched numerals into five of the broadheads, thereby destroying the point on the sixth. He shot the first marked shaft in a long arc over the wall. After wobbly, erratic descent, the arrow cracked resoundingly against Anthei's door; rebound spun it clattering end over end down the stair by the entry.

Korendir adjusted his position against the tree trunk. Affected by the Blight, his shafts would win no tournament, but for the purpose he intended they would serve. Twilight settled swiftly over the land; only minutes remained before darkness spoiled his marksmanship.

From the tower's lancet window, Anthei watched Korendir drop arrows at intervals along her garden path. Their eccentric flight betrayed makeshift origins, and admiring a skill which mastered the adverse effects of the Blight, Anthei released the catch on her casement. Leaning outward, she began the song which had lured the horse the previous evening; only this time she tuned her spell for the archer who had ridden it.

Korendir's hand held steady on the bowstring. His final arrow bit just inside the gate, scattering white gravel in the gloom. Well into her song of summoning, Anthei waited for the man to display the first spoiling traces of restlessness. Korendir dropped lightly to the ground. Shadow flickered at his heels as he paused by the fire to collect a rusted heap of ironware. Deaf to the smith's encouragement, he removed the scrap to the gate and arranged a crude barrier between its posts.

Anthei frowned from her seat by the window. Had the man been susceptible to her spell, he should have entered her garden without any delay for precautions. Intrigued by his resistance, Anthei placed a perfectly shaped fist on the sill and pitched her call an octave higher.

Korendir glanced at the tower. His manner reflected no urgency as he arranged his remaining arrows point first in the dirt. He tested the tension of his bow, then raised a booted foot. Careful to keep his flesh from any contact with the bronze, he eased the bar from its setting and kicked the gate sharply inward.

Anthei abandoned her call mid-phrase. Against this man, the lure was useless. The witch's eyes narrowed with fresh interest as she assessed his poised stance between her gateposts. Korendir had withstood the murder of his beast and a summoning geas; Anthei waited to see how he would manage her guardians.

The bronze grill grated to a stop to reveal a pristine expanse of white walkway. But the path with its borders of flowering shrubs stayed empty only an instant. Motion flurried the plants on either side, and the cat-shaped forms of Anthei's guardians hurtled forth. They numbered three. Black-and-white striped coats rippled over muscle as they sprang for the intruder at the gate. Manes of stiffened quills framed eyes like coals and needle-fanged muzzles bared to snarls.

As the beasts bore down on him, Korendir bent his bow. With steady eyes he sighted their run, and the gravel which scattered under the stretch and spring of each stride. Lethal as they seemed, their charge was indirect; Anthei's guardians swerved to avoid the broadheads left imbedded in the path. Conjured from earth magic, they appeared to be chary of cold iron. Gratified to see his hunch confirmed, Korendir kicked a kettle into a clanking roll across their path.

The leading guardian spat. It dropped into a crouch, forepaws flexed to expose claws like skewers, with barbs to entrap as well as maul.

Korendir fired his arrow. The shot took the creature point-blank through the eye. Smoke boiled from the wound. The beast's scream shivered the night, a sound that engendered terror to freeze the heart. By the fireside, Haldeth buried his head in his arms.

At the gateway, deafened by wax, Korendir nocked another shaft.

The remaining guardians circled their fallen, whose convulsions plowed furrows in the path. They paced to the barrier of ironware, ringed tails lashing with agitation. Korendir drew his bow. The nearer guardian hissed. It raked out with a barbed forepaw, and disturbed currents of air brushed Korendir's knuckles. He aimed for the soft triangle of the throat and released.

The arrow flew true. Maddened by the bite of iron in its flesh, the beast launched into the air. Smoke billowed from its muzzle. Korendir backstepped clear. Undeterred by its baleful, screeching cry, he sent a second shaft into its exposed underbelly. The guardian crashed full length across his barrier. Pots scattered from the impact and the beast's form unravelled into fumes. Stung blind by stinking vapor, Korendir blinked away tears and saw the last guardian leap over the corpses of its fellows. He nocked another arrow; and the Blight-cursed cotton bowstring snapped between his fingers.

The guardian sprang for the kill.

Korendir dove flat. Frantically he scrabbled for a fragment of metal as the guardian hurtled overhead. His hands hooked on nothing but weedstalks. The beast landed, whirled and charged again. Korendir rolled and fetched bruisingly against a farmwife's flatiron. Too late, his fist closed over the rusted handle. The guardian regained balance and lunged with a snarl for his throat.

Braced for impact, Korendir raised the iron. He thought to ram the beast between its gaping jaws, but understood his plight was hopeless. Claws would rake him before the silly wedge of metal could connect. His agonized death would follow swiftly.

Locked to the gaze of murderous red eyes, Korendir did not see the pan hurled in from the sidelines until it bashed the creature in the flank. The guardian twisted mid-leap and spun with bared teeth toward Haldeth, who ran weaponless into the fray. Cat-muscles bunched for attack. In desperation, Korendir chopped his flatiron into the creature's neck. Smoke plumed from the contact. Choked by fumes, Korendir seized his last arrow and rammed the guardian through to the heart. Its dying swipe caught him in the calf. Hooked by barbed claws, he crashed to the ground while around him the conjured mass of bone and muscle unbound into ugly coils of smoke.

Haldeth dragged him clear. Coughing and dizzied from the acrid tang of spells, the smith labored to catch his breath as Korendir stirred, rolled, and violently vomited his supper.

Haldeth steadied his friend's shoulder until the spasms ceased. "Are you all right?"

Korendir ignored him, shivering. After a moment he picked the wax from his ears and raised a face transparently pale. "What a cruel end for Snail. Those horrors ate even his hooves."

"He's avenged," Haldeth said shortly. Unreassured by the small talk, he hauled Korendir to his feet. "Come back to the fire and let me tend that leg."

"Not yet." Korendir shook free and straightened. "I'm going in." His gray eyes shifted pointedly to the corpses left steaming on the path. "If I wait, Anthei will have another spell guarding her gates. I must go now, or not at all."

Haldeth responded with reluctance. "Will you be careful?"

Korendir brushed rust flakes from his hands and laughed low in his throat. "I'll watch the odds."

Haldeth looked on, appalled, as his friend tossed his tallow plugs aside. No words were suitable for the occasion, but as always Korendir did not care. He strode limping to the garden wall, and without an instant's hesitation, scaled the stone and dropped on his feet in Anthei's rose bed.

Curled comfortably on cushions in her tower window, the witch wrinkled her nose at the stench of ruined spells. "Clever man," she whispered.

Had Korendir entered through the main gate, he would now be quite dead. Since he had not, Anthei switched tactics to counter. Leaning her elbows on the sill, she framed the man between the angle of her thumb and fingers, and her voice measured phrases to a different tune. Darkness spread like a pall over her garden. Shrub, path, and starlight vanished, as if Neth's creation had never existed.

IV. Anthei's Tower

Shadow snared Korendir in darkness. His eyes seemed wrapped in felt, and the air went strange and thin in his nostrils, devoid of any scent. Certain blindness alone would prove no handicap unless Anthei had set other perils against him, Korendir groped for a landmark to orient himself. His hands met emptiness. Garden foliage had disappeared; the very ground before his feet had dissolved into air, leaving him one step from oblivion.

Korendir straightened and unslung his belt. The buckle shone ghostly white against that unnatural void. As if the proximity of iron weakened the spell, faint radiance traced the outlines of rose leaves against a black as absolute as death. Korendir extended an arm into the glow and felt thorns hitch at his sleeve; with no pause for thought he dropped the buckle like a plum bob. It slithered through foliage and struck earth.

Korendir lifted his foot. He felt the solidity of the garden vanish into nothing as his boot left the ground. Guided by the gleam of the iron, he eased forward. His toe touched soil, but his heel remained suspended over emptiness. With painstaking caution, he slid his foot further into the sphere of the metal's influence and shifted his weight. The rosebed held firm. Step by deliberate step, movement was possible; but no margin remained for mistakes. Estimating his bearings from memory, Korendir made tortuous headway through the cross-tangle of briar and hedgerow. At last he felt gravel grate beneath his sole. He had reached the central path.

Faint light pinpricked the darkness an arm's length to his right. Korendir reached down to touch. His fingers scraped gravel and closed over honest wood wound with twine; the illumination arose from the iron tip of his arrow, left embedded in Anthei's front walk. The broadhead bore the numeral five, and by Korendir's calcula-

tion, the tower door lay fifty paces north. He swung the
belt and proceeded, progress marked by the nebulous
glimmer of his arrows.

He recovered his last shaft at the foot of Anthei's front
stair. The marble risers stayed firm without need of iron's
virtues to bind their existence. Korendir ascended and
gained the landing. Abruptly the pall of darkness lifted.
The latch tripped, and brass-bound door panels swung
inward, spilling candlelight over the stoop. Anthei waited
at the threshold. Framed beneath the carved agate lintel,
she was robed in floor-length crimson velvet. Gold braid
belted her waist. Her delicate oval features nested like a
gem beneath masses of coiled blond hair. The beauty of
her stunned Korendir like a physical blow; he had expected a crone.

Amused by his surprise, Anthei laughed with a sound
like the ringing overtones of coins falling on glass. "My
ways are not those of mortal women. Did you forget? I'm
a wizard's daughter, and to that heritage I have added the
powers of the White Circle's greatest wardstone."

She considered her visitor with eyes the changing, iridescent green of a peacock's plumage. "Sixteen men out
of seventy-four lived to reach my stair. I offered them
the choice I now grant you. Leave with my forgiveness
for the desecration you've caused within my gates, else
enter at your peril. Be warned. No man has yet crossed
my threshold and survived."

Korendir laid his broadheads on a jutting shelf of
molding and threaded his belt to his waist. He spoke no
word, but his gaze flicked to the latch beneath Anthei's
gloved fingers. Wrought in the form of a dragon, its
scaled surface glinted the frost-blue of burnished steel.

"You are a brave and clever man," said Anthei.
"Don't prove yourself a fool. Once inside, no iron forged
can save you."

"I'll take my chances." Korendir stepped forward.

Anthei inclined her head as he entered. She pulled the
door to, and the latch fell with a sullen clank, echoed
over and over by agate walls. Anthei lifted her candle
from its sconce and started up the stair. Korendir followed, aware that wits were his only weapon.

The chamber above was carpeted in white wool.
Carved agate nymphs pillared the roofbeams, and the

collection of armor and weaponry displayed on the walls between might have been the pride of Aerith's royal treasuries. Precious metals and gemstones threw back reflections like stars, yet their luster seemed dim beside the jewel cradled on a tripod above the mantel. The wardstone of Torresdyr shed all its awesome splendor in that confined space; though no fire burned in the grate and every wall sconce remained dark, the chamber held the warmth and radiance of midsummer noon.

Anthei extinguished her candle and sat on a white fur hassock. Her brilliant eyes followed Korendir as he turned from the wardstone and paced, studying swords, bucklers, mail and helms with evident interest.

"Those are my trophies," said the witch. "Every man who died for the king's quest bequeathed me trinkets for my walls. Have you any ornaments to add?"

Korendir faced her, unruffled. "None that would complement beauty such as this."

"Indeed?" Anthei clasped her hands at her knees. "It need not be wondrous to look upon."

She rose, all grace and stretch like a cat. From the far wall she removed a dagger from carved ivory pegs. The weapon was stubby and plain, notched steel betraying a history of careless usage; a clouded, uncut stone set in the pommel crowned its ugly appearance. Anthei fingered the blade, her face pensive; then with a sudden flick of her wrist, threw the knife at Korendir's chest.

He spun on light feet. His hand shot out and intercepted the dagger's spinning arc. Steel slapped flesh, controlled with no more penalty than a slender red nick on one thumb.

"Ah," said Anthei, regretful. "So soon you find your bane. That weapon was wrought by the White Circle. A small cut it made, but one that will never heal. Morey of Dalthern thought to take my life so. He has claimed yours instead."

Blood welled across Korendir's palm, splashed in soundless drops to the carpet by his boot; without remorse he noted, "I'm going to leave marks on your sheepskins."

He examined the dagger with deliberation, then settled himself on a divan and turned his gaze upon Anthei. Seated once more on her hassock, she arranged herself with artful abandon, until like the wardstone, her magnif-

icence hurt the eyes. The effect was not lost on Korendir.
But where other men quickened their breath and sweated
in bewilderment, this one sat like a struck bronze image.

"You're a well-controlled man," Anthei observed. For
a time she watched the slowly spreading stain which
marred the brocade beneath his hand. Korendir made
no response. Nettled, she traced her fingers suggestively
through fur and added, "What a pity you're meanly
dressed. I could bring you Morey's tunic and surcoat to
brighten your final hours."

"No." Korendir balanced the little knife on his knee.
"I prefer my own."

"You've nothing to lose." Anthei gestured toward the
buckle at his waist. "Iron only affects sorcery derived
from the wardstone, since any spells fashioned through
its powers are bound to answer earth law. But Iraz's lore
transcended such basics. His teaching holds all metals
alike. Cling to your tinker's trinket if you wish. You will
find it proves worthless against me."

Korendir offered no reply. Anthei spoke with conviction,
but her gloved hands belied her words. Her basic strength
might indeed be impervious to iron; nonetheless she was
careful to shield herself from its touch. In the hours which
remained before he bled to death, Korendir saw no need
to yield up even so questionable an advantage.

If Anthei was disappointed by his refusal she masked
her feelings well. Bored with his taciturn company, she
rose to depart. Reflections from the wardcrystal empha-
sized her iridescent eyes as she paused a last moment by
the door. "You'll be comfortable here, at least for
awhile. I'll return your corpse to Torresdyr for burial, as
I have seventy-four others. Your belt buckle will adorn
my east wall. Take comfort from the fact. You were the
first to counter a summoning song with a lump of wax.
That was the triumph of your life."

Anthei stepped from the chamber. The latch clicked
gently shut. Though no lock turned, Korendir entertained little doubt that sorcery sealed the portal beyond
the virtues of iron to open. He had no desire to risk
being torn limb from limb because he rushed to try the
obvious. Instead he thrust Morey's dagger through his
belt and roved the breadth of the chamber. The worth
of the weaponry would easily have ransomed a dozen

princes. Between maces and tasseled halberds, four lancet windows opened at each point of the compass. Bare slits at their widest aperture, they would never permit escape. But the wardcrystal lay upon the mantel within easy reach; if Korendir could toss the jewel from the window where Haldeth might retrieve it, all effort might not be in vain. Children would no longer die in Torresdyr, and its pitiful king could shed his burden of guilt.

Without sparing thought for consequences, Korendir unslung his belt. He ignored the bolted catch, but set his buckle against the hinge, his intent to force the pin. Contact roused a dazzling flare of light. Agony lanced his body, ripped screams from a throat which had never opened for any torment of the Mhurgai. Thrown backward onto the carpet, Korendir lay unconscious. He sprawled under the stony shins of the nymphs for close to an hour, while his hand seeped steady drops of blood. Alarmed when he wakened to discover a pool of spreading scarlet, he abandoned attempt on the casement. Anthei's tower was a prison beyond means of man's endeavor, and with each minute he bled, his options diminished. Korendir pushed himself to his feet.

He paced the chamber until dizziness spoiled his balance. By the time dawn glimmered through the casements, he sprawled on the rug by the mantel, his forearm streaked to the elbow, and his lips tinged blue against flesh translucent as steamed glass.

Sunlight threaded copper glints through Korendir's hair when at last Anthei chose to return. White wool lay speckled like a slaughterhouse where her prisoner's restless steps had carried him; prone by the hearth, the man himself was ivory pale against a scarlet mat of carpet. Anthei tossed her head, sharply disappointed. She had come to make his passing unpleasant only to discover he had collapsed far earlier than expected. Cheated of her sport, she crossed the chamber on slippered feet. If Korendir was simply unconscious, she would restore him and make him suffer; his remote facade would shatter and he would beg for death. Lovely as a succubus, Anthei bent and grasped his wrist to check for pulse. She did not notice the boot left braced against the firedog.

Long, loose hair slipped over her shoulders and caressed the line of his cheek.

Korendir exploded into motion. He twisted like a dropped cat and pinned Anthei's hair beneath his shoulder. His motion jerked the snared tresses taut, and Anthei overbalanced. Startled laughter rang in his ears as she crashed across his body. Through dizzied vision, Korendir glimpsed widened, green-blue eyes and an expression of murderous delight.

"Clever man," said the witch. But her amusement changed pitch to alarm as he rolled again, and her silky locks snagged on the unfinished edge of his belt buckle.

Smoke plumed from the contact. Metamorphosis travelled swiftly up the strands, graying their youthful resiliency. Wrinkles spidered Anthei's forehead. Her remarkable eyes clouded with cataracts, and smooth cheeks puckered with wrinkles as the iron's fatal unbinding engulfed her face. Years of aging claimed her form in a single instant, puffing slim hands and shrivelling spell-wrought beauty to skeletal ugliness. Red velvet caved and sagged over more angular contours. With a breathy, startled sound like an infant's cry, Anthei shuddered and collapsed.

The man disentangled himself from her corpse with savorless practicality. The gatekeeper had correctly named the wardstone responsible for Anthei's prolonged youth. Subject to earth law, the plain beggar's iron which fastened his belt had grounded her with reality; shock proved too much for her heart. But the accomplishment left the victor exhausted.

Korendir rose on unsteady feet. Dizziness sucked at his balance as he braced himself against the mantel and lifted the wardstone from its tripod. He wrapped the jewel in his cloak and rocked drunkenly down the tower stair. The latches on the doorway were fastened without enchantments. Korendir fumbled them open and emerged in the full light of morning.

Anthei's front path burned his eyes like a snowfield. The bronze gate shimmered at its end, impossibly distant. A blurred form appeared beyond, wildly shouting: Haldeth.

Korendir blinked and forced concentration. With great effort he lifted the wardstone from his cloak. For an instant, two thousand two hundred and forty facets blazed like fire in the sunlight. Then Korendir swayed and tumbled headlong down the steps.

He was still struggling to rise when Haldeth reached him. Sure hands gripped his shoulder and settled him gently against the stone of Anthei's stoop.

"Neth's everlasting pity, lad, you're decked like a cock from the fighter's pit. Is the blood yours or the witch's?"

Korendir stirred, opened bland eyes, and raised his thumb. But the slice opened by Morey's enchanted dagger was now miraculously healed; apparently contact with the wardstone had closed the spell-cursed cut. Not even a scar remained. Speckled with rainbows thrown off by the gem's prismatic facets, Korendir laughed. "Haldeth," he said when at last he regained his breath. "There's a fortune in that tower."

Haldeth lifted the wardcrystal from his friend's unsteady grasp. Even lit by its radiance his eyes shone much too bright. "You've won crown and kingship also," he observed.

Korendir winced. A pained look crossed his face. "I'd forgotten." He followed with a vulgar word and hammered his knee with his fist.

Four days later, he and Haldeth arrived at the palace of Torresdyr, the wardstone slung in a cloak between them. The tired old gatekeeper winched back the portals and stared through astonished eyes at blossoming orchards and lush new grass. Across the kingdom, farmers were plowing weeds from the fields, and though spring lay six months distant, the seeds they sowed sprouted and matured almost under their feet.

The king wept shamelessly. His steward accorded Korendir the courtesy due a prince and babbled excited plans for coronation.

"Cancel that!" Korendir said sharply. "I came for Anthei's gold. Loan me an apple cart, and I'll leave with it."

"You'll take no reward at all?" said the king, distressed to realize the ruffian meant every word.

"A draft horse and a harness," Korendir replied, faintly vexed. He accepted no more than that.

Later, as the wagon rattled empty toward the tower which housed their winnings, Haldeth studied his companion; he knew the flush of triumph on those features could never last. Korendir was not a man to put aside his restlessness. Yet had he dared to speculate, Haldeth would never have guessed they would seek to challenge the dreaded Cliffs of Whitestorm, where gales keened over the bones of dead dragons, and not even wizards dared landfall.

The brig's captain regretfully regarded the bronze-haired man who had just proved that his gold was not offered in jest. "I'm sorry, young master," he said at last. "No coin ever struck will buy passage to Whitestorm Cliffs. It's mutiny I'd have, if I charted a course through those waters, and cut throats for us both ere we rounded Irgyre's Rocks."

The stranger, who named himself Korendir, took the refusal in calm stride. Untitled, rootless, and apparently without surname, he had recently acquired both fortune and reputation by rescuing Torresdyr from a wizard's bane. Rumor had branded him reckless. Still the captain was startled when the young man inquired next of Fairhaven's shipyards.

"You'll meet your death, lad," he snapped.

A bland, chilly smile touched Korendir's features. "Perhaps not. Would you recommend a shipwright? I'll need a responsive craft with sturdy construction."

"Are you daft?" The captain spat over the seawall. "The best vessels built become fishbait off the Cliffs of Whitestorm. Foul weather aside, icefloes have the bottoms out o' them twixt one gust and the next. I'll not lend my advice to the murder of good timber. That's begging ill luck."

Korendir's smile disappeared. He turned abruptly to leave, and confronted by the determined set of his shoulders, the captain felt strangely moved. He called out. "Ask for Sathig! He's got an eye for a sound plank."

Korendir glanced back, jostled by the press of the fishmarket. "Fortune to you," he said. "Sathig it will be."

The captain watched the adventurer's black tunic disappear into the softer beiges of the crowd. Suddenly sorry he had spoken, he sighed and shook his bald head. The idiot would never return alive.

Parchment was barely laid out on Sathig's design boards before every sailor in port at Fairhaven had heard of Korendir's desire. The madman intended to challenge the Cliffs of Whitestorm for the dragon's hoard trapped in a chain of caves at the tidemark. Once the quest had been common. But at the time Sathig inked the lines for a two-man boat, adventurers no longer talked of treasure. The dragons themselves were bones, solidly frozen in the ice at White Rock Head. Folk whispered at the dockside and sadly stroked their chins. The young fool would die, even as the dragons had, victim of the weather elemental which stirred the shores of Whitestorm to a nightmare of gales and freezing current for the past century and a half.

Unconcerned by the fate which awaited him, Korendir sat in Sathig's study and reviewed drawings for a twenty-five-foot sailboat of lean contours and shallow draft. She would be fitted with a double set of rowlocks in anticipation of unfavorable winds; thoughtfully, Sathig added a leaded swing keel against the inevitable shoals. Well-pleased, Korendir left the parchment unrolled, and weighted at the corners with a princely sum in coins.

Sathig fitted the little craft well, though onlookers smiled over his work from the day the keel was laid. Korendir was a whistling lunatic if he thought to best a weather elemental with a brace of oars; and nowhere in the Eleven Kingdoms could he hope to find another as crazy as himself to man the second pair.

Korendir met their jibes with features like blank slate. Bent over an adze among Sathig's craftsmen, he chose not to mention the companion who currently commandeered the forges at the chandler's shop.

Grateful for that small privacy, Haldeth released the handles of the bellows, wiped callused palms on his apron, and reached for his hammer. He had no stomach for taunts. Standing over the anvil with his hair slicked to his temples and neck, he pounded out the tines of what soon would be an anchor. He berated himself for a lack-wit. The hook he forged was oversized, even for a mackerel boat, and any current requiring such weight was more than mortal man should challenge. But Korendir was determined.

"The hoard of Sharkash alone is rich enough to build a stronghold from foundations to battlements, with wealth left over to fit out the armory," his friend had justified firmly. "The opportunity is too great to ignore."

Annoyed by the memory, Haldeth shoved the anchor into the coals and hauled on the bellows. Korendir would go alone if need be. Hardship had touched the man's sanity to the point where the fortress he dreamed of building meant more than life and breath. Haldeth cursed and licked a blistered thumb. He hated the sea. But his friend would need someone to splint his silly, shattered bones, if by the grace of Neth he survived the venture at all.

Haldeth made himself scarce as work on the sloop continued. Her mast was stepped by late spring, and artisans fussed over her brightwork. Korendir spent his days reddened by the reflection of tanbark-treated canvas, while the sailmakers labored to sew a doubly reinforced storm jib.

" 'Tis more an elephant sling than a sail," grumbled the master designer.

Taut-lipped, Korendir silenced the craftsman's complaint with gold. The sloop was launched the next morning; named *Carcadonn* after the winged unicorn no man could hope to capture, she sailed in early summer. A crowd lined the wharf to see her off. Sathig stood with the rest, certain he had seen the last of his handiwork. The sloop would not be returning to Fairhaven, even in the baskets of a salvager's skiff.

Driven on a broad reach by the summer trades, *Carcadonn* made comfortable passage despite her short sheer line. Absorbed by charts and dividers, Korendir reverted to silence. Although sail changes and gear repair kept Haldeth busy, long hours at the tiller left his thoughts free to brood. Once, White Rock Head had been a favored harbor with safe anchorage. But since the weather elemental had claimed the territory, tempests raged unabated, savaging the shoreline until the cliffs lost all semblance of their charted contours. In Fairhaven's taverns, tales were told of Whitestorm's weather that caused Haldeth to shiver in full sunlight. No curse could ease his misgivings. He detested the cold.

Carcadonn sailed through the Dragon's Eye and ran east. Though summer reached its height elsewhere, past Irgyre's Rocks, the temperature began remorselessly to fall. Standing watch one moonless night, Haldeth was first to notice that ocean phosphorescence no longer sparked in the wake. The waters foamed cold and dark beneath *Carcadonn*'s keel, and blown spray bit his skin like sleet. When Korendir took the helm at midnight, Haldeth wrenched open a locker and tossed his companion a cloak of oiled wool.

"You'll need it," he said crossly.

Korendir's sole answer was a shrug.

Seven days later, *Carcadonn* lost her weather. Wakened by a bang of canvas and the yawing pitch of an unplanned jibe, Korendir clawed out of his bunk. On deck, Haldeth wrestled the tiller, drenched and swearing. The gusts shrieked, rushing in like a boxer's punch across sixty degrees of change. Overcanvassed, *Carcadonn* reeled through steepening seas.

"Heave to!" Korendir jammed his feet into seaboots. "We'll reef the main and switch to the smaller headsail. Which tack steers easiest?"

"Neither!" Haldeth ducked an icy sheet of spray. "Mark me, we'll be under muscle by morning."

Korendir vaulted the hatchboards and headed for the foredeck. Gently he said, "You're a pessimist."

But the wind belied his outlook. By afternoon *Carcadonn* bucked over wavecrests blasted to spindrift. Pummeled by gusts, her gear rattled and crashed aloft. The tiller plowed against Haldeth's hands with the force of a gut-speared boar. Old Sathig's handiwork could assuredly stand up to punishment; but as Korendir took the helm at dusk, the smith wondered how long the sloop could stay seaworthy. Conditions hereafter would only get worse.

By morning the wind backed and blew from the northeast. *Carcadonn* beat to weather, clawing over swells half the height of her masthead. On starboard tack, Haldeth

glimpsed land between the waves. The low dunes of
Dunharra were replaced by rock-crowned crags which
broke the slam of the incoming surf like an unending roll
of thunder.

Haldeth shook water from his hair and shoved the tiller
hard alee. *Carcadonn* ducked, came about with a whipcrack of slack canvas, and turned the hazards of the coast
astern. The cliffs were proof she made progress. But
when Haldeth retired below and discovered the galley
fire doused by the damp, he separately cursed every
league he had sailed out of Fairhaven's harbor. Abovedecks, a block squealed warning. He grabbed for the rail
and missed.

The boom lifted and crashed to the opposite tack. The
mainsheet parted like thread. *Carcadonn* slewed, tossing
Haldeth against a bulkhead. Cold oatmeal splattered his
chest, and his oath brought Korendir in a bound from
the helm to measure the scope of the disaster.

Haldeth sat scraping porridge from his beard, while
his companion hunkered on his heels and grinned with
infuriating calm.

"When you're wiped up," Korendir said, "we're going
to take in sail."

The smith glared, rose, and jammed his arms into oilskins. The wet patch left by the oatmeal settled like icy
fingers against his chest as he emerged unwillingly for
labor. While the sloop wallowed under bare poles, he
helped Korendir slot rowlocks into her toerail and
benches to the cockpit lockers. Much as Haldeth detested
rowing, oars were preferable to riding a whirlwind under
banging yards of canvas.

Stripped of sail, *Carcadonn* made better headway, but
her crew suffered for the improvement. Waves broke
over the bow, and repeatedly flooded the cockpit. Worn
by the drag at his ankles as the water sucked out through
the scuppers, Haldeth found rowing a miserable contest
of endurance. Cold and fatigue dulled his mind, until
time itself seemed suspended.

When the first icefloe reared above the wavecrests,
dirty white in the currents which tumbled past the keel,
Haldeth shipped oars in silence. He went below to brew
hot tea and found no reassurance as the beat of Korendir's stroke continued unabated above decks. Every pull

of the oars brought them closer to Whitestorm, where the elements would batter them beyond hope of survival.

The next day dawned thick as unbleached wool. Fog swallowed the mast down to the spreaders, and gusts screamed through the rigging like the ribald laughter of hags. *Carcadonn* bucked, graceless as a death-wounded deer. Her crew jounced against the benches, their team-work at the oars gone ragged. With his eyes streaming runnels of seawater, Haldeth waited for Korendir to admit his folly and turn back. Yet hour after weary hour the man leaned into his stroke. No word passed his lips, and no glimmer of reason relieved his expressionless face.

That night, secured under double anchor, Haldeth stood first watch lest the moorings drag. He huddled in the cockpit and tried to remember what it felt like to be warm, while gusts played a song of endless winter through the stays. The hours crept. With no star over-head to reckon by, the dark seemed to freeze in place. Stiff and shivering, Haldeth retired at midnight. He found Korendir still awake, intently bent over the chart table.

The smith cracked crusted ice from his oilskins. "You're a maniac, and very soon you'll be a frozen mon-ument to stupidity. It's colder than the Mhurga's third version of hell out there."

Korendir looked up, eyes impervious as mirror glass in the gimballed swing of the lanterns. "We're nearly there." His voice sounded bemused over the rush of wind and waves.

Braced against the heave of the deck, Haldeth exam-ined the chart. The inked line of *Carcadonn*'s running fix ended almost under the shadow of White Rock Head. Less than two leagues to the north lay the lairs of the dead dragons, and the vortex of the elemental's force.

"What we are is witless," muttered Haldeth. For one wild moment curiosity overrode sense; then his thrill of excitement died out at remembrance that his boots sloshed with seawater, and the galley fire was a mess of wet ashes. He cursed aloud at the chart, never noticing the tolerant amusement which touched Korendir's face as he swung himself up the companionway to finish his turn at watch.

V. White Rock Head

Morning dawned dim with cloud. Korendir labored on the foredeck, drenched to the skin by flying spray long before the anchor broke free of the sea bed. Too miserable even to curse, Haldeth manned oars in the cockpit, his eyes squeezed shut against the sting of salt water. He pulled his looms by reflex. Years of ingrained habit allowed him to adjust to compensate as his companion joined stroke at the forward bench. *Carcadonn* shouldered clear of her anchorage into the teeth of the gale.

Battered, pitched, tossed upon their benches until their flesh bruised, the two men labored for a league. Seas broke with hissing fury over the beleaguered sloop. The cockpit swirled with green water and seaboots chafed against shivering flesh with the abrasive irritation of sandpaper. Haldeth could spare no resource to fret over folly now.

The weather worsened, its force more viciously concentrated than any concoction of nature. Wind frayed the mist to shreds like tattered spectres. *Carcadonn* shuddered with each pull of the oars, while contrary, spindrift-crowned waves slammed her time and again, a hairsbreadth shy of broaching. Whipped at last to exhaustion, Korendir and Haldeth dropped double anchor. Too chilled even to stand watch, they huddled over the galley stove while *Carcadonn* pitched against her lines like a pain-maddened bull.

Storm brought early darkness. The mast whipped against the stays. Lines chafed and fittings rattled, and the rudder banged at her pins, despite stout lines of lashing. Toward midnight, drifting ice ground into the aft anchor rode. Chain snapped off at the hawse, and *Carcadonn* slewed in a bucking arc, dependent on her thinner second line. The yank as the slack caught short flexed every timber in the hull.

By miracle, the bow hook held.

The lurch upended lanterns in their brackets. Fortunately their reservoirs were emptied, an extreme precaution for rough weather. Haldeth took refuge in his bunk with his arms clamped over his head, and for once yielding to common sense, Korendir did not stir aloft. Conditions were too desperate to risk slacking off line to set the spare anchor. If *Carcadonn* broke loose in such current, no remedy might spare them from wreck on the reefs.

The night passed; if Korendir managed sleep, Haldeth most assuredly did not.

Daybreak arrived through louring layers of cloud. First to rise, Haldeth cracked the cockpit hatch and blessed luck that he still was alive. Everywhere the sloop showed punishment, from varnish and paintwork stripped down to wood, to lines snapped into tassels. Even Sathig's meticulous handiwork could never withstand another night like the last. Korendir seemed not to care. He hastened to raise anchor like a man set after by demons. Too worn to argue, Haldeth sat his bench and bent to the rhythm of the oars.

Carcadonn heaved sideways. A wave slapped her thwarts, and spray showered over mast and deck and cockpit. Haldeth shook water from his eyes and shouted warning, just as the anchor cleared the sea. The sloop slewed like a cork in a millrace. Somehow Korendir kept his balance. He made fast the chain and swung aft with the agility of a monkey to take his place at the bench.

Both men pulled to the limit of their strength, to no avail. Against the tumbling grip of the current, sinew and oars proved inadequate and the sloop ripped out of control.

Haldeth saw the iceberg first. Glistening white, and sharp as trap jaws, it reared off the bow while the current sheared eddies on either side. Shouting, the smith heaved on his loom to deflect the sloop to leeward.

Water resisted his pull like iron. *Carcadonn* spun sideways, married to her course like a suicide. Haldeth braced for the inevitable impact.

"Keep rowing!" Korendir screamed.

He slammed his oars clear of the rowlocks, then rose

with the shafts in his hands. Braced against rail and cabin top, he leaned out to fend off like a madman.

Beechwood met ice with a screech and dislodged a spray of flying chips. The oar blade ground into splinters. Korendir shouldered into the stub, his face a snarl of effort. The planking beneath his back and feet groaned as if the bulkhead would crack. Then the sloop bucked. Water sucked at her keel, and she shot clear with a lurch. The iceberg retreated dizzily behind.

Korendir never looked back, but bounded in a stride for the foredeck. He freed a halyard, but his valiant effort to hoist sail ended in flogging defeat. The wind was impossibly strong. Whipped into retreat by a snarl of rigging and burst canvas, *Carcadonn*'s master abandoned the mast. He dropped to his knees on the deck and slashed the ties which restrained the anchor. Hook and chain fell free, swallowed by boiling foam. The line burned out with a scream of friction. White-lipped, Korendir counted footage and belayed off to a cleat.

At last able to help, Haldeth dragged hard on the oars. He strove against what seemed the unleashed fury of hell to ease the strain on the anchor. Still, the line snapped taut with a hum like the cock of a siege arbalest. Droplets smoked from stressed plies. But the cable held.

Haldeth nearly wept with relief.

Korendir straightened on splayed feet by the foredeck. He glared at the ruins of his trysail, then shouted, "That thing would've served better as an elephant sling!" He hacked the mess free of the shackle, slung himself aft, and thrust an armload of dripping canvas at Haldeth. "Stow the cussed thing in the forepeak, in case we have need of a hull patch."

At a loss for comment, Haldeth obeyed. When he returned from below and found Korendir unlashing the tender from *Carcadonn*'s cabin top, his nerve at last gave way.

"Just how far do you expect you'll get in that?" Bent by the force of the gale, the smith clenched both hands on the lifeline just to maintain his footing.

Korendir jerked his head toward the cliffs, where a spray-drenched islet arose, marked by geysers of spume as breakers thundered past toward the headland. He shouted over the tumult. "We'll want to mount bolt rings in the channel. Sathig would never forgive me if I left his boat hanging by one anchor, untended."

"Neth!" Haldeth slapped ice from his collar. "You're mad! If you think to manhandle that eggshell in there, don't expect pity when you capsize."

Korendir paused. He looked up, and his lips split with an expression that passed for amusement. "I'm not daft. Not when I know the weather elemental of Whitestorm by name."

Haldeth sat heavily on the cabintop. "Where in Aerith's Eleven Kingdoms did you learn that? You had no enchanter's upbringing."

Suddenly absorbed with his knots, Korendir said, "I won Anthei's library, didn't I? Her father left notes in the margins of a spell scroll that called for nine coinweight of dragon's teeth."

This revelation was remarkable only for brashness. While a man trained to power could sometimes influence an elemental through the binding properties of its name, Korendir was no wizard.

Haldeth took a breath of cold air. "Since when does knowing penmanship make you an expert?"

Korendir tossed off the last rope. He glanced up with eyes that were much too steady. "Do you want to turn back?"

"No, the more fool I!" Haldeth flung away in emotional contrast. He sought comfortless refuge in the cockpit while Korendir slung the dory from the main halyard, then wrestled against the pitch of the seas to launch the craft over the rail. Not until he tossed his tools and line beneath the oar seat did the smith surrender to the inevitable. Haldeth emerged to steady the painter, while his companion kicked over the lifelines and settled himself on board.

Korendir signalled his wish to be cast off.

Haldeth gripped the line in white knuckles. "Is there nothing that moves you to fear?"

Korendir shrugged, supremely reluctant to answer. Then, on a whim, he changed his mind. "The death that's in front is a known thing, already faced and accepted. But the end that catches a man without grace from behind, that one drives me to terror. There I will raise walls in defense, Haldeth. Until then, nothing else matters."

Brusque now, Korendir freed his oars. As though his conclusion was inevitable, he added, "Stone masons demand great piles of coin." Almost gently, he reached up and pried the line from the frozen fist of his friend.

A swell rolled green beneath the sloop. Lifted on its crest, the dory spun away, snatched off by the twist of the current. Haldeth watched, his chest all aching and hollow, and his throat closed to sound.

Korendir made no attempt to row, but instead struggled upright, propped against his oarshafts in the dory's pitching stern. Wind cracked his cloak like a flag and the punch of the waves rattled the boards beneath his feet. Tossed like a chip before the might of the elemental, the man's braced figure reflected all the futility of a twig propped upright against an avalanche.

Had means existed, Haldeth would have dragged both dory and occupant back to *Carcadonn* by main force. Since that was impossible, the smith pondered the merits of earnest prayer for the first time since Mhurgai had murdered his family.

The next instant, Korendir flung a shout like a herald's cry against the ice-runged cliffs. "Cyondide!"

The word echoed back, baldfaced enough to provoke war between neighboring kingdoms. Haldeth's emotions were quenched with the speed of a pinched candle.

"Cyondide!"

Whitestorm's elemental gave response in a rush of wind and wave. *Carcadonn's* dory spun like a cork compass, and spray plumed over her gunwales. Balanced on sloshing floorboards, Korendir fought to stay upright. As if the roiling waters posed no significant threat, he raised his voice again. "Cyondide, I come to Whitestorm as envoy. Would you founder my craft before I deliver my message?"

Water slapped the dory's bow. Her keel settled so abruptly that Korendir was slammed to his knees. Then the wind parted to carve a circle of calm around the tiny boat. Into air frozen in sudden silence, the elemental replied, its voice the hiss of breaking surf. "Cyondide is here. Who sends a mortal man as envoy? No wizard would so dare."

Korendir recovered his footing. He answered with a calm that chilled Haldeth's blood. "Ishone, from the east sends me. As bearer of his message, I demand safe harbor and leave to moor my craft against the rocks."

Seawater exploded into froth beneath the dory's keel. The little boat tipped not a hairsbreadth, but stayed cradled on an apex of forces that threatened her capsize at any moment. Korendir neither crouched nor grabbed at thwarts in self-protection. Instead he laid aside his oars as if the elemental's assurance of his safety was already foregone conclusion. Shamed to favorable decision, Cyondide tamed the seas. Waves foamed and flattened; as far as the eye could see, the ocean lay like sheet glass against the feet of the cliffs.

Korendir sat down unperturbed and threaded his oars. The echo of his stroke as he rowed fell like a shout on eddyless air. His manner reflected no haste, yet Haldeth observed that he worked without wasting movement. In less than an hour, he had mounted the hardware to berth his sloop between islet and shore. Although the temperature plunged like a stone, not a cat's paw of wind troubled him as he returned and warped *Carcadonn* from her anchorage. Haldeth helped secure the sloop to the rocks. Although at Fairhaven, the smith had seen twenty-ton ships less stoutly moored, he refrained from disparaging comment. Against the fury of Cyondide, steel cable would chafe like simple hemp; a man would be supremely lucky if even forged chain did not break.

Korendir loaded the dory with food, spare clothing, and coils of pale new rope. To these basics he added a square of uncut sail cloth, a climber's axe, and a tied bundle of pitons. Haldeth dogged the hatches and silently boarded up the companionway. The quiet made him ache with uneasiness. Although weather elementals lacked any sense of sight, when aroused, their hearing could be preternaturally acute.

Carefully, Haldeth dropped from *Carcadonn*'s deck into the laden dory. As Korendir took up the oars, the smith settled in the stern seat and asked the question that had fretted him throughout the hour. "Who on Aerith is Ishone?"

Korendir leaned into his stroke and returned a whisper. "Another elemental."

Unreassured, Haldeth sat braced as the dory ghosted forward. "And your message?"

Korendir's mouth stiffened obstinately. His oars rose dripping from the sea and descended again without pause.

Soon after, a gust cracked the calm. Ripples shivered the reflections of the rocks, and Cyondide's impatience rebounded from the ice-scabbed cliffs overhead. "Mortal, your safe-conduct wearies me. Deliver your message."

Korendir dragged an oar blade and turned the bow. A fragile wake of bubbles trailed astern as the dory nosed past an ice floe.

"Mortal! Answer Cyondide, or be dashed to a rag on the rocks."

Korendir cried back in annoyance: "Is Cyondide without honor, that a messenger from Ishone is met with threats?"

Haldeth tucked his head between his shoulders, expecting at any moment to be spilled from his seat and whirled to his death in the sea.

Yet Korendir's stroke resumed undisturbed. One league, then two passed beneath the dory's keel. Stillness pressed against Haldeth's nerves until he felt he must split from the pressure.

Oars poised, Korendir leaned forward at last and whispered into his companion's ear. "Start looking. If the tide's out, we ought to find a small ledge. The entrance to Sharkash's lair should lie just above."

"Mortal!" boomed Cyondide. "You do me no service by squeaking in the manner of a mouse. Speak louder, that I might hear what tidings Ishone sends in the mouth of a man."

The dory glided ahead. Black with wet, and glistening under rungs of ice, the rocks showed neither ledge nor cave mouth. Discouraged, Haldeth peered down into depths too cold to grow weed. There, beneath a fathom of water, he found the outcrop. Cyondide's interference had upset the tides since the bygone days of the dragons. The entrance to the lair lay submerged, hopelessly inaccessible to a dory laden with tools.

Haldeth waited in dismay as Korendir shared the dilemma of discovery. Committed beyond retreat, they would suffer the fate of the dragons, drowned, or maybe frozen, all for an elemental's caprice.

The dory rocked; Haldeth looked up in time to see his

companion fill his lungs with arctic air. "Cyondide! I have been six weeks upon the sea, and my feet grow weary of boats. Give me solid ground, and I shall deliver Ishone's tidings."

A wave arose and smacked against the cliff base. "There are ice floes about, mortal, that offer footing as firm as any land. Choose one of these, and swiftly, for my patience wears thin."

"What is ice but water frozen?" Korendir's tone turned scornful. "Does Cyondide lack the might to drop the tide one fathom, that Ishone's envoy have dry rock for his feet?"

"Cyondide could ebb the tide until the sea bottom crumbled and grew desert fern. Stand warned, mortal. Cyondide could blast your bones to powder also."

"Words are only bluster," Korendir returned with bitten insolence.

Haldeth cringed through a moment tight-drawn as the calm before killing storm. Then the ocean sucked away from the cliffs in a roaring, eddying rush. The dory spun. Water curled over her gunwales. Korendir caught the rowlock to keep from falling. Then he sat and threaded oars. The instant he recovered steerage, he jerked his chin at the smith.

Haldeth leaped across to the ledge. Fast as he dared, he unloaded tools and ropes into the dripping mouth of the cave.

"Mortal, your message!" Icy wind froze the droplets as they fell; Haldeth shivered as salty, unnatural sleet bounced down the rim of his collar. Cyondide's impatience charged the air with the ozone of an immanent lightning strike.

Korendir inventively strove to stall. "The words that Ishone charged me to deliver to Cyondide are complexly phrased, and lengthy. They concern a most delicate subject."

Haldeth listened, a prickle of dread giving rise to suspicion: his companion's strategy was no plan at all, but only a brazen bluff.

Korendir shipped oars and stepped ashore. "Cyondide offers grave discourtesy, to force important matters on a messenger still weary from travel. Surely Cyondide can forbear, that Ishone's chosen envoy might rest."

"Then beware your fragility, mortal!" the elemental boomed back. "Your demands have not pleased Cyondide."

Haldeth helped drag the dory onto the rock. Then he hurried to unload the remaining supplies. Elementals had touchy natures; possessed of towering pride, a few had been known to hurl themselves into tantrums violent enough to obliterate their own existence. Power alone commanded their respect. Arrogant of their might, they challenged enchanters for sport; few wizards in Aerith owned lore enough to contest with the beings and survive. All that restrained Cyondide from destroying the trespassers on the ledge was the implied slight to his omnipotence.

Had the elemental at Whitestorm possessed sight to observe the men upon his cliffs, he would have dashed them into the sea to drown. Yet since mortals lacked the aura that clung even to the weakest of wizards, only sound could betray them. Korendir muffled the climbing axe with sail-cloth, then gestured to his companion. Haldeth accepted the tool. While Korendir stood vulnerable on the ledge, the smith ascended the rock shaft that angled upward from the waterline.

Whitened bands of salt marked the floods of countless tides. Though his hands and feet froze to numbness, Haldeth pressed stubbornly forward. No ambassador's courtesies could avert retaliation once Cyondide pressed his demands. The smith had no desire to be drowned like a rat by the rage of a duped elemental, not with the dragon's lairs and safety just a few yards higher overhead. Haldeth did not bother with pitons and axe, but forced his shivering frame up the black throat of the shaft by touch. In time the rock walls widened. A hand-hold, a kick, and a slither, and the smith rolled onto a shelf that extended an unknown distance in the dark.

He sat, breathing hard, and rubbed his fingers. Then he unlashed the spare rope from his waist. Sweat dampened his temples by the time the knot came free. Haldeth loosened the coils. He flaked the line down the shaft to Korendir, who tied a pack to the end. A twitch signalled back, and the smith raised the rope hand over hand. He hoisted the bundle over the lip of the shelf. Tired of fighting the darkness, Haldeth dug into the pack after flint, stakes, and a wad of oil-soaked rags.

Spark snapped in the smith's palm. Flame kindled round his new-made torch as he knelt and raised his arm. Fire fluttered to brilliance and sparked a glitter from the shadow. A sapphire blazed like splintered starlight from a hollow not a pace beyond his elbow.

Haldeth sprang up in exultation. His head cracked rock with a force that stunned him dizzy, but his excitement remained. Passageways branched outward in three directions just past the overhang that had bruised him. There the caves lay polished, ground smooth by the scales of dragons; the sapphire twinkled in promise. Surely Sharkash's main horde awaited in caverns higher up.

Haldeth jammed his torch in a cleft. By the loops still coiled at his feet, he judged his climb had covered close to three hundred feet. Whether Cyondide could drive the tide that far was a point best left untested. The remaining supplies must be hoisted without delay.

Korendir caught the line at the cliff base, aware his ruse was wearing thin. The air over White Rock Head hung cold as death; had a man attempted sleep in such conditions he would have frozen solid, as Cyondide no doubt intended. The sea seemed to mirror the elemental's pique in brooding, green-black depths.

Numbed past hope of dexterity, Korendir labored urgently over knots that should have taken seconds to complete. As he raised the final bundle from the ledge, a piton slipped from the wrapping.

Korendir fumbled the catch. With a thin, ringing chime, the metal bounced and splashed into water. A circular band of ripples fled the site. Korendir lost a moment to horror. Then he dropped the pack and slashed the cord free with his dagger.

"Mortal!" The voice of the elemental shivered the air like a thunderclap. "Speak, mortal! Cyondide will wait no longer."

Korendir flung off his gloves. He caught the rope barehanded and secured a loop to his waist.

Tremors shook the ledge underfoot as the elemental shrieked a command. "Deliver Ishone's message to Cyondide!"

A wave arose from nowhere. Doused to the waist, Korendir slammed forward into rock. Blood dripped from a gash in his forehead as he planted his weight to resist the drag of current against his shins. Cornered now, and left but one alternative, he raised his voice.

"Cyondide!" Anger chiselled his shout. "Know that you have offended Ishone through abuse and injury to his envoy. For this insult, in the name of Ishone, this envoy issues challenge to Cyondide. Never shall peace exist between Cyondide and Ishone until a duel of power brings settlement."

Before his echoed words had faded, Korendir dove for the cave mouth and frantically hauled on the rope.

The sky split. Lightning seared the ledge, and rock splinters flew where his feet had rested barely an instant before. The sea sucked back with a rush like an indrawn breath, even as the man threw himself upward with all of his desperate strength. For a moment the wind screamed maledictions; then water smashed up from beneath with the battering momentum of a log ram.

Korendir never felt the cold. Crushed headfirst into stone, he went limp. Blackness claimed his awareness, even as the waters crested in a rush up the shaft and foamed over his body.

The rise of the tide echoed upward like the roar of an infuriated dragon. From the ledge in the upper cavern, Haldeth bellowed in wordless rage. Aware that the rope now supported the fleeing weight of his companion, the smith pulled, driven to heroics by fear. He never saw the water that boiled over the lip of his outcrop, though wavelets soaked his feet and kicked the stacked supplies on a tumbling roll into darkness. Haldeth heaved mindlessly. Coil after coil splashed from his hands. The flood chuckled and slapped over stone, and then as abruptly subsided. Sea water gurgled downward. The rush of its ebb tore greedily at hard-won cordage, and whirled the supply packs like dice.

Hemp burned through Haldeth's fingers. He cursed, and kept hold, though callus tore from his hands and his footing was nearly sacrificed. Maddened by the sting of flayed palms, he separately damned every body of water in Aerith. Scared witless at the prospect of a lonely end at Whitestorm, he recovered his stolen yardage. Foot after foot, the rope arose from the shaft, until torchlight caught on a spill of bronze hair. Haldeth's muscles knotted one last time. He heaved Korendir's frame over the brink and sprawled him face up on his back. Gray eyes were fixed and sightless. Water dripped from a slackened mouth, and blood that shone black in the torchlight flowed over temple, forehead and cheek.

Haldeth bent, trembling with shock. He laid hands on sodden cloth, but felt neither movement nor life. The ribs beneath his touch stayed stone still. He shouted, overtaken by rage. "Die on me, will you?"

Only echoes answered. Mocked by their repetitive sound, the smith succumbed to fury. Riches, fortress, safety itself seemed a fool's dream, as far past his reach as the family left slaughtered by Mhurgai. Crazed by grief, Haldeth gripped his companion by the shoulders. He shook Korendir's lifeless torso as if violence by itself could negate the finality of defeat.

Korendir choked. His head rolled back. A flare of sparks from the torch showed a flicker of pulse at his neck. Shocked back to reason, Haldeth changed his grip. He turned the unconscious man over and administered a sharp blow to his back. After a moment Korendir sputtered. Water spilled from his nose and mouth, and his chest shuddered weakly into motion.

"Praise Neth!" Suddenly aware of the cold, the smith stripped the clothing from Korendir's body, then wrapped him in his own dry cloak. The packs lay wedged in a fissure. Haldeth drew his dagger and cut them free, praying furiously that the tinder inside was not entirely soaked through.

Korendir awakened to the warmth of sunlight on his cheek. Furs bound his limbs in clinging warmth, and a fire snapped at his back. One of his eyes was swollen entirely shut; almost everywhere else he was bruised. His chest ached. His face stung. The sunlight, and the shadow of his form against rock grated against his awareness with a wrongness he could not identify.

"Cyondide has deserted Whitestorm to duel Ishone," said a voice; Haldeth's, by its Southengard drawl.

Memory returned. Korendir tried to move, changed

his mind, and grimaced. He managed a rough-edged whisper. "I'd hoped for that." It hurt, even to speak.

Motionless beside the fire, Korendir listened as Haldeth told of his search through the caverns that laced the strata of the headland. Early on the smith had discovered a tunnel which accessed the summit of Whitestorm's cliffs. In more detail, he described the dragon lairs, and the first, torchlit inventory of Sharkash's legendary hoard.

"There's enough gold in these rocks to pay every mason in Aerith," the smith finished. "You'll have your holdfast, if we can find a way to move such a grand weight of treasure."

A companionable silence passed before Korendir stirred himself to question. "What of the dory?"

Haldeth shook his head. "I burned bits of the transom for firewood. That's the only fragment I could find."

Yet the thorn trees which grew in black, impenetrable stands on the clifftop offered hope to solve this setback. Though unpleasant to work, the trunks yielded passable timber. Already Haldeth had begun construction of a raft to ferry jewels back to *Carcadonn*.

Korendir grunted approval. "While you're busy, better cache some kindling in the driest, best ventilated lair you can find." He caught his breath, then continued with a trace of the timbre that had outbluffed Cyondide. "Whichever elemental wins that duel will return in high passion for vengeance."

Already worried over that, Haldeth shoved to his feet. "If we're caught before we sail, we're both dead."

"We'd be pursued, regardless," Korendir finished matter-of-factly. While his companion unhappily pondered the complications of that, he closed his good eye and slept.

Korendir rested soundly until dusk, when Haldeth swore a vicious oath in his ear. The anger behind the curse was sincere. Startled half out of his furs, the injured man whirled, drew his dagger, and lashed out to skewer an assailant who was not there.

The ledge by the campfire stood empty. The packs, the food stores, the spare coils of rope: all were stacked undisturbed. No footsteps fled down the passage which led toward the dark of the dragon lairs. Korendir was utterly alone. The imprudence of sudden movement made itself felt in a multitude of aches. Still, he did not lie back. He waited, poised in thought, for reasonable explanation to present itself.

A second later, Haldeth repeated his malediction. This time a reference accompanied that placed blame on his Neth-forsaken climbing axe.

Korendir frowned. He slipped clear of his furs and coaxed stiffened muscles to bear weight. His companion's epithets rang preternaturally clear, as if the smith sat adjacent to the firepit. Korendir was certain he suffered no hallucination; neither had the words been the product of a wizard's spell. Some trick of the rock must have deceived his ears. Intrigued, the adventurer reached for his breeches and boots. He clothed himself, preoccupied beyond noticing bruised limbs and swollen cuts.

When Haldeth returned, he found his companion perched, cloakless, on the brink of the four-hundred-foot drop that fronted their campsite. Chill winds whipped Korendir's hair into tangles, and the coals at his back had gone cold.

"What in the Mhurga's many hells are you doing?" The smith threw down his sack of tools and knelt irritably to rebuild the fire.

Without turning, Korendir recited Haldeth's earlier oath with a pitch and inflection that were maddening for their mimicry. "The weather's mild," he added. "And I can't stay bundled in furs like a babe any longer."

Haldeth dumped his logs, then sneezed as he inhaled a disturbed cloud of ash. "You'll rest if I have to forge chain to keep you down."

Korendir let that pass. He pursued his earlier train of thought as if the smith had neither threatened nor interrupted. "Where were you, and what made you curse with such enthusiasm that I was wakened from sleep?"

"What?" Haldeth stopped with his flint poised motionless over the bark he had shredded for tinder. "Neth, man, you're raving. You couldn't have heard me. I was in a tunnel east of Sharkash's hoard."

Korendir turned awkwardly from the cliff edge. His eyes quite pointedly fixed on Haldeth's left hand. "Did you hit yourself by accident, or did you bruise that thumbnail purple to attract a lover? The whores of Arhaga started the fashion, but they generally use paint for the purpose.''

Haldeth's roar of outrage became swallowed without echo by empty sky. Through swelling and bruises, and a forehead still scabbed from mishap, Korendir might have smiled. "Be more careful of the axe, my friend. And don't forget where you drove that piton. Our lives might soon depend on it.''

Korendir's strength returned gradually. At first unable to manage the heavy labor of raft construction, he spent his days exploring the cliffs of Whitestorm, both the inside chains of caverns and the crags without. The treasure proved too extensive to tally; and freed of Cyondide's influence, the headlands themselves embraced change.

Summer winds blew the chill from the air. Though the flinty, white rock remained armored in ice, the soaring lift of the crags caught the eye with a stark and forbidding beauty. Korendir roamed across the heights, the thorn trees an impenetrable tangle at his back. Where Haldeth cursed the inhospitable barbs, and twisted black branches that seemed to claw like tortured spirits at the sky, Korendir saw a bastion against invasion. He listened for hours to the cries of the gulls, and was moved. Whitestorm haunted him, waking and sleeping, until finally he set words to his thoughts.

"I want to build here," he announced over the flames of a late night fire. "This is the most perfect site in all Aerith to raise my holdfast.''

Startled in the midst of cooking, the smith spilled an overdose of herbs in the stew. "Neth!" He scooped with the ladle, but bungled the recovery; glumly he watched the seasoning sink beneath the gravy. "You're mad. Mad! And possessed with the gall of Cyondide. How do you propose to match the wrath you've stirred up among the elementals? Mhurga's hells, man! We have gold enough to build mansions and stuff them to the eaves with pretty servants. Can't you choose a plan that won't wind up getting us both killed?''

"You shouldn't have smashed your thumb," Korendir

said obliquely. "Are you going to mix meat with the rosemary, or should I make bannock in self defense?"

Haldeth looked blank. Then, red-faced, he threw down the ladle and spattered the campsite with broth. "Suit yourself. Burn the gravy." Explosively, he stood up. "You can bet on the fact I'm not hungry."

Unruffled as his companion stormed out, Korendir slung the pot back over the coals. Soon the sounds of furious hammering drifted down from the cliff top; Haldeth expended his temper upon the boards cut from thorn forest. If, beyond an hour, he had not recovered his appetite, Korendir resolved to toss their overspiced supper off the cliffside.

Four days later the raft was completed and launched. Burdened low on the waterline with treasure, the craft proved unwieldy but stable. Korendir and Haldeth attempted the return trip to *Carcadonn* at ebb tide. The sun struck patterns in the shallows, and the drip of steadily melting ice spilled melodious trickles down the rocks. Though treacherous still with ice floes, Whitestorm's natural patterns of surf and current proved mild and unthreatening. The sloop remained secured to her moorings; but the winds of Cyondide's departure had dismasted her ten feet above the decks.

Haldeth climbed the strakes. He fought his way aboard through snarls of stays and thrashed rigging. Bedecked with gold chains, and sporting a twisted string of pearls for luck, he managed to withold any curses until the companionway was unsealed. Water had overrun the bilge and soaked his favorite blanket; the fact that Korendir already manned the pump did little to ameliorate his temper. If flooding was reversible, matters of scarping and carpentry were not so easily solved. Timber was needed from Thornforest before *Carcadonn* could carry sail. Their departure must be delayed at least several turns of the tide.

"Sathig will have you murdered when he sees how you've treated his brightwork!" The smith withheld what he knew was the truth; more likely they would not live to make port at Fairhaven at all. Foolishly, boastfully, or maybe from surly stubbornness, Korendir had set his heart on winning the coast of Whitestorm from the elementals.

"The luck of the dragons is on this place," was all he would offer for excuse. Haldeth abandoned argument, too chary of his friend's chancy temper to point out that nothing remained of the dragons beyond tales and unburied bones.

VI. Master of Whitestorm

Cyondide returned to Whitestorm just at the fading of
twilight. Haldeth and Korendir were caught exposed on
the ridge, sweaty from the labor of cutting timber.
Warned by a sudden plunge in temperature, and a
scream of wind-whipped water that bounded across distance to reverberate beneath the cliffs, they dropped
their tools where they stood. Side by side they bolted for
shelter, leaving planks cut with adze and plane abandoned half-dressed on the ground. They took refuge in
the depths of the caverns. The lair they chose was dry,
smoothed by time, and well removed from any opening
to the outside.

The whistling cold of the elemental's breath touched
them, even there, while the smash of ice-ridden waves
beat a furious tattoo through the rock. "Mortal! Cyondide duelled Ishone, and triumphed. Ishone is now nothing but a lament sung by the breeze. Ishone, delivering
to Cyondide his final word, said no envoy had been sent
in his name."

A gust eddied snow across the outside cliff face. The
melted runoff from the glaciers froze instantly to the
hardness of quartz. "Mortal, you have lied. Cyondide
will pick apart the rocks to find you. Cyondide can hear
the whisper of your breath."

Korendir flung off his cloak. He glanced at his nervous
companion and said, "Loan me your torch. I'm going to
take Whitestorm from Cyondide."

A gust drove a rattling fall of hail against the cliffs.
"Mortal! You progress from lies to insolence. Cyondide
will tear away your life."

A sudden snap of frost pried an avalanche from the
heights. Boulders fell, tumbling and grinding down the
slopes to splash geysers of spume from the sea. The spray

blew in sheets on the wind. Droplets iced into hail which battered the cliffs with a rattle like shaman's bones. Gale winds tossed through the thorn forest, and the ancient network of dragon caves rang like a flute to its passing.

Korendir threaded through the gusty drafts of the caverns. He passed through an opening of natural stone and entered Sharkash's lair. The bones of the King Worm remained there, entombed on the mound of his hoard. Korendir climbed a hillock of priceless treasure. He threaded a path through the dead dragon's ribcage, and gold coins, rang beneath his boots. The torch burned raggedly above his hand. His breath plumed like smoke in flickering, wild light, while relentlessly, Cyondide sucked the warmth from the air.

Korendir swung his leg over the barrier of the skeleton's breastbone, then vaulted over razor-finned vertebrae to reach his objective. Ahead, above the vacant eye socket of the skull, a shaft rose into the ceiling. Korendir set the end of the torch between his teeth and clambered up a ladder of reptilian incisors. He stood on the dome of the dragon's crown and felt amid cobwebs and darkness until his fingers touched cold metal; the piton Haldeth had driven when he mistakenly hammered his thumb.

Korendir approximated the stance the smith must have assumed to set the pin. As he did so his ears were battered by the tumultuous thunder of the elements. He listened to the effects of Cyondide's rage as if he stood exposed upon the cliff face level upon level above. The illusion was uncanny. The scream of the winds and the crash of storm waves sounded real enough to provoke a shiver of dread.

Korendir gripped the torch in sweating fingers. He raised his voice with all the contempt he could muster and directed a shout up the shaft.

"Cyondide!"

Like Haldeth's curse, the acoustics of rock deflected the sound. Korendir's outcry reverberated through tangled, dragon-smoothed passageways to the outer cavern once used as a campsite; ringing defiance, it broke over the cliffs of Whitestorm, audible even over the roar of gale and tide.

Cyondide responded instantaneously. A shaft of light-

ning seared the ledge from whence the sound issued.
Thunder snapped and rolled, shaking the caverns and
deafening the ears of the man who stood with an upraised
torch many yards beneath the surface.

Korendir filled his lungs with air that held the sheared
scent of ozone. "Weak are the lightning bolts of Cyondide, that a mortal stands against them!"

A howl of rage tore the night. The darkness cracked
open, flickering and lurid as full noon as charge after
charge of electrical force hammered the ledge. The
growling crash of thunder shook rock and ice from the
heights, and debris plummeted downward into the millrace of current beneath.

"Weak is Cyondide!" yelled Korendir. He dropped the
torch and flung both hands over his ears. The endless,
rumbling boom which followed all but shook the life from
his body. He sank to his knees, curled with his face
against the bone of the king dragon's skull. Still the thunder pealed. The brimstone smell of scorched rock wafted
down the shaft. Sweat dripped from his brow and heated
air stung the linings of his nostrils. Huddled and helpless
before a violence that paralyzed thought, Korendir
closed his eyes.

A final, smoking bolt tore across the ledge on the clifftop; enraged beyond self-preservation, Cyondide chan-
nelled the sum of his being against the mortal who had
mocked him. The rock glowed red, melted, and reformed
into a permanent epitaph of wrath.

Thunder slammed like a blow upon the air. Echoes
bounced and roared across the cliffs of Whitestorm, then
faded away into silence. For a time, nothing moved along
that gale-whipped coastline except the dash of waves and
dwindling eddies of wind.

Cyondide the elemental existed no more.

Far beneath the earth, Korendir stirred. He lifted
trembling hands from his ears, then fumbled among the
time-polished horns of a dragon and recovered his fallen
torch.

"Great Neth," he said gently.

His words roused nothing but stillness. Korendir leaped
to his feet. A smile surged over bruised features, and a
wordless shout of victory escaped his throat. Funnelled
outward by the very rock which had tricked Cyondide to

his end, the cry reverberated like the triumph of a god over the crags of White Rock Head. The weather-stripped skulls of a thousand dead dragons rang with the sound, and spirits whose fires had been quenched by an elemental's icy tyranny at last were freed to find peace.

The warmth of high summer cracked the ice from the cliffs of Whitestorm. Frost left the ground for the first time in fifteen decades, and life reawakened in the thaw seemed all the more vibrant for its dormancy. Grasses raised blond heads to the breeze and spread a living, sun-burnished carpet over the heights. The close-woven boughs of Thornforest burst into blue-violet blossom, then shed scented showers of petals to unveil shiny, black-green foliage. Overnight, White Rock Head transformed from the frigid, wind-ridden hell of an elemental's caprice to a wide place between sea and sky where the seasons turned with savage, unspoiled grace.

Yet nature no longer ruled the site undisputed. A jumble of great, gray blocks had been imported by sea from Southengard, then raised by means of ox-driven winches to the summit of Whitestorm cliffs. There, Korendir raked a hand through sweat-tangled hair. Shirtless, clad in breeches dusty and torn as any craftsman's, he regarded the line of foundations newly laid for his holdfast. For a heartbeat his features softened with contentment as deep as the summer.

Baileys, walls, and keeps had been designed in harmony with the landscape. Though the levels of gold coins in the coffers decreased with shocking speed, Korendir had not compromised. Whitestorm keep on paper promised the most impregnable defenses in all the Eleven Kingdoms. The ring of the stone mason's mallets, the creak of the massive winches, and the calls of the ox-drivers blended to rhythms like music in Korendir's ears. As he measured the progress he had earned with his hands and his wits, his spirit knew rare satisfaction.

Haldeth saw, and paused with his mallet poised over his chisel. The moment of apparent fulfillment did not fool him. The adventurer who had three times accomplished the impossible still woke sweating from his sleep, the outcries from unknown nightmares stifled behind iron control. Other nights, Korendir avoided his dreams altogether; hours at a stretch he would pace the cliffs by moonlight. Through days of summer dust and weeks of backbreaking labor, the restlessness never left him.

Once the walls were raised, with roof slates secured and great engines of defense set in place behind the battlements, Haldeth prayed to Neth the tension would pass. Likely his hope would prove futile. Like a wound that festered beneath an apparently healthy scar, the driving recklessness which had won their freedom from the Mhurgai lay dangerously near the surface; however much Korendir might yearn to settle behind secure walls, Haldeth wondered how long such a life could hold him.

As if he sensed the observer at his back, Korendir suddenly turned. "In that pose, you'd make a splendid model for a gargoyle."

Haldeth shook off a shiver at the intensity of his friend's gray eyes. "The moment I hauled you out of that blasted, water-cursed shaft, I knew I was going to regret it." He lifted his mallet, prepared with all of a smith's trained strength to direct a stroke onto his chisel. But his arm poised at the height of an arc that never completed. Around him, the clang of the stone mason's sledges wavered and died. Silence descended over the construction site, heavy with the muffled beat of the sea.

Korendir's levity faded. His eyes darkened as he looked to the edge of the clearing. "That's no craftsman of ours."

His tone had changed like a blast of cold. Haldeth followed his companion's gaze in time to see a hunched, miserable figure stumble through a gathered crowd of craftsmen whose tools hung idle in their hands.

"He looks like he just crawled through Thornforest," Korendir observed bleakly. He threw down his measure and chalk and broke headlong to a run.

Haldeth dumped his mallet with an oath. The statement was no exaggeration; even from a distance, he could see the unfortunate's clothing lay shredded almost to ribbons. The flesh underneath would not be much better. Beneath their mantles of shiny leaves, the trees atop Whitestorm were close-woven, impenetrable, and vicious. Not even deer inhabited Thornforest's dark depths. Whoever the stranger was, and whatever his reason for hacking a passage through the briar wastes, Haldeth already hated him for shattering the peace.

The smith shook stone chips and dust from his apron. He threaded his way reluctantly between ditches, granite blocks, and the abandoned teams of the oxen, his heart braced for trouble.

The masons had closed about the stranger by the time Haldeth arrived. Unable to see through the crowd, he waited on the sidelines while others took matters in hand. Presently his forebodings were confirmed.

"Fetch Jonnir's wife," said Korendir, his voice raised and terse. "Tell her to come with her herb basket."

"If her bread burns, there'll be hell to pay," remarked a man from the middle ranks.

Korendir's reply drove every other worker within earshot to an involuntary step back. "Fetch her *now*!"

A mason broke away at his bidding. The crowd parted to let him through, and Haldeth stepped into the gap. He saw what prompted the call for a healer's skills, and immediately wished he had not.

Supported in Korendir's arms, the stranger knelt on the beaten soil. His jacket and tunic of cured leather hung in tatters from shoulders gashed bloody from the thorns. The fleece lining dripped dirty crimson, and a clotted snarl of hair obscured the man's features. Yet when he raised his head, the onlookers shuddered with horror. One eye had been gouged from the socket. Weeping tears of blood, the man drew breath and spoke in the accent of a farmer. "I seek the Master of Whitestorm."

"You've found him." Korendir accepted the title as if destined to position from birth. "Your need must be great if you saw fit to crawl the breadth of Thornforest."

"No ship out of Northengard would sail the coasts of White Rock Head." Self-conscious embarrassment showed even through the stranger's pain.

Haldeth considered the man's raw courage and felt cold. By now, Korendir's reputation for perilous undertakings must span the breadth of two continents. Sailors who hailed from Fairhaven had loose tongues and a penchant for sharing tales; that folk threatened with disaster now came asking at Whitestorm for assistance should come as no surprise. Haldeth studied the bleeding, hopeful face of the farmer, and bit back an oath of sheer anger. At the least, he wished the inevitable could have waited until just one building had a roof.

A shout from Jonnir's woman broke the spell of horrified fascination. "Move aside! Sure's thunder, I won't be walking over any man's backside, not for some clumsy lout what's bashed his thumb."

Bent beneath her wicker herb hamper, the frowsy, frizzle-headed woman cleared laggards from her path with the tongue of a harborside fishwife. As the onlookers thinned to let her pass, she realized her patient was no careless stonecutter. The railing string of oaths that followed drove all but Korendir from the site.

A safe distance removed, Haldeth watched the confrontation.

"You're going to need help," the master said as the plump, diminutive healer shook her fist in his face. "This man is my guest. He'll not be treated like a horse, in the open."

"Stubborn, you are, and quite justly you'll die of it," the healer snapped. But even she could not hold that steady gaze for long. Defeated, she knelt and examined the stranger with hands that were learned, and astonishingly gentle.

Haldeth moved off after the departed workers, grateful to escape the task of bearing the litter. His own past held tragedy enough. Determined to avoid involvement, he applied himself wholly to the shaping of stubborn gray granite. Later, when muscles and fury both failed him, he would drink himself into a stupor. If he was lucky, the stranger would perish of Jonnir's wife's rotten tongue before he gave voice to his plea. Then Korendir could dig a new grave at Whitestorm, and the fortress with its promise of impregnable safety could be completed without interruption.

Sundown forced an end to the labors of Haldeth the smith. Tired, but not from exhaustion, he laid aside hammer and chisel. Clouds crimsoned the sky above Thornforest. The wind off the sea blew damp with the promise of rain. Resigned to another night of wet blankets in a tattered tent that would chill him to aches come the morning, the smith stretched, then sauntered off. He did not go to the fires to share laughter, complaints, and boiled stew. Instead he sought his ale jug, fortuitously refilled the day before by the master of a ship out of Fairhaven.

Yet even as Haldeth stooped to enter his miserable dwelling, a shadow stepped between.

"I'm leaving for Northengard," Korendir said into the gathering dark.

Haldeth curbed the oath that waited on his tongue. In an appeal already futile, he caught his companion's shoulder. "What prompts a four-week passage, and an overland journey of fifty leagues, when all that you value lies here?"

Korendir shrugged clear of the touch. "Gold." His voice was stripped of nuance.

Half-sickened by the reek of the healer's herbs which clung to his friend, Haldeth gave way to temper. "Great Neth, man! Already you have everything riches can buy. What are you, obsessed?"

Deepening night hid Korendir's expression; Haldeth waited, sweating, unsure what reaction his outburst might provoke. The crickets sang obliviously on in the grass, and breezes musky with the perfume of dying thorn-blossom stirred the air. Softened, perhaps, by the land where he had chosen to sink roots, Korendir sighed.

"You saw Torresdyr before the Blight lifted," he said quietly. "Even when fitted by the finest stone masons, Southengard granite cannot withstand an attack by sorcery."

Haldeth lashed back with a sarcasm prompted by memories as ghastly as any that haunted Korendir. "What can a mortal do against a wizard? Buy the White Circle's favor for a wardstone? Man, you are obsessed. How much gold will that take, does any soul on Aerith even know?"

"I'll find out," Korendir said.

"You'll find out alone, then!" Haldeth heard the hurt in his tone, and strove unsuccessfully to harden delivery of his next line. "I've known men of your stamp before. They start with only a little more ambition than most folk. But somewhere between one adventure and the next, they acquire a taste for danger. Then, like pipe drug, they find themselves addicted. Risk becomes a thrill they cannot live without."

Haldeth tried to push past; Korendir only fell into stride beside him. The smith cursed. "I'm not that sort of fool. Luck has spared my life for the last time, young master. No gold on Aerith, and no illusions of White Circle charity will make me change my mind."

Korendir met the tirade with amusement, the cold sort reminiscent of a hell-ridden sail out of slavery. He paused by a loose spill of stone chips, and his maddening, steely voice answered: "I don't recall asking you to go along."

As his friend tried again to shoulder past, Korendir moved and obstructed him. "If you're going off to get drunk, at least take a sober half-minute to hear my instructions beforehand. The stone haulers and the masons have to be paid next fortnight, and the plans for the south keep have been adjusted to allow for another armory."

"Neth's pity, you won't stop!" Reminded, suddenly, of the stranger who had come with a quest, the smith sought a nearby foundation and sat down. "What sort of terror are you going out to fight?"

"Wereleopards." Korendir spoke matter-of-factly, as if creatures born of hell itself were no more consequential than rabbits. "The beasts found a way through the mountains, and villagers along the Ellgol River are being slaughtered."

Haldeth felt as if the wind had been kicked from his lungs. "When do you leave?"

"Tomorrow. The ship which brought your ale weighs anchor on the dawn tide." Like a shadow, Koredir departed. He took with him the odor of sour unguents, and left winds that smelled of grasses and empty dark.

Haldeth took a long, lonely time to resume his interrupted intent. He could not shed the suspicion that a point of significance had escaped him; that something outside his comprehension underlay Korendir's motivation. Now, even more than before, the smith needed comfort from his ale jug. Aerith held no beasts more fearsome than the wereleopard. Man-shape during night hours, and cat-formed during daylight, the shapechangers were irremediably savage killers. Their bite was venomed, and their reflexes, faster than sight. Korendir would be a dead man the instant he stood ground in Southengard.

Haldeth banged his shin against a log paling and cursed in a muddle of self-pity. Whitestorm castle would shelter nothing but echoing, empty halls, and across the Eleven Kingdoms, only one idiot of a smith was crazy enough to ache as if that were a tragedy.

Late summer heat wilted the leaves by the time the trader made landfall at Northengard. Too impatient to wait through the lengthy negotiations for dockage, Korendir personally rowed the captain's longboat ashore.

The farmer who accompanied him had healed well enough to walk. Clumsy yet, and unaccustomed to his new eyepatch, he followed through wharfside crowds, surprised when Korendir flung wide the door to the way-broker's and impatiently motioned his intent to enter.

"But we can't go on by sea," the farmer objected. His backcountry accent caused heads to turn in the foyer.

"The overland walk doesn't bother me," Korendir said shortly. "Now will you come in and witness signatures, or must the rest of your countrymen bash through Thornforest because chicken-hearted captains from the mainland won't sail past Irgyre's Rocks?"

The farmer widened his remaining brown eye. "Coin won't move them," he warned. "Believe me, I already tried."

Korendir lifted his hand, and the counter-weighted door swung closed with a thud that shook the rooftree. "I don't pay people who annoy me."

His sword sang from the sheath, gold lit by the flame of the wall lantern. The farmer gaped as, like a sable hawk in a henyard, the Master of Whitestorm shouldered a path into a crowd of merchant magnates and overwhelmingly made his point clear. He left behind shrieks of outrage, result of a half dozen judiciously slashed brocades; but no bloodshed. The parchment he dictated to ensure the villagers gained access by sea to Whitestorm acquired signatures with hysterical alacrity.

Then, before the traumatized waybrokers ceased bewailing their finery, farmer and mercenary left town.

From the coast they traveled overland, a tortuous journey through mountains with narrowed passes that only pack ponies might cross. Rather than break the legs of a blooded horse, Korendir went on foot. By now, the farmer had learned not to interrupt the silences that sometimes extended for days; Korendir of Whitestorm was not a man who loved talk. Effusiveness did not impress him, and even the wittiest jokes failed to brighten his sword-gray eyes. Cold as the frost which carpeted the ground in the mornings, he followed his guide into low country, where fields and pastures stitched the landscape like a crabbed old grandmother's patchwork.

"Yonder lies the trade road." The farmer gestured as evening spread shadows over the valley entered that morning. "Our journey will be easier from there. Once we tell of our errand, no carter will refuse us a ride."

Korendir showed no sign of apprehension that only a few leagues' travel would deliver him into danger. Lean and dusty from days of hiking over grades, he strode at a pace that was cat-footedly graceful, even over freshly ploughed furrows. The farmer stumbled after, red-faced, sweating, his good nature suffering sorely from short wind. He regarded the black-cloaked champion he had summoned with a respect that bordered upon awe.

Rain might fall, or grit rise choking from the roads, but Korendir never cursed. The animals he snared for the dinner pot fell cleanly under his dagger; so sure was his hand at dealing death, the farmer might have doubted his humanity. Bronze hair and gray eyes were unknown among the mortals of Aerith; the killer who walked wrapped in silence might have been a demon sent from the spirit world of Alhaerie.

Except that after nightfall, crouched beyond the embers of the evening's cook fire, Korendir drew out an ordinary whetstone and honed the edge of his sword. Wrapped in blankets upon soil still soggy with rain, the farmer fell asleep to the sound.

Ten leagues down the trade road, they forded the river Ellgol and bargained for space on a barge bound upstream to Karsford. Beyond that town, they walked again, for since the migrations of the wereleopards, neither riverman nor trader would venture farther.

Once the town of Mel's Bye was a prosperous community with a market renowned down the Ellgol. Yet on the day during harvest that Korendir and the farmer arrived, the central square stood empty. The wooden stalls remained tenantless, their canvas covers flapping forlornly in the breeze off the river. The desolation of the place brought no surprise to the mercenary; for the past five leagues their travels had crossed through acres of unharvested fields. The stalks of oats bent weathered and gray, and what livestock remained in the pastures had grown ill-kempt from neglect. Cottages were shuttered tightly, or abandoned, and cart ruts on the roadway sported cockscombs of weed.

Where Korendir saw emptiness with new eyes, the farmer was haunted by memories. Life-long he had toiled for the autumn market, with its creaking, laden wagons, piled pyramids of produce, and the boastful bargaining of traders eager to buy. But on that windswept afternoon, the echo of their footfalls in the deserted square at Mel's Bye rocked the simple man to his core.

"My folk should surely offer better welcome than this." He shrugged in shaken apology. "The wereleopards cannot have slaughtered them all. Not in the course of one summer."

Korendir grasped the man's shoulder. "They aren't all dead." With a firmness that steadied, he pointed toward the public tavern. Although the shutters were closed and the main doors tightly barred, smudges of woodsmoke arose from the chimney over the kitchens.

The two men crossed the courtyard. Breeze scattered leaves before their boots, and not a single stray dog skulked in the shadows by the stoop, hopeful of a handout from the cook. Unremarked, and almost as travel-worn as the day he had bowed before the King of Torresdyr, Korendir hammered with his sword hilt upon the inn's oaken door.

The panel did not open; instead, the shutter of a nearby window cracked slightly. A dark eye peered suspiciously through. Then the shutter banged closed, and behind the door came voices, then rattling chain, and at last, the clang of a bar being drawn back.

Korendir thoughtfully sheathed his sword. Then the door swung wide. A pasty man in a tavernkeeper's apron beckoned across the threshold.

In contrast to the sunlit courtyard, the taproom was

smoky, dim, and fetid with the odor of confined humanity. The innkeep refastened his door. Shut in darkness only partially alleviated by an oil lamp, the travelers waited while their eyes adjusted.

The patrons of the tavern held no such disadvantage, but the farmer's leather eyepatch stalled immediate recognition.

"It's Lain!" a woman shouted, "My own husband, an' by Neth, I hardly knew him. Lain, ye've grown so thin. Did ye get to Whitestorm, man, and horrors, what's happened to yer eye?"

Too overcome to speak, Lain returned a shrug; suddenly, bewilderingly, he found himself accosted by a press of jabbering townsmen. The wife had to push to reach his embrace. Lain buried his scarred face in her loosened, gray-streaked hair, and shamed to respect, his countrymen gave him space. The tumult of talk died. At last the folk in the taproom noticed the stranger who waited at Lain's back.

Clad all in black, his presence had been easily overlooked. Now, in the subdued glow of lamplight, the bronze hair, the level gray eyes, and the hands crossed and still over an unadorned sword drew every eye in the room.

"Lain has brought us the Master of Whitestorm," a man whispered.

"It's true, do you see," murmured another. "He really does have hair the color of coin bronze."

Korendir did not warm to the comments, but remained, stone quiet, before the doorway.

The innkeep was first to recall manners. "Carralin!" he bellowed over the din of a dozen excited voices. "Bring beer for Lain and the Lord of Whitestorm."

A dark girl in a linen smock left the crowd. Graceful despite her size, she made her way to the tap and returned with brimming tankards. Unnoticed at first, her hands were large, and chapped from hard work at the spit. The first draft she handed to Lain, who raised a nervous shout. "To the death of the wereleopards!" He quaffed a deep swallow and leaned down to kiss his wife.

As the townsfolk cheered, Carralin offered the second tankard. Korendir accepted with a dry murmur of thanks; his glance lingered. The shapeless shift of a serving maid could not quite hide her soft figure, and if her bones were big, and her jaw too square, she handled herself with a deftness that spared her looking clumsy.

Aware of the stranger's regard, the girl blushed. "Lord, are you hungry?"

Korendir's interest underwent a subtle change. "Thank you, but I'd rather hear about wereleopards."

At his mention of the enemy, the bystanders all raised their voices, anxiously eager to speak. The innkeep intervened to instill order. Hesitant to presume friendliness with a swordsman, he caught Lain by the elbow and steered for an empty table. Korendir followed, beseiged, while unnoticed in the commotion, the maid effected an embarrassed retreat.

The taproom grew thick with pipe smoke as the afternoon progressed. Men drank, and their tongues loosened; one by one they related the horrors which beset their town and farmsteads. They told of children dragged from their beds, to be found mauled in the morning; of wives, cousins, and livestock savaged, and stout doors unhinged by razor claws. Korendir listened, intent, to accounts of death by venom. His beer tankard warmed, barely touched, while unseen beneath the table, the fist which rested between his knees slowly, dangerously clenched.

"The fields were abandoned before harvest," the current speaker lamented. "Had to be, and no question. The hell-spawned creatures even kill during daylight, particularly just before rains."

Korendir raised his tankard and took a sip. Sailors had told him similar tales. Two things a wereleopard could not tolerate: water, and changes in air pressure. Wetlands they avoided out of distaste; but the lows that brought in a storm, or the rarefied air of high altitudes, invariably drove the creatures to fits of bloodthirsty slaughter. Indigenous to the dry wastes of Ardmark, wereleopards seldom strayed. Routes into inhabited lands were protected by boglands, or to the east by the peaks of the Doriads. Given that Mel's Bye suffered the worst attacks before rainfall, the creatures' avoidance of altitude still held; which meant some other feature in the landscape must have changed.

"Where does the River Ellgol originate?" Korendir asked at last.

The folk of Mel's Bye regarded him as if he had downed an imprudent quantity of beer. Yet the tankard at the mercenary's elbow remained three quarters filled. His hand was steady on the table, and his eyes shone disturbingly sane. "Do I have to take a hike to find out?"

Across the trestle, a burly, black-haired fellow banged a fist on the boards. "Did we all beg loans from the merchants for this man to take air in the countryside?"

"Emmon, hold your tongue!" snapped Lain.

Korendir shifted his regard to the one who had called him from the cliff site that meant more to him than life. His voice went suddenly cold. "That doesn't answer my question."

"A jaunt upriver won't kill wereleopards," shouted Emmon in surly provocation. Wild-eyed, and muscled like a bull under his patched and faded doublet, he looked crazed enough to murder.

Under the table, Korendir's fingers tightened on his sword hilt. His body angled forward, ready at an instant's notice to kick clear of the table.

Only one in that tensioned atmosphere dared interference. Silent as a sprite, Carralin appeared at the huge man's elbow. Up close, their resemblance was striking, and only possible between siblings. The girl murmured something, and Emmon subsided with a frown. The rest of the folk in the taproom sighed as one with relief.

Korendir waited still, his posture indicative of extreme impatience.

The innkeep was quick to speak up. "The River Ellgol springs from a fissure in the hills, my lord. Onmak Tarris raised sheep there, years ago, before his wife died of a fall. Nobody else ever settled that way. The path is steep, and very rough."

"Not for a wereleopard," Korendir said softly. Few in the room overheard him. With a swordsman's disciplined grace, he rose and called out to Lain. "Find me a guide willing to walk this town until sunset. The autumn rains are not far off. Unless the wereleopards are confined to Ardmark before then, not one of your people will be safe."

VII. Wereleopards of Ardmark

Between mid-afternoon and sundown, Korendir walked the breadth and length of the settlement of Mel's Bye. He encountered doorways that had been clawed to wreckage, and the mangled bones of livestock. He saw graves. He listened to tales of assault and tales of loss, standing in the dooryards of weed-grown farmsteads, while those inhabitants bold enough to accompany him clustered at his heels and started in terror at shadows. No safety lay in numbers where the wereleopard prowled. The Master of Whitestorm had been told as much. Still, he strode the roads and fields with no other precaution than a hand left half-curled on his sword hilt.

At this Emmon Hillgate's son shouted derision. The mercenary the town had hired was certainly a fool; or else he had no concept of the speed a wereleopard could charge. The rest of the farmers held their opinion. With winter closing in, they had no choice. The optimistic among them read the mercenary's attitude as an expression of extreme confidence; the keenly perceptive saw differently: the man seemed fearless primarily because life mattered little to him.

As one who had arranged the loans for the mercenary's fee, the chief councilman might have raised outcry over this, except that Korendir's indifference did not extend to his job. When the party stumbled across a freshly slaughtered deerhound, the mercenary's concentration was daunting to witness. He knelt in the spattered dirt and explored the still-warm corpse with bare hands. He measured the depth of the fang bites with his dagger, examined the ground for signs of struggle, and of course found none. The wereleopard was a creature of grace, lightfooted as wind itself; its venom worked with terrible speed. The torn grass, the claw marks in the sod, all had been carved by the hound's own death throes.

The wereleopard proved to be finicky; it gorged on the choicer entrails and left what remained for the crows. Korendir straightened with a disturbed frown. He cleaned his dagger and sheathed the blade with hands still bloodied from the dog. Then, as the townsmen nervously inclined toward departure, he lingered to study the pad marks left by the cat-form demon. He marked off the sixteen paces of the beast's closing spring, and its satiated stride as it departed. At the end, the onlookers who expected comment were disappointed. In absolute silence, Korendir vaulted a stile and strode back toward the town tavern.

Day was fading. Shadows striped the lanes with purple and the western sky blazed red. Korendir set a brisk pace, and the short-legged chief councilman had to strain to keep up. After a time it became more than plain that no information would be offered. Gathering his nerve, the plump official ventured inquiry. "What will you do?"

"Kill wereleopards." As if unwilling to be bothered, the mercenary's stride increased.

Frustrated as much by his brevity, the chief councilman broke into a trot. Unaccustomed exertion caused his tunic to ruck above the belt; his belly jiggled, and his face turned redder. He would not yield to indignity, but gasped between puffs to Korendir, "How will you do this? Wereleopards have outrun the postrider's horses. One snapped the spine of a bullock in a single bite."

The Master of Whitestorm glanced aside, that moment aware of the councilman's discomfort. He slowed at once. "Tomorrow, when I've explored the river in the hills, I'll tell you."

The chief councilman frowned, absorbed by the need to tug his tunic straight. This answer was far from satisfactory, not when every man in Mel's Bye had pledged his next harvest to borrow gold. If the mercenary hired with the sum failed to rout the wereleopard, there would be no crops, and no hands left to sow seed. The farmers and their families would be ruined. Breathless, sweating, and badly in need of reassurance, the chief councilman surrendered to rumpled dignity with a sigh. He regarded

the taciturn man at his side, and something indefinable
warned him against pressing with further questions.

An adventurer who had singlehandedly lifted the
Blight of Torresdyr, then freed the cliffs of Whitestorm
from a weather elemental could not be expected to welcome the chore of justifying his intentions with talk.

Night fell over the settlement of Mel's Bye. Townsmen
and farmers crowded the taproom in the tavern until
chairs and stools ran short. Latecomers perched upon
trestles. When every available space had been taken, others stood or leaned against the walls, some of them mothers with infants in their arms, others commandeering
floor space for toddlers asleep in blankets. Every cranny
in between became filled with boisterous children. A few
elderly denizens drank themselves senseless to escape the
pandemonium. The young men chose other options.
Emmon Hillgate's son climbed a joist and lounged in the
roof beams, which were smoke-stained and dusty, but
broad enough to accommodate even his muscled bulk.
From there he surveyed the scene with dark, mad eyes,
and observed the one place in the tavern that was not
jammed with townsfolk.

The corner where Korendir of Whitestorm sat was
empty for a yard on either side.

Earlier, while the mercenary sharpened his sword, the
reach of the blade had forced would-be bystanders to a
distance. Now finished with his steel, his whetstone laid
aside, the space around him remained. In solitary, Korendir settled before the trencher brought to him by the
tavernmaid. Nobody else intruded on his presence. He
ate his meal without inviting conversation. Even Lain,
who had shared his company on the road for six weeks,
hesitated to renew the acquaintanceship.

The evening progressed. Carralin cleared away the
crockery, and closed the tap for the night. Despite her
bulky frame and square jaw, her kindly endowed figure
and honest manner had attracted a string of suitors who
outdid each other to win her attentions. But tonight, as
she made her rounds with bucket and cloth, it was the
mercenary's table she lingered over.

Her brother noticed, and frowned from his perch in
the rafters.

When finally the beer mugs stood emptied, the talk among the townsmen faltered. The silence and the darkness beyond the inn's shuttered windows seemed to weigh upon everyone; except Korendir, who sat at the trestle pushing breadcrumbs into patterns with his thumb.

"He's considering strategy," ventured someone, but at a whisper that the mercenary would not hear.

Emmon Hillgate's son held no such restraint. He called loudly from the eaves, and asked how a wereleopard could be intimidated by the arrangement of a banquet suited for mice. The nearer of the townsfolk shifted in embarrassment, but the insult failed to provoke a response.

Korendir raised eyes like northern ocean and announced his intention to retire.

Carralin showed him to his chamber, the inn's best, situated at the end of a gabled corridor on the second floor. The furnishings included hand-sewn rugs, chests fashioned of cedar, and a bedstead tasseled in scarlet, green, and turquoise, more tailored to the tastes of Southengard merchants than to the comfort of a hired sword. Korendir tossed the pillows against the footboard without compunction. He followed by reversing the blankets and quilted coverlet.

Carralin watched his movements with huge eyes as she lit the candle on the nightstand. Diffident, almost wistful, she gathered her courage and asked, "Would my lord like his boots removed? The lad downstairs could oil and polish them."

"Thank you, no." The Master of Whitestorm lifted the candle from under her chapped hands and moved to the window. There he became engrossed in the study of catches, latches, and hinges. Carralin lingered, absorbed by a longing quite at odds with her brother's provocations. Aware of her worshipful presence, Korendir said pointedly, "Your inn has seen to my needs well enough."

"Then I bid you goodnight, my lord." Carralin retreated quietly; and because she turned down her wick to save oil, her disappointment was lost in the shadows.

While her step faded down the stair, Korendir left the window. He snuffed the candle and settled against the footboard with his boots still on. The tasteless dangle of the tassels never influenced his decision; he had simply selected the position that offered the only clear view

through the casement. That left him vulnerable through
the door at his back, but the folk at the inn were no
threat. Danger in Mel's Bye came from wereleopards
changed to man-form at nightfall, and well able to climb
mortared stone, or cross the sloping shingles shared in
common with the innyard stables.

Poised between vigilance and sleep, Korendir reflected
upon the deerhound's corpse lying disembowelled by one
long swipe of claws. The animal had known no chance
to turn, fight, or flee. The carnage had happened faster
than reflex, swifter even than thought. One glance had
confirmed to Korendir how pitifully inadequate mortal
resource would be against the golden killers from Ardmark. Yet if the prospect of ridding Mel's Bye of their
predations daunted him, he fretted not at all. He rested
motionless, thinking, his hand settled loosely on his
sword. Sometime after midnight, he dozed. A half moon
rose in the east and glazed the mullioned windowpanes
in light.

Sound roused him, a furtive scrape followed by the
creak of a floorboard. Korendir's fingers clenched to his
weapon the same instant he opened his eyes.

A shadow eclipsed one square of the casements.

Driven by explosive reflex, Korendir shot from repose.
Barely had his feet struck the carpet when sword steel
sang from his sheath and flashed, point first, to kill.

Yet his adversary was no wereleopard, nor even a thief
come for plunder. Draft from the opened door wafted
an odor of perfume, a cheap scent similar to ones worn
by women who traded their favors for coin. Korendir
registered this at the last second. He recoiled in mid-
lunge and turned his blade, just barely. The flat, not the
edge, grazed the importunate female across the throat.
Momentum was never so easily bridled. His follow-
through hammered one quillon against her collarbone
and jarred her back on her heels.

Korendir caught her left-handed as she tottered. He
spun his own body with the last of his control, and managed to cushion her fall. The hard edge of a clothes chest
bashed his ribs and his sword pommel clanged on the
basin which rested on top. Wash water flooded in a sheet
over his shoulders, soaking his dark tunic, and the hair

of the doxie, which was silky, long, and sweetened with the smell of cherry blossoms.

With the girl's soft breasts against his chest, Korendir leaned forward to ease his bruised side. The slight shift of weight exposed her square jaw to the moonlight.

Recognition caused him to drop his steel as if burned. "Carralin!"

She twisted against his neck, hoarsely gasping for air. Korendir pushed aside her collar and explored her throat. He felt no cuts, no smashed cartilage, only inflamed skin. She would show a bruise by the morning, a small enough penalty. Neth alone knew how close she had come to being skewered. Korendir expelled a quivering breath.

"Why did you come here?"

The words came out harshly. Carralin collapsed against his shoulder, weeping. Convulsed by the aftermath of shock and fear, she could not answer. Kneeling with her young body pressed to his chest and flank, Korendir was aware how scantily she was clothed. Draft from the doorway chilled her flesh, and her small, hardened nipples thrust against the thin muslin of her shift. Even the abundance of perfume could not mask the healthy, female attraction of her.

Korendir moved as if goaded. He gathered his scattered composure, adjusted his legs, and rose with the girl cradled in his arms. Two steps saw him across the floor. Then, as if her flesh might scald him, he shed her clinging weight onto the coverlet of his bed.

Carralin snuggled into the still warm hollow left by his body. Her weeping eased slightly and she reached for him, plain in her need for comfort. But lightly as shadow, Korendir evaded her. Moonlight revealed him; across the room, he bent and recovered his sword from the floor. Then, with barely a creak of floorboards, he returned and sat upon the mattress by the tavern girl's knee. The sword, gripped in too-white knuckles, rested point downward against the scrubbed boards of the floor.

"You shouldn't have come here, Carralin."

His tone was hoarse, as if he had been running and fought to control his breathing. Carralin extended her hand, but the dark of his tunic lay just beyond reach of her fingertips. Frustration, and the memory of the blade that had attacked out of nowhere crumbled her fragile composure. She fought her voice steady. "Lord, I wanted comfort. I wanted to give comfort. My father, my younger brother, my sister, my mother—all are dead. Emmon is the last of my family that wereleopards haven't slaughtered, and he is mad with grief. Now you'll go out, and also be killed—"

Korendir stopped her words with a curt shake of his head. "That isn't what your councilmen are paying me for. Not to come here and die."

Carralin did not argue, but gulped in a spasm that rocked her body. "My lord, you must listen! They are murderous and fey, those creatures. The dark is their time of terror, and I can't sleep for the nightmares."

Korendir sucked in a ragged breath. He rose and trod briskly to the casement; for a long time he stood staring out over fields where the wheat lay rotting like mudflats sheared by a storm tide. "Fey they may be, but the wereleopards aren't invincible. They can be made to bleed and die like any man."

"How?" Carralin's voice showed more hysteria than belief. "How will you kill a thing that moves faster than a man, and carries a poisoned bite?"

Korendir turned with a vicious smile. "When I find out, I'll skin the pelts of the slain for your hearth rug."

Carralin sat up, shocked. The coverlet crumpled under her hips as she swung her long legs to the floor. Moonlight touched her shift like smoke, and the ripe, rounded body underneath. "You have no plan," she accused.

Korendir said nothing. Backlight from the window masked his expression, as though he deliberately hid something.

"*You have no plan*," Carralin repeated, frightened. She fingered her shift with hands that in shadow no longer seemed chapped. Her thread of composure broke. She hurled herself across the chamber, painfully in need of male contact to bolster her failed reassurance.

Korendir's hands caught her shoulders, not gently. Unprepared for the roughness of him, Carralin cried out. Her discomfort softened nothing, but seemed only to sting him to further harshness. She glimpsed his face as he twisted: impervious to pity as sleet-smoothed granite.

Then he spilled her gracelessly onto the windowseat, and retreated to the darkest corner of the room.

Disheveled, disturbed beyond tears, Carralin listened to the rasp of his breath. With a shock of intuition, she interpreted his distress as avoidance. Surprise supplanted her terror. She blunted her edges of uncertainty with husky, female command. "My Lord of Whitestorm, how long since you shared your bed with a woman?"

He did not answer. Painfully still, Carralin waited while he recovered a control that chilled the heart to contemplate. When his breathing steadied, and still, he did not speak, she tossed back long hair and shamelessly stepped forward so the moon would highlight her body. "How long, my lord?"

Korendir shifted slightly in the darkness. Carralin could not see him to know that his eyes were closed, his jaw clenched hard against words. His hands stayed clamped to his face, as if the feminine beauty of her called up some private hell that seared his sanity to envision. Only one thing held meaning for him in this world. Like a litany, he locked his mind upon memory of Whitestorm's windy heights; the dream of the holdfast begun there seemed to steady him.

His throat unlocked. Most of the sweat dried from his brow, and he framed the best words he could manage. "Lady, there is only one comfort a man like me can offer." Taut as the hair-trigger latch on a crossbow, he snatched his sword from the bedstead. On through the opened door he hastened, and never once looked back.

The girl on the windowseat stared after him, confused and startled to anger. "Great Neth, you've gone crazy!" She called again, unwilling to believe his tread on the stair. "Go out by dark and you'll be torn to screaming pieces."

Korendir never answered. He did not return. Touched by unassuagable sorrow, Carralin hurled herself onto his empty bed. He had gone, been driven away by the very consolaton she begged to offer and receive in turn. The sheets where his lean, swordsman's body had lain seemed suddenly chill as a grave. Carralin muffled her weeping in his pillow. As her tears soaked the linen beneath her cheek, she exhausted herself finally into sleep.

* * *

The taproom of the inn was not empty when Korendir reached the bottom of the stair. Oil lamps still burned over the trestles; between starred swaths of shadow and light, the master of the tavern sat guarding the door, a pipe of Sithmark clay clenched between stumpy teeth. He turned his head as Korendir crossed the floor. His eyes glinted through a haze of smoke and his dark brows lifted in surprise.

"I thought, when you asked to retire, that you'd put aside your quest until morning." And he grinned, sure indication that he knew of Carralin's excursion up the stair.

Korendir tested the sharpness of the swordblade which rested unsheathed in his hands. "Not anymore." He set the point down, leaned the quillons against his knee, then caught his cloak from the peg in the common room. His wrists moved, once, and cloth settled soundlessly over his shoulders. "Open your door, good man."

The innkeeper jumped up and gestured with the hand that clutched the pipe. "You can't be serious! In the dark, the wereleopards are changed to man-form, and—"

Korendir flashed a glance that killed the man's protest to silence. The lanterns burned steadily as he adjusted his garment to free his sword arm, then lifted his weapon from the floor. "Your townsfolk hired me to kill were-leopards."

The baleful intensity of him daunted; the innkeeper stared at the unnaturally still face, then the poised blade. The angle of the steel was not friendly. Caught at a loss, he stood aside. "We've gone into debt for a suicide," he muttered as Korendir brushed past.

The mercenary set to work upon bolts and bars. Moved by the man's brash courage, the innkeeper reached behind his chair and lifted a heavy, bronze lamp that once had served a freight raft as storm lantern. "Take this along," he urged. "Merciful Neth, out there you may need a light."

Korendir thrust his wrist through the carrying ring. "Light the wick," he said quietly.

The innkeeper bit his pipe and complied with hands a great deal less steady. Spark snapped from the striker, and flame flared with a hiss and a reek of hot oil. Korendir closed the shutters and set his fingers to the door latch.

As he pushed the panel wide and stepped out, the inn-keeper groped for words to wish him luck. Not a sound left his lips. The Master of Whitestorm crossed the board stoop and descended the stair beyond, then his cloak blended indistinguishably with a night pitch black with threat.

The innkeeper's nerve vanished with the mercenary. Overcome by shivering panic, the portly man banged his door shut and dropped the bar with a crash that shook the lintels. Then, bereft of confidence, he scrabbled in the gloom for the tobacco pouch he had laid aside, but could not remember where.

The moon dropped behind the wooded slopes that flanked the River Ellgol. There the water flowed in a shallow, reed-choked channel, dragged to white snags where the current tumbled over obstructions. Korendir did not walk the banks to trace the river's course, but instead picked his way along the ridge top, where the chuckle and rush of the foam did not fill his ears to distraction. The heavy, shuttered lantern swung on his arm and his sword was poised ready in his hand. He had crossed the bare fields of Mel's Bye without disturbing so much as a shadow, but reassurance did not follow. Only during daylight did wereleopards prowl the open; in man-form, they preferred to lurk under cover. Korendir made his way forward with slow, tentative strides. He waited for the rustle of each footfall to end before starting his following step.

Between times, he listened to the infrequent croak of frogs, the rasped songs of crickets, the sigh of wind through evergreen boughs. For a league or more, the forest night seemed tranquil. His nose burned with the reek of hot oil, and his palm sweated on his sword hilt. He eased himself over a deadfall; his cloak scraped across rotting bark with a soft slither of sound. Abruptly the crickets stopped chirping. Korendir stiffened, took another step, paused. Then, from behind came a staccato snap as a twig broke.

Korendir threw himself flat. He rolled headlong down the slope, heedless of the lantern which bounced and bruised against his side. The shutters clanged back, and sparks winnowed and danced through a flying whirl of damp leaves. Korendir rolled faster with the increased pitch of the slope. His wrist cracked painfully into rock as he held his naked blade from his body. He gave the discomfort no thought, but looked back over his shoulder. Through a tumbling whirl of light, he gained a first glimpse of his attacker.

The wereleopard bounded down slope after him, its eyes slitted with lust, and its fanged, triangular jaws dripping venom. Tufted ears lay flattened back against a skull uncannily human. Clawed, five-fingered hands extended from lightly furred arms that even now reached to rend and slash. The speed of the creature's rush was uncanny. It saw with precision in the dark.

Korendir fetched up against a fir tree. Dry needles showered his head. Some fell into the opened lantern; a flare of pitchy flame showed the wereleopard gathered for a leap that must end with deadly, venomed jaws tearing flesh.

Hopelessly outmatched, Korendir raised his sword arm. He tossed the cumbersome lantern into the trunk that pressed like a fence at his back. The casing struck with a crash. Bronze shutters clanged open, and thrown sparks touched needles and dry resin and ignited.

Flame blossomed. The river bed flared with sudden light that outlined the wereleopard with all the clarity of a nightmare.

Korendir braced to fight.

That same moment the beast hurtled in a bound from shadow into fiery brilliance. Slit pupils contracted to compensate; and the sudden shift in illumination catalyzed startling transformation. The wereleopard's clawlike hands blurred, shortened, and abruptly reshaped into paws. The savagery of its rush continued, but in a form gone eerily fluid. The facial structure altered, became wholly that of a beast. Weight, bone, and muscle redistributed into cat-form, and during the immediacy of the moment, the creature's reflexes were slowed. Unbalanced, almost clumsy, the wereleopard crashed short of its prey.

Korendir reacted without pause to analyze. He lunged away from the fir trunk. His blade thrust deep into spotted hide, even as venom-wet teeth snapped closed, and claws raked out to rend.

The steel pierced the wereleopard through the heart.
Even then death came with difficulty. The creature spun
with a hair-raising, coughing yowl that rang throughout
the forest. Its claws plowed furrows in the earth and its
tail lashed up dead leaves. Over and over the fey thing
thrashed in the throes of its dying.

Korendir felt his sword twisted violently from his hand.
He jumped clear, barely ahead of disaster. Fanged jaws
clashed where his calf had been only an instant before.
Droplets spattered his legging, a fresh threat; wereleopard venom was poisonous enough that contact with the
skin could be fatal. Korendir backed off instantly. He
cut away the tainted cloth and tossed the smoking fabric
in the coals. Then, wary of his dying enemy, he hooked
the lantern ring with his sword and dragged it clear of
the brushfire. He set it upright upon the ground, arranged his cloak to protect his hand from burns, and
readjusted the wick.

The wereleopard shuddered at last into stillness. Even
dead, it was a sight to inspire dread. The venom-flecked
muzzle was drawn back to reveal five-inch fangs, and
incisors aligned like razors. The eyes were jewel green,
banefully opened wide. The pelt, sleek, golden, and mottled in diamonds of black, might have been the delight
of a royal lady; jolted from reaction, Korendir recalled
the piteous terror that haunted Carralin. Foolish he may
have been, to linger where a wereleopard's dying might
draw others in to retaliate. But as if his promise to the
girl was the driving motive of his life, the mercenary
drew his dagger. He knelt in the unguarded open to skin
his kill by lanternlight.

The creature's flesh was unnaturally hot and the blood,
when Korendir cut, almost scalded. He worked without
flinching and wondered if wereleopards were connected
with the alter-reality of Alhaerie, that otherworld existence that White Circle enchanters tapped to power
spells. Not all wizards had benevolent intentions, and
the creation of shape-changing killers might stem from a
conjured curse.

Korendir peeled the pelt from the forepaws, cautious
of the razor talons. The tendons ran like cables from flat
sheets of muscle to bone, every sinew knitted with an
artistry designed for death. As the hunter dressed out his

pelt, he kept his ears tuned to the forest. The brushfire
had burned to embers at his back, and frightened by the
heat into silence, the crickets no longer sang their measure of assurance. A wereleopard attacking now might
find easy prey if a man grew inured to his danger.

Korendir arose and wrapped the bloody skin into a
bundle. Sword resting against his thigh, he used a bit of
sinew to lash the pelt to his waist. Then he wiped the
knife on his leggings and reached down to pick up the
lantern. He stopped with the gesture half complete. A
wereleopard watched from the dark, its eyes glaring ovals
of green just at the edge of the flamelight. It hissed as
Korendir saw it. Clawed fingers twitched in agitation, yet
it hesitated, strangely reluctant to attack.

Korendir lifted his sword. In the process he knocked
the dangling tail of the pelt into motion; and the man-
formed thing in the shadows shied back.

Fired by a leap of intuition, the mercenary divined why
he had not been slaughtered outright. The wereleopard
seemed intimidated by the fate of its fellow. As if the
fur of the slain were a talisman, Korendir feinted then
followed with a throw of his skinning knife.

His aim went true and the dagger struck. A terrible
cry split the night. With a rattle and a crashing of brush,
the creature spun and fled into darkness.

Korendir shouted in exultation. Lamplight showed a
spatter of blood on the leaves, steaming in the chilly air.
His fingers clamped tight to his first pelt, the mercenary
pushed forward to track.

Daybreak saw the Master of Whitestorm returned to
the square in Mel's Bye. The lantern dangled cold from
his belt loop; one sleeve of his shirt was shredded, the
wrist beneath furrowed where a near-pass with a wereleopard had shallowly gashed his hand. The blood which
spattered his boots did not issue from any wound, but
drained in clotting strings from the raw, diamond-spotted
pelts strapped three deep at his belt. Towed through the
dust at his heels by a tawny crown of hair, the man-
shaped corpse of a fourth horror dragged in loose-limbed
death. This one his sword had slain before sunlight could
catalyze the shift into cat form.

The inn's stout door remained barred as Korendir

reached the entry. Unfazed, he dropped the wereleopard corpse with a thump on the wooden stoop. Then he settled his shoulder against the signpost, and with a rub rag, began cleaning his sticky blades.

Chain rattled a minute later, followed by the grinding slide of bolts being drawn. The door opened. Without looking up from the work in his hands, Korendir said, "Someone tell Carralin I've brought her a present."

Silence.

Korendir glanced up. He found the innkeeper, the chief councilman, and all the folk of the town crowded in a pack past the threshold. Their eyes were flat with unfriendliness, and though four dead wereleopards offered cause enough to celebrate, not a man stepped forward to congratulate the mercenary who had accomplished the feat.

With a thin ring of sound, Korendir set sword and knife into their sheaths; his manner changed from hard to unremittingly grim. "Maybe you should tell me what's happened," he suggested.

No one answered.

Korendir's regard shifted from one hostile face to the next, and only after exhaustive search uncovered the fact that Carralin was not present.

Always, since the moment of his arrival, she had tagged his presence like a shadow.

Without speaking again, the mercenary slipped the thong which bound the pelts at his waist. Bloody furs unfurled in a heap around his ankles as, still without words, he stepped clear. The wooden stair boomed hollowly under his tread. The wereleopard corpse might as well not have been there for all the notice he gave as he strode into the press beyond the door.

Folk melted away to let him pass. But though he crossed the taproom unimpeded, mutters arose sullenly at his back. The air smelled close—a mix of sweat, and raw anger, and a staleness of lingering pipe smoke. Korendir shed his cloak and added the reek of burnt pitch and blood. He threaded through trestles and benches, passed the stools by the bar with a stride that seemed unhurried. But folk who were brazen enough to follow discovered they must hasten to keep up.

Korendir took the stairs beyond, first two, and then

three at a time. He crossed the darkened landing, ducked down the corridor, and wrenched open the door to his chambers.

Just five hours earlier, he had left a young girl weeping safely on his bed.

Now, the room was close with the scent of cheap perfume, and another smell more cloying. Daylight from the window lit carnage. The whitewashed walls, the floors, the tassels adorning the bedstead wore ropy garlands of blood. Carralin lay with her head thrown back.

Her throat was torn out; the mangled bones of her spine showed white through a mess of slashed gristle. One chapped hand trailed from the bedclothes, huge and limp and forever finished with pouring ale for thirsty patrons.

Korendir stopped as if kicked.

He took one breath, then another, and his eyes flicked from the dead woman to the sill. Bloody marks remained where the killer had made its exit. The casement hung open. Latches had been torn from their settings by claws and ruthless strength. No one had bothered to close out the draft; the mullioned frame swung creaking in the wind off the fields.

Korendir started forward to remedy the lapse when a heavy footfall dogged his track. A hand reached out to restrain him.

He spun very fast. Emmon Hillgate's hulking son missed his hold and grasped only empty air. For a moment both men locked eyes, one still and waiting, the other shivering with anger and grief and a wild, untenable madness.

Emmon's fists bunched. "Man, you took your pleasure and then abandoned her to die!"

Townsfolk gathered in the hallway; out of fairness to the mercenary, one man strove to restore temperance. "Emmon, leave be! The lord went hunting wereleopards, and by the look of things, bagged four."

But Emmon Hillgate's son was lost to all things beyond the girl lying slaughtered on the bed. Huge, threatening, he advanced upon his slighter adversary. "You might have done your hunting right here, then. For your cheap toss in the sheets, my sister deserved a defender."

Korendir denied none of the accusations. His face

showed no feeling, and his movement no shred of hesitation as he stepped past Emmon's bulk and smoothly shut the casement. Returned without pause to the bedside, he raised hands that did not shake and veiled the corpse like a bride in her bloodied sheets. He smoothed the last strands of hair from view with fingers stained still from his wereleopard kills. Then he raised his eyes.

Anger burned there, electrically intense, and deep beyond rational understanding.

Emmon misinterpreted. He took leave of his senses with a scream of rage and lunged to strike, to mangle, to pulp the wretch who had abandoned his sister to an unthinkably, horrible death.

Korendir spun calmly. His attacker towered a full head taller, and at least half again his weight. He deflected the first punch with his forearm, ducked the blow of the second. Light on his feet as a dancer, he snapped his sheathed sword from his belt, then kicked a footstool into Emmon's shins. The larger man blundered through with a clatter of splitting rungs. Korendir stepped aside and hammered the pommel of his weapon on the back of the giant man's neck.

Emmon buckled at the knees, then collapsed across splinters of furniture. Korendir picked his way past. Whatever emotion had moved him was gone; the dumbstruck knot of villagers saw nothing except eyes gone silver with cold.

"Somebody stay with him," the mercenary said in regard to Emmon, who sprawled on the blood-spattered floor. Stiffly he added, "When the great oaf stirs, tell him I'll guard while he buries his sister."

Then, steel still in hand, the Master of Whitestorm advanced in the direction of the stairway. Even in outrage over Carralin's fate, not a man from the town dared prevent him.

In the taproom Korendir chose a trestle and set his dusty boot on one corner. He leaned on his knee and gave the taproom crowd a harsh scrutiny. "I'll need a dozen men who are unafraid to bear weapons, and six more skilled with a bow. The wereleopards enter Southengard through the caves of the Ellgol, and there, with Neth's grace, we can stop them. Choose your twelve. Tell them to rest, for I'll need them wakeful at dusk."

Korendir paused, his hands too still where they rested on the blade across his thigh. "I also want the boots each man will wear, and the services of your cobbler for today."

He added nothing more; no excuse for his desertion of Carralin, no boastful account of his kills. He did not ask the healer to attend the scratch on his forearm, but instead disappeared through the outside door. The townsfolk stood rooted in surprise, and even their garrulous chief councilman struggled at a loss for words.

VIII. The Caves of the Ellgol

The party gathered in the common room at twilight, twelve men packing torches and rucksacks that bulged with weapons and supplies, and six more with filled quivers and bows. The boots of each, from Sethon the miller's son, to the sinewy bulk of the village blacksmith were newly topped with wereleopard pelt, scraped, but of necessity uncured. Korendir had insisted that the cobbler treat his own footgear the same. When the squeamish craftsman raised objection with words concerning trophies and vanity, the mercenary gave him short shrift. The company from Mel's Bye relied upon one fact: living wereleopards faltered in their attack if they scented the hide of their slain. That split second of hesitation was all the edge a hunter might get. In that instant a quick man could escape being massacred and make his kill.

Consequently, at sundown the entire party donned their stinking footgear without complaint. They checked their weapons, adjusted pack straps and sword belts, and bemoaned the lack of beer with the bluster men use to bolster each other's nerves. Korendir sat unconcerned upon a trestle, rebinding his wounded forearm with strips torn from a linen napkin. He finished the knot with his teeth, then tucked the trailing ends into his cuff.

"Are we ready?" he said to his company. He slipped from his perch on the table and made for the door. The innkeeper slipped the bar to let him out. As the panel swung wide, Korendir stepped into gathering night without a glance to see who followed.

The master smith broke the general air of reticence. "Well, lads, can't leave him to claim all the sport by himself."

"Oh, easily," quipped a farmer who wore shovels strapped to his backpack. "I'll keep my burnt stew and

nagging wife, and leave fey beasts to those who hafta
prove they got parts to fill their britches."

Someone else shouted out from the rear. "Now didn't
I hear your woman singing a different tune, words on
the matter of closing yer points with her needle, since
what dangled inside seemed lazy as the rest o' you?"

A shout of laughter answered, while the farmer howled
and turned red. "Sheesh, now, who listens to a woman
what's got a mouth so big and bitter you could cure a
ham inside?" He trooped down the stair, and almost collided with Korendir, stopped still without warning and
all but invisible in his dark clothes. The farmer recoiled
into his fellows as the mercenary spoke out in clipped
threat.

"You cannot come to the caves."

Stung, the farmer drew breath to protest; then his vision adjusted to the gloom and he realized the outburst
had not pertained to him at all. A hulking shadow
blocked Korendir's path; Emmon Hillgate's son, with his
great thick fists clutched to a pole weapon salvaged from
his father's attic. Failing light touched his mad eyes, and
the newly sharpened halberd that gleamed in a crescent-
edge of silver above his shoulder.

"I'm going," said Emmon.

His demand would be argued. Korendir's tight stance
forewarned as much. Moved to boldness by a flood of
fear and resentment, the nearest of the farmers said
sharply, "He deserves the right, I think."

Others behind called agreement. Carralin had filled
their mugs since she was tall enough to heft a pitcher.
Her large-boned, diffident presence was missed at the
tap, and in the dark, about to risk themselves against
wereleopards, the men of Mel's Bye readily gave way to
disgruntlement. Korendir might deliver their town from
danger, but he would be remembered as a man who had
pressed his advantage on a girl in a time of misfortune.

"If Emmon is left, I stay also," said the miller's son.
His closest companions stood with him, their voices over-
loud in agreement.

Korendir turned his shoulder toward Emmon. As if
the pike did not tremble in hands that yearned to take
satisfaction for a sister's dishonor and death, the merce-

nary regarded the villagers one by one. Silence fell, stubborn as old rock; Korendir understood its temper.

"There will be death and sorrow if Emmon goes," he cautioned. "Not of my making; no more can I promise than that." And quickly, he passed on his way.

Left braced for a challenge that never happened, the villagers reacted belatedly. They shifted packs and tools and swords, and uncomfortably moved to follow. None looked at Emmon; yet when the big man joined the rear of the party, nobody prevented him. They started across the market, while the door boomed closed behind them. Nailed to the oaken panels was the hide of the man-formed wereleopard Korendir had slain the previous night, as talisman to augment the safety of the wives, children, and craftsmen left behind.

Full night had fallen. Korendir led through the town, past the stake he had left with the skull of a wereleopard kill as sentinel over empty houses. The farmers at his heels gave the trophy wide berth, except Emmon, who paused to spit in the blood-dried pits of each eye socket. "So will I treat the one who killed Carralin," he muttered viciously. Those who overheard could not tell which he referred to—the murdering cat-form, or the mercenary.

The trek from the outlying farmsteads proceeded without talk. Many of the farmers had not crossed their fields since spring sowing, and the rankness of weeds where crops should stand high at harvest weighed sorely upon their hearts. Late-singing mockingbirds called, but corn did not rustle, and the pastures were thick with grass that in better years was grazed short.

Past such evident ill fortune, the unchanged woods seemed a haven. The air under the trees hung thick with the scent of pine. No wind blew, but the footsteps of men who were unskilled at hunting frightened the crickets to silence. Other nocturnal wildlife that might have forewarned of an ambush took flight before the disturbance. The early-rising moon ducked often behind banked clouds; during such intervals the dark beneath the trees became total. Men blundered cursing into branches and roots; except Korendir, who assessed the obstacles as the light dimmed, then paused between steps until his eyes adjusted. Rather than stop and lecture on woodsmanship there and then on the path, the mercenary ordered torches lit. Shortly every other man carried a brand, the unencumbered left to wield weapons.

The party paced onward through oily fumes thrown off by the cressets. If wereleopards lurked close, they stayed concealed in the shadows. The men pressed ahead more confidently. In time they crossed the blackened swath of ash where Korendir had accomplished his first kill. Now not a trace remained of the flayed corpse; the ground lay tracklessly smooth, and even the scratch-marks of carrion crows did not mar the scorched soil of the site. More sinister still, the burned tree stump where Korendir made his stand had been uprooted and clawed to white splinters.

The discovery was sobering, that wereleopards held regard for their dead. Men felt their mortality more keenly after that, and Korendir, grimly silent, questioned whether the hide bands stitched to each man's boots held power to inspire anything but rage from the creatures they marched to eradicate. The torches burned just as brightly, but the heady, close air of late summer seemed to drag at the flames, shortening the circle of light. Korendir looked back to take stock of his men and realized that two lagged behind. Emmon and the miller's son lingered in the swath seared by last night's fire.

"I see no sign of a wereleopard killed here," Emmon said loudly.

"You will, and very quickly, if you don't close ranks and keep moving!" Korendir strode past the column, his intent to assume rear guard where he could keep better watch over stragglers.

Emmon's chin lifted mulishly. "Look, Sethon, we're getting a babysitter."

That moment the wereleopard charged.

Mate of the one slain at that site the night before, she had been stalking in the brush. The scraps of pelt had first deterred her, but now, she sensed dissent among the prey who blundered through the trees. She pressed her advantage and sprang, a bolt of molten gold in the torchlight.

Barely a leaf rustled warning. The men from Mel's Bye watched to see how Korendir would handle Emmon's provocation; for only a moment they neglected to remember the forest which hemmed their backs. The crash of a torchbearer and a cry caused them all to spin round in horror. Two bodies rolled in the leaves, one tawny yellow and spotted, the other clothed and struggling.

Korendir dodged past a man too stunned to react, and another one yelling in fear. "Steady those torches!" he shouted. He freed his dagger and completed a whipping throw.

The blade buried with a thump in the ruffed torso of the predator, which was nakedly female. Korendir kept moving. Even as the wereleopard's death cry reverberated through the forest, he crouched down, barehandedly grasped the beast's shoulder and flung her off her prey.

Fangs raked the air; venom drops flew like jewels through torchlight. Despite Korendir's swift recoil, spatters caught the linen that bandaged his wrist. The material blackened instantly. Korendir slipped the knot, shredded the tainted fabric off, and with no break in motion, grasped the man and dragged him clear of the wereleopard's death throes.

Blood leaked in trails from the wounded man's body. In agony, striving to stifle screams, he flopped wretchedly in the leaves. Boiled leather wrist guards had spared him the wereleopard's venom, but the elbow savaged by her foreclaws was a mess of mangled bone.

"Merciful Neth," murmured a bystander. Someone else doubled over and retched in the brush.

"Stay together," snapped Korendir. His hands, the same hands that had killed on an instant's notice, now explored the downed man's body with gentleness and dispatch. Yet even had he owned a surgeon's skill, no succor would avail. The smell of blood and feces hung heavy on the air and even the squeamish who averted their eyes understood that the injured man's plight was hopeless. The wereleopard's spurred toes had raked open his abdomen, then shredded the gut inside.

Even Emmon's deranged scorn abated at the sight. A man could not die cleanly from such mauling; if luck ran against him his agony might drag on for a fortnight.

The stricken man was aware. "Don't bring me back to my daughters like this," he pleaded. "I beg you, don't."

Korendir regarded the clustered bystanders. "Does Vwern have kin present?" That he knew the man's name startled no one at the time; their minds were shocked numb by catastrophe. "Is there one friend brave enough to complete this man's request?"

Feet shuffled through leaves; hands loosened from the hilts of weapons, and no man would meet any other man's eyes. Emmon stood with bent head, his great fists sliding up and down the weathered shaft of his pike.

At some point the wereleopard's thrashing ceased. She lay on her back, her surprisingly human breasts upthrust and gleaming in firelight. No one seemed anxious to approach her, but even less willingly would they contemplate what must be done for their comrade.

"Very well," said Korendir, his voice like steel against silence. "Sethon, take Emmon's pike. Bind up the killed beast and sling her on the pole. Then, all of you, move out upstream."

The men did not have to be reminded to stick together. Spurred by an embarrassment of relief, they offered their belts and bootlaces and helped Sethon lash the carcass.

Korendir remained kneeling in fir needles. One hand supported the wounded man's head, while the other eased the collar loose at his neck.

"I am glad it's to be you," gasped Vwern, valiantly trying to shed hurt that had nothing to do with torn flesh. "At least you're a man who knows the best place for the knife."

Korendir said nothing, but slipped his dark cloak and arranged it over the victim's chilled flesh. Then he settled on his heels, waiting, while around them the men finished off with the wereleopard. Trembling with nerves, Sethon returned the mercenary's dagger. Someone had wiped the blade clean. Korendir accepted the obsidian hilt. On the inside of his wrist, where Vwern could not see, he carefully tested the edges. Satisfied that wereleopard bones had left no nicks in the steel, Korendir nodded dismissal to the miller's son.

The farmers banded together and departed. Torchlight flickered and faded between the trees. Alone under the moon's fitful gleam, the motionless man and the doomed one each took a breath in preparation.

"Strike now," urged Vwern. The quick shock of accident was wearing off, and suffering tugged at his voice. "—T'would just compound my mistake, if you got attacked on account of me."

Korendir's reply held a gentleness no ears left living had ever heard. "Not yet." He reached out in darkness and unerringly found the victim's fingers, then grasped with a grip that was warm, as if death did not hover in the wings. "First tell me the names of your daughters."

Vwern stifled a sob. "There are three. Nessie, Mallie, and Tesh. She's youngest, and blond, like her mother, though Mallie, maybe, is prettier. I love them all," he added, as if the mercenary might not understand; as a father, he had no favorite.

"Nessie, Mallie, and Tesh, who is blond," Korendir repeated. He made a small movement, then added, "They'll be safe, Vwern. On my life, I swear they'll prosper, and marry, and live to raise children in your memory."

The hand that held the wounded man's gave no twitch in warning, but abided, steady and firm. The knife seemed to come from nowhere; it entered fast, painlessly clean, precisely below Vwern's left ear. His awareness ebbed swiftly in a flood of arterial blood.

Korendir did not rise. Beside him, the corpse ceased to shudder; the chest quit breathing and sagged motionless, finished with struggle and life. Still, the mercenary remained. He unlaced his fingers from the dead man's and wiped the warmed blood from his knuckles. Meticulously he cleaned his blade. He closed the eyes that gleamed empty within a pillow of leaves and covered the slack face with his cloak. Then he straightened. Moonlight revealed what Vwern, or any other in Neth's Eleven Kingdoms might never be permitted to see.

Tears rinsed Korendir's fine-boned face; as he wept his expression was stripped by an ache of compassion that flowed straight from the heart.

"By my mother, you were brave," he said to the still form at his feet.

That moment, a wereleopard might have taken him without a blow struck in token defense.

The interval ended suddenly, like the immolation of too dry tinder snapped into flame by a spark. Korendir blotted his cheeks. He returned his cold knife to its sheath, retrieved his abandoned sword, and moved off without a backward glance. By the time he caught up with the others, his expression was impervious as quartz.

"That's one on your soul, to equal the one on mine," he said softly to Emmon as he passed.

Hillgate's son slapped a hand to his belt knife. The Master of Whitestorm never so much as flinched, but kept going until he reached the head of the column. Emmon was deranged enough to strike from behind when provoked; but whether Korendir cared at all, or whether some instinct convinced him that the seventeen survivors who had volunteered for this march would have acted to defend him in that moment, remained unclear. The mercenary from Whitestorm had completed a mercy stroke that others shrank to contemplate; the deed had been accomplished with such lack of ceremony that no man's pride became brutalized. For that grace, Korendir earned a respect that admitted tolerance for his presumed abuse of Carralin. The townsfolk would never forgive her murder. But now, only madness offered cause to prolong resentment; Emmon Hillgate's son was left to nurse his grievance alone.

Night was beginning to fail. On his previous expedition, Korendir had found that twilight was a time of transition for the wereleopards. He had neither been attacked nor had he observed any movement through yesterday's daybreak. Now he banked upon the presumption that the creatures preferred to retire during their vulnerable time of change; in cat-form, in daylight, the beasts were far more difficult to kill. If this band of inexperienced villagers was to win reprieve for their families, their safety must be secured before sunrise.

The River Ellgol sprang from a cleft at the base of the shale cliffs that footed the Doriads. No trees grew there; against the knees of the mountains, the forest ended as if sliced. Seeds that sought foothold on the cracked and moss-rotted stone beyond grew to crabbed saplings, then died, leaving skeletons like fingers hooked in an agony of torture. The river issued from a seamed maw beneath; waters welled up from the earth's dark and roared down a ravine, to carve a more meandering course through the valley.

The party from Mel's Bye paused beneath the crest of the outcrop. In the gray half-light before sunrise, Korendir hurried them through a meal of bread, cheese, and sweet ale. Then the mercenary placed half of the archers in crannies overlooking the forest. Their task was to arrow down any wereleopard who left the cover of the wood, while companions razed the trees in a swath a hundred yards wide by any method that would serve; fire, axe, or landslide, Korendir made it clear he did not care, so long as the glade surrounding the cliffs was cleared to the last standing twig. Seasoned logs from the deadfalls were to be hewn into firewood, and stacked alongside the river mouth.

On the heels of a nightlong march, the work he proposed was brutal enough to wilt the stoutest spirit; yet there were no slackers. Having tasted the blood of the wereleopard which had preyed upon their kinfolk for so long, the villagers felled trees with determination. Even Emmon took up an axe. His frame sweated with hell-bent exertion, and his eyes shone fanatically bright; he labored as if by brute strength he could absolve his part in the misfortune that had ended Vwern's life.

In contrast to Hillgate's son's passions, Korendir applied himself with the chill of new steel forged for bloodshed. Stripped to breeches and swordbelt, he assembled a bundle of unlit torches and set the remaining men to climbing. Barely visible in the early light, and dampened by mists of falling water, his picked party toiled upward toward a shelf of rock undercut by the current of the Ellgol. Korendir insisted that wereleopards entered Southengard through the mazes of water-tunnelled caves that riddled the mountains behind. He planned to seal their access by engineering a rockslide above the river, but work could not commence until the caverns had been secured from inside.

Korendir explained in snatches as he climbed, the gist of his strategy based on the wereleopards' compulsion to shift form when exposed to transitions in light. The stone of the cliff face was rotten with weather and age; shale crumbled unexpectedly underfoot, to clatter downslope and crash through the undergrowth below. The most skeptical villager allowed Korendir his point. Protected by bonfires, a work team with pick axes and shovels could undermine the loosened shale, fashion shoring of timbers and plank, then tear such bracing away to precipitate a rockfall.

The men who attempted the ascent pressed forward
with a will. Hard the mercenary who led them might be,
and lacking in decency and warmth, yet the Master of
Whitestorm had proven himself capable. Mel's Bye might
be a poor town, if he lived to collect his fee; but his
direction offered hope that the farms might be safe to
recover prosperity in the future.

Korendir reached the cave opening. Through whorls of
mist from the falls, the lead men saw him grasp a crevice
and heave his body inside. By the time those following
reached the outcrop, he was busy lighting torches. An arc
of them burned at his feet. Heat slicked his face like a
gypsy entertainer prepared for an exhibition of juggling;
except his frown held no hint of gaiety, and his sleeves
were crusted with the blood of a man and a beast.

"Sethon goes last," he said without looking up. "Not
because he lacks courage, but because he's the youngest." The striker flared between Korendir's hands.
"Bachelors march at the fore, behind me. Fathers with
young children will follow in back." When the last torch
was set blazing, the mercenary's gaze touched each man
in turn. "The order of march is a formality. Any one of
you careless enough to get killed will find your own way
to hell, because the others outside cutting trees have no
choice but depend on us."

Korendir pressed a torch into Sethon's hands and drew
his blade. Then he stamped the wooden grip of the cresset lying nearest and flipped it like a trickster's flare into
his hand.

Eastward, the sky had brightened; mist off the falls
changed from blue to subtle rose, forewarning of the
dawn to come. Korendir dropped onto his belly. With a
scrape of fabric over shale, he dragged himself into the
aperture which accessed the caves. The men picked up
torches and trailed after in single file. Sethon the miller's
son entered last, eyes burned by the soot thrown off by
oiled rags. He breathed damp, heated air, and the sourness of other mens' sweat. His ears heard little beyond
the confined roar of the watercourse which thrashed and
tumbled through the caverns, fed by the drip of countless
subterranean springs.

Korendir crawled to the end, where the stone widened
out. His cresset guttered and whipped in the draft as he

straightened as far as his knees, shuffled forward, and at last gained space to stand.

"Hurry," he encouraged the man who came at his heels.

The cavern brightened as the villagers emerged. Raised torches revealed walls that sloped upward to a ceiling that sparkled with mineral deposits. Korendir advanced across a floor sleek-wet with run-off. His cresset threw orange reflections off his swordblade, the puddles scattered underfoot, and from his wrist, scraped open and freshly bleeding after his traverse through the passage. The sting of split scabs must have pained him, yet when one of the men expressed concern, he spurned both help and companionship.

"Stand together!" His rebuke echoed outward like the crack of a marble chipper's mallet. "Pool the light from the torches, and keep your eyes to the walls." Then, as if knowing he had rejected an honest act of courage, he said, "Expect an attack at any moment."

A spill of gravel rattled from the darkness overhead. Pebbles bounced and rolled and scattered ripples across the puddles.

Already Korendir had thrown himself aside, his steel upraised and ready. "Get Sethon to light more torches!"

The wereleopard dropped that moment. Man-formed, muscled for murder, it landed with the recovery of a tiger. Steel sang through air as Korendir lunged. His target twisted clear in a reflex too fast for sight. Somebody shouted. That sound spared the mercenary's life. The wereleopard spun, slit-eyed, and sprang at the farmers clustered before the passage.

"Throw down your torches!" screamed Korendir.

The three men not panicked obeyed. Flame struck wet stone with a sizzle of oil; grease-soaked rags spread a slick on the puddles, and fire flared instantaneously wider. Sudden light rinsed the crannies, and forced the wereleopard to metamorphosis.

Its stride faltered, changed in mid-charge to a stagger.

Korendir swung his sword. "Light more torches. Quickly!"

Sethon fumbled after rags and oil, while someone else cut the ties that contained the bundled wood. Quickly as frightened men responded, the wereleopards moved faster. Another one launched from the shadows.

The first still thrashed, impaled on Korendir's blade. The swordsman fought to stay upright as the wereleopard kicked and slashed. The razor length of steel twisted in its chest, then wedged immovably into bone. Korendir yanked, unable to clear his sword, while the unwounded predator sprang.

Desperate, one of the farmers threw a torch. Flaming rags and a billet of beechwood impacted the wereleopard's flank. It twisted with a ringing snap of jaws and caught the light full in both eyes. Change followed; its outlines blurred. The delay gave Korendir space to free his steel, but the stroke that slew his attacker was dealt by a woodcutter from Mel's Bye.

The caverns rang with the howl of dying enemies and the rough cheers of men. Sethon arose with an armload of ready torches and distributed them among the villagers.

"Quarter the cave," the Master of Whitestorm directed. "Find every entrance that might possibly admit a wereleopard, and flank those holes with torches. If we're lucky the change will disadvantage whatever beasts charge through. Bowfire can take them safely from a distance."

All saw wisdom in the tactic. The woodcutter who had skewered his first wereleopard moved off with a swagger, and the others followed, except one.

"What about yourself?" he questioned Korendir.

For the mercenary made no move to lead, but stood checking his bloodied sword edge for flaws. He found none, wiped his fingers on his hose, and impatiently regarded the speaker, a farmer named Nevel whose face showed the labors of seasons exposed to summer sun.

"I'm going on," the mercenary said. "Somewhere these caverns connect with the watercourse of the Ellgol."

Taller by half a head, Nevel shrugged wide shoulders. "Why not balk the wereleopards from here?"

The Master of Whitestorm looked up with incredulous astonishment. "Neth, man, this place is a warren of holes and shadows. A man caught alone here would die in a minute, and there's no safe haven to fall back to. Need I go on about space to store supplies and dry wood? There are men left out in the open. Every minute we delay, they remain in terrible danger."

Nevel fingered his weapon, an axe designed for hewing

planks. "Just you shouldn't be going alone. At least take Sethon, to hold the torch."

"Never Sethon," Korendir returned, abrupt to the point of viciousness. "Vwern was one too many. Now clear my path."

Slow to think, slower still to move, the field hand squared his jaw. "I'll go, then, and no word from you will stop me."

"You're more mad than Emmon." Korendir gestured ahead with his bloodied sword. "That way."

Torchlight showed a seam cut through cavern walls. Beyond a gleam of wet stone, shadows lay thick as the felt used by priests to shroud tombs. Nevel showed signs of misgiving; but Korendir strode on without a glance to see whether his self-appointed escort would follow. Stung by that imperious self-assurance, and too proud to accept that his offer lay beneath regard, the field hand collected two torches and dogged the mercenary's tracks.

The ceiling sloped sharply past the entrance. First forced to stoop, and then to crawl, clumsily fighting the impediment of weaponry and smoking flares, Korendir and Nevel made their way down the damp passage. The light became lost behind, along with the echoed conversation of the others. The air turned thick with the silence of the earth, punctured like harp notes with water drops; always like a litany behind ran the thunder of the Ellgol's mighty current.

Torch smoke made the eyes sting unbearably. Hardly able to discern Korendir's heels in the gloom ahead, Nevel dragged stubbornly onward. The stink of uncured hide filled his nostrils. Slime and mud caked his clothes; once something live squirmed under his palm, and though by nature he respected religion, he cursed the variety of Neth's creation.

Korendir paid no mind, but continued, the scrape of his sword sheath the only sound of his passage.

"What if the wereleopards are able to swim the river?" the field hand gasped. "If so, no rockslide will block them, and all our troubles will continue."

The Master of Whitestorm paused and kicked once; his feet disappeared. The roar of the river swelled to deafening proportions, and his voice, in reply, floated strangely thin through the passage. "That's the other thing we're here to find out."

IX. Rockfall

The shaft quite suddenly felt damper, and the air swirled with draft. The field hand from Mel's Bye hiked forward, torches clamped in both fists. The axe haft strapped to his back scraped shale with a note that set his teeth on edge. Then his shoulders cleared an obstruction. The passage abruptly widened. He slid forward, gained his knees, and looked out from the mouth of the opening. Beyond lay a dizzying vista.

The cavern ahead was vast. Above, the torrent of the Ellgol pelted from an origin lost in darkness; the waters plunged, dashed to arrowed cascades by the rocks through a sixty-foot drop into a cauldron of boiling foam. Far below, picked out dimly in the torches' glare, a snake of black current coiled upon itself and spiraled into a maelstrom that sucked down through some monstrous sink hole beneath the channel floor. Where the river coursed until it resurfaced into sunlight beneath the shale cliffs, only the devil might know.

The field hand shifted grip on his torches. Korendir's cresset bobbed halfway down the shaft. The mercenary's tunic blended into shadow, but the blade he held shone baleful with reflections. He had set his torch between his teeth to free his hands for the descent, and the bronze hair so tragically admired by Carralin was in peril of singeing at the tips.

Unsteady with nerves, Nevel fumbled to rearrange his own cressets for the climb. He edged closer to the drop, cursed softly, and raised a soot-streaked sleeve to blot his brow. Attack that moment by wereleopards seemed less risk than picking a path down rocks made slick by the falls.

"If heights make you dizzy, don't come," Korendir called from below. His words were punctuated by a rattling fall of shale. The farmer shut his eyes and waited for a splash that never came. Korendir's voice resumed without concern. "The footing's not the best and if I have to leave in a hurry, I'd rather know that shaft where you sit stays clear of spotted intruders."

"Got less sense of caution than Neth gave to butterflies," Nevel muttered as he scrambled back from the drop; but his admonishment held admiration.

The crash of the falls into the sucking violence of a whirlpool might satisfy most men that the Ellgol's watercourse was impassable. Only a fanatic might presume differently; out of folly, or madness, or perhaps a mix of both, Korendir seemed driven to search a cavern infested with wereleopards to make certain. The price required to hire the mercenary had been steep; but as Nevel settled gratefully to wait, he allowed that Korendir returned fair exchange. If his plan for a rockfall succeeded, Mel's Bye would be unquestionably secure.

Time passed without measure in the deeps of the earth. The passage was cold enough to cause a man in wet clothing to shiver. The field hand on guard huddled over his torches, then finally wedged the wooden handles in a crevice of rock and tucked his chilled hands beneath his jacket. The night-long trek left him weary. At length, he sat down with his axe unsheathed across his knees. His head nodded; he jerked out of a drowse and swore to Neth he must stand up, slap his knees, do something to keep himself awake. Lethargy kept him rooted. Before long sleep overcame him and he slouched into dreams while the torches near his head burned lower.

Nevel roused to a crack of stone and a wild flicker of flame light. One of his torches had gone out; the other burned wanly, a charred stump of spent fuel. The farmer stumbled to his feet. Gasping with fright, he clawed at his pack for fresh supplies, and only recalled his axe as the blade fell with a horrendous, echoing clang that barely missed severing toes.

"No wereleopards have ventured through the passage, I see," Korendir observed from the dark.

Caught between shame and embarrassment, Nevel understood he had been wakened by a chunk of shale, pitched with spiteful aim into the rock beside his ear.

"Be glad I wasn't the enemy," Korendir finished. Impatient with clumsiness, he recovered the spent torches and set to work with rags and oil. Light brightened swiftly under his hands. His face, underlit like a demon's, showed bronze hair dripping with wet and eyes over-bright from exertion.

"How long was I asleep?" the farmer asked suspiciously.

Korendir finished with the cressets and gathered up his sword without any break in movement. The blade appeared strangely dulled, and Nevel took a moment to realize the sheen was masked with fresh blood.

"How long?" he demanded more urgently.

Before he replied, the Master of Whitestorm recovered the fallen axe and pressed the haft into the farmer's unsteady hands. "Enough to ascertain that the wereleopards enter through another opening higher up. Also long enough for me to set a trap and lure, and entice a live beast into a fall where the river disappears down that sink hole."

Nevel considered this through a sickening recurrence of vertigo; with a nervous catch of breath he recalled the jagged snags of boulders which surrounded the subterranean rivercourse. That any man could stand with his hands on a bloodied sword and list such accomplishments with a calm that bordered on disinterest in itself inspired terror.

The farmer shuddered. "Neth, man, nothin' wholesome lives down there. What hell-spawned thing did ye find to use for bait?"

Korendir's brows lifted with exasperation. "You were sleeping. You don't want to know."

Nevel stared in horror, certain now, and loathing his conclusion. Quite deliberately the Lord of Whitestorm had set himself up as bait in the darkness; what else could attract an unholy predator to tread on bad footing and fall into that sucking cauldron of water?

Through a strained silence, the farmer studied the mercenary's face. He read there an exhaustion that left the flesh bloodlessly pale; Korendir presently maintained alertness on nothing at all but raw nerves. Gold by itself could never drive a man to such lengths; the possibility of what else might made hell seem merciful by comparison.

"Pity on us all," gasped Nevel. "Ye're crazed as

Emmon Hilgate's son, and more like those fey things you hunt than any man born to a mother." Heart pounding, hands clenched in fear on his axe and his torch, he spun and fled into the passage.

The crawl back to the outer cavern seemed interminable. Nevel breathed stale air mixed with the rankness of his own sweat; he heard like some monstrous impossibility the scuffle of the man who followed at his heels. Nevel scrabbled faster and cursed as he gashed a knuckle on something sharp. Then he hitched himself around a crook into a searing blaze of flame light.

"Hold fire, that's Nevel," shouted Sethon from beyond the dazzle.

The field hand blinked, his spooked imagination slapped squarely back to reason. Very tired, and made aware by the heat against his skin how chilled he had become, he dragged himself clear of the hole.

"Where's Korendir?" somebody demanded.

The farm hand dropped his axe. Aggravation showed through the mud on his face as he snapped, "Neth! Wherever else but behind me?"

"He hates life, that one," Emmon Hilgate's son observed. Come daylight, the huge man had taken refuge in the cavern with the other workers, although he sat apart. No one felt comfortable with his presence; yet if his comments were heard without welcome, he finished his musing regardless. "I should know. I hate life. That's what makes our Master of Whitestorm so accursedly difficult to kill."

At twilight, the contingent from Mel's Bye searched for the wereleopard which had hurtled headlong into the sink hole beneath the falls. The creature lay dragged against a log snag downstream, a tangle of limbs only recognizable by the diamond spots gleaming wet on its matted coat. Its neck was bent backward until one ear touched a shoulderblade; even from the bank a man could see that most of its bones had been broken.

Emmon Hilgate's son was first to find his voice. "They don't get through from Ardmark by swimming, that's sure as snow." But his tone was mocking and his fists stayed clenched at his sides.

Korendir shrugged without rancor. "I'd thought not.

But I had to make sure before risking any others from the village."

The days after that passed in backbreaking work. Every man strong enough to wield tools blistered his palms breaking shale. The stone was loaded into baskets, emptied into farm wagons, and hauled off to be dumped and spread across an ever-widening expanse of cleared ground. Korendir had ordered the forest stripped still farther back from the cliffs to afford untrammeled sight for the archers.

Cut timbers were sawed into beams for shoring, and the dead branches split for fuel to keep the inner caverns lighted. The bonfires were tended night and day, that no wereleopard could pass without being forced to change form. Ones who tried were caught in that instant of vulnerability, and brought down by a posted guard. In time the compound before the caves became ringed by a paling of staked skulls. The reek of woodsmoke, and rotting flesh, and sour, poorly cured hide mingled with the smells of cooking as the farmwives and elderly men tended open air kettles to feed the hungry in relays.

Korendir of Whitestorm labored with the rest, but never side by side. Carralin's death had soured the villagers' welcome, and he, aloof by nature, did not seek to win forgiveness. Stripped to his hose and swordbelt, he chipped shale, chopped wood, curried and harnessed the draft teams, or helped the wheelwright make linchpins and spokes, for wagons broke often on the rocky terrain.

Yet for all his reticence, the mercenary seldom worked alone. Like some glowering, muddy giant, Emmon Hilgate's son shadowed his side. As though by dint of zealous work the huge man could resurrect his lost sister, his pick chipped stone in unison with Korendir's, and his shovel tossed gravel until his body trembled in fatigue. Hour upon hour with the Master of Whitestorm, Emmon ignored the changes in shift.

At eventide while weary men rested, Korendir sat separately, wrapped in his black cloak with his hands busy. He mended the fletchings of arrows, or twisted new bowstrings from dried strips of wereleopard gut. Carralin's brother looked on with eyes intent as a starving beast. He had no patience for small tasks; still he slept only in snatches as the mercenary did, and arose in the hours after midnight, to stand watch with the archers in the smoke-shot flicker of firelight within the caverns.

The days of killing labor gradually bore results. By the time the autumn winds sang down off the upper peaks, and frosts touched the leaves to red-gold, the outcrop overhanging the Ellgol stood timbered like a meeting hall with neatly hewn posts and shoring. Still, when the rains fell, driven by biting gusts, men did not shelter beneath that undercut rock. The timbers groaned with their burden of earth; sand and loosened pebbles trickled down between cracks in the planks, and if that in itself did not wear a man's nerves, the storms without exception drove the wereleopards to frenzied fits of slaughter. Archers died on such days, mauled even after they fired a killing shaft.

So died Sethon, grown too cocksure of himself after half a dozen kills. Korendir was informed where he stood, shoulder-to-shoulder with Emmon, and gasping as he labored to free a wagon that had mired. Without a word, the mercenary set aside the staff he had used to raise the axle. He retrieved his soaked tunic from the buckboard, pulled it over streaming hair, and adjusted his swordbelt at his waist. Then he stared through the curtains of falling rain.

The mountain loomed like the shadow of doom over the thrashing waters of the Ellgol; timbers that seemed slender as match-sticks propped tons upon tons of weather-rotted shale, glistening now with streamlets which trailed silver around the skeletal roots of saplings. Korendir regarded the site, thin-lipped and still to the core. As if he could measure the waiting mass of soil and rock, he stirred at last and spoke.

"Tell the teamsters to harness every horse in the camp. Then make the chains fast to the kingposts. The slide comes down today, now. Waken the off duty watches." Then, as if the order held nothing of particular moment, the Master of Whitestorm started up the hill. Reflexively Emmon Hillgate's son made to follow.

The mercenary rounded in barely leashed fury. "I'll take the last watch by myself, son of Hillgate. From this time forward, no other lives than mine will be set at risk in the caverns."

Emmon glowered. He stepped away from the mired wagon so suddenly that the team jerked back in distress. Water snapped from sodden manes, and spattered his mottled face. "By the death you brought my sister, you have no right to prevent me."

For an instant, the eyes of the mercenary seemed weary, rinsed to emptiness by rain, long nights, and days of nerve-driven labor. Then his look hardened, determined as Emmon's own, but icy, where Hillgate's son's boiled with emotions like stirred lava.

"Don't try me on that score," the Master of Whitestorm challenged, almost too low to be heard. He left then, a crow-dark figure half lost against fields of shale gravel.

"Strange one, he is," muttered the teamster. Paunchy in his cloak of sodden leather, he shook himself and unfurled like a rag from his seat. With reins wadded in his fist, he sneezed runoff from his beard in self-pity.

"Help unhitch my bays, then," he asked of Emmon, his pragmatism a bastion against the grinding misery of the weather. Not at all certain that Hillgate's son would comply, he slapped his hand fondly on the nearest steaming rump, then bent to unhook the traces.

For a moment Emmon stared after Korendir in fixed and surly resentment. Then, for no apparent reason, he shed his sullen mood and began tunelessly to whistle. His unlikely bent of cheerfulness endured, though the sky opened up and lashed rain on his unprotected head, and the team sidled and made tiresome the chore of their unhitching from the mud-mired dray.

Other teams already stood harnessed by the time Emmon and the stout farmer reached the clearing beneath the outcrop. Over the roar of the Ellgol and the ceaseless spatter of rain rang the shouts of men, and the chinking rattle of chain. Horses stamped and snorted in the chilly air. Tempers were short, only partly due to the fact that everyone's boots were drenched, the stockings inside crushed to miserable wads around blistered heels; all the folk of Mel's Bye had striven for this moment. Lives had been lost, families had been separated, and crops had gone rotten in the fields to prepare for the rockfall that would bar the wereleopards from Northengard. Now, as horses were jockeyed into position, and chains were dragged and hooked round tackles and kingposts, every man of the town felt poised on a knife-edge of fear.

If the shale did not fault above the excavation, if the cliff face did not crumble and fall, if for any reason in nature the passage failed to seal, no recourse remained. Mel's Bye would be under siege for the winter, the trade routes impassable for the import of supplies; starvation would kill any wretches the wereleopards spared.

Tense, drawn by cold and exhaustion, the villagers tested buckles and harness straps, checked shackles and linchpins and chains. Some of them prayed, others cursed, and a few stayed grimly silent. At length the workers were joined by the men Korendir had excused from watch. The confusion redoubled until the newcomers had been assigned jobs, and all the while the rain beat down, blinding men's eyes and numbing their fingers until even the simplest task required curses to complete.

A horse shied, and one of the chains fouled under the roots of a stump. Men struggled and swore and split the skin of their knuckles to work the wedged links free.

"Where in hell is Emmon when his damned brute thews are needed?" someone carped.

The work team answered in grunts, too involved to concern themselves with the man, mad as he was, and unpredictable. The root splintered and gave. Chain slithered free, and bodies overbalanced into mud to a chorus of blasphemies. By the time the company sorted itself out, two score teams of horses stood quietly in line, heads down, tails flattened against the driving damp. Nothing remained to do but send a quartet of men to retrieve the supplies from the cavern, and recall Korendir from fire guard.

The men appointed this detail started for the caves with a fat child's pony and lightweight cart to load the gear.

The chief councilman arrived. His cloak of dripping burgundy wool exactly matched his nose, which also dripped, and for that he carried a lace handkerchief in sore need of wringing out. "Where's Emmon?" he asked.

"Where is he ever, but in the Master of Whitestorm's shadow?" the smith called sourly. "The others will have to bring him down. Neth curse this weather, did you think to bring up a wineskin?"

The council chief sneezed, shook his head, and paused with his hanky half raised to his face. Something in the quality of his stillness caused the men clustered nearest to look up.

In the gloom between two outer kingposts stood Emmon Hillgate's son, his hair plastered to his skull with rain, and a loaded crossbow in his hands.

"What in the Eleven Kingdoms is that madman doing up there?" the leader by the ponycart snapped.

"Go and find out," the chief councilman commanded through his handkercheif. "If Emmon makes trouble, ask the Lord of Whitestorm to handle him."

"Right." The man clucked to the pony and tugged irritably on the reins. Wheels turned with a rattle of shale, and the party round the cart started in a knot up the slope.

"Stop there!" shouted Emmon; his ragged pitch of hysteria could be heard even over the creak of the cart and the ceaseless batter of rain.

The chief councilman hesitated. The man at the pony's head glanced back in uncertainty. When he received no further orders, he kept going.

"No!" Emmon shouted. Carralin would have recognized his mood; there were times her brother would brook no reason from any man. Yet her poor departed spirit could not warn the living. Emmon flung back his head, dark hair flying in the wind. "Fools and sons of fools! My sister died on a wereleopard's fangs, and I say her killer will meet the same end."

He raised the crossbow to his shoulder.

The chief councilman shouted for the villagers to cease their advance. But the wind plucked his call away.

Emmon pulled the trigger.

The bolt struck flesh with a sickening, flat whap, and the pony jerked up its head and screamed. Scarlet bloomed at the juncture of its throat and chest. Crazed with agony, it reared. The reins tore the hands of its driver. Up the animal went, until it overbalanced and fell kicking amid a splinter of traces and a grate of steel-rimmed wheels.

Blood smell saturated the air; every horse in the column tossed and shied in their traces. Drivers shouted, white-faced. Too late they reached for whip and rein; the teams surged away in blind panic, and the chains to the kingposts clamored taut.

There followed a tortured creak of wood, then a run of maniacal laughter from Hillgate's son. Hooves skated and clattered on shale, and the blocks disgorged chain with a rattle like multiple ratchets.

Emmon flung his hands up, as if exhorting Neth. Then the beams over his head shifted as the nearer of the central kingposts twisted from its setting and toppled.

Cracks widened above the outcrop. The first boulders trembled and rolled and fell in what seemed like slow motion. Then more posts canted and the mountain itself gave way. Crushing tons of shale let go with a grinding, earth-shaking terror of sound and vibration.

Emmon was lost under a booming rush of debris. The ground shook. Downslope, the figures of horses and men fled in panic for their lives.

A rolling wave of shattered stone engorged the land, the river, the rows of five-foot palings topped with were-leopard skulls. The first ranks of trees became engulfed, chewed up like so many matchsticks. Several of the horse teams became snagged by their chains. Two men paused and tried to slash traces to free the animals. The slide caught them all without mercy, pulped their flesh and slivered their bones. The Ellgol moiled and ran dirty. To the men who survived to reach safety, the rending, shattering roar of moving earth seemed to last interminably before subsiding.

Yet silence returned at last. The air held a drifting curtain of fine dust, rapidly cleansed by rain. Drenched, miserable, heartsick with awe, the men of Mel's Bye emerged from cover and gazed upon the changed face of nature.

A great scar marked the place where the cliff face had fallen away. Where the honeycomb mouths of the caves had been, a jagged field of boulders lay heaped at the foot of the outcrop. The head of the gorge was choked off, and ribbons of water sluiced through a sieve of invisible gaps. Bark-stripped trees poked out of the devastation, and the shattered curve of a wheel rim; but nothing more. The passages that had let in the wereleopards had been milled under, utterly, by unshiftable tons of stone.

That the man who had engineered this feat should be

left, trapped inside in the darkness for death by mauling
or starvation, was a tragedy no man cared to contemplate.

"Go home," said the chief councilman, sodden and
small before that vista of ravaged landscape. "He cannot
be helped."

Slowly, reluctantly, wearily, the folk of Mel's Bye
turned their backs against the rain. No one suggested a
monument. Emmon's act was compounded of insane
grief and justice; not one farmer who made his way home
in the rain gainsaid a man's right to exact vengeance for
his sister.

Only the issue of the gold remained; and where matters of finance prevailed, the townsfolk prided themselves
on a tradition of scrupulous fairness.

Sleet rattled over the unfinished battlements at Whitestorm. Iced-over puddles gleamed like hammered metal
in the compound that Korendir had dreamed would become his castle's inner bailey. Construction had ceased
for the winter; in the absence of any craftsmen the site
lay desolate, whipped by sea winds, and loud with the
crash of the breakers that storms hurled endlessly against
the cliffs. Though inhospitable, Whitestorm keep was not
untenanted. A crook in the half-finished stonework stood
roofed over with sod and enclosed by mud-chinked walls.
There, his feet on a hot brick and his shoulders cloaked
in blankets, Haldeth huddled before a blaze of thorn
logs. Laziness, as always, got the better of him. He could
see from where he sat that his fuel supply would not last
until morning. Hating the cold and the long, lonely
nights, he grumbled, shed his mantle of quilts, and arose.

He unlaced a doorflap of oiled leather and stepped out
into the dusk. A rutted footpath led from there to the
smithy with its open-air forge and tool shed. A clutter of
scrap iron lay piled untidily about the yard; in the gloom
of another shelter rested the results of Haldeth's labors,
a seemingly random assortment of tether-rings, hinges,
latches, fastenings, gate-bars, winch pulleys, and other
sundry hardware necessary to the raising of a fortress.
Later, he would temper steel and hire in a master weaponsmith to begin on the armory; but at present his
thoughts ranged no further than the tarp which protected
the woodpile, which lay inconveniently flat.

Haldeth cursed. Yesterday's indulgence had caught up with him; he should have fixed the axe haft and gone foraging for brush while the weather was mild and sunny. That he must remedy his lapse in darkness and driving wind now could not be helped; he had only himself to blame. Vexed that Korendir's commission in Northengard should keep him from Whitestorm so long, Haldeth stumped out through the gap that would someday become the main gate.

Freezing wind slapped his face the instant he cleared the walls. His eyes burned with cold and he blinked, at first too preoccupied to complete his habitual search of the sea. When the gusts subsided and his vision cleared to allow a squint beyond the cliffs, he stopped in his tracks and forgot everything to do with the insatiable requirements of woodfires. Against the indigo line of the horizon lay a glimmer of light.

A ship rode the waves toward Whitestorm.

At this season, with the spice fleets battened snugly in harbors and next year's wool trade mantling the backs of the grazing flocks, a vessel in these waters could mean but one thing. Korendir of Whitestorm had returned.

X. Wizard's Tower

The ship's lights steadily drew nearer, yellow against the sea by the time Haldeth replenished the wood stores. At dawn, the vessel backed sail and dropped anchor in the harbor beneath White Rock Head. The smith busied himself setting out kettles and stew, then washed his chipped mugs and fussed over his dwindled hoard of tea. Come the ebb tide at mid-morning, he descended to the beach to greet his returning companion.

The bark at anchorage was a merchanter, squat and low waisted to ease the loading of goods. Her canvas was furled neatly, and her paintwork recent if scuffed from careless dockage. Haldeth waited, shifting from foot to foot while crewmen swayed out a longboat. He cursed himself for omission; a ship's glass would have served him well, for the tender did not immediately depart, but dallied to on load some chests that were heavy enough to commandeer several halyards and a commotion of shouted orders. The gold, of course; Korendir's fee. Haldeth swore again, for forgetting. Eyes narrowed against the flash of sunlight off the waves, he waited. Yet no dark-cloaked figure descended the battens to claim the stern seat in the longboat; instead several farmers in dusky cloth jackets completed the party bound for shore.

Korendir, Master of Whitestorm, was not among them.

Touched by foreboding, Haldeth saw the craft draw away from the merchanter's lee. Oar shafts rose and fell through a fine-blown scatter of spray, driving under the shadow of the cliffs until the boat put aground in the shallows.

Looms flashed upright and were hauled inboard by the oarsmen, while the sailors nearest the bow leaped the thwarts. Haldeth stepped into the icy surf to help steady the craft. As the following comber raised the stern, he hauled with a vengeance for the beach.

The chests made the craft keel-deep and awkward. More oarsmen had to wet their feet and heave before the longboat became manageable. In thick silence, Haldeth watched two farmers disembark; the third had a familiar face, behind an eyepatch and a green mottling of seasickness.

"Yegods, lookit 'im, 'e's mebbe going ta puke," laughed a sailor.

Certainly ill, but clinging to dignity as chief delegate from Mel's Bye, Lain rolled his eye to the cliff face, with its ragged crown of foundations pricking the sky overhead. The sailors lifted him ashore, where he sat as if felled on dry sand and muttered about an absence of roads for a wagon.

From this Haldeth miraculously divined a meaning. He waved back the sailors who strained to raise the first chest from the longboat. "There's a loading winch up top, built for lifting granite. If you wait while I thread on some cable, no one will need to bust a gut."

The farmers on their feet conferred, and agreed to oversee the loading at the beach head. Lain tottered up-right and followed Haldeth toward a barnacle-crusted portal in the rocks. The opening was black as a pit and reeking of tidewrack. The departure of Whitestorm's elemental had dropped the sea to its former level; what had been the lower entry to Sharkash's caverns opened out on the narrow strand where the smith escorted the jelly-legged envoy from Mel's Bye.

Much else had changed, since summer. Past the first crook in the walls, Haldeth retrieved the burned down stub of a torch. Flame from draft-fanned embers revealed a puddled, sandy floor, then stairs cut into rock all but buried under drifts of seaweed.

Miserable with nausea, Lain began the ascent at Haldeth's heels. Early on they passed through a heavy steel trap that opened by winch from above. Although the sea had been at work on both, the chain was new, and the bolts yet bore marks from the forge. Haldeth did not close this defensework, to Lain's overpowering relief. He imagined besiegers pinned against such a gate by the rising well of the tide, and the sickness that still lingered from his voyage redoubled and left him gasping.

Too preoccupied to notice much beyond his own distress, Haldeth led through two more grilles and passed the level of the high water mark. The upper access to Sharkash's lair had been fortified into an abutment, pierced with cruciform apertures for crossbowmen. Sea wind sang through those slits, and others cut through the walls where the stair continued the ascent. Lain shivered, not only from chill. He placed one foot mechanically after another, and wondered whether Faen Hallir's royal archers were numerous enough to man the defenses built into White Rock Head.

The stair ended in an unfinished outer bailey. Haldeth paused to secure the final door, a steel plate that rolled on a track by means of a windlass and counterweight. Sweating in unexpected sunlight, Lain regarded the massive bulwarks, at present just eight feet high, but built of blue granite to uncompromising specifications. Everything about the incomplete keep bespoke the man left trapped in Northengard, behind tons of fallen shale; the wereleopards infesting the passages would not have shown him mercy. Unnerved afresh by the tidings he bore, Lain faltered in his tracks.

Haldeth quenched his torch in a puddle, and noticed the farmer's white face. "You're ill," he said contritely. "Why not sit in the sun while I attend the winches? There are corners sheltered from the wind, and I'll heat water for tea."

Still speechless, Lain shook his head. With forced determination he braved the cold on the heights, and lent his weight to the ropes while the chests shipped from Northengard were hauled from the beach to the summit.

Exertion restored his equilibrium. Drained and tired, Lain accepted tea from Haldeth and sat down on the nearer of the iron-bound chests. The smith took a seat on the other. His tumbled hair needed a trim, and clothing much mended from briar snags smelled pungently of woodsmoke and forge coals. He gripped his mug with anxious hands and pointedly avoided questions.

Lain had exhausted his reasons for withholding bad news any longer. "Mel's Bye sends the fee for Korendir of Whitestorm, who successfully completed his contract."

Solemnly, the farmer drew a chain over his head; the iron keys at the end chimed sourly as he relinquished them to the smith.

"He died, then," Haldeth stated flatly. He shivered at the touch of the metal against his palm.

Lain nodded, and thereby crushed the final, outside hope, that the bronze-headed fool might have gone straight on from Northengard to fill another commission.

The smith snatched a breath to steady himself. "Tell me how."

Lain stared with his single eye into the dregs of his tea. Haltingly he began to speak.

By the time he recounted the rock slide he was shaking. He perched rigidly on the bullion chest, his knuckles laced together, while his memory echoed yet with the grinding, thunderous crash of falling shale.

Haldeth said something sharply. Lain took a moment to focus, then muster his thoughts and find answer. "Aye, there were supplies in the cave. Wood, canvas, a stockpile of food for the sentries."

An interval passed, filled by the shrill calls of gulls.

Then the smith hammered a fist against his palm in outraged disbelief. "Korendir certainly survived!" As if he addressed a lackwit, he qualified. "There must be other access to those caverns, higher in the mountains, where altitude would deter wereleopards. Why come here with this gold? Instead your people should have hired search parties to scour the Doriads for caves. Neth's mercy, man, the Master of Whitestorm saved your town! Could you not at least endeavor a gesture in his behalf?"

Lain shifted sadly, head down; his collar laces tapped in the breeze. "Because of Carralin, the council was opposed."

Haldeth drew breath but found no inclination to curse. He arose instead and savagely kicked at a coin chest. Oaken boards bound with hobnails and iron absorbed the blow without budging; for his fury the smith gained only a sullen clink of gold and several painful stubbed toes. Limping, a frown on his face, he strode to the half-completed battlements and stared unseeing at ocean.

He could not bear to look behind him, at the partially finished main hall. Here lay the foundations of a magnifi-

cent fortress; once the dream of a man obsessed by his
need for security. The hope of a haven behind which to
appreciate living, Haldeth profoundly understood. Mhurgai cruelties had driven many a man to madness;
Korendir's had just been more logical than most. Haldeth tried embracing the scope of the memories left behind, and the home he inherited by default; lastly,
achingly, he considered the circumstances which had
brought this tragedy to pass.

Something inside him rebelled. He exhorted Lain for
details. "Did you keep records? Exactly how much wood
and food did Korendir have at his disposal?"

Lain stared open-mouthed, while Haldeth rounded
from the wall in a fury. "*Answer* me, man, how long
could he stay alive on those stores?"

"But the wereleopards!" Lain shoved halfway to his
feet, incredulous.

Haldeth allowed the farmer no quarter, but towered
over him and flexed his blacksmith's shoulders. "But the
Lord of Whitestorm proved himself a match for shapechangers, yes? You sit on the gold that proves it."

Lain sank miserably back. He fingered his tight-
buttoned cuffs and would not look at Haldeth. "At the
outside, the food left behind might sustain one man for
two months. The firewood should have gone much
sooner. Without light, the wereleopards would be free to
slaughter. By this time, only an idiot could believe that
Korendir of Whitestorm remains alive."

The farmer's assessment was just. Yet the mercenary
would never have sat and built fires until the predators
came to make a meal of him. He would have moved,
and fought; and the prospect of winter and loneliness on
the summit at White Rock Head made folly much easier
to contemplate. Amazed at thoughts more Korendir's style
than his own, Haldeth asked Lain his last question.
"Where's your trader bound when she leaves this harbor?"

"Northward, into Heddenton, and then on to Northport for careening." Lain shrugged lamely. "The season
for southbound trade's ended. If chance and luck both
prevailed, your master could never in all the Mhurga's
hells hold out unsupported till spring."

The pronouncement of sound logic fazed Haldeth not
one bit. "I'm going north," he snapped. "You can holler

down to the beach and tell your bosun, while I step inside to fetch myself a clean shirt."

When Lain returned a blank look, the smith rubbed his axe blistered hands and qualified. "I plan to sail, and every Neth forsaken coinweight of this gold is going back to that merchant brig's hold."

Windblown and queasy from bitter tea, Lain raised his brows in exasperation. "Whatever for, to buy search parties to comb the caverns for a skeleton? By the time the passes thaw, naught else will remain."

Haldeth stood with his fists braced on stone and said nothing.

Lain shoved his dirty cup aside and stood up. "You're as mad as your master was."

That perhaps was true; certainly before escape from the galleys, Haldeth had never shown such contempt for the impossible. Yet his refusal to believe in Korendir's death demanded no less than action of the sort the man himself might have chosen.

Decisively Haldeth started for the winch; his next words threaded through the clang and rattle of chain. "Another means of passage exists that has no regard for seasons or time."

"Sure," said Lain, still obstinate. He made no move to shed his jacket for labor, but continued on a note of dry sarcasm. "White Circle enchanters cross whole continents through the alter-reality of Alhaerie. Except they won't do spellcraft for mortals, and their towers are built without doors."

Haldeth chose not to argue the fine point that the rumor of doorless towers was a mistaken belief from a children's tale. Instead he spread the sling on the ice-rimmed earth and set hands to the nearest chest. Twelve thousand coin weight in gold would establish whether enchanters did business with mortals; and scarcely three leagues from the merchant port of Heddenton rose the tower of the wizard Orame.

The trader dropped anchor in Heddenton harbor on a day of driving rain. By dint of the fact he paid handsomely, Haldeth had himself and his chests delivered to the wharf by sailors who cursed their captain, their brig, and their shipmates for the duration of a wind-raked crossing. There, stinking of soaked wool and lamp soot, and glad to be quit of the miasma that arose from the bilges of a vessel that carried pigs as well as passengers, Haldeth stood hatless in the downpour and regarded his destination.

The docks were old and sagging, creaky under their burden of stacked barrels and lumber and heaps of much mended fishing net. Beyond lay cobbled streets slimy with run-off from the fish market, which now was deserted except for flocks of scavenging gulls. Stone buildings with shutters painted in patterns arose along the quay side. The more imposing had balconies and widows walks, built over the course of six centuries to a hodgepodge of changing tastes. Wrought-iron rubbed corners with gingerbread, while without regard for fashion, each facing and cornerbeam stood scoured with gull guano.

Haldeth hitched at his cloak and winced as a runnel of water tracked a new course down his spine. A sensible man would have lightened Korendir's cursed chests, and replenished his wardrobe against the onslaughts of winter storms. Frowning, soaked, and regretting his harebrained sympathy for a friend's impossible predicament, the smith stumped off to the harbor master's shed and rousted three stevedores from the fireside.

"Damn me, she's heavy," the first of them complained as he hefted his appointed load from the dock. "That, on account o'rain too, cost ya extra."

"You say?" Haldeth returned a glare of practiced menace. "We'll see how much extra if you like, but I promise no payment in coin."

"Neth, but ye've no sense of humor," the stevedore groused, and then swore in earnest for allowing himself to be intimidated as he slung the chest to his shoulder and heard metal chinking within.

"Off you go," Haldeth ordered sharply.

With a grimace more to do with lost opportunity, the stevedore obeyed. His two companions followed with the other chests, muttering among themselves. "First rich man to come to Heddenton, and he has to travel crazy in the wet."

At the innyard, beneath a swinging, weather-checked livery sign, Haldeth hired a wagon and a nag. The rig came dear, due to an inopportune comment by one of the departing stevedores. But the smith considered time more precious than the money he might save by haggling. Out on the road, with the buckboard jolting loose under his feet, and the driver's seat giving him splinters, he came to regret his compliance. That the rattletrap vehicle should be rented at all was a robbery of criminal proportions, even had the hack in the harness not kicked like a donkey with hemorrhoids. As its rear hooves hammered the planking repeatedly over the leagues, Haldeth shook his whip and threatened torture if the animal would not level out and haul.

An ear twitched back. The beast tossed its head above the shafts, its eye a half moon of rolling white; and Haldeth exclaimed with enlightenment. He had been rented a harness without blinders. Perhaps the ostler at the tavern had been careless; more likely, he was hoping for a wreck, and the salvage of coins from a burst chest. Whatever the reason, his omission was wasted effort with a smith. Haldeth knotted the reins and dismounted into the soupy mud of the roadside. He strode to the horse's head and wadded his scarf around the cheek straps of the luckless beast's bridle.

He resumed driving and the kicking stopped. Unable to see the wagon which followed, and no longer distressed by its rattle, the horse jogged down a turn off from the road that no man in Heddenton cared to travel. At the end, couched amid dripping evergreens, rose the tower of Orame of the White Circle.

Built of polished stone, and octagonal in shape, the structure rose sheer from the forest floor. The turreted top lay blurred by mist, and though there was an oaken door carved with runes and leering faces, not a single window relieved the imposing expanse of black wall. The mirror-smooth stone reflected the rain and the swaying boughs of the pines, as well as the damp and red-nosed visitor hunched in his rickety cart.

Haldeth looped the reins to the buckboard and stiffly climbed down. Chilled from more than wet clothing, he regarded the tower and shivered. Brash as Korendir had been, he had never attempted anything so harebrained as begging aid from a wizard; that he had avowed the intent before his departure for Northengard seemed a folly far better forgotten.

Stubborn as iron when he wished to be, Haldeth ignored the wisdom of turning back. Instead he left the cart where it stood and paced the tower's perimeters.

While he squelched over matted pine needles and splashed his way through puddles, he felt he was being watched. The tower yielded no secrets. Seamless stone gave back nothing but his own reflection. The door beneath the pillared arch had neither knob nor keyhole, but only the horned and leering faces of demons and border upon border of runes. The smith stamped across wet flags to the stoop. Rain dripped in his eyes. He longed for a seat in a tavern and a foaming tankard of beer, except Korendir must be wishing for similar comforts, in a cave infested by wereleopards.

Haldeth raised his hand and knocked. The oak was hard and the runes bruised his knuckles. He shifted in trepidation, while more rain dribbled down his collar.

Nothing happened.

The rain continued to fall, and drip, and splash from the needles of the evergreens; the cart horse stamped and snorted runoff from its nose. Irked and feeling stupid, Haldeth knocked again.

He waited, poised for a spell that never came. He would have run at a sound, or the slightest glimmer of magic. Indifference was the last reaction he had expected from a wizard who belonged to the mightiest order on Aerith. And yet, his presence was not entirely disregarded. The crawling goose-flesh between his shoulderblades did not ease. He *was* being watched, and closely, but with patent disregard for manners. Snug and dry in his tower, Orame made no offer of hospitality toward the visitor who froze on his door stoop. That he was a White Circle enchanter and as such not entirely mortal made little difference to Haldeth's uncomplicated outlook. Orame's oversight added up to insult.

Haldeth regarded the closed, rune-carved door, then strode across the wizard's yard to the cart left parked by the trees. He unhooked the traces, marched the hack from between the shafts, then looped the reins through his elbow and cut a pine switch.

"Orame!" he shouted. The wood absorbed his call without even echoes for reply. "There's a man awaiting your consultation who has traveled a long way to see you."

The wizard gave no response, yet the air took on a waiting stillness, as if someone's attention sharpened.

Too annoyed to take heed, Haldeth removed the scraps of scarf he had earlier twisted through the bridle. Then he backed the run-down horse up to the demon-carved portal, firmed his grip on the reins, and slashed the air with the switch at the edge of the animal's peripheral vision.

The nag arched its bony spine, heaved up its quarters, and let fly a resounding kick at the door panel. Oak slivers and runes bounced with the impact; the boom re-echoed through the windowless well of the tower like the fall of the hammer of god.

Hugely pleased, Haldeth raised his crop for another go.

"Just what do you think you're doing?" said an acerbic voice from behind.

Haldeth dropped his stick. He spun around just as the cart horse spoiled his balance with a hard shy backward against the reins. "Whoa!" cried the smith, and braced himself mightily. Brought up short, the horse settled, blowing gusts and rolling its eyes.

The wizard stood two paces off. His age was impossible to guess. The rain fell relentlessly, but his charcoal gray robes showed not a trickle of wet. His hair was very dark auburn, and his eyes piercingly black. Tall he was, and slender, and unquestionably put out.

Haldeth diffidently stepped backward until the door blocked his retreat. He raised his chin, masked fright with defiance, and spoke back in flustered desperation. "I knocked, your wizardship. Twice. What's a visitor in the freezing rain to do when you choose not to answer your door?"

Orame gestured with extreme impatience. "Great Neth, man, I was a thousand leagues away at the time! What you felt was the spell that wards my tower. I did hear you, even from such a distance, and I was coming. You had only to wait."

Haldeth recoiled in horrified disbelief, his spine gouged by the knobbly horns of a half dozen carved demons. That moment the horse shook like a dog, and splattered him from head to foot with dirty water.

Orame raised peaked brows in reproof. "Take that beast off my door stoop, you great lump of a blacksmith. Remove its harness and tether it where it can graze. Then I expect you're hungry, and want a fire, and also have a boon to ask. Though why I should listen after suffering this abuse to my woodwork is a riddle that would perplex the Archmaster at Dethmark himself."

Haldeth gathered his rented gelding's reins, and with a look of unvarnished skepticism towed it toward the verge of the trail; little use, he thought, to belabor the fact that the beast could not forage on pine boughs.

"Neth's image, you mortals," grumbled Orame from behind. "Seek out a wizard for miracles, and then with gymnastic illogic presume the arrangement of fodder could be any less than impossible." He snapped his fingers.

The earth seemed to lurch underfoot. Suddenly knee deep in oat grass, Haldeth stumbled through a tangle of seed tassels. The instant he recovered his footing he bent a sour glance at the wizard.

But the yard once again stood empty. Orame had gone. So had the door with its decorative runes and demons. Apparently that imposing front had been an enchanter's confection of illusion. Revealed beneath the arch was a portal bound in brass, and cut, at waist height, with the crescent indentations made by a startled horse. To the smith's embarrassment, the latch had been left unhooked. The panel stood ajar in invitation.

Anxious to be quit of the rain, Haldeth attended the livery nag with all speed.

Orame's tower held the predictable spiral staircase overseen by stone gryphons and gargoyles. Strangely enough from the inside, there seemed an abundance of casements latched and snug against the rain. The library on the landing above proved comfortably furnished with fur hassocks. The books on the shelves bore no titles. Though curious, Haldeth withheld from comment. The ways of wizards were not his to fathom, and White Circle enchanters were widely renowned for their knowledge of perilous secrets. Orame stood flanked by shoulder-high candlestands wrought in the form of scaled dragons. He motioned his guest to a chair before a tortoise-shell table set with tea and refreshments.

Any thought of indulging in comforts grated, given Korendir's straits; but after his gaffe in the dooryard, Haldeth was determined to mend his lapse in manners, lest the enchanter take offense and turn him out.

The smith moved toward the offered chair, drew breath to apologize for his rank odor and dripping cloak, and realized with a start that somewhere between the outer door and the landing all of his clothing had dried. The smell of wet horse had miraculously gone with the water. Tongue-tied in amazement, Haldeth sat with a thump that shook the table.

"I know why you've come," the wizard said, before Haldeth could lose the flush on his face. "I know already what you journeyed here to ask me, and before you left, you should have known that gold buys no influence with the White Circle."

Haldeth reclaimed his poise. "Korendir, is he alive?"

Orame enigmatically poured tea. He set a roll on a napkin before Haldeth, and helped himself to another. "Why should this man's life concern me?"

Having neither appetite nor words for the occasion, Haldeth could find no answer. After a moment, Orame said, "He's alive." A frown marred his olive skin as he took a bite and chewed thoughtfully. "But not for very much longer, I should think."

Haldeth shoved the bread aside in dismay. "What do you mean?"

Orame flicked crumbs from neat fingers. "Mean?" He sighed. "See for yourself." And the polished glaze of the tea pot suddenly acquired an image.

Haldeth beheld darkness and torchlight; but the flame was failing, flickering wildly in a draft. Through a weaving murk of shadows, he received the impression of rock walls glazed shiny with water. Then, with a start that all but stopped his heart, he made out a tangle of bronze hair. The torch was held in the white-knuckled fist of Korendir, who climbed with his dagger between his teeth and his sword thrust unsheathed through his belt. The crossbow slung at his shoulder showed blood on the grip, and one whole side of his tunic was sliced to gore-drenched ribbons.

"Neth, he's hurt," cried Haldeth.

As if he could hear, Korendir turned his head. It became apparent then that he was engaged in a climb through a shaft that seemed bottomlessly dark. In the wizard's tower, staring at an image in a teapot, Haldeth saw his friend's face was worn with exhaustion and hunger, and that something else stalked him from below. Now and again the flicker of torchlight caught on green-golden crescents that were eyes.

"Wereleopards!" Haldeth reached out, bruised his knuckles against heated ceramic, and cursed. The image disappeared, and he frantically looked to Orame. "Neth's grace, you can't just let him die."

The wizard considered, his eyes impervious as obsidian. "To save your friend would require use of a wizard's gate, and a crossing to Northengard by way of the alter-reality of Alhaerie."

When Haldeth looked blank, the enchanter qualified conversationally over his tea. "You do know that every ill that has ever plagued Aerith has entered through such rifts into the otherworld. The demons that overran Alathir originated from Alhaerie. High Morien's holding was destroyed, and all of his following, and he was Archmaster before Telvallind."

"Then sit there nibbling raisin pastries and do nothing!" Made bold by desperation, Haldeth ranted on. "You said you were a thousand leagues away at the time I knocked on your door. If you'd open a wizard's gate to answer a mortal's call, why not to save a life?"

"Because the route from here to Dethmark is guarded well by wards. The passage where your friend flees for his life is a place in the wilds, unfrequented by wizards, and naked of the most basic protection." Orame laced long fingers around his chin. "But should I let Korendir die? That's another risk altogether. I'm inclined to believe I dare not."

The odd implications hinted by the enchanter's words were too abstruse for pursuit in the face of crisis. "You'll take the gold, then," Haldeth offered eagerly, and pushed in haste to his feet.

"No." Orame set his cup down with a click. "Certainly not. The suggestion alone is preposterous."

Haldeth bit back an insult. With all the diplomacy he could muster, he said, "Whatever moves you, just ask."

Orame sat back in his chair. His hair shone in the candlelight, combed and smooth as an owl's plumage, while he folded his hands in his lap. "If I do this, you will ask Korendir who his parents are," he said obliquely.

The smith nodded with baffled impatience and stepped back. "The Master of Whitestorm may kill me rather than answer, but I'll question him."

"And," added Orame, "at your first opportunity you will fashion for me a grille of wrought iron. A decorative one, but stout enough to spare my front door from abuse if other travelers use horses that kick to gain entrance."

"Done," said Haldeth promptly.

Orame arose without hurry. He folded back the cuff of his robe and withdrew a ring from a pocket. Haldeth recognized the glitter of a tallix jewel setting. Frightened by the adventure he had suddenly committed to undertake, he wished he had never left Whitestorm as Orame of the White Circle slid the ring on his forefinger and raised it in the air above his shoulder. Haldeth felt his wrist gripped by narrow, bony fingers. Then the wizard let fall his arm.

Where the tallix crystal passed, a line of light shimmered upon the air. Haldeth blinked, dazzled by glare. When he opened his eyes next, the seam had parted, and he gazed upon a sight that wrenched all his senses to behold.

XI. Visions of Alhaerie

To look through the gate Orame had opened upon the air was to experience the living face of chaos. The alter-reality of Alhaerie was color and movement with no pattern, a churning swirl of energies that the eyes could not reconcile without relinquishing all grip on reason. Haldeth gazed upon a film of pearlescence that had no analogue to anything understandable in Aerith. The universe that existed beyond the gate possessed neither up or down, nor any other measurable dimension; time itself was skewed there, stirred and non-linear as spilled fluid. Haldeth felt crawling discomfort. He looked away swiftly, but the hair continued to prickle at his neck, and his stomach clenched with nausea.

"You *travel* through that stuff?" he asked tightly.

Orame returned an abstracted reply as he traced a pentagram before the gate. "With extreme caution, yes."

"Neth!" More than ever, Haldeth wished himself back at Whitestorm. His better sense told him he should flee at once, even surrender Korendir to his fate; that way he might survive to know peaceful old age.

Except that Orame caught his wrist in a grip like prisoner's shackles, then propelled him forcefully forward.

The first step carried Haldeth across the bounds of the pentagram. Electricity caused every hair on his body to rise. Spellcraft and safe-wards pressed his being on all sides; the magic constricted him physically to the point where the scream that arose from his lungs could find no escape through his throat. Half choking on unuttered sound, the smith felt himself dragged onward. His unwilling feet carried him across the spell's far boundary and on through the wizard's gate beyond.

The strangeness that was Alhaerie flowed over Haldeth and ripped away everything familiar.

His senses tumbled into chaos. Sound, smell, sight, and orientation disappeared. His boots trod upon *nothing*, and yet he did not fall. Neither did his steps convey any measurable sense of movement. The nerves in his feet transmitted no feel of solidity beneath his weight; his eyes saw only mad swirls of color. In desperation, Haldeth looked at his body, but not even the fabric of his cloak and tunic remained in understandable form. In place of clothing, he wore a churning mass of visions, as if events had been stewed in a pot, and all the cloth's creation was simultaneously made visible: from the seeds of the plants that produced the fibres, to the sweat of the dyer's labors, to the click of the weaver's loom, to the rot of moths and mildew that awaited in the future to come.

Haldeth felt sick. He wanted, no *needed*, to bend double and spew the contents of his stomach. Orame's hold prevented him. Through disorientation that wrung him dizzy, he opened his mouth to protest.

A hard hand sealed his lips, and at the same time a warning not spoken in words rang through Haldeth's inner mind: *You must not speak in this place.*

Orame's precaution served to focus scattered thoughts. Only then, through meaningless waves of sound that buffeted his ears like an assault, did the smith come to notice that the wizard chanted spells in a sing-song held down to a whisper; the prohibition against talk proved no arbitrary restriction. Alhaerie's reality transformed even sound to a thing which defied credibility. Each phrase that left the wizard's lips became manifest; silvery, razor-thin ribbons that were words cleft the roiling atmosphere and left no doubt of their solidity.

Haldeth's heart banged in his chest.

Orame's spell chant alone affirmed continuity. The stuff of his wards unreeled with precise control; in time, through his pervasive unease, Haldeth observed that the shimmering strands did not disperse into chaos as random sounds might have done. Instead, like braiding, the recitation interwove to form a cord of netted energies. This the wizard bent into a pentagram. He released Haldeth long enough to cast the figure around himself and the mortal he escorted. Immediately, although nothing visible resulted, the smith felt as if firm ground supported his feet. His vertigo subsided, and with it, the cramps that crippled his gut.

He opened his mouth to give thanks, then recalled his peril and snapped his teeth shut without speaking.

Backed by the indefinable chaos that was Alhaerie, Orame of the White Circle smiled. "You may talk if you wish. We are behind wards now, and protected."

"But I don't see anything." Haldeth gestured, baffled.

Orame tapped the shining band of the pentagram with his finger; at his touch the structure rang like the struck peal of a bell. "Senses are deceptive in this place," he added, patronizingly complacent. "Trust only what you feel."

"Sick," Haldeth said sourly, although in truth that discomfort had faded. His boots might *seem* like they trod upon bedrock, but he preferred ground that he could see tree roots, pebbles, and dew upon.

"Alhaerie does affect the mind," Orame agreed. "Its energies can cause insanity in a man too long exposed without shielding spells." He tapped the ward again and roused a repeat of the same clear tone. "D flat," he concluded after a bird-bright glance at Haldeth. "The pitch seems steady enough. Shall we go on?"

"I'm not a singer," Haldeth said obstinately. "I wouldn't know D flat from the thump of an acorn falling."

Orame's brows lifted into an acerbic peak. He stepped onward; the pentagram moved with his motion, and rather than get sliced through the ankles by the following boundary of the spell, Haldeth stumbled forward.

Oblivious, the wizard continued his discussion. "Acorns don't fall in Alhaerie, unless a mortal not under the protection of wards chances to think that they do. Then there would be trees and acorns aplenty, until the stability of the man's being was entirely unravelled to provide them."

This esoteric drivel made no impression on Haldeth, who was trying to reconcile the solid ring of his heels with *nothing* beyond the eerily glowing pentagram which continued to travel in stride. The smith was scared out of his skull, and without credulity to spare for riddles. As if those affronts to rationality were not enough, D flats meant even less to a man born tone deaf to a sixth generation ironsmith.

"Well," Orame concluded, as if he could guess the nuance of mortal contemplation as he walked. "Even without D flat, you would know if my spellcraft was unstable. When I struck the ward, the pitch would have risen to a dissonance that made you wince. Musician or not, most men can distinguish between the yowl of a cat in heat and a tuning fork."

Haldeth gave no reply. He had no interest in figuring how a wizard might offer insult, and still less in understanding the alien splendors of Alhaerie.

Toward that end, Haldeth finally clamped his eyes shut. He walked on trust alone. The occasional brushing touch of Orame's sleeve became his only assurance that he remained in the wizard's protection. How long the crossing lasted was impossible to determine. Departure from the tower might have been minutes, hours, even days in the past; or unlikely as the concept seemed, that moment when the tallix scored the gate through the void could have taken place in the future.

Orame might have said for certain, if the mind of any wizard on Aerith could reliably know such things; Haldeth could not escape his morbid doubts. His nature was not like Korendir's, to be drawn to fascination with the unknown. Reconciled at last to a permanent self-affirmation, Haldeth wished for nothing beyond surety that he would forever after this keep his place within the world he understood.

And yet for all his longing, the transition back to Aerith happened by surprise. A sound intruded like a rip upon the air. Haldeth did not react in time to unseal his closed eyes. His next step carried him from the glassy smooth surface of spells onto the rocky and unforgiving slope of a mountainside.

He stubbed his toes on jutting shale, then tripped into the thorns of a gorse bush. Too late to save himself, he flung out his arms in time to get slapped by a nettlesome sting of branches. His oath of annoyance tangled with Orame's last incantation, to the detriment of both. The wizard's spell shaped sluggishly. Fell gusts tore through the closing slit of the gate to Alhaerie; the wizard's robes flapped like whipcracks around his ankles, and Haldeth overbalanced backward.

Disgruntled by Orame's exasperated scrutiny, this time the smith was wise enough to stifle complaint. The ground was unpleasantly damp; threat of more rain lurked in the clouds that bunched like combed cotton over the peaks. The gate had delivered wizard and smith to a windswept crag. The weather here was milder than that which froze the north shores at this season; since the caves of the Ellgol were situated well south of White-storm's latitude, Haldeth presumed the enchanter had been correct in his navigation across the void. The wilderness where they emerged must be located in the Doriad mountains.

Thorn-studded branches tore the smith's shirt and ripped at skin as he pulled clear, yet scratches seemed of small consequence beside the fact that Orame had drawn his pentagram after him into Aerith. The thing drifted in the place where the gateway had closed, a silver-bounded shape with no discernible thickness and a center brimming and boiling with the kaleidoscopic chaos that was the essence of this world's opposite.

"Great Neth, get rid of that thing," Haldeth burst out. The dance of non-colors hurt just to look at, made his eyes water and his stomach spasm. "Please," he added, as Orame returned a glare of naked irritation.

The enchanter made no move to banish his figure with its contained seethe of Alhaerie. "Mortals," he muttered in disgust. "Why do you all most obstinately fail to appreciate the fine things in life?"

Orame glanced keenly up, then down the mountainside. He stroked his chin as if his companion had ceased to exist. "Ash," he said thoughtfully after a time. "And rowan wood inlay." Then he frowned at his drifting pentagram and spoke a word.

The air near his feet seemed to explode. Light flashed, and a wash of shed heat made Haldeth blink. His vision cleared to reveal the presence of a finely polished table, carved and inset with rowan wood into patterns of exceptional beauty. Astonishment made the smith shout.

"Quiet." Orame scowled. "I'm busy with decisions." He tapped his foot briskly on rain-damp shale, as if he had furnished kingly trappings to the crags of the Doriads

every day of his life. Haldeth looked on with a mix of
amazement and worry, for the sting of gorse prickles in
unmentionable places had affirmed that despite his quak-
ing nerves, he was safe, and in Aerith; somewhere
nearby, Korendir's life was in consummate danger.

Orame paced sharply left and then right. "Ham, one
rye loaf, cherries and cream, and fresh goat's cheese."
He stopped, slapped his forehead with his palm and
added, "Ale, five years old, from the best Torresdyr
brewery."

The list was preposterously inopportune, but Haldeth
noted the last item with pity. In his traverse of Alhaerie
the wizard had assuredly lost his wits. The request for
five-year ale was the sheerest impossibility, since every
brewer in Torresdyr had suffered under blight for the
three quarters of a century prior to Korendir's victory
over Anthei.

Apparently this fact escaped both Orame and his spell
because the named victuals appeared, including a chilled
crock that foamed unmistakably with ale. The labels list-
ing vintage, brewer, and kingdom looked inarguably
genuine.

Haldeth looked for a rock to sit down, remembered
his thorns, and stayed standing.

"Napkins," continued Orame. Then, as if in afterthought, he tipped his head to one side and described a
final request. "Chairs with red velvet cushions and silver
braid, five in number, and let's have legs that match the
terrain, for I don't fancy getting overset onto wet
ground."

The furnishings appeared in brisk order; at last drained
of power by their creation, the pentagram drifted lifeless
as smoke upon the air. Orame waved away the fumes.
He perched on the nearer chair, and by some unseen
artifice of magic the legs conformed to compensate for
rocks, and the extreme pitch of the slope.

Haldeth stared with his mouth open.

"Sit down!" The wizard waved toward an empty cushion. "Eat." He glanced at the surrounding bleakness of
the hills and shrugged. "Or don't eat, but you won't have
a better chance, I'm thinking. It's past the season for
berries."

Haldeth's temper flared. "You choose a poor time for

foolishness. What about Korendir? While we dally over ham and cherries, there are wereleopards hunting him."

Orame grasped the rye loaf in long fingers and broke it into halves. "Forgot the butter," he noted peevishly, then focused eyes like chipped obsidian on Haldeth. His manner seemed outwardly unchanged, but through some indefinable subtlety, his presence acquired an air of command. "Sit down. At this moment your companion is in less danger than you are. If you don't trust my judgment on the matter, you'll pay for that folly with your life."

Inscrutable as a crow, Orame turned to his repast and started slicing cheese and ham; except there was a watching stillness about his pose. His eyes did not track the motions of his hands, but darted often to assess the surrounding hillside. Not quite brazen enough to disregard the warnings of a White Circle enchanter, even one who apparently acted upon fancy, Haldeth pulled up a chair.

He had no wish to ask after the magic which kept his seat stable on a footing of soggy lichen and shale; neither did he incline toward filling his belly with bread and cream concocted of wizardry. "Tell me, you're expecting guests," he said with a sour glance at the empty places which surrounded the table.

Orame lifted his knife, speared a morsel of ham, and chewed carefully. "I am expecting company. But not the invited sort."

The meat smelled delightful. Haldeth swallowed once, twice, and berated himself for a fool. The idea of eating struck him as absurd. Even if he could bring himself to trust in victuals summoned by spells, concern for Korendir took precedence. His frustration found expression through sarcasm. "By the spread, I'd guess you expected your mother-in-law, and maybe her aunts in the bargain."

"I'm not married," said Orame succinctly. "Most White Circle enchanters aren't, and for good reason." He sipped his ale, and the tiniest spark of amusement flashed in his eyes. "Appearances can deceive."

Haldeth studied the chairs more carefully. He had moved his own when he sat down, surely; and yet the spacing of the remaining three, along with Orame's, described a perfectly symmetrical pentagram. Insight dawned belatedly. "A ward figure? This?"

Orame made no reply. Instead he dropped his eating

knife and shoved with shattering speed to his feet. The silver landed with a clang on the ham platter, overlaid by the wizard's shout. At once his chairs fashioned of spells unravelled into snapping bars of light. Thrown down without ceremony onto stony soil, Haldeth had no chance to cry protest. The breath left his lungs with a painful whoosh, and for a moment his eyes saw darkness.

Orame started chanting again, from an indeterminate point nearby. The air split with a ripping sound, and Haldeth blinked. He still seemed enveloped in shadow; but emerging from the deeps of the murk was a form that rippled and flowed to a shape of impossible contours. Dimensional laws could neither encompass the thing, nor define it; but decidedly it lived, and attempted to enter Aerith with Neth knew what destructive bent in mind.

Haldeth knew fear. A clawed foot raked through the dark and crashed into the ham platter. The blow sent both meat and Orame's knife flying. The silver blade clipped a talon, which promptly burst into ill-smelling smoke. The monster attached to the nether end screeched. It rocked forward in pain and set weight upon the ash table; claws furrowed ruinously into baroque scrolls and rowan wood inlay.

Orame shouted again, unmistakably triumphant.

And the creature, with its bristles, hooks, and barbed, odiferous scales, turned a blinding and incandescent red. Haldeth covered his eyes, then wished he had extra hands to stop his ears as a yowl broke from the monster's throat, piercing enough to deafen the fish on the sea bottom.

Then Orame framed a word in bitten consonants that miraculously restored silence.

Haldeth dared a cautious look. A burnt smell lingered upon the air; the ham and knife lay tumbled on the ground, while various platters and an ale jug drifted incongruously at table height. Of the ash and rowan wood furnishing little remained but a charred and steaming tangle of sticks.

"Neth's mercy," muttered Haldeth.

Orame paused in the act of straightening disheveled robes. "Hardly that."

Haldeth remained blank until he focused and fully realized that absolutely nothing supported the ale jug, the cherry bowl, or the cheeses and cream.

The smith's stupefied exclamation prompted Orame to explain. "Every spell not derived from earth magic draws power from the alter-reality of Alhaerie. The separation of the void between opposites becomes weakened through such use, which is why wizards take exhaustive precautions. But a gate which allows passage from one reality to another does more: it actually mingles the separateness of Aerith and its counterpoint universe. Traces remain on both sides, if the breach is not promptly sealed. Sometimes creatures try to break through before the barrier has fully knitted. We are not in a wizard's tower where defenses are permanently laid down to compensate. Therefore I expected trouble, and prepared for it."

Unremittingly practical, Orame plucked up a goblet, caught the floating ale jug, and poured out a healthy draught. This he handed to the smith.

His earlier reservation forgotten, Haldeth drained the glass and licked the last drop from the rim; the label unquestionably had not lied, and the damp which soaked through his breeches and cloak no longer chilled with such viciousness. "Why the table and chairs?" He asked when he could be certain his voice would hold steady.

Orame raised his brows, as if the reason was obvious. "Beings from Alhaerie don't like silver, ash, or rowan."

"Well your style is certainly flamboyant." Haldeth hitched himself clear of a rock, caught a punitive prick from a thorn, and winced.

"Not at all." Orame grinned, plainly entertained by his companion's discomfort. Obligingly he poured more ale. "I knew something had followed us, and wished to flush it without giving reason for suspicion. Alhaerie's inhabitants can be quite ruthless. Sometimes the best defense is surprise."

"That strategy can cut both ways, enchanter." Haldeth downed his second helping of ale and fussily pushed to his feet.

Impervious to bitterness, and fastidious to the least detail, the enchanter collected the food platters. From the occasional flash and backwash of heat, Haldeth presumed Orame worked new spells, but he had lost any interest in watching. His head ached already from too

much magic, and his concern for Korendir intensified
with each passing minute.

"You're not burdening us with more ham and bread,
I hope."

"Hardly that." Orame's tone stung with reproof.
"You've a companion, I think, being harried by wereleopards?" And he extended to Haldeth a bundled length
of new rope.

The smith accepted the coils with a flush of embarrassment. Worry left him mannerless; brisk Orame may
have been with regard to his fearsome craft, but he had
helped a mortal without stinting. Haldeth struggled to
swallow his pride and apologize.

Orame forestalled him. "Time is short, master smith.
If your friend is to be saved, we must leave at once."

The wizard strode downslope, toward an outcrop that
speared like a sentinel through a hillock mantled with
gorse. As if privy to Haldeth's thoughts, he added,
"Your contrition is misplaced. I came for my own
motives."

Such sudden and stinging arrogance permitted no
space for reply; Haldeth did not try, but breathlessly hastened to follow. Daylight was beginning to fail. The wizard's charcoal-colored robes melted almost invisibly into
cloudy twilight and a sky that unkindly threatened drizzle. The wind had acquired a chillier edge as it rattled
through tough stands of gorse; but cheerless weather perhaps might help deter wereleopards. Haldeth strove to
wrest comfort from that hope as the last gleam dimmed
above the peaks, and darkness closed over terrain that
was treacherous with roots and loose rock.

Orame pressed on without misstep. Haldeth kept pace,
cursing as his ankles turned, and his elbows skinned into
jutting edges of shale. He thought wistfully of lanterns,
and almost slammed into Orame as the wizard suddenly
stopped.

"Your pardon!" exclaimed the enchanter. "My kind
see well in the dark." He made a pass with his hand and
a cold light flared above his palm.

The illumination burned with an energy that stabbed
the eyes; the ground underfoot became rendered in
patches of fiery brilliance and shadows deep as pits. As
the wizard started forward once more, Haldeth found

himself stepping over objects not worth the bother, and tripping on things that seemed to spring out of glare and snag his ankles like malice given life.

His curses grew more heated.

Orame paid no mind, but paused finally before an aperture that yawned between the rocks. "Here."

Blinking to see through the dazzle, Haldeth said, "Where?"

Abruptly the smith wished his question unspoken. A yowl to freeze the blood erupted from the earth below his feet. A slither of leather on stone tangled with a din of reverberations, and finally made aware that his light was unsuited for clarity, Orame dimmed the brightness by half.

Granted an untrammeled view, Haldeth discovered he stood on the lip of a drop overlooking a shaft that led to a subterranean cave. There was movement within, something that may have been a bronze spill of hair.

"Korendir!" shouted Haldeth. He unlimbered the rope and frantically shook out coils.

A hand glimmered deep in the darkness, and magewrought light suddenly caught on an uplifted, bearded face. "Haldeth?" The voice was hoarse with stress, and also a tentative, incredulous hope. "Neth, you crazed smith, is that you?"

A second yowl obscured the smith's call of encouragement, identifiably the hunting cry of the wereleopard; already fey killers closed to corner their prey. All too aware of his peril, Korendir heaved himself bodily up the shaft. He was hampered by injured knuckles and a sliding fall of loose rock. Haldeth whipped the end of the rope into a loop and fumbled with knots, furious with himself; why had he had not thought to prepare himself for trouble sooner? Orame's unbroken competence had put him off guard, and now he rued the lapse. The time required to secure the safety rope cost dearly.

"You have only seconds to effect your rescue," Orame said dispassionately from a point not far behind.

"Try offering help instead of pointing out the obvious." Haldeth jerked tight his last knot and cast the line.

Rope snaked downward into the shaft. A coil caught on an outcrop, and the smith was forced to waste precious seconds flipping and shaking the line in an effort to free the snag. He cursed and sweated and banged the heel of his hand on sharpened shale. The rope slipped clear, and the loop knotted into the end flicked straight and dangled, an arm-span above Korendir's head.

The starved yowl of a wereleopard echoed up the shaft, close enough to harrow a man's courage. The cry was joined by others, bloodthirsty and eager, the celebration of a pack on the hunt.

"It's after dark." Orame observed with nerveless steadiness. "The creatures will be in man-form, and well capable of climbing."

Haldeth did not bother to reply. "Korendir!" he shouted, desperate to be heard over the snarls of closing predators. "Look up, man!"

Korendir clawed for a higher hand-hold, but did not tip his head. The rope spun slowly, unnoticed. Haldeth repeated himself and flapped the line to attract attention. The loop swung and tapped the rocks on either side of the shaft. Pebbles bounced down like sparks in the wizard-light.

Still Korendir did not respond.

"Rouse him," cried the smith to the enchanter. "We're too close to lose him now!"

Orame declined answer. Haldeth glanced furiously aside and spotted the wizard perched unconcerned on a boulder. The smith drew breath to utter something heated, but a sudden, sharp tug on the rope killed his epithet unspoken.

At long last Korendir had caught the line.

Haldeth swung hastily back. He stared down the shaft to find new blood glistening on the wrist that grasped the rope, and by that came to realize: his friend was hard-pressed by an attack from the caverns beneath.

"Hang on!" screamed the smith.

He heaved on the line without waiting for Korendir to hook the loop over his shoulders. As his friend kicked off from the rocks, fangs gleamed where his feet had been. Sharp over the echoes of the pack's cries, Haldeth heard the clear clash of jaws.

A shiver swept his skin. Fear lent him strength as, hand over hand for the second time in life, he raised his friend toward safety. His palms sweated against a line already damp. The rope itself did not help. Spell-woven cordage was slick, and the plies slipped at the slightest provocation. Haldeth tightened his grip.

The rope jerked suddenly.

Hard won footage burned through Haldeth's palms; he gritted his teeth, cried aloud from the sting of abraded skin. "Hold still, man, for love of life."

But in the shaft below, his safety precariously secured by a fist wet with gore, Korendir fought frantically for survival. More agile than a man, the wereleopards scratched and scrabbled holds in near vertical stone. They snapped at his suspended ankles, and droplets of venom flew like jewels against the dark. Korendir shoved a jutting ledge with his toe and set the rope spinning to thwart the jaws that clashed at his heels. He swung his sword with his sound hand and managed to harry a beast off its niche. It plunged into darkness with howl that set its companions into frenzy. The one in the lead launched upward. Talon-like hands swiped air and caught Korendir in the calf. Claws sank deep into flesh.

Haldeth's yell tangled with Korendir's scream of agony.

Jerked to the brink of disaster by doubled weight on the rope, the smith braced mightily and held, though his hands quivered and his palms felt flayed by fire.

Korendir kicked out, smashed the wereleopard in the face with his unencumbered boot before it could sink teeth and poison him. It spat through broken fangs. Korendir kicked again, and the creature ripped free and fell twisting into darkness.

Haldeth's burden immediately lightened. He hauled, straining, gasping, his vision swimming with the effort. Coils piled at his feet. An eternity seemed to pass, all wrought of crippling pain and overtaxed muscles. Then a bloodied hand emerged from the hole. Fingers groped and caught at the rock by the smith's braced ankles. An equally crimsoned sword blade followed.

"Drop that cursed weapon," Haldeth gasped.

Korendir was beyond hearing, long past rational thought. He continued to react on reflex. Poised by one arm on the lip of the shaft, he twisted round to battle the enemies who yet clambered upward to kill.

As the drag of the rope slacked off, the smith dropped his hold. He bent at once, dodged Korendir's reflexive sword swing, and seized a wrist that felt thin as a stick. Haldeth jerked his companion bodily upward, and out into rain-dark night. Wereleopards swarmed up the shaft after their prey, eyes glinting green by wizard-light.

"Toss the rope into the shaft," said Orame succinctly. Unnoticed, he had moved to Haldeth's shoulder.

The smith released Korendir in an unceremonious heap, then kicked the loose coils over the brink.

Line unreeled downward with a hiss that had little to do with disturbed air. Before Haldeth's eyes, the hemp vibrated with light, then reverted with a shriek and a blinding flash into the sorcery that originally created it.

The wereleopards were incinerated in an eyeblink. Not even fumes remained to mark their passing.

Orame tilted his head to one side over the suddenly deserted shaft. As if in afterthought, he stepped to the boulder where, earlier, he had chosen to sit. Calmly he set elegant hands against its rain-streaked shale. The stone groaned, shifted, then rocked with an energy that defied the still earth and every law of inertia. Orame spoke in a coaxing tone, as if he entreated a beloved hound to fetch something unpleasant. The rock hesitated like a live thing. Then it trembled and tumbled awkwardly on its side, to lodge with a great, hollow boom directly in the mouth of the shaft.

No wereleopards would emerge from that cave forever after.

Orame dusted his hands. Satisfaction softened his countenance as he joined Haldeth, who already knelt in concern over the ragged survivor delivered safe from the caverns of the Ellgol.

XII. The Grief of South Englas

The blood proved to be as much the wereleopards' as Korendir's; beyond his mauled leg, a shallow slash on one shoulder, and some scabs on his left wrist, the mercenary from White Rock Head was remarkably unharmed after his trials in the caves. Haldeth tightened the knots on the last make-shift bandage and sat back on his heels with a sigh of intense relief. Attenuation from scanty rations and exhaustion would mend swiftly, given rest and food; clean-dressed wounds would heal.

Permitted finally to move, Korendir's first act was to recover his sword. The blade was sticky red, and dulled from too much use without sharpening. "You wouldn't by any chance have oil and whet stone about?" he asked of his companion.

Haldeth returned a curse. "Thank Neth, I don't." He shook his head, wondering upon the haggard features of the man before him. Korendir's eye sockets were bruised from lack of sleep; his hands shook, despite every effort to conceal weakness. Unable to imagine the months and the terrors he had survived under the mountains, the smith shifted his glance to include the sword. There were chips missing from the cutting edge, visible even through congealing layers of gore. "That steel's not worth sweating over. Give it up. I'll forge you better when we return to my smithy at Whitestorm."

Korendir gave back a blank glance, then settled with wiping the weapon on the tattered and already fouled hem of his tunic. After that he turned eyes large as coins in his gaunt face, and measured the shadowed figure at Haldeth's shoulder.

Starved Korendir might be, and hurting, but his reaction stunned thought. In an instant he was on his feet, wary, poised, but prepared to be courteous in his stiff-mannered way. "You're White Circle?"

Orame inclined his head. Then, before Korendir could phrase even rudimentary thanks, the enchanter laced slim hands at his belt. His gaze raked the mercenary from bronze hair to torn boots, then flicked in expectation to Haldeth. "My payment, master smith," he prompted sternly.

Haldeth pushed apprehensively to his feet. He had no stomach for crossing Korendir while sitting on his backside in shale; even worse, the gorse still lodged in his britches added irritation to what now seemed a regrettably bad bargain.

The smith closed his ham hands into fists, faced his companion, and spoke in a rush before his courage failed. "For your rescue I was forced to make a promise. You must tell me the name of your parents." Next he flinched in expectation of swift and merciless retribution.

Anger tightened every joint in Korendir's body. He gripped his naked blade, unmistakably poised for attack. Then without warning he checked and shifted focus to the wizard who waited stone-still in the darkness and the rain.

Gray eyes met black through a charged moment of challenge.

Finally a muscle jumped in Korendir's jaw. "For Haldeth's honor only," he allowed. His tone was edged as beaten metal, and directed solely at the White Circle enchanter.

"I am illegitimate." The sword blade remained, a line of deadly stillness in the air. "The Widow of Shan Rannok may have been my mother. She fostered me. When I reached my twentieth year, I was to be informed of my parentage, but that secret died untold." Korendir paused, then forced the last words past his teeth. "The Lady of Shan Rannok and all of her following were slaughtered without reprieve by Mhurgai raiders."

Silence fell, filled by a soft sigh of wind. Without regard for the poised blade, Orame tipped his head to one side and nodded to himself. "Did the lady herself say you were born out of wedlock?"

Korendir moved not at all, but the tic in his cheek went still. He matched the wizard's expectancy with icy restraint. "That is not for your hearing, enchanter. My debt to you, and Haldeth's, is discharged as of this moment. If you think otherwise, then kill me where I stand."

Orame smiled and quietly demurred. "The debt is cleared. If you find any comfort in truth, the gossips at Shan Rannok lied cruelly. The widow was not your natural mother. She stayed faithful to her dead lord, always. The secret of your origins in all probability died before she ever took you in."

But if the wizard had perceived and answered some deeply hidden longing, his words drew no reaction. Korendir heard this news without gratitude. If Orame hoped to prompt an appeal for additional information, the mercenary's lips remained sealed, and his sword stayed implacably raised.

With what seemed dry amusement, the wizard turned toward a taut and unnerved Haldeth. "I take my leave of you both. The gold you left at my tower shall be returned to Whitestorm keep. The draft horse, I believe, chewed through its tether and wandered back to the roadway. It has already been recovered by the livery stable."

"And the cart?" asked Haldeth.

Orame's eyebrows rose in evident mirth. "That, dear man, had been designated for the junk merchant a fortnight before you chose to rent it."

The wizard stepped back then. His charcoal gray robes vanished abruptly into the darkness, and if any discernible disturbance marked his departure, the event became obscured by Haldeth's invective against the ostler at Heddenton who had taken good silver with all the honor of a thief.

When the smith at last ran out of breath, he found himself alone. Korendir had taken his sword and gone off to search for wood to kindle a fire. The rain was perversely falling harder, and with a pang of regret, Haldeth recalled the ham and the cheeses on Orame's table that he had indignantly refused to sample. The nearest settlement of shepherds was leagues away, and his belly felt empty as a drum.

The evening progressed in miserable silence. Korendir sat wrapped in his cloak, light eyes fixed on the flames.

Except to mention that the farmers of Mel's Bye had left him a stock of supplies, he chose not to speak of his ordeal in the caves of the Ellgol. Raindrops seeped from his hair and dripped off the beard that had grown unchecked through his months of privation. The mercenary may have been brooding; possibly he speculated upon innuendos raised by the final words of Orame; but when Haldeth accidentally brushed Korendir's flank while adding wood to the fire, the glare flung back at him warned otherwise. The Master of Whitestorm viewed the bargain which surrounded his rescue with cold, inexpressible fury. Aware of a pressure beneath his quiet that burned and seethed like trapped lava, Haldeth strove to deflect the bent of his companion's thoughts.

"When we get back, and the keep is built, you can give up adventuring and settle down. Orame of the White Circle told me, without question. His kind never sell their services for gold."

Korendir's gaze stayed fixed. "Then gold must be raised to buy whatever it is that White Circle enchanters desire."

"Neth, I swear, you were fathered by a mule!" Haldeth flung a billet on the fire with excessive force. Embers scattered; sparks whirled skyward and momentarily lit the rain like some grisly fall of blood. "A stone responds to reason more readily than you do. Will you never let be and stop?"

Korendir redirected the exclamation with a pointed question of his own. "How goes the construction at Whitestorm? Are the walls shoulder high yet?"

Haldeth answered only when he ran out of expletives. As cold drizzle fell and fell, and light from the campfire traced the tired, too gaunt profile of a man who had fought off wereleopards through three solitary months of confinement, the smith described the state of Whitestorm's fortifications. He added exhaustive detail, and listed everything from the game paths in Thornforest, to the fish in the tide pools beneath the cliffs. All the while, he could not help but despair inside.

"Your quest is a hopeless waste of life," he announced in a shattering change of subject. "Don't expect me to go with you, or save you again, when you rush headlong into risk."

"No," said Korendir with a simplicity that implied far too much.

Haldeth stared at the coals and cursed the smoke for making his eyes water. The rescue from the jaws of the wereleopards had most assuredly been futile. In time, some unfortunate wretch would send an appeal to Whitestorm, pleading help in behalf of his countrymen, and offering gold in return. Somewhere, anywhere in the Eleven Kingdoms, trouble and woe would be stirring. . . .

The guardsman who brought word of the tragedy had to be half-carried into the king's audience chamber, so weakened was he from loss of blood. His surcoat had been rent by a scimitar, and dust-caked stains all but obliterated the device.

"Your Royal Grace," he managed, swaying on his feet despite the support of two sturdy squires. "The princess's caravan has been overtaken by Datha raiders. All in her service were slain in her defense. Myself, Neth's Accursed left for dead. Sire, I searched, but no trace could I find of Her Grace, Iloreth, nor any of her tiring women and maids."

The queen's anguished wail fell upon a court stunned to stillness. Shocked courtiers were soon disturbed by the hurry of the royal healer, who shoved past the gaping chamber steward with his smock in disarray. An old man skilled in his trade, he sketched obeisance before the throne, looked once at the guardsman's gray features, then rounded without ceremony on the king.

"Your Grace, this man is dying. Have I your leave?"

The king ignored the healer's impertinence and somehow managed a nod. He watched in stony-eyed shock as the guardsman was led away, stumbling over a gold and purple carpet now marred with bloodstains and dust. The first seneschal of the realm spoke urgently to the queen's ladies. They moved like ghosts in response, and veiled her weeping face behind silk. On the highest level of the dais, the king roused himself. He gripped his throne with shaking hands and spoke.

"My daughter Iloreth is dead." The pronouncement was met without a rustle from the courtiers seated in the galleries on either side. "If there is life in her body, pray

Neth extinguishes it, for the Dathei are an honorless race. Let South Englas mourn for the princess's soul. When the candles burned in her memory are spent, let no man speak her name in my presence."

Bells tolled in South Englas by royal decree, shivering the air over the desert sands. The king's loyal donned the black of mourning, and every priest in the land burned offerings for the merciful deliverance of Iloreth. Yet the sole and beloved offspring of the sovereign of South Englas was not dead.

The princess had twice tried to take her own life. As the victory screams of the Datha horseman had quavered over her fallen escort, the dagger she turned on her wrists cut well and deeply; but death had not come swiftly enough. Her captors had staunched her bleeding, their cruel, peaked brows shadowing their eyes as they worked. Words in their guttural tongue flew thick and fast between them. They pulled her from the scented dimness of her litter into merciless sunlight. Harsh hands pinioned her limbs, held her helpless before laughter and jeers while other, uglier hands prodded at her young flesh.

Scarlet with shame, Iloreth tore one hand free and seized the curved knife from the belt of her nearest captor. This time she tried for her heart.

The weapon was snatched from her grasp. A ringed fist slammed across her face and opened her cheek to the bone. One of her maids screamed as she sagged upon the sand. Yet the blow in the end proved merciful.

The princess who had never in life known mistreatment swooned into deep unconsciousness. She did not suffer when the thumbs were severed from her hands; she felt nothing of the callused fingers that pried her jaws open, or the knife that hacked the tongue from her mouth. The shock of such mutilation claimed the lives of two of her women. They were the fortunate ones.

Iloreth woke to the tickle of flies around her lips. Pain ran in waves up her arms and over her face; her subsequent attempt to move revealed an agony of cramped muscles. She opened caked eyes and received a whirling, blurred impression of sweat-sheened hide and jewelled leather. She had been lashed like baggage to the saddle of a Datha horseman. The rider was currently dismounted. He and his beast drank from a desert spring in great, sucking gulps; the sounds drew the princess's notice to the dried and swollen state of her own mouth. That moment Iloreth encountered the horror that remained of her tongue. The discovery made her retch.

The rider heard. He spat water into the sand and turned to find his captive restored to consciousness.

"Yhai," he exclaimed. Thin, mustachioed lips parted over white teeth. Sunlight gleamed on his muscled back as he bent and dipped his leather cup in the spring. He jingled as he moved. Brass ornaments sewn to his riding leathers scattered reflections of desert sky; slung from his studded belt, he carried six knives, a scimitar, and a sharpened set of quoits.

Iloreth retched again as his smell filled her nostrils, rancid and sour from the fat smeared on his skin as protection from the desert's drying wind. The Datha closed his knuckles like a vise in her hair. He yanked back her head, then poured a warm stream of water into her mouth.

Iloreth choked, forced to swallow or drown. Nausea racked her and emptied her stomach the instant her captor released her. His laughter stung her ears. Weak, dizzy, and barely aware, she lay limp, head down over the horse's sweated side. Her captor hooked the cup to his belt, then spun on his heel and remounted. He spurred his horse to a canter, and tormented once more beyond consciousness by the jolting lurch of the ride, Iloreth missed the raiders' entry through the gateways of Telssina.

Datha metal workers held no equals in their craft, and the city that housed their sultan possessed enchanting beauty. The wrought grilles of window and balcony gleamed like gold lace in sunlight, and colonnaded porticos stood patterned with delicate enamelwork. Telssina was the image of paradise of earth, but to the thousands of thumbless slaves who labored to keep its opulence unspoiled by tarnish and the erosive depradations of desert sand, this splendor was accursed by Neth.

Iloreth learned early to hate what lay beneath Telssina's graceful trappings. Delivered into the hands of the Master of Tribute, she and her surviving maids were pushed, prodded, or dragged into a pastel room with fountains. There they were stripped and examined like beef, the pretty ones selected for the sultan, and those too plain for his taste culled off for return to the raiders for personal pleasure or sale, at their whim.

The Master of Tribute turned Iloreth's chin one way and then the other in his fat and sweating hands. He smelled of citrine; the eyes deep-set into creased flesh missed nothing. Such lustrous hair and brown eyes betrayed promise, even through the dust and stains of capture. A nasal order set Iloreth aside with those retained. She was given care by a perfumed healer who packed her face and wrists with poultices and forced possets down her throat to make her sleep. Her cheek healed badly despite his efforts. The failure cost him a whipping. Cursed with a long, puckered scar that twisted her lip and pulled her left eyelid downward at a grotesque angle, the princess was reduced in rank yet again. Her deformities were too offensive to ornament the sultan's couch, but her body was deemed pleasing enough for a palace maid. Veiled in a servant's gauze, the once-cosseted princess learned to scrub floors and empty chamber pots; only then did she fully appreciate the inventive cruelty of her masters.

Thumbless hands could not manipulate door latches. They could not effectively handle a weapon or resist a beating. Slaves lived at the mercy of the titled lords or royal favorites who resided within the palace, for labor or for pleasure. Though Iloreth's scarred features spared her the attentions of most men, others whose tastes ran to vice were attracted to her. Life became an endless torment. Aching for the solace of death, Iloreth grew to detest the clever scrollwork that decorated the chamber pots, rendering it possible for the eight-fingered to dispose of their contents without mishap.

Two years from the date inscribed in the memorial chapel, the King of South Englas received word of his daughter. It came in the form of a ragged square of silk carried by a camel trader who sometimes did business at the oases. The fabric bore tortuously written lines that spoke of mutilation and mistreatment, some of which went beyond even the worst rumor out of Datha. Familiar names appeared, heartbreakingly set about with circumstances: Neshiane, assigned to the Sultan's heir as a breeding woman. She had delivered a stillborn child, and for a week she had screamed under torture in a sacrificial ritual intended to restore the prince to favor with the fertility deity she had offended. The words described Daide, who had birthed a healthy son, but one with blue eyes; an ancient Datha prophecy warned that a light-eyed man would bring about the fall of the current dynasty. Daide's baby had been hung from a pole in the square until vultures fed on its entrails.

Iloreth ended with a plea to her father that an army be raised against Datha. She signed with her name, and included a description of her childhood nurse to prove her missive was no forgery.

The camel trader shifted his weight on slippered feet. Ill at ease with the formality of the audience chamber, and unprepared for the royal tears, he masked impatience behind obsequious courtesy. He had risked much to deliver the princess's message. All he desired was compensation and leave to depart.

When the king twisted a ruby from his finger and pressed its massive weight into the camel trader's palm, the man flushed scarlet. He had been bestowed the wealth of a lord. He cared not a whit for the princess he had served, but conscience momentarily lent him principle.

"Your Royal Grace," he said, and bent his ample middle into a bow. "I have heard of a man, a mercenary, who might assist you against the Dathei. His name is Korendir of Whitestorm. He holds a reputation for undertaking the impossible. Word goes that he charges dearly for his sword, but he has never failed to deliver his contracts. The sailors out of Fairhaven speak his praises. If you ask, I'm sure they'd tell you more."

The king did not answer. His eyes seemed locked by invisible force upon the appeal penned by his daughter. The camel trader was ushered out by a courtier, the ruby clenched in his fist. His part was done. What followed concerned him not at all.

The King of South Englas neither ate nor slept for three days. He did not laugh at the revels, but sat like a painted icon in his hall of state, uncaring whether judgment was passed over the subjects who appeared with grievances. The queen hovered anxiously at his elbow, ignorant of the white square of silk that had lately been smuggled from Telssina. On the fourth morning, the king summoned his scribe. In the privacy of a locked chamber, he dictated a document which offered gold and command of the royal guard of South Englas for the purpose of war against Datha. Affixed to the parchment with wire was the scarf sent by Iloreth; set in a flourish above the seals, the inscription begged the attention of Korendir, Master of Whitestorm.

"Send this with the next captain bound for Fairhaven," the king instructed. Then he waited, galled by the knowledge that his cherished only daughter washed chamber pots in Telssina, pleasuring by night any barbarian who might fancy her.

In springtime, three years after the stone was laid for the foundations, the fortress on the cliffs of White Rock Head reached completion. High on the topmost battlement, Haldeth leaned on a flagstaff that flew no standard. Beneath him, the slate roof of the keep which housed the library reflected back the heat of morning sunlight; farther down breakers flashed in unending rows against the headland, and beyond the line of the horizon lay the mast of a trader most likely northbound for Heddenton.

But the ship was all that moved in the circle of Haldeth's view. Fortifications designed for warfare and siege, and the bustling strife of life, instead wore an incongruous mantle of tranquillity. Not a single man at arms sparred in the armory yard; no sentries patrolled the gatehouse. Sunlight fell untrammeled through the lancet windows of a hall unsoftened by tapestries or furnishings, and empty of servants and hunting dogs. Dust ruled in place of a chatelaine, and guests did not visit to feast. The master of the hold was in Heddenton bargaining for honey and broadcloth. Since his stint against wereleopards, Korendir had stayed on at Whitestorm and overseen completion of his holdfast.

Haldeth basked in the comfort of spring, and prayed to Neth the peace would last.

Twice messengers had come to offer contracts for Korendir's services. Both had been sent packing without so much as a meal offered in hospitality.

"Wars," Korendir had reiterated to an inquiring Haldeth, after the second of the two couriers was launched aboard the longboat which had delivered him. "The King of Faen Hallir is haggling over his borders. Again. Just men fighting their neighbors with repeated and senseless ferocity. The Mhurgai raid the coastlines upon principles very little different."

"Hardly that," Haldeth corrected. "Faen Hallir's enemies are invariably the aggressors."

To which Korendir had shrugged, closing a subject Haldeth was content to let die. If the Master of Whitestorm accepted no other contract, if the keep on White Rock Head never hired a single man at arms, the smith would pick no quarrel; women, maybe, and a servant or two for the hall, that was a subject altogether different.

But instinct warned Haldeth against broaching that matter. Korendir's temperamental nature had not mellowed at all.

The steady blaze of sunlight in time made Haldeth drowsy. He turned his shoulder comfortably against heated stone, settled into a cranny, and closed his eyes to nap.

The shrilling of a signal arrow split the sky above the wall. Haldeth started from sleep as the missile wailed overhead and plunged with a crack into the bailey. He bounded erect and looked out. The trader ship noticed earlier proved not to be destined for Heddenton; instead, she lay anchored beneath Whitestorm, the flag of a courier streaming at her masthead.

Recovered enough to swear, Haldeth rubbed sleep from his eyes. A longboat cleaved toward the headland, an emissary bearing a parley flag lodged like a vulture in her stern. Glad of his master's absence, the smith kicked open the postern to the stair. After sunlight, the sudden plunge into shadow raised chills on his cloakless back.

Yet by the time Haldeth passed the gamut of Whitestorm's defenses and arrived upon the strand, the boat with its blackrobed emissary was already being rowed back to the ship. Haldeth expelled a deep breath. The shore party was already beyond hailing distance; if the message had been urgent, the emissary would surely have lingered on the beach head. Grateful for his solitude, and panting from his run down tiresome flights of stairs, Haldeth set his back against the sea-damp cliffs and muttered a prayer devoid of blasphemies. Not until he turned to go did he notice the item left wedged in a cleft beside the entry to Whitestorm keep.

The emissary had delivered his message after all. It took the form of a folded square of parchment, crusted with ribbons and seals. Fastened to one edge with a twist of wire was a length of silk, jagged across with script in a hand that sprawled like a child's.

Haldeth lifted the missive from its niche, his heart touched numb with foreboding. The seals proved to be royal, the desert hare blazon of his Grace, the King of South Englas incised into rare purple wax. Border disputes would not be the issue this time. Pinching the missive like carrion between thumb and forefinger, Haldeth ascended to the upper keep. He could not bring himself to examine the silk, or read its piteous message. Whatever plea it harbored was no affair of his; he left both envelope and cloth on the desk in Korendir's library, then bolted the brass panelled door as if securing an enemy inside.

The message remained undisturbed for a fortnight, until Korendir returned from Heddenton and chanced to require a book. When he found the door to his library inexplicably barred and fastened, he stopped cold still in his tracks.

His shout raised echoes all they way down to the bailey. "Haldeth!"

No voice answered.

Quite without warning the smith had departed to go hunting; Korendir discovered as much in the course of a swift investigation. The horn bow reserved for game was gone from the hook in the armory. The fact that the smith's boots remained on the hearth rug, and his cloak still hung on its peg, spoke less of scant stock in the larder than of desperate, stop-gap escape. Korendir raked back bronze hair. His eyes were chips of ice as he retraced his way to the library and irritably unfastened latches.

The door swung soundlessly open. Fading daylight from the window cast a sheen on ribbons and royal seals; not the scarlet of Faen Hallir this time, but the purple

and gold of South Englas. The ruler of that land was a
king famed for timidness, a fact resoundingly exploited
by the rapacious Datha Sultan adjacent to his eastern
border. Korendir crossed swiftly to the desk. With none
of Haldeth's hesitation, he ripped open the seals and read
lines which promised riches in exchange for mercenary
service. The lure of the gold alone invited consideration
and might have bought acceptance on its own merit; but
the piteous tale scratched in blood upon silk was the
reason the Master of Whitestorm departed at a run for
his sword.

He all but collided with Haldeth beneath the arch by
the seaward postern. Though the quiver at the smith's
back was empty, the gamebag at his hip dangled suspiciously flat.

"Kindle a signal fire on the east tower," Korendir said
briskly. "I'm going to require a ship."

The smith regarded Whitestorm's master, clad as always in black, from plain cloak and tunic, to the soles
of boots well worn from nights spent walking the cliff
tops. The only concession to color was the band of wereleopard hide stitched to the cuffs, unchanged since Korendir's service in Northengard. The scabbard and baldric
were the same he had carried into the caves of Ellgol,
and the sword, sharpened over old chips, had not been
replaced. Haldeth had always found an excuse rather
than re-forge that blade; now, his stubborn adherence to
a former oath made him sorry. Fool he had been to think
Korendir might settle for a quiet life at Whitestorm. The
man's reasons for refusing the two contracts from Faen
Hallir had never arisen from any reluctance to face risk.

"Let me at least repair your weapon before you go,"
the smith pleaded. "One day more cannot matter when
that letter sat for two weeks."

"Two weeks!" Korendir curbed a wild blaze of anger.
"Did you read that square of silk?"

Haldeth shrank miserably against the arch. "No. I told
you once. The adventures you undertake are your own
affair. No more help will you get from me."

"Meddle again, and I'll kill you." Korendir ducked
aside and strode on through the gate.

"Damn your arrogance!" Haldeth flung after him.

"After this, I'll think twice before I trouble to climb stairs and light any hell-begotten signal fire!"

The echo of Korendir's receding steps was all the answer he received.

Haldeth slammed his fist into stone. "Get yourself killed, then," he shouted into the empty night. "I'll worry less, for one thing, and a woman or two in this rock pile would make winters a sight more bearable."

Grumbling over bruised fingers, the smith stumped off to gather firewood. If Korendir chose to wait in the open until the next ship happened by to answer summons from Whitestorm, only a fool would try to dissuade him. The master was rotten company most any time, with his queer distaste for talk; when he wished, he could be vicious as the deadwood in Thornforest. As Haldeth lugged logs in a sling on his back up the spiraling stair to the upper battlement, he wished upon his companion a case of boils in places a maiden would blush to contemplate.

XIII. City of the Sultan

Ye crowned prince of Rachad's seed
   beware the Light-Eyed Man,
He of foreign birth and breed
   thy bane lies at his hand.
Datha's Scourge, the Light-Eyed's deed
   before which none shall stand.

Seven months passed, unrelieved by seasons. The sun shone hot over southern lands, and reflections like chipped diamonds flashed off the breakers which rolled from the Tammernon Sea; carried on winds from higher latitudes, ships made port from Fairhaven. The sovereign of South Englas had acquired the habit of gazing out his casements toward the harbor. Alert for the clutter of servants and heraldry that accompanied mercenary captains, the king was unprepared when at last the man he had summoned arrived on South Englian shores.

Confronted in his chamber of audience by a black-clad northerner with a grim face and impeccable manners, he bade the visitor rise. He found his person touched by an unfathomable gray gaze.

When the stranger spoke, his words were devoid of boastfulness. "I am Korendir of Whitestorm, Your Royal Grace. I've come to engage the Dathei, and to bring your daughter home."

Touched by deep disappointment, the King of South Englas regarded the mercenary before his dais. The sailors had neglected to mention that the man possessed rare coloring; in South Englas folk were seldom born with light eyes; and never with hair the rich, red-brown of spring honey. Aware that his silence had lasted discourteously long, the king cleared his throat. Decency demanded a response.

"I will pay your expenses." The king toyed regretfully with his signet ring, then sighed in outright unhappiness. He looked again at the man who waited, too still, before his throne. "For honor's sake, I dare not bind you to contract. Datha prophecy holds that a light-eyed man will destroy the sultan's dynasty. Sight of your face would seal your death in that land. My realm has endured grief enough from such enemies without adding murder to the score."

Korendir of Whitestorm laughed, but without any resonance of humor. His hand rested quietly on his battered scabbard, empty, since the sentries in the hallway disallowed weapons in the presence of royalty. But even swordless, his presence felt dangerous, and the scars which traced the backs of his knuckles marked him out for a killer. "Compensation for my troubles shall not be necessary, Your Grace. If the Scourge of the Dathei is to be a man with gray eyes, that's my advantage, not my bane."

As leary of conflict as his door guards, the King of South Englas yielded with gratitude. The sailors from Fairhaven had spoken high praise for the Master of Whitestorm's talents. If half what they claimed was true, the Datha prophecy might have been made against this same mercenary's arrival. Prepared for demands of troops and immediate quantities of weapons, the king was startled enough to question when Korendir asked instead after the camel trader who had delivered Iloreth's message from Telssina.

The bronze-haired swordsman inclined his head with chilly courtesy. "Your Grace, when men at arms are needed, I'll ask for them. Until then, I work alone." Korendir bowed and stepped back. From the seneschal's hand he accepted the camel trader's address. Then, without pause for refreshment, rest, or ceremony, he left the palace.

Since the sale of the king's finest ruby, Elshaid the camel trader disdained to deal in livestock. He inhabited a mansion on a quiet street and lived in indolence, attended by slave girls garnered through dealings with black market smugglers from Arhaga. The illicit possession of flesh made Elshaid leary of visitors. He paid an ex-assassin to guard his premises; another, all muscle and loyalty, both answered and safeguarded his door. The services of these brutes cost dearly. The former trader was therefore irate when a black-clad, sword-bearing northerner arrived unannounced in his bath chamber.

"I'm here to demand your service on the king's behalf," the intruder snapped out in clipped accents. He had bronze hair, light eyes, and an air charged as a stormfront with the promise of trouble.

Immersed like a walrus in hot water, suds, and rare oils, Elshaid roared a blasphemy. He heaved himself erect, and the slave girls who tenderly sponged his neck became drenched by the sloshed contents of his tub. Though their silken garments became plastered to their nubile skins, the man in the doorway remained cold-bloodedly undistracted.

Elshaid concluded that northerners must love boys before he barked a command to his women. They shed perfumed towels and sponges and fled through a carved screen behind the bath. The erstwhile camel trader glared at the stranger and coughed soap from his mustache. "Get out."

"Not yet." The swordsman set his hip against the nearest panelled wall, braced up one foot, and regarded his length of bared steel. The edge was sharpened razor thin, and well nicked with use.

The bath water abruptly seemed cold. Defenseless and nakedly fat, Elshaid cupped both hands at his crotch. "How did you get past my servants?"

The stranger smiled in a manner that chilled. "The guard and that ox at the door? They dream the visions of the faithful, unconscious. Both will recover with headaches."

Elshaid understood when he was disadvantaged; experience at swindling Datha horsemen had taught him not to buckle to threats. "Who are you? What do you want of me?"

"I'm called the Master of Whitestorm." The swordsman did not look up from his weapon. "And I need to know how you got a certain square of silk from Her Grace, the Princess of South Englas.

"Oh, that." Elshaid restrained an impulse to smile with relief that his slave girls were not at issue after all.

But the northerner was quick; he saw the glance his victim darted toward the screen. Before the merchant could reply, he added, "The welfare of your comforts depends on how carefully you tell the truth."

Now Elshaid's smile turned fatuous. He considered himself wronged; in good faith he had recommended this mercenary to his king, only to have the man burst uninvited into the most private sanctum of his home. Elshaid phrased his answer in vindication, certain the Lord from Whitestorm could gain nothing of value from the information. "I received Her Grace's message from one of the sultan's porters. He was a slave loaned to Del Morga to convey gifts of state to the port."

Korendir absorbed this without setback. "Then I'll need you to assemble a caravan to admit me to the sultan's city of Telssina."

Elshaid shot splashing to his feet, his shrivelled manhood forgotten. "Impossible!"

Korendir measured the camel trader from head to dripping privates. His hand tightened ominously on his steel. "Don't claim you have no experience with contraband," he cautioned. "Unless your slave girls are gifted at swordplay, your survival is a forgone conclusion."

Scarlet with indignation, Elshaid bent over. He groped a fallen towel from the floor beneath the screen and sullenly began rubbing off soapsuds. "The sultan's defenses include a double ring of walls!" He twined the towel around his girth, plainly unhappy about the force required to make the two ends meet. "And I'm no conjurer, to arrange for a spell of concealment. Telssina's guards never slack duty. They take pleasure in flaying the skin off anyone in the company of a man with frog-spawn eyes like yours."

"Then that's a problem you'll have to solve quickly," the northern mercenary said. The last of his tolerance vanished. "Get dressed!" He snapped his blade aside, and with a move most enviably fast, hooked and tossed back a silk robe which lay heaped on a nearby chest. "Ready or not, we leave for Telssina by noon."

Five days later a packtrain carrying scented oils, brocades, marten furs, and rare wines approached Telssina

from the northeast. It had originated from the sultan's
port of Del Morga and gone on to cross the desert under
pitiless late summer sun and curtains of ochre dust. The
heat had turned the pelts rancid. Poorly cured to begin
with, their taint threatened to spoil the cloth goods, and
in a gesticulating display of temper, the merchant who
stood to lose profits scrambled from his litter in a haste
that nearly tore his trappings. His camels succumbed to
riled nerves and spat on his silk over-robes.

Elshaid's cheeks flushed purple. "Fetch out those
Neth-blighted furs!" he screeched to his beast goad, a
turbaned man with a squint that all but buried gray eyes.
The merchant took pleasure in his ranting. "Then find
some cord. Tie the pelts on your head, and bear them so
until we arrive in Telssina's great market." Here Elshaid
smothered a spiteful chuckle. Under his breath he added,
"And, Neth hear my plea, may the stink of three dozen
dead martens addle the functions of your brain."

The gobbets of beast spittle had soaked in, leaving a
residue of hay shreds. While the king's precocious mercenary applied himself to bundling smelly furs, Elshaid
howled for his body servant to unlash his chest of spare
clothing.

The caravan moved on within the hour. Burdened by
a headdress of corrupted skins, the camel goad eased his
squint long enough to study the city of Datha's Sultan,
laid out on the plain like a desert chief's jewel in a setting
of high stone walls. Sentries in plumes and scimitars
guarded the five arched gates. Horsemen in double-file
companies patrolled the outer perimeter throughout each
hour of daylight; by night their numbers would be tre-
bled, and archers would stand watch at fifty-foot intervals
along the torchlit walls.

The camel goad reviewed these defenses with his eyes
unreadably in shadow. As Elshaid's caravan approached
the market gate, his sole concession to risk was to droop
the furs lower on his brow, and to develop a hitch in his
stride that required him to constantly watch his feet.

The camels bawled and halted, and stirred dust spread
over a compound trampled bare of desert fern. Bronze-
studded gates loomed overhead, and the towers on either
side threw shadow in swaths across the earth. Beasts jostled and sidled against their halters to seek relief from

the heat; only the half-wit wretch who managed them remained in the glare of the sun, pelts piled sloppily atop his head, and his camel goad looped at his wrist. He looked too lazy to present any bother. The guardsmen assigned to inspect caravans focused on the loud-voiced merchant who sweated through the labor of dismounting.

"Elshaid, by the Hells!" exclaimed the most seasoned of the guardsman. "Squandered thy fortune and had to retire to merchanting, I see."

"Certainly not." The fat man stuffed his handkerchief in his cuff. He straightened pearl-stitched lapels and tried through discomfort to look dignified. "This caravan carries an order for a favored customer."

Bristling with weapons, the guardsmen closed for a routine inspection of the goods. Elshaid dispatched servants to fetch out his lists.

"Special order smells spoiled to me," observed the officer who passed near the camel goad. "If furs constitute thy delivery, and if thy client is Lord Ismmail, thou wilt surely get thy butt bastinadoed."

Elshaid shrugged. "My client is not Lord Ismmail. These furs are bound for another, one I warned that this was not the acceptable season for buying pelts. Scarcity was sure to compromise the quality. Oh yes, I assured this much. But he stubbornly insisted." Smug now, Elshaid folded his hands on the dome of his belly. "Of course, I made the fool pay for his martens in advance."

The guardsmen chuckled their appreciation. "His persistence became thy good fortune, Elshaid?" teased the one who was an acquaintance.

"Just so." Elshaid waved to the wine tuns, carefully lashed under linens to keep off the sun. "Those, now, they're another matter. I brought several extras, for the sultan's guard to share among themselves."

The officer in command stiffened suspiciously. "We cannot drink wine while on duty. If thou thinkst—"

But the guard acquainted with Elshaid interrupted. "The merchant is wise to our laws. In the past we provided our address, and Elshaid delivered his gift to our dooryards."

Elshaid nodded with obsequious diffidence. "I trust such arrangement will be acceptable?"

At this, the sultan's faithful clustered about the merchant, who, after tedious rounds of repetition, collected directions from each guard. Beyond the compound, the next caravan in line was forced to wait. Driven to vociferous impatience, its head drover assailed the officer with imprecations. The guards stirred reluctantly back to duty. Since their captain suspected a bribe, they inspected Elshaid's wares meticulously, then left the camels to their bad temper. There remained only the beast goad's putrescent load of pelts. The man sat crouched with his eyes closed. The sultan's finest had been in shade long enough that the shift to full sunlight made them blink; by now, the stench of rotted furs had attracted a buzzing cloud of flies. The soldier commanded to take inventory was in no way inclined to duck down and peer beneath the bundle for a look at the face underneath; and the accounts tallied without discrepancy.

"Get ye on, then!" snapped the officer in charge.

As the guards passed by, the camel goad straightened indolently. He shuffled off to drive beasts, while with silent but profuse prayers to heaven, Elshaid heaved back into his litter and clucked his sour beasts to their feet. In shambling disarray, his caravan crossed through the arched double gateway of Telssina, and entered the bustling main street.

The thoroughfare was packed with palanquins, foot slaves, hand carts, and camels in caparisons and twisted silk bridles bearing wealthy trade magnates. Elshaid's packtrain jostled a path through the press, but his beast goad was given wide berth. In a city prided for cleanliness, where servants of the great lords burned incense on their balconies, the stink of bad furs stood out like a corpse in a flower bed. The caravan which included the bundle was shunned as if it carried leprosy. Embarrassed, and on edge lest he damage his reputation, Elshaid turned his pack train into a side street after the barest of prudent intervals. There, in the shadow of an alleyway, his camel goad shed his burden of pestilent furs.

"Let me be clear," whispered Elshaid, his damp brow furrowed in aggravation. "I cannot get you out of this city, and I'll not be responsible for your safety. If you're caught, I'll claim I never knew you."

Korendir unwound his turban, which reeked pervasively of dead skins. He shook loose bronze hair more pleasantly scented by the desert fern that had pillowed his head during camp in the open. "We never were partners in any case." He raked the camel trader with a gaze grim as granite, then tore a strip from the nearest bolt of brocade.

Elshaid winced, but dared not protest. He watched his contemptible camel goad bind his hair under cloth embroidered with peacocks that should have been sold to clothe a prince. Stung afresh by squandered profits, the merchant added, "I won't be smuggling Princess Iloreth out, not if you threaten to kill me."

Korendir's quick hands tucked and knotted his headdress as he answered. "That task, I entrust to no one."

Then, while Elshaid stood in straddle-legged defiance over a heap of spoiled furs, the mercenary commandeered two packbeasts in the king's name, and with them four tuns of rare wines. After that he stepped back without apology and vanished into the depths of the alley.

"Neth!" Elshaid twisted his rings in red-faced, impotent fury. "The gods of the Dathei should punish such arrogance." Murderously irritated, he kicked the furs left rucked at his feet. Flies buzzed; high overhead, a horn blew thrice from the timekeeper's tower. Three hours remained before sundown. Then the sultan's edict which forbade strong drink was relaxed, but Elshaid would not be easing his losses by sampling the contents of his wares. Thanks to one insufferable mercenary, Elshaid-the-No-Longer-Retired was required to deliver the rest of his precious spirits to the homes of unappreciative guardsmen.

The Princess of South Englas awoke with a start in the locked chamber where she spent those nights she was free to sleep alone. Roused by a touch on her cheek, her frenzied effort to rise was caught short by a grip on her shoulder. A fast, implacable hand stifled the scream that arose from her lips.

"Your Grace," the man who held her whispered clearly. "Your royal father sends his love."

Iloreth choked back a second more agonized cry. She stopped struggling and looked up into eyes touched luminously silver by the moonlight let in by the narrow window overhead. Her message had reached South Englas;

realization caused her to break her proud composure as she had not since she first lost her freedom. She wept, held lightly against the shoulder of the stranger sent by her father. Her tears soaked soundlessly into cloth spiced with the musk of desert ferns.

The man maintained his passionless embrace until she quieted. When her breathing steadied, he reached into his tunic and pulled forth a card marked with letters in the looped script of South Englas. This he laid at Iloreth's knee, providing the tongueless a means for accurate communication. Almost, the Princess wept afresh; yet gratitude came mixed with fear that the Sultan's guardsmen might snatch opportunity from her. Iloreth straightened and leaned into the moonlight that spilled in a square across her mat. Her greeting was nervously short.

Neth bless you, she spelled. *You are the Scourge of the Dathei.*

A brief, barely audible laugh answered her from the dark. "No," whispered the stranger. "I'm Korendir, summoned south from Whitestorm to take you home."

Iloreth's hands tapped swiftly over the script. *Careful, guards.*

Korendir nodded encouragement. "Tell me more of them. All that you know."

Iloreth answered his questions until her eyes ached from following the letters by the moon's wan light. Just when she thought Korendir would never be satisfied, he rose to his feet. Iloreth settled back on her mat. She followed with her eyes as he paced the breadth of her chamber. His demands had encompassed more details of the sultan's city of Telssina than the princess realized she knew; some points had been phrased repeatedly for clarity, but the subjects reviewed in such depth seemed hardly worth interest and without descernible pattern.

Korendir had even demanded to know what sort of fitting fastened the scrollwork which railed the upper galleries of the merchant's mansions. Iloreth had provided an accurate enough description; like most slaves, her hands were callused by polishing cloth and compound, and the aching hours of toil required to keep the wrought brass bright. Too weary for curiosity, the princess waited without questions for Korendir's restlessness to end.

He paused finally beneath a window tinged pink with

dawn. "Look for me at the dark of the next moon, Your Grace."

A smooth leap gave him a grip on the sill. A kick and a slither, and he raised his body through the slit high above. The next instant he was gone so thoroughly that the narrow opening showed empty sky.

Only the musk of the desert fern lingered to affirm his existence. Iloreth subsided on her mat. She ached with the need to call out, to beg him on her knees to return. Speech being impossible, she fought an undermining tide of hopelessness. The dark of the moon lay a fortnight hence; if on that night some noble chose her for his bed, she would be helplessly unable to keep the rendezvous.

Korendir spent the day asleep underneath a trough behind a vintner's shed. Next night, he skulked through alleys and byways until he learned every quarter of the city. He mapped the guard posts on the walls and noted the location of barracks and stables. Once his reconnaissance was complete, he left through the main gates, clinging to the underside of a wagon bound for Del Morga.

No one noticed him when he tumbled clear in the dust raised up by the wheels. He recrossed the desert on foot. Past the borders of South Englas, he engaged a post horse and rode north to the City of Kings. The wall sentries admitted him on sight. His hair gleamed like a brand in the sunlight, and his lithe, swordsman's stride set him apart from the merchants, priests, and foot servants who fared on the royal road.

Upon his return, Korendir demanded immediate audience with the king. His request was passed on. Despite the chamber steward's distaste for the dust which filmed his leathers, and the pervasive musk of the desert fern as yet unwashed from his skin, Korendir did not wait for admittance to the royal presence. The instant the great doors opened, he delivered word that Her Grace, Iloreth had retained both her health and good spirits.

"Have you a plan to storm the city and arrange for my daughter's release?" Strained and hopeful on a throne studded with amethysts, the king thumbed at a hangnail while the mercenary completed proper courtesies.

"I ask use of your armor's services, and a carpenter's

apprentice for one day," Korendir said. "Also add a length of new rope. Then we'll see."

"No soldiers?" snapped the king, loudly enough that his bodyguards started at their posts. "Do you mock me?"

But Korendir declined to elaborate.

Unsatisfied by the modesty of the mercenary's requests, and anxious for his daughter's rescue, the king clapped his hands. A page fetched the official scribe and seal bearer, and the sovereign Lord of South Englas dictated an edict. In formal script, on finest parchment, Korendir, Master of Whitestorm was granted service from the royal smith, along with whatever resources he might require from any joiner and ropewalk in the kingdom.

Korendir accepted the writ without comment. To the transparent relief of the chamber steward and certain high-ranking nobles, he left court and proceeded to the smithy where his demands were a good deal stiffer.

The master armorer of South Englas braced muscled arms on his hips. Charged with forging two score throwing knives whose weight, balance, and spin were perfectly matched, he cursed long and vehemently over the seals which footed Korendir's royal document. Assured in triplicate that the blazons were no forgery, he clamped his jaw and rubbed his bald head.

Until Korendir mentioned his deadline.

The armoror drew breath like a bellows and laughed. "You want your knives complete in six days?" He shrugged incredulously. "Impossible."

Korendir folded the king's document with fingers still grimed from the desert. He wasted no breath in protest, but added a list of further specifications that caused the smith's apprentice to be rousted with an obscenely phrased order to split more wood for the forge.

Then the king's over-priviledged mercenary became the recipient of the armorer's temper in turn. "Leave me to my work, you!" The man presented his sweating back, and between rude words began hefting his stock of new steel. When he turned with his chosen bar in hand, the mercenary from Whitestorm had departed.

The joiner faced his task with better cheer. He spun the four-inch brass pin provided by Korendir between his fingers and squinted to estimate diameter. "As it happens, I do stock spicewood in my sheds. But just for ornamental scrollwork, understand? The wood lacks hardness. Dowels turned from such lumber will splinter under the slightest stress." He tipped his head at an enquiring angle. Cedar shavings trickled from his hair as he studied the mercenary who confronted him.

Korendir returned a level stare.

"But you know that spicewood doesn't endure already," the joiner amended diffidently. Inquiry after the mercenary's purpose met with an uninformative reply, and stung by the rebuff, the craftsman adjusted his lathe in faintly resentful silence.

Late day saw Korendir changed from riding attire into tunic and hose of unornamented black. He visited the chandler's on Ships Street and returned with fifty feet of cordage. Settled by the fountain in the king's private garden, he pulled out a marlin spike and displayed the skill of a trained seaman to the half dozen pages who gathered to watch. Afternoon passed as he spliced a set of loops at intervals along the length of rope. The fascination of the boys became shared when the king arrived with furtive lack of ceremony to observe behind the curtains of a second-storey casement. Believing himself unnoticed, the sovereign of South Englas was startled to receive the courtesy due his rank when Korendir finished working.

The mercenary knelt without fuss, ringed by admiring young boys. His eyes lifted unerringly toward the monarch who sat in concealment as he said, "Grant me the use of three horses. Your daughter will be restored to South Englas in a fortnight, and the ruin of Datha shall follow after."

The king sprang erect and clapped his hands. No servants answered. Irked by his lapse, for he had forgotten where he was, His Grace dispatched his bodyguard to run his errand to the grooms. Then, embarrassed that a stranger should witness impatience unseemly for a ruler, the king looked askance at the courtyard. Korendir had already gone. The pages were absorbed in practice, weaving splices out of grass, and the shadows that slanted from the guard tower recalled the time. Dinner was nigh. Hungry as he had not been in ages, the king made his way toward the feasting hall.

                        *   *   *

Korendir rode from court at first light seven days later.
The lengths of rope he had altered hung in coils across
his shoulder, and the master armorer's throwing knives
gleamed, thrust through leather loops in his belt. A sack
tied to his saddlebow bulged with the spicewood dowels
made to demand by the joiner. Except for two riderless
horses hooked to his wrist with braided cord, the mercenary rode unaccompanied. His final word to the king was
his promise to return from Telssina with the princess.

But just before the appointed day of rendezvous, Iloreth's fortune ran out. That afternoon Telssina's gates had
opened to admit an envoy from Arhaga, and a ranking
official in the ambassador's train had picked her to warm
his bed.

This latest unkindness of fate brought Iloreth shattering despair. Delivered to the emmissary's chambers at
sundown, she paced fretfully, tormented by awareness
that the dark of the moon was only one night hence. The
last slave who displeased a palace guest had been slowly
tortured to death; her screams remained vivid in Iloreth's
memory, but the risk of similar penalty mattered little
by the time the envoy returned, drunken with overindul-
gence of the sultan's hospitality. The princess resisted his
advances as well as her thumbless condition allowed. She
prayed through tears of frustration that brute Arhagai
lust would sour and crave another in her stead before
morning.

The official overpowered her before he succumbed to
his liquor. Iloreth endured, as she had countless nights
in the past; through the quiet hour that followed, she
appealed to Neth's mercy that the Arhagai as a race preferred submissive women. Her prayer went unanswered.

Daylight brought the official a fierce hangover and no
recollection of his evening activities. He rose nursing an
overblown mood of self-pity, and ordered Iloreth to fetch
his clothing and boots. Once dressed, he departed in
search of hot drink and a sweet roll. When the house
steward inquired after his pleasure, he cradled his suffering hangover and pleaded no change in accommodations.
Left the task of straightening tumbled sheets, Iloreth
wrestled hopelessness, that the freedom so near at hand

should relentlessly pass her by. If she could have laid hand on a knife, she might have ended her misery, but even embassies to a land as savage as Datha carried no arms; the furnishings of the guest suite contained no suitable substitute.

Released at midmorning to make rounds of the palace chamber pots, Iloreth hid among the flowering shrubs inside the sultan's seraglio on the bald-faced chance she might elude the Arhagan's attentions. The head gardener discovered her and at once second-guessed her intent. His report earned her a beating. The house steward took care not to mark her, since she was presently favored by a guest. Yet welts that stung red and then faded offered nothing by way of consolation; more lasting punishment would await the envoy's departure.

Returned under guard to the guest chamber, Iloreth stared at the street beyond the scrolled brass grille across the window. Her thumbless hands were incapable of drawing the pins that secured the ornamental grate; and the medallion which framed the central aperture was barely a palm span across. A sparrow might have sailed through between wing beats; a slave was helplessly imprisoned.

Tropical dusk fell swiftly. A shaved crescent moon sank over the roofs of Telssina and stars burned like lamps on blue silk. Huddled forlornly on a hassock beside the hearth, Iloreth sat with dry eyes and wondered whether Korendir would wait long in the room that housed her sleeping mat. She thought of her parents as the wall sconces were lighted in the street, and the distorted shadow of the window grille leapt and wavered across the floor. Hours passed. Songs from late-night revellers heralded the closing of feasting halls and taverns. Knowing the Arhagan would be along soon, the princess sat listlessly. At any instant the bleak comfort of solitude would end, along with her last hope of home.

That moment the wall sconce by the window hissed and went dark.

Normally in Telssina such lights burned until morning, but Iloreth had no chance to reflect why the torch had precipitously failed. The latch of the guest suite tripped up and the door opened. Moved by less welcome than she would have awarded the palace executioner, Iloreth arose, her scarred face set with distaste.

The Arhagan crossed the threshold. "Come to me, ugly one," he invited. He leaned on the panel as it swung shut, his lips parted over teeth that gleamed faintly from the shadows. He was quite sober.

"A fine thought, thee had, to leave my chambers dark. We shall make sport together, yes?"

The Arhagan smiled again.

A shadow moved at the grate. Steel flashed in an arc through the bars and struck with the speed of a snake. The Arhagan's look of lust froze into horror. He gurgled, clutched at the blade embedded in his throat, then crashed full-length on the floor.

Iloreth recoiled from her tormentor's dying struggles, and stared wide-eyed through the window. A man crouched there, black-clad and nimble. Before the Arhagan gasped his last, a brass pin chimed on the tile. The grille swung open and in wafted the unmistakable scent of desert fern.

"Come quickly, Your Grace," whispered Korendir. "Dead envoys are bad luck in any country."

XIV. Scourge of the Dathei

Iloreth rushed forward. The mercenary in the window caught hold of her. His sure grasp raised her up and over the sill, then bundled a cloak over her thin silk robes. Half stunned by her change in luck, Iloreth felt herself hurried across the palace street and into a side alley, where a rope dangled from the grille of a gallery.

"Climb," said Korendir in her ear.

Loops had been spliced into the rope, forming a ladder for thumbless hands. Iloreth swung herself upward. Steadied by the hands of the northerner, she went quickly. Before the Arhagan left behind in the guest chambers ceased bleeding, she reached the roof and clung to the ceramic of the rain gutter.

"Hold here, Your Grace." Korendir reached past her, grasped the lip of the tile, and kicked free of the rope. He slung himself up with the agility of a lizard, then crouched and caught Iloreth's wrists. Hoisted in the grip of the swordsman, she landed, breathless, above the eaves.

"Go across," Korendir instructed. "Over the rooftop on the far side, you'll find another rope fastened to a chimney. Start down if you can. I'll be along."

Determined to carry her own weight, Iloreth choked back her fear of falling. She scaled the slippery roof tiles and located the line Korendir had left. She caught her fingers in the top loop, clenched her jaw, and slid over the lip of the rain gutter.

The mercenary arrived at the roof edge just as the princess reached the ground. The rope previously used for ascent was hooked into coils over his shoulder; the other he severed at the knot. Iloreth gathered up the length which cascaded to her feet, while above her, Korendir swung onto a gallery. A movement saw him hanging full length from the brasswork adorning the lower railing; from there he dropped the short distance to street level.

The second he recovered his balance, he was flanked by a hunched figure in black.

Iloreth was startled into panic. If she became recaptured, the agonies that awaited at the hand of the sultan's torturer raised a horror that overwhelmed caution. A scream arose in her throat, stopped by Korendir's hard fingers.

He shook her once, sharply, and his whisper restored her to reason. "Look again."

Shaking with rattled nerves, Iloreth discovered who sheltered beneath the cloak hood. Tears welled in her eyes. Korendir had stolen Daide from the sultan's seraglio, but his sympathies did not extend to delay for sentiment or gratitude. The mercenary grasped the hands of both women and hauled them urgently into a run.

Telssina's thoroughfares were never quiet. Caravans from the south commonly scheduled night arrivals, and last watch's guardsmen loitered between gambling halls and wineshops, making each street corner a hazard. Korendir had chosen his route to compensate; he and his refugees utilized rooftops to cross the most crowded quarters of the city. They were challenged only once, while Daide descended by rope from a second floor balcony. Korendir answered the soldier's query with a throwing knife, and pressed on without pause to recover his weapon. The gravest risk lay ahead. Between the inner city and freedom lay the double walls of the sultan's fortifications. The avenue which paralleled these defenseworks was the haunt of beggars, blackmarketeers, and disease-ridden, one-coin prostitutes, every one of them desperate enough to turn informer for the hope of a guardsman's copper. At no hour of the day or night was the street deserted, and a division of the sultan's cavalry patrolled constantly to manage the crime.

Korendir had no intention of fighting what could not be changed. He sheltered Daide and Iloreth beneath the canvas cover of a refuse cart, then catfooted through the gutters to an alley two streets down. There he broke into the warehouse which held the confiscated goods of Elshaid the erstwhile camel trader. In short order he left four tuns of fine northern wines to roll unattended into the avenue beneath the walls.

Excited shouts proclaimed their discovery by the resident riff-raff. The barrels were broached with abandon, and as celebration drew every lowborn citizen within earshot, the spoils of Elshaid's misfortune were shared out and imbibed and fought over.

Korendir slipped off into shadow. He ducked beneath the cart that hid the women and waited while Telssina's eastern quarter brewed up a riot of swaying bodies, drunken laughter, and brawlers who cheerfully cursed and cracked heads and battered one another with an assortment of ill-gotten weaponry. The Sultan's horsemen descended like a swarm of yellow hornets upon the site. Forced to dismount and dirty themselves manhandling commoners, their angry oaths rang out above the noise.

Korendir chose his moment and started ascent of the wall. He slung his first rope over a merlon behind a gate house and climbed to the top without sound. The guardsman on duty died with a shudder and never a chance to cry out. The mercenary leaped before the body stopped twitching and swiftly doused the watch torch. Quick as a spider he swung onto the roof of the battlement which joined the guard embrasure with the far wall. As the soldier on the outer defenseworks peered across to determine what mishap had befallen the light, his face showed briefly in silhouette. The third of the armorer's throwing knives found its mark, and a second corpse crashed on the stone. Korendir completed his crossing of the arch, blackened the next torch, and set the rope for descent over the spikes which crowned the outer rampart.

The margin he had before discovery at best could be counted in seconds. Racing to beat odds, Korendir retraced his steps and fetched the two women from hiding. He delivered his instructions in a voice breathlessly curt. Iloreth and Daide were to climb, covered from the rear by his weapons. They were told where horses awaited, tethered in a hollow under cover; orders were to ride without thought for whatever might arise behind them.

"Her Grace leads," Korendir finished. "Go, and on your lives and honor, don't either of you look back."

The fugitives hurried across the avenue and faded into shadow by the gate house. Korendir set his shoulder against the wall, the last rope hooked loosely through his elbow. He caught Iloreth's waist and hefted her upward, hastening the start of her climb. Daide followed more awkwardly. Five months with child by the sultan's heir, she raised not a murmur of complaint, though pregnancy added clumsiness to her hardship. As Korendir boosted her after the princess, her frail hands caught the rope as though it held her last hope in life. Daide climbed at Iloreth's heels, her hooded head tilted upward toward the battlement and freedom.

In that most vulnerable moment, the night echoed with approaching hoofbeats. Down the street a staff messenger sent after reinforcements spurred clear of the riot. As his sweat-lathered horse jibbed through an unruly corner, the rider chanced to look up; he spotted dark-clad figures in the act of scaling the wall.

Korendir's thrown dagger found the man's heart too late to prevent outcry. As the messenger toppled from his saddle his dying scream rang the length of the avenue.

Sentries in the adjoining gate houses raced out at the disturbance; mounted patrols abandoned the fray that still raged in tangles around the wine tuns. Someone on the battlements sounded an alarm bell, and pursuit converged from both directions.

Korendir flipped the rope from his forearm. He spun and faced the galleries that overhung the thoroughfare along the inner wall. His throw sent coils snaking upward. Multiple loops snagged over ornamental spikes and grille railings that extended along the balconies above his head. Earlier, the pins which secured the brass panels had been replaced with the dowels from the carpenter. Unobtrusive twists of wire joined one panel to another above the level of the street. Grim as death, and as ruthless, Korendir bent the tail of the line around a lamp post. Then he slammed his weight against the end.

Spice wood slivered under stress. Jerked askew, a six-foot panel dove over the brink. Korendir tugged again. Wrenched in chain reaction that carried the length of the block, the grilles on the second-storey galleries cartwheeled into the air and fell twisting over the lances of the oncoming cavalry. Upset like a row of dominoes, ponderous pounds of wrought brass scythed down horses, men, and bystanders with the mangling force of a cataclysm.

The dissonant chime of metal blended with the screams of casualties. Pinned like insects, the victims scrabbled to escape the shift of tumbled grilles which snapped limbs and crushed skulls without distinction. An officer unhurt in the wreckage tried vainly to bellow orders.

Korendir shrugged clear of the rope that had set his diversion in motion. He footed across jumbled panels to the wall and glanced skyward. Iloreth was safely up and over the upper battlement; Daide negotiated the topmost spikes.

An arrow glanced, chattering over masonry. Korendir ducked a gritty fall of mortar. Somewhere, perhaps in the adjoining gate house, an archer remained with a clear head. The mercenary set the rope swinging to hamper the bowman's aim, then furiously began to climb. Darkness made him a poor target and a relief charge sent in by the cavalry commander served only to abet his escape.

The mounted division swept through the wine riot at full gallop. Beggars and drunken prostitutes shied clear, shrieking imprecations; not a few were trampled down. The horses surged past unimpeded. Korendir never looked back as the cries of the lead riders cut like a knife through night.

Their mounts were first to suffer. Slender forelegs clanged through the open scrollwork of the fallen grilles and momentum did the rest. Caught short, the thousand-pound chargers flipped like trouts on a line. Their riders were messily crushed. A tangle of snapped limbs and agony, the war horses thrashed. Their hooves rained smashing ruin upon those unfortunate survivors pinned within range.

Korendir topped the wall as the second rank of cavalry pressed haplessly to ruin by the riders that galloped behind; twenty-two horses were broken before the charge could be halted. The rear ranks avoided the carnage only to find themselves preoccupied by mounts that shied from the smell of fresh blood.

Only the archer in the gate house remained to defend the walls. His aim was righteously vindictive.

Korendir crossed the bridging arch amid a clattering fall of shafts. He caught the descent rope by touch and flung himself over the brink. Before he dropped, a war arrow hammered into his forearm. His grip tore loose. Left one hand and friction to brake his fall, he plunged in an uncontrolled slide. Skin ripped from his palm. He lost the rope, hit ground in a rolling sprawl that allowed no chance to correct mistakes. The war shaft jabbed earth, drove cleanly through flesh and muscle, and snapped off. Korendir struck a ditch with a force that slammed the last air from his lungs. For a prolonged and dangerous moment he lay doubled, utterly unable to rise.

His chest unlocked at length. Breath and then movement returned. Korendir shoved to his knees. Daide lay in a heap of wilted cloth to his left, an unlucky victim of the archer. Iloreth had gone on to the hollow where horses awaited. Against orders, she returned, leading all three mounts by their bridles.

Korendir swore. He drew out the headless fragment of the arrow, threw it down, and regained his feet. Telssina's walls were still manned, and the disaster unleashed in the streets would no longer serve as protection. The sultan's faithful would regroup and pursue in a passion for vengeance, while guards would recover from shock. If Iloreth attracted notice from a wall sentry, reparation would be instant and this time no cover was prearranged.

Korendir bent swiftly over Daide. A check with his good hand established the fact she still breathed. When the princess arrived he commanded her to help lift, and with combined effort the injured woman was hauled across the saddle of a nerve-jumpy gelding. A cut length of rope secured her unconscious body over its withers. Korendir gestured Iloreth up behind, then vaulted astride the larger of the remaining two mounts. He whipped both animals to a gallop, driving the riderless one ahead.

The thunder of horses in flight raised noise impossible to overlook.

The throaty wail of a horn split the night at their backs. Lights blossomed in the guard tower, while to the east, Telssina's steel-wrought gates swung wide and disgorged a yelling company of horsemen. Oiled bodies shone beneath streaming cressets, and each man's drawn scimitar deflected needle-thin reflections against the darkened wall.

Korendir measured the situation at a glance. He directed the princess and Daide under cover in a thorn thicket, then headed off the spare horse. A one-fisted haul on the bridle turned his own mount after the gelding's high-flung tail. Korendir rode with eyes narrowed against pain. Carefully he judged distance, then veered his pair of fear-maddened horses in an arc across the warriors' charge.

When the company wheeled to give chase, Korendir dropped his reins. He unsheathed his next to last knife and flicked his wrist in a throw. The blade spun flat and buried hilt deep in the flank of the riderless horse.

Tormented by the bite of the steel, the gelding coughed and shot ahead. Korendir felt his own mount quicken to keep pace. He freed his toes from the stirrups and snapped off in a flying dismount. His injured wrist marred his balance; instead of landing upright, he stumbled head over heels and smashed to a bruising stop in a thicket. Nettled by more than clumsiness, he looked up to ascertain that both horses pounded in panic ahead of the oncoming cavalry.

Like a flaming serpent from hell, the sultan's finest screamed warcries and whipped up their mounts.

Korendir pulled clear of crushed thorn leaves. He gripped his last knife in grazed fingers and crouched against the sand. Motionlessly he waited as the horsemen hurtled by. Shadows from their torches flicked his face. Sand flung up by the milling hooves stung in showers over his cuts. He endured, patient, until the last man and animal thundered past. Then in one move he straightened and made his throw.

The steel flew and sank with clean accuracy in the trailing rider's back.

Ruled by the pride of his race, the warrior toppled without sound. His rigorously trained mare stopped in her tracks and resisted the herd instinct which urged her to flee with her fellows. She pawed, ears flicking nervously, and waited for her master to rise.

Korendir intervened to ensure the man would not. While his victim lay stunned, he leaped from cover and stuffed his cloak in the Datha's mouth. Then he bound the braceletted wrists with cord, cleared his weapon from its sheath of enemy flesh and staunched the bleeding that followed. Once assured that the man would survive, he seized the oiled flesh of one bare shoulder and flipped the warrior over.

The mercenary's gaze held no mercy as he confronted a face pinched with hate.

"I've a message for your sultan," he said to his captive. "You're my appointed envoy. Tell your sovereign that Korendir of Whitestorm was responsible for the murder of his Arhagan guest, and also for the theft in his seraglio. Invite him, in my name, to satisfy the insult to Datha's honor on the knoll beyond Erdmire Flats. I will await His Excellency's presence in a fortnight's time. Now, repeat that to me."

Korendir jerked off the gag. Met by insult the instant the warrior found his voice, the mercenary returned an ungentle measure that left the man miserably retching. Afterwards, his message for the sultan poured in a torrent from the whitened lips of his victim.

"May Irdhu's Fires consume your flesh, and that of your misbegotten offspring, light-eyed man," the Datha gasped at the end. He was afraid. The curse was not the worst he could have uttered.

Unmoved by threat of divine retaliation, Korendir replaced the gag. He vaulted into the warrior's empty saddle and rode off into the night, the fingers of his sound hand busy stripping off the brass which bedecked the mare's battle tack. The spangles he flung into the sand underfoot, lest their glitter betray him to the sultan's patrols.

Desert dawn spread gilt across the sky by the time Korendir overtook the princess. Doubly laden, her gelding had lost its early freshness; though Daide had ceased to breathe during the night, Iloreth refused to abandon her body to be picked by scavengers. Korendir had not gainsaid the princess's sentiment. When the sun climbed high enough to shimmer heatwaves over the gray-brown tassels of the desert fern, he ordered a halt in the shade of an outcrop.

Tired and sore beyond patience, he helped the princess from the saddle. Although the effort taxed his hurt arm, he gathered the body in the black shroud of his cloak, and laid it straight upon the sand.

He spoke then with piercing directness. "If this is an

unsuitable place for me to dig a resting place for Daide,
bear in mind that she might cost your horse his life. I
will run the gelding until he breaks, should the sultan
send a patrol. Daide will be left where she falls. I'll not
risk your safety for a corpse."

Head bent, Iloreth sank down beside the body of her
former companion. Almost an hour passed before she
extended a rope-burned finger and traced her reply in
the sand. "I'll take the chance," she wrote. "Daide's father will be grateful, and I want South Englas to know
she died free of the sultan. For trying, you deserve my
people's reward."

Korendir surprisingly capitulated without argument.
"Your Grace," he said, and knelt in acknowledgment of
rank as if he were a vassal given royal command.

Puzzled by a courtesy contradicted by his edged manner, Iloreth wondered upon the nature of the man who
had saved her. Plainly the honor she sought to bestow
was least among Korendir's intentions.

In silence, the princess and her rescuer shared rations
from the Datha's stolen saddlebags. Then Iloreth sank
down and garnered a much needed rest. Korendir kept
watch. Moody, restless, driven by emotions that never
showed, he settled finally against a striated shoulder of
rock. While the Princess of South Englas lay asleep, he
built up a tiny fire, peeled the sleeve from his arm, and
boiled fresh water to cleanse his wound.

The Sultan of Datha sent no more patrols. Confronted
over breakfast by a sand-flecked guardsman who brought
news that a light-eyed northerner had violated the sanc-
tity of the palace and escaped, his Excellency left pastries
on his platters. While meat congealed uneaten between
the crested handles of his cutlery, the doors of the armory gaped wide to admit a bustle of officials clutching
royal requisitions. Datha's sovereign intended to meet
Korendir's challenge. Heir to a prophecy that assigned
the ruin of his House to the deeds of such a one, the
sultan would not expose his person to danger. He would
satisfy honor and the slight to the Arhagai delegation
with a war host ten thousand strong.

*　　*　　*

Ladies wept in South Englas's City of Kings when Korendir of Whitestorm returned. The long-lost princess was greeted with tears of joy, and Daide with those of sorrow. Celebration commenced with courtiers clad in the black-bordered robes of mourning, and the scene at the palace was repeated in halls the breadth of the realm.

Badgered by scribes for an account of the rescue, Korendir remained uninformative. When the court minstrels repeated the same plea, they found themselves summarily dismissed. The mercenary's conduct might have earned him a satire had Iloreth not been tireless in applauding his courage; her ladies repeated her story, but the northerner cast in the hero's role avoided court company from the outset. Against the entreaties of the king, Korendir took lodging in a boarding house.

Daide's kin sent thanks in the form of a resplendently jewelled set of arms. The mercenary delicately requested their equivalent worth in coin, and heartened that the finest of the ancestral heirlooms would not pass from the family, Daide's father doubled the sum directly. His generosity was quietly accepted.

Though South Englas became engrossed in festivities, the king could not forget his beloved daughter's captivity. Confronted at every turn by her ruined hands and scarred face, and by the silence of her mutilated tongue, he ignored the queen's pleas that he revoke his resolve against Datha.

"How many sons and daughters from South Englas still polish the sultan's brass?" he demanded, spinning his untouched goblet between nervous fingers. "If a way exists to stop their accursed raiders, Neth grant us means to subdue them."

A voice answered, almost at the king's shoulder. "The talents of the Almighty shall not be necessary." Korendir of Whitestorm met the ruler's startled glance with words inflexibly direct. "Allow me fifty chosen men, and all the arrows in your armory. Your prayer shall be granted within a fortnight."

The king rose. He clapped his hands for his scribe, and while guests sat waiting with empty stomachs, a document was drawn up and impressed with the royal seals. The writ was placed in Korendir's hands before either ink or wax had set. This time, in place of questions, the king wished the Master of Whitestorm success in his endeavor.

Korendir bowed and took his leave. The paper granted him unlimited access to anything he might demand; wielding the writ as he would a weapon, the mercenary compelled a select group of men to leave the feast and prepare for his challenge to the sultan.

The palace seneshal, the master fletcher, and the captain of the archer's guard were first to suffer Korendir's summons. Drunk, sober, or sleeping in the arms of their wives, they were rousted to immediate duty. The fletchers were shown bins of war arrows lying dusty in the vaults and instructed to replace the conventional points with bats of quilted linen. Korendir's demands included that each shaft be rebalanced to compensate for the shift in weight. Then the captain's archers were called out one by one, and subjected to rigorous interview. Those not culled off were sent on to more grueling practice at the butts. The Master of Whitestorm took four days to select his fifty; within the hour the final list was read, he had them on the march beneath the desert sun, accompanied by three teams of oxen and sand sledges laden with oil casks and sharpened logs.

Korendir and his picked following arrived at the knoll that overlooked Erdmire two days ahead of the date appointed. The flats themselves were a level strip several miles wide that bridged the sand hills of Datha and the sea with its harbor at Del Morga. The land between was desolate. Coarse, salty soil supported no life but the desert fern, and there, that brittle, musk-laden plant thrived as nowhere else. The acres east of the shoreline lay mantled under dun, knee-high fronds whose hollow, grease-filled stems whispered in the breezes off the sea.

Korendir ordered the sledges unloaded. Cover was built for his archers behind stakes angled outward at chest height; when the log embrasures were completed, they formed a crude line along the dunes for half a league on either side of the knoll. Korendir had selected the positions with the care that he used to sharpen knives; the archers in the encampment quickly learned not to trouble him when whetstone and steel occupied his hands. Only when preparations were satisfactory did the mercenary reveal his intentions.

Conversation over that evening's meal was scant and grim. Korendir's plan was deadly simple. If he failed, not a man would survive; but if his tactics succeeded, the Master of Whitestorm was indeed the Scourge of Datha prophecy, and the sultan's accursed raiders would ravage South Englas no more. All that remained was the wait until the moment Telssina's army marched forth to answer challenge.

The sultan's war host reached the edge of Erdmire Flats early morning on the appointed day of rendezvous. Scouts rode in with word just after dawn, and by the time the chill had warmed from desert air, the archers of South Englas strung their bows. They assumed position before midday; alone behind inadequate defenses, each man squinted against the glare as the army drew swiftly into view. The numbers of warriors sent against them were enough to assault a fortified city.

Men swallowed and found their throats parched from nerves. They sweated, irritated by the scrape of sand crickets and the cloying musk of desert fern. Mercifully, by noon when the war host crossed the flats, the mounting heat eased with the wind which freshened over the dunes from behind. Steady ocean breezes stiffened the banners of the approaching host, and plumed the manes and tails of the horses like silk. Sunlight sparked blinding reflections off the spangles that adorned each warrior and mount.

The archers waited. Korendir had delivered their orders in a terse sentence, then followed with a promise to kill any man who acted before the appointed signal. His threat at the outset proved unnecessary; not an archer from South Englas wished to be first to draw notice from an enemy ten thousand strong.

Korendir stood alone on the knoll that overlooked Erdmire. He surveyed the army that spread like jewelled cord across the flats below. The ranks were close-packed to allow passage between the sand hills and the sea. From plumes and feathered bows to studded caparisons and spangled breast-straps, the war host out of Datha was a sight to inspire dread. Yet the mercenary made no move to hide his presence. He waited on the crest in the open; sweat dripped down the neck of his tunic, and his face stayed fixed as a mask. All had proceeded as he anticipated. He had only to stand and observe the fruits of his sowing.

"*Ahail, ahail!*" The cry trembled on the brittle air, and light tingled in reflection off a needlepoint row of raised scimitars. The Datha cavalry prepared for their charge with a ritual that had terrorized and disheartened many a defender before the killing strike.

"To our brave Captain General, *ahail!*"

Banners waved in salute of the Datha commander. Korendir's archers drew their linen-tipped shafts from pots of oil and reached for tinder and flint.

"To His Excellency, the sultan, *ahail, ahail!*"

Sabers dipped as honor was paid to Datha's reigning lord. Pale flame blossomed behind the defenseworks that bordered the dunes, and fifty hand-picked archers from South Englas nocked arrows and bent their bows to full draw. The approaching lines of warriors shimmered as men sighted through smoke-heated air.

"To Irdhu, who claims all life, *ahail, ahail, ahail!*"

Bowstrings sang, and arrows arched up. Smoke streaked in wisps from heads that blazed with the flames held most sacred to the deity the Dathei saluted. The shafts rose high across the sky, then plunged, crackling to earth ahead of the sultan's lines. Fires licked the stems of desert fern. Fanned in the grip of the sea breeze, small blazes caught well and swiftly. The archers nocked shafts a second time. They fired another volley, and a third; beyond that, no more were necessary.

In the act of sounding the charge, the Captain General's crier found himself confronted by a wall of snapping flame. He had time to wheel his horse before the conflagration overtook him. His scream rent air above the boom of drums as his oiled flesh touched off like a torch.

The desert made perfect tinder. Dry, greasy fronds exploded with zealous violence and hurled drifts of windborn sparks. These caught and fiercely ignited the manes and tails of the horses. Fire lapped from plant to plant. Whirled up into crackling curtains, it closed over the glossy, fat-smeared contours of the riders. Within minutes, Datha's finest became embraced in a fatal holocaust. Mares screamed and plunged and reared, to no avail. The proud host of ten thousand transformed to a living

pyre from end to end. In vain the rear ranks broke for-
mation and fled for their lives; no man among them had
a mount whose legs could outrun the wind.

Behind the breastworks, Korendir's archers gazed with
deadened eyes at the disaster; their ears were pierced
by screams that destroyed the very memory of silence.
Although the killer winds bore the smoke from the carnage away from them, it seemed the stench of seared
flesh would never clear from their nostrils. Horses and
men rolled in dying agony upon charred and blackened
ground, while the remains of the sultan's banners drifted
on the breeze, immolated to wisps of ash.

Korendir left his position on the hill. He roved the
length of the breastworks and roused South Englas's men
from stunned and horrified stupor. With shouts and
blows and imprecations, he forced them to harness the
oxen.

"Your task is done," he snapped to any who were slow
to respond. When the last man settled in his place on
the sledges, the mercenary mounted his horse and moved
on, a dark figure against a horizon dirtied with smoke
haze. He harried his following forward with fast and merciless order, while across the flats at his heels, the fire he
had arranged in cold blood finished its murdering work.

Though entitled to spoils, no one under Whitestorm's
command dared to question his order. The Datha dead
were left smouldering where they lay, while the fifty
archers responsible turned their stunned faces toward
home. Mechanically they moved feet and legs on the
three-day march to South Englas.

Every citizen in the City of Kings turned out for a
hero's welcome. The streets by the gates stood lined by
crowds who threw coins and luck charms and flowers.
Few smiles of triumph brightened the faces in the
archers' ranks. Korendir swore viciously at a child who
tossed him a victory wreath, and he interrupted the king's
speech of honor with a flat demand for his fee.

"Your daughter sits safe at your side. The sultan is
ruined, and Telssina is yours for the taking, if you stir
your men at arms before the Arhagai." Amid shocked
and spreading silence, the mercenary bowed with impa-

tience. "My work is done, Your Grace. I require nothing but my gold, and your leave to depart."

The king magnanimously forgave discourtesy and summoned his seneschal on the spot. The draft for the mercenary's pay was signed amid awkward stillness. Korendir made no effort to smooth feelings, but with dangerous, quick-strided grace, took his leave. While the crowds with their flowers and tokens dispersed from the city's main square, the Master of Whitestorm presented himself at the treasury vault. With a frown locked immovably on his features, he set about collecting his due.

He secured a berth on board a brig bound for Fairhaven within the hour. The king watched the ship weigh anchor off the point, short-tempered as a man with a grievance. Not until sundown did he send for his captain of archers and ask for account of the battle. The telling left a knot in the royal gut that no glow of victory could loosen.

"Neth have mercy," the sovereign murmured when he recovered enough presence to speak. His voice shook with appalled and cruel shock. "I'd not have the Master of Whitestorm's conscience for any sum in gold, nor his heart of ice. Pray South Englas is spared the need to hire his kind again, even to vanquish a race as fiendishly cruel as the Dathei."

XV. Summons from Tir Amindel

Korendir returned on the edge of autumn, aboard the same ship that brought in the new iron Haldeth had ordered to replenish his depleted forge. That day the clouds lay in raked gray sheets, warning of killing frosts to come; in Thornforest the leaves showed edges of red like dipped blood. Alone in chambers that turned chill at eventide, and weary of footsteps that echoed down empty, unfurnished halls, the smith met the trader brig's arrival with a soaring lift of spirits. At low tide he descended to the beach to greet the longboat, a whiskey flask tucked under one arm, and new bread left cooling in readiness on Whitestorm's spotless trestles.

The boat made slow progress, laden as it was with crated ingots and Korendir's chests of bullion; the oarsmen were poorly teamed. They battled a headwind, and each mistimed stroke spat spray over the bow to drench the cloaked occupant in the sternseat. By the time the craft gained shore, Haldeth's impatience had reached the point where he willingly wet his boots to speed the landing.

"Welcome home," he called, as a familiar, black-clad figure arose and leaped the gunwale into the shallows. Haldeth had time to notice that his friend's face seemed more haggard than usual. Then a wave slewed the longboat bruisingly into his groin, and he was forced to redirect his attention toward muscling the wayward craft straight.

"Why not give a hand, you lazy louts," he snarled to the crewmen who had yet to ship their oars.

A model of graceless coordination, the sailhands groused and eventually sorted themselves into order.

By then, Korendir had left the beach. Haldeth forgave the precipitous departure. If the incompetence demonstrated by the oarsmen was typical of seamanship aboard the brig, the voyage had likely been a shambles. Doubtless the Master of Whitestorm craved dry clothing and shoes that did not chafe from a crust of ingrained salt. Haldeth dumped the wet from his own boots, then regarded his crates of new ingots; Korendir's chests of gold easily doubled their cargo weight. Rather than strain his back, the smith elected to winch the load over the battlements.

Minutes later he cursed his impatient plunge into the surf. His feet weighed like lead, and his socks rucked soggily around his heels as he climbed the stair to the upper fortress. Worse, Korendir was not in the hall when Haldeth stamped through to check; still hopeful, the smith climbed more stairs in the north tower to reach his friend's private chambers. The rooms there all remained empty; even the clothes chests lay undisturbed under a season's layer of dust.

Puzzled, Haldeth let himself onto the windswept terrace of the watch tower, where a ship's glass rested always in a niche by the postern. The smith set cold brass to his eye and scanned the clifftop and at first pass spotted a black-clad figure walking the crags above the sea.

"Damn your miserable mood, anyway," Haldeth grumbled into the wind. Belatedly he remembered the flask which hung at his hip; as he retraced his steps to man the winch, he unslung the thong, yanked the stopper, and consoled himself mightily with spirits.

By the time the last crates and bullion chests lay stacked in the keep's inner bailey, Haldeth had forgotten wet feet; five months of unremitting solitude had left him starved for company. Loosened from exercise, and expansive with strong drink, he forgave the sailors their incompetence and descended again to the beach head to invite them for beer and sausage.

Their refusal was immediate, which surprised him.

"Your captain must be a fair task master," Haldeth sympathized.

His sarcasm seemed lost on the sailors, who exchanged glances.

"Not exactly." The larger of the four tipped his head, as unofficial spokesman for the group. "Just we don't fancy hospitality with your Master of Whitestorm about.

Got eyes like death, he has. Puts the living shivers on a man."

"Korendir?" Wind tumbled hair in Haldeth's face. He shook it back in annoyance. "His Lordship's off on the cliffs somewhere, brooding. Bound to be gone for hours, if that's all you're worried about."

"Well," said a sailor with a squint. "I'd watch yourself, were I in your berth. The crew who gave yon master passage from South Englas swore on their beer he'd gone insane. We thought they were drunk and telling tales, in port. At sea we found out different. Your Lord of Whitestorm drew steel on anyone who stepped too near his back. Through the nights and the storms, he paced the deck. Sometimes he took a turn at watch in the cross trees. He must've napped then, but our captain never caught him. Not for want of seeing, mind. The master o' yon brig's got an eye like the devil for slackers."

Haldeth became suddenly still. The whiskey in his belly no longer made him warm; reluctantly he said, "I think someone should tell me what happened with Korendir's contract in the south."

The question unnerved the sailors. Not a man would meet the smith's eyes, and the rearmost pair edged toward the longboat. Worried by their discomfort, Haldeth could not let the brig's oarsmen depart without explanation.

Quickly, the smith revised his earlier offer. "At least stay for a meal. I can let down a cask and bring victuals. We can eat here, sheltered in the lee of the longboat. Korendir won't bother you, and should your captain complain, I'll smooth his inconvenience with silver."

The tall man muttered, uncertain, but the opinion of his companions prevailed. The promise of beer and an idle hour beyond reach of shipboard discipline was too good a chance to turn down.

Overhead, the clouds had thickened to a featureless blanket. Gusts off the sea carried an edge which threatened rain. Concerned that more than weather might change against his favor, Haldeth cast an eye to the tide line; full ebb was already past, and the beach would become flooded before midafternoon. He had perhaps three hours to get four hard-living sailhands into their cups enough to talk.

The next round trip of the stair revealed that he suffered an early hangover; the pangs left by the whiskey compounded discomfort as his balled up socks galled his heels. Haldeth revised his priorities to wish Korendir and his troubles back at sea. Better, the smith might ship out with the brig for a port that had women and taverns, and leave one madman turned mercenary to suffer alone with his woes.

Except the thought of leaving Whitestorm keep somehow was not possible. Haldeth paused in a cornice cut for crossbowmen and angrily raked up his hose. For some stupid reason he regarded this Neth forsaken rock heap as home; that and misguided obligation for the freedom recovered from the Mhurgai kept him stubborn past the time a wiser man should have quit.

Never at ease with logic, the smith rolled two casks into the winch sling and lugged sausages, fresh cheese, and bread back down to the beach. By the turn of the tide, he had drunk more beer than he wished to see in a tenday of carefree celebration. Worse, the moment he stood up, he discovered himself in no condition to walk. His thoughts, in contrary obstinacy, remained disturbingly sober. The sailors had related Korendir's decimation of the Dathei; at flood tide, as Haldeth reeled his way up the stair, he desperately wished back their silence.

Only one conclusion could be drawn from the event at Erdmire Flats: Korendir had turned his addiction to risk and violence toward murder. Neth take pity on any soul who stood in his path, for in all the Eleven Kingdoms, there lived no more perilous man to cross.

Day dimmed early under drizzling veils of rain. Haldeth built a huge blaze in the hearth and nursed a headache that threatened to sear out his eyeballs from behind. He did not hear Korendir come in. His first indication of the mercenary's presence was the scrape of a softly closing door, and later, a light that burned from the upper window of the library, discovered on a routine trip to haul firewood. Haldeth stood in the open and considered, while rain slowly wet his fresh clothes. He cradled his pounding head and in the end decided to go up, but after he had brewed a tisane for his pains. In fact the remedy was an excuse. Not until after midnight did the smith finally muster up his nerve.

The entry to the keep which housed the library was neither bolted nor locked. The outside door swung easily at Haldeth's touch. The staircase beyond spiraled upward into shadow, still as the inside of a conch; the Master of Whitestorm had not troubled with lanterns. Haldeth owned no such affinity for the dark. To spare his blistered feet the added affront of stubbed toes, he fumbled the striker from his pocket and brightened the lamp on the landing.

Aside from the smith's own quarters, the library keep at Whitestorm was the only comfortably appointed suite. The stairs were laid of polished agate from Torresdyr. Oaken hand rails were chased with brass, and ended in scrolls before double doors: panels carved of ash wood, and inlaid with ebony and abalone. Haldeth raised the latch with caution. He eased the portal open and gazed into a circular chamber carpeted in scarlet and gold. Books lined the walls from floor to ceiling; these were not the spell tomes inherited from Anthei's library, but other volumes acquired between commissions and catalogued by Korendir's own hand. At a heavy table, seated between rinds of burned candles, the Master of Whitestorm lay asleep with his bronze hair spilled across a pillow of opened pages.

Haldeth crept close. Korendir's eyelids were bruised and twitching with exhaustion. The fingers curled on the chair arm were tense even in sleep. The nails were dirty, the knuckles stained dark with the tar from rope and rigging, but surprisingly fine boned beneath. Haldeth hesitated between steps. As long and as well as he knew the man, this detail had escaped him. In a strange way the oversight troubled him as much as the summary execution of the sultan's army.

When the smith observed that the print under Korendir's cheek was an illuminated stanza of verse, he seriously questioned whether the sailors' account held truth. The singlehanded slaughter of ten thousand warriors seemed impossible to attribute to a man who dreamed like any other mortal overtaken by too much care.

The mercenary and he were closer than most brothers, Haldeth would have sworn; the hardships shared at the bench had forged bonds as strong as blood kinship. The smith reached past a snarl of salt-tangled hair. In a gesture of spontaneous sympathy, he straightened crumpled cloth across a shoulder muscled like gristle.

Korendir roused screaming.

The transition happened fast, from sleep to waking nightmare. Only fatigue stayed the Master of Whitestorm's reflexes. His outcry of uninhibited terror choked back to silence in less than a fraction of a heartbeat; his surge to rend the intruder who handled his person escaped his control altogether.

Haldeth flung back. Spurred by fright, he dove in a roll for refuge under the table. Sword steel clanged and bit splinters only inches from his retreating back. The smith rammed his shoulder into a support strut. Cornered, weaponless, he twisted at bay and looked up into the face of madness.

"Korendir!" Panic split Haldeth's voice as the sword flashed again in descent.

The shout spared him.

Korendir flinched. His body shuddered in a violent spasm, then went frighteningly still. The lips drawn back into a snarl relaxed, and the mask he habitually presented to strangers twitched into place on his features.

The Master of Whitestorm drew breath after a moment, but did not sheath his steel. Instead, he regarded the gouge his stroke had left in the table leg. Hoarsely he said, "Don't ever try that again."

Haldeth sank back. Trembling himself, he uttered a dozen phrases, every one of them rude.

Korendir said nothing. Dangerously expressionless, he settled himself crosslegged on the carpet, laid the sword flat by his side, then closed his eyes and massaged his temples.

Haldeth stared at the blade, narrowed and razor thin from repeated sharpening; the edge showed inward curves where chips had been filed out, legacy of Ellgol and the wereleopards. With a pang of unwarranted regret, he recalled he had promised Korendir a new blade; yet although the smith had fashioned all manner of wrought-iron for the stables, and bolt rings and fittings for doors, not one of his creations had been weaponry. The Mhurgai had forever spoiled his concept of honorable war. Reminded that the silent man by his side was equally scarred in spirit, Haldeth said gently, "Do you want to talk?"

Korendir's head snapped up and his eyes showed a smothered flare of rage. "Not ever."

Shocked by the depths of raw savagery held in check, Haldeth pushed abruptly to his feet. He left the library without a backward look, and proceeded straight to the smithy. There, out of anger, he lit the forge fire. While rain slashed at the windows, and the winds that heralded winter raked the roof slates, he pounded out a blade. That his hangover ached in sympathy with the ringing clang of his hammer he regarded as natural justice; for on the day his wife and his daughters had died, he had vowed he would never forge weapons.

The next day, when a third and more desperate summons arrived from the King of Faen Hallir, Korendir's acceptance was immediate. Haldeth watched the mercenary's departure from the battlements. The gleam of new steel in the sheath at his companion's side failed to thaw the smith's forgiving heart.

"Neth and grief, man, what a fool I've become," he swore, then continued for ears that could not hear. "The violence of your trade has overtaken you, I'm afraid. The gold for the wizards is an excuse. Somewhere in your quest for protection you've learned to live just to slaughter."

But by then Korendir was in the boat. The war frigate which bore the royal standard carried him south across the straits, and the days shortened relentlessly. Haldeth prepared for another northern winter. He stocked the pantries and root cellar, and sent to Heddenton for bowstrings and a matched set of crockery for the table. Then he wrought andirons for the hearth in his bedroom, and forged a new chain for the stew pot. When a freak early snowstorm caught him with shutters still open in the main hall, he did not bother to shovel out the drifts. The walls had no fine tapestries to save from mildew, and it would require more than wetting to rot the boards of Korendir's bullion chests. Haldeth hunted game and made candles and wished he had patience for reading books. He once went as far as entering the library; but the titles on the shelves haunted him with memories of a companion who no longer existed, one who had split his knuckles with the stone cutters who helped carve his hearthstone, and who had not quite forgotten how to laugh. After that the ash wood doors stayed locked.

Haldeth rolled his blankets around his tools and fared north to Heddenton, where he lived two months with a sailor's doxie. His attempt to break monotony with companionship failed miserably. The girl argued like a shrew, and finally threw him out. On the street, surrounded by an untidy clutter of belongings and staring neighbors, Haldeth found himself stripped of his pocket change and also the glass ornament he had saved from the Mhurga galley. Too embarrassed to raise an outcry for the theft, he returned to the cheerless hall at Whitestorm.

On midwinter's night, a late trader braved the northern gales to deliver a contract from Tir Amindel.

Haldeth returned the packet to the sailors as if plain parchment could burn him. "The Lord of Whitestorm is south, in service to the King of Faen Hallir. Find him there, if he's needed."

Yet storms sealed the harbors soon after; the missive with its ribbons and ducal seal moldered in the brig captain's chest until spring, when ships resumed trade to the south. Haldeth tended the empty hold with an untroubled conscience. Never once did he imagine the delay might cause more than a season of borrowed lifespan for the enemies of Tir Amindel's duke.

The days lengthened and grass sprouted green over southern meadows. Still in Faen Hallir after solving a string of inexplicable assassinations, Korendir had lingered in the king's service as advisor to the royal army, which now laid siege to the holdfast of the outlaw baron who was last autumn's proven culprit. The messenger from Marbaen port delivered a battered, salt-stained packet with the sigil of Tir Amindel to the Master of Whitestorm's campaign tent.

The dwelling within its sun-whitened canvas was neat to a fault, and the blankets on the cot unwrinkled. The inhabitant was thankfully absent. The courier left his missive by the water pitcher on the clothes chest and departed from the camp in relief. Across the kingdom the rumor was whispered that this swordsman was apt to kill if his privacy was disturbed inopportunely; at the royal palace in Faen Hallir, a gravesite existed in the servant's quarter with an epitaph that lent truth to the gossip. The mercenary from Whitestorm keep might be formidably competent, but he walked the thin edge of insanity.

Korendir returned to his tent after nightfall. He noticed the document the instant he lighted the first candle. Abruptly still, one hand clenched on his sword hilt, he scoured the shadows for movement. Although nothing stirred, he failed to relax. Still gritty with dust from the field, he drew his dagger and cracked off the seals.

The message by now was months old; the outer parchment showed the wear of many pairs of hands. Inside, elaborate state language charged the Master of Whitestorm to travel to Tir Amindel, and for a period of nine months, to serve as bodyguard for the duke's infant heir. The fee for the contract was three hundred thousand coinweight in gold.

Korendir let the parchment fall on his field pallet. With barely a pause to splash water over his face, he flung on his cloak and interrupted Faen Hallir's Lord of Armies at supper.

"I need the fastest horse from the picket lines," the mercenary demanded without apology for his precipitous entrance to the command tent.

The king's officer blotted sallow lips with his napkin. By now attuned to the Master of Whitestorm's queer temperament, he reflected that at least his meat would not have a chance to grow cold. Of all men, this one never dawdled over words. "You're going, yes? What shall I tell my liege?"

Pale and unnatural in the candlelight, Korendir's eyes never flickered. "Tell him that sieges are won on careful planning and time. I've provided the first. The last is a resource I no longer have to spare."

"I see." The Lord Commander reached for his eating knife. Warned by the sudden jerk of muscles in the man who stood opposite his table, he remembered in time to slow his hand. Gifted the king's mercenary might be, but his hair-trigger wariness was a liability the camp would be thankful to miss. "Give the Lord of Whitestorm whatever mount he chooses," the Commander barked to his aide de camp.

Korendir smiled with a gratitude that was shocking for its intensity. Then he spun on his heel and left, with the aide forced to rush to attend him.

"Neth," swore the steward who served the table. "The man's insufferable."

"Effective," amended Faen Hallir's most seasoned commander. He shook out his napkin and did not say what he truly felt. The mercenary's departure was a relief; for as he judged character, the Master of Whitestorm was inherently unstable, and no man to keep under stress on the field of war.

Korendir chose a black stud with an undying streak of viciousness toward all things two-legged and human. Its meanness fuelled an energy that burned like volcano fire, sullen and tireless and hot. Aware the brute would run on its hatred until it dropped, the mercenary spurred past the encampments of Faen Hallir's royal army. Once past the siege ditches, he reined west, on direct course for the Wastes of Ardmark.

The groom and the aide who watched shook their heads; no one rode into Ardmark unless he craved death.

"Wereleopards'll do fer him," said the groom.

"Might not." The aide looked off into darkness, where the hoofbeats diminished rapidly into distance. "Might do fer the wereleopards, that one. Want to lay odds?"

The groom laughed. "Never. Wife'd skin me if I lost. And besides, I say the stud'll win out. That snake-devil of a horse will kick the head clean off the fool's neck the minute he unsaddles to take a leak."

Three mornings after Korendir's departure, a messenger in Tir Amindel's livery made hasty appearance at the command tent. His duke had learned that the prophecy which foretold harm to his child referred to no plot, but to the misfortune of fatal disease. A bodyguard would avail nothing. The rider carried a token fee for cancellation and orders to intercept the mercenary enroute.

Interrupted from parley with his field captains, the Lord Commander met the query with exasperation. "You'll overtake that one in peril of your life. The letter from your duke arrived late, so to save time he shortcut across the Wastes of Ardmark."

Tir Amindel's rider showed skepical astonishment. "Surely you jest."

The Commander shook his balding head. "Not about that man I don't. Your duke should be cautioned, if the mercenary arrives on his doorstep. Korendir is a killer pitched on a sure course for suicide. When he snaps, and he will, Neth help any living creature who happens to be caught within sword reach."

Nothing remained but to take a fresh horse and leave camp. Disinclined to risk death on the fangs of a were-leopard, the duke's rider took ship for Dethmark with his missive to Korendir undelivered.

Unseasonally fresh winds carried the messenger back to Tir Amindel before the mercenary. His report and his warning were received unhappily. Responsible for incon-venience to the most expensive mercenary in the Eleven Kingdoms, the duke understood that an act of courage undertaken in his behalf demanded reward in proportion to the risk. Whether a feat of insanity or not, Korendir's Ardmark crossing might cost the palace treasury half of the contracted fee; and since the first mention of were-leopards, the Lord of Tir Amindel had been vexed by the hunch that the madman would survive to claim his due.

The ferryman's smile showed broken teeth as he pointed toward the splendor of north keep gate. "Yon's the main entrance to Tir Amindel," he lisped proudly. "Bards say the water tries always to match it in reflec-tion, but never succeeds. They say also that the stone-work was laid by a sorcerer. Do you believe such?"

His sword hilt gripped tight in agitation, Korendir of Whitestorm offered no reply from his seat in the ferry's stern. He had seen wonders created by wizards in Tor-resdyr, and again in the court gardens of Faen Hallir. Poisoned by remembrance that some of the most beauti-ful could kill, he forced his gaze to linger over the city reputed to be the fairest in all the Eleven Kingdoms.

Tir Amindel did not disappoint; black and white spires and red slate roofs shone gilt-edged in sunlight, airy as a dreamer's painting on sky. The portals of the north keep gate splashed reflection across the landing on Kel-harrou Lake. The city towers were indeed exquisite, but uncannily, unnaturally so, like a maid possessed.

Above the stairs from the ferry dock, an avenue of flagstone invited travelers and merchants into the city. Korendir tossed the bargeman his fare. He joined the inbound traffic with a hurried stride. Accident had killed his horse; forced to cross the mountains on foot, his arrival had been impossibly delayed.

Bronze hair and gray eyes were less rare among Tir Amindel's inhabitants, but dark, unornamented clothing was unusual enough to draw notice. An informant carried word to the duke while the mercenary summoned from Whitestorm pressed through the commerce that jammed the streets.

Unaware his welcome had been retracted, Korendir asked directions at a furrier's stall. Colonnaded galleries shaded the shops on either side, topped by statues and spires, and roof peaks crowned by crystals that splintered the light into rainbows. Although at every turn, Tir Amindel's wonders begged pause for admiration, Korendir continued as though bedevilled. He threaded between the shimmering wares of the silk merchants and hurried along Baker's Lane, untempted by freshly sugared pastries or inviting smiles from the flower maids.

The squall of a kitten stopped him short.

Trapped in a culvert with sides too steep to scale, its cries echoed in piteous contrast to the laughter of some children who had abandoned their play to watch.

Korendir frowned. "I'd not treat my pet like that."

The youngest boy removed plump fingers from his mouth. He screwed up his cheeks and giggled. A girl recognizable as his sister grinned through tears of hilarity and said, "Please. Help her out. We can't reach that far."

Oddly placed as the appeal was, Korendir lacked patience to question. He dropped prone on the pavement and reached into the dank recess.

The kitten did not wait to be caught by the scruff, but seized on the chance to escape. Korendir was clawed from wrist to shoulder before he could straighten and pluck the animal from his sleeve. On his knees in a busy

street, he bit back an oath and transferred the creature
into the hands of the girl.

The child smothered a giggle in the fur of the kitten's
ruff. "Oh, thank you, sir!" As if on cue, her brother and
all of her companions burst into shrieking laughter.

Korendir rose and brushed grit from his tunic, his
brows crooked in annoyance. Tir Amindel might be fair,
but its youngsters were by lengths the rudest he had encountered anywhere. He resumed his interrupted course,
jogging to make up lost time.

No palace the breadth of the Eleven Kingdoms could
compare with the dwelling of Tir Amindel's duke. Sea-
gray marble from South Englas formed the walls, alter-
nately banded by black and gold agate from Torresdyr;
pillared embrasures held casements paned with amber
glass. The levels above were cut from quartz, with galleries and catwalks and lover's nooks set under cupolas of
silver. Lost to inadvertent admiration, Korendir was
brought back to himself by a crushing pain in his toe.
His sword was half clear of his sheath before he recovered the wits to curb his reflex.

"Your pardon, sir," said the overweight matron who
had trodden on him. Most oddly, as if she had not narrowly evaded the brunt of an armed attack, her smile
was accompanied by a throaty chuckle of amusement.

Caught at a loss, Korendir slammed his steel safely
home in his scabbard. The threat to the ducal heir was
the only concern that drove him; the eccentricities of Tir
Amindel's citizens were not his trouble to unravel. He
hastened on to the palace entrance, gave his name, and
found himself ushered down a series of vaulted passages.
Tir Amindel's artistry was not confined to facades.
Korendir strode past gilded wainscoting, his steps cush-
ioned by lushly patterned carpets. At the anteroom of
the audience chamber, a liveried steward demanded that
the mercenary surrender his weapons.

Korendir returned a scowl like a weatherfont. "That I
do only for royalty."

The steward tapped elegant fingers across the insignia
sewn on his tabard. He had been carefully instructed.
"There's crisis in this city that you have taken five
months to answer. Don't try the duke's patience with
pointless requests to change protocol."

Unwilling to set a child's life above a salve to his ruffled dignity, Korendir folded his arms. Tersely he said, "If you want my weapons, then remove every one of them yourself."

He endured, smouldering in distaste as the servant's beringed hands roved across his person and divested him of sword, daggers, and boot knife.

"Neth, you carry an armory," grouched the steward. He stepped back in patronizing scorn and rubbed his palms as if he felt dirtied.

Korendir gave the man's contempt no response, but watched to see which of several chamber pages stepped in to take charge of his blades. He committed the boy's face to memory before the great, doubled doors swung wide, and the steward whispered instructions on the etiquette of greeting Tir Amindel's duke.

The forms proved ridiculous beyond anything Korendir had suffered in audiences before crowned sovereigns. He advanced into a room grown suddenly hushed. Steady steps carried him down a parquetry aisle that extended to the stair by the dais. Guardsmen in full armor lined the approach. Their trappings were gilded and enamelled, and their tunics of patterned silk. The courtiers behind wore brocades like peacocks; beside their splendid dress, the mercenary's black stood out like blight in a flower shop.

Precisely eight paces before the dais, Korendir dropped on one knee. He remained for a slow count of ten, then rose with his head bent in deference and requested the reigning lord for permission to raise his eyes.

"Korendir of Whitestorm, you are late." The duke's basso voice held overtones of pettish annoyance.

Eyes locked on the flooring, Korendir said, "Lord, grant me grace. Wereleopards slew my mount while crossing Ardmark, and the mishap delayed my arrival."

The duke made a sound through his nose. "To battle a wereleopard is an excusable necessity. But to defer my need by adorning your boots with fur trophies was a vain and egotistical waste of time."

A flush swept upward from Korendir's collar; prepared for instantaneous action, the duke's guardsmen shifted on their toes.

But the Master of Whitestorm only raised his head.

As his gaze met and locked with that of the ruler who met him with insult, the duke was forced to conclude that the assessment of Faen Hallir's Lord Commander was in error. Nothing could be read in the mercenary's eyes but a bleakness that disallowed pride.

"My Lord," said Korendir without insolence. "As your summons required, I am here. If my service is no longer wanted, I'll accept honor gift for past hazards and depart on the next outbound ferry."

The duke returned a shout of laughter, but no merriment prompted the sound. The Lord of Whitestorm might be crazed enough to cross Ardmark, but his instabilities did not extend so far that rudeness would serve to provoke him. His reputation for fairness spanned the Eleven Kingdoms; were he dismissed without compensation, news of shabby treatment would travel with him.

The shame to Tir Amindel could not be abided.

The duke set his fists on the lions carved into his chair posts. "Your negligence has displeased me. Since I choose not to compromise honor by duelling a bastard, I hold your free will forfeit. You were summoned to protect my heir. This you will do, according to the terms of my contract, but with one change. Should my son die before midsummer's day, his loss shall be balanced with your life."

Korendir released a sharp breath. Charged by what onlookers presumed was conceit, he delivered his word to the duke. "I accept." Then he spun without regard for the halberdiers who stationed themselves at his shoulders. Caught at a flatfooted standstill, his appointed escort marched out of stride to flank him before he passed the doors.

XVI. Ithariel's Tower

In short order the mercenary found himself posted in the ducal nursery at the bedside of a comatose infant. A strained desperation marked his manner that Faen Hallir's field commander would have recognized; Korendir moved taut as an over-wound spring that threatened to snap at any instant. His weapons had not been returned. Guards stationed outside the doorway forestalled any chance to seek the page assigned to their keeping. Although he still possessed his dirk and the dagger won from Anthei's tower concealed in sheaths at each wrist, he was distraught to be left with an empty scabbard.

That placed the threat of execution in a wholly different light.

Sworn to responsibility for the survival of Tir Amindel's heir through the advent of midsummer's eve, Korendir paced and sweated, enraged at the deceit set to trap him; for the plight of the child was hopeless. Fever had wasted the boy's body. Already his complexion showed a corpse's bluish undertones, and his pulse beat weak and rapid, erratic as the flutter of a night moth.

The only soul in the palace who refused to abandon faith was the duchess. Between noon and the evening meal, the nursery doors swung wide to admit the wrinkled, squint-eyed figure of yet another herb woman. The surcoats of the guardsmen stationed in the hallway were eclipsed by the voluminous brown cloth that swathed her from head to foot.

As the panels boomed closed, the veiled woman glanced briefly at the mercenary, then crossed to the child's crib. There she conducted a busy examination, lit her portable brazier, and began mixing possets as if the boy had not already faded beyond help.

The mercenary forced to share the deathwatch resumed pacing, while the nursery filled with the crushed grass scent of aromatic herbs; whatever the woman had mixed gave off a miasma of vapors. Their effect slowed the mind and caused an overwhelming sensation of drowsiness. Korendir moved toward the casement, his intent to trip the latch and let in the breeze to clear the air. A detail made him hesitate. Beneath the cloying medicines lurked another thing, not an odor at all, but a creeping, intangible force that prickled the flesh.

Korendir checked in suspicion.

Perhaps the duke's heir suffered no natural plague, but an affliction wrought of dark spells. Enemies might wish the boy dead. Not all mages held to principles as stringent as the White Circle; herb witches existed whose loyalty might be bought, and whose potions could poison and cause illness. Korendir spun between steps and studied the healer.

Her cheek might seem sagged and wrinkled, yet her body was too well formed for a crone. From the neck downward she was youthful, a fact cleverly obscured by stooped shoulders and layer upon layer of tawdry wrappings.

Korendir hooked his fingers beneath his sleeve and carefully loosened his dirk. He crossed the carpet like a cat, clamped a hand on the witch's shoulder, and whipped the blade to her throat.

The woman did nothing but mumble a guttural phrase; yet the posset on her brazier flashed light. The smell of restoratives seared away, leaving magic like the tang of sheared metal upon the air.

Korendir's awareness unravelled into dizziness. He tried to sink his blade into falsely shrivelled flesh, but the arm that gripped the knife went numb. Both reflexes and balance forsook him. Overcome in the space of a heartbeat, he toppled to his knees. Vaguely he felt his shoulder strike the floor; the clang of his fallen weapon and the herb woman's sibilant whisper pursued him downward into dark.

"What do you know of healing, mortal man? This posset will save life at a time when naught else could avail."

Korendir fought for words, for breath, for even the smallest shred of strength upon which to frame a resistance. Yet the spell overpowered him, utterly. Lost to the duke, incapable of attending the dying heir of Tir Amindel, Korendir knew nothing as the hands of the herb witch snatched his wrists and flung his body into oblivion.

The Master of Whitestorm woke to a chamber shadowed like dusk by hangings of royal blue and silver. Fine furnishings adorned a floor of checkered agate. The view from the central carpet revealed a spread of brocade upholstery and divan legs patterned with shell inlay. The air smelled cleanly of lilacs.

Korendir reviewed these details with wariness. No clue existed to inform how he had been conveyed from the ducal nursery to this new, unfamiliar site. He lay on his side, unbound, and lighted by tiers of candles set on a stand of spindled iron.

A woman observed him from the divan. She might have been a princess; her poise was that elegantly schooled, and her beauty stunned. Inadvertently Korendir caught his breath. Had he died, he could not have freed his gaze in that moment. Robed in dark satin, adorned with pearls, she had skin as perfect as her jewels, and a face that balanced high cheekbones and brows without flaw. Auburn hair encircled her head in twisted braids. Her eyes were gray as his own and as icily devoid of sympathy.

So might a goddess appear, limned in silent mystery. Unquestionably her aspect was remote as any star that ruled the night.

The herb witch's potion left no weakness; Korendir recovered senses and memory without confusion. Although this lady was not the one who had worn the guise of healer, the mercenary held no doubt he confronted the mind behind her. He snapped his left wrist, caught his last dagger as it slid from the sheath beneath his cuff, and in a movement gained his knees.

Candleflame glanced off the knife's pitted blade, the same that Morey of Dalthern had hoped would end the Blight of Torresdyr. The steel was a fit weapon to present against a witch; one cut from its spell-tempered edge and the woman on the divan would die bleeding.

"Who are you?" Korendir demanded.

The lady inclined her head without alarm. "I am Ithariel, enchantress of the White Circle. And steel wrought by magic cannot harm me."

Her tone chased chills across his skin. Cornered by loveliness too potent to be natural, Korendir struggled to breathe. The lady's allure roused compulsion that obeyed no sane reality. Against overwhelming male instinct, he set the distrust that ran like a crack in crystal through every aspect of his being.

The enchantress spoke only words, and the dagger was all the weapon he possessed.

Ithariel sensed his disbelief. A smile crossed her lips; too swiftly for mortal reaction she sat forward and nicked her wrist across the blade.

Korendir recoiled, his gasp as her blood splashed the tile entirely involuntary and his face wracked by horror that escaped all attempt to conceal.

"You fear for nothing," Ithariel said quietly. "Raise your head and see."

The mercenary mastered his expression before he looked up. Wildly guarded, even braced as if threatened by assault, he discovered the lady's presence still taxed his concentration. She sat with her hand gripped around the wrist his blade had opened; but when she removed her fingers, only the skin was smeared red. No trace remained of the cut but a scar that faded even as he discerned its presence.

The Master of Whitestorm moved to his feet. He sheathed his dagger with a hand that trembled outright and said, "Had you deigned to do as much for a certain ailing boy, I'd be more impressed."

"If you refer to the duke's heir, there was no hope for him." Ithariel rose also. With a grace that could harrow a man's spirit, she crossed to a side table and rinsed her fingers in an ewer. The curve of the breast just visible beneath her gown shone soft and finely lustrous as her pearls.

Korendir ripped away his eyes. His groin ached. He dared not contemplate what he might feel if he touched her. Dizzied by desire, he strove to maintain detachment; she moved within layers upon rings of spells. Mortal beauty did not sear with such intensity. With every fiber of his being savaged by temptation, Korendir confronted the enchantress.

"Return me to the duke," he said finally. "If your talents cannot cure a dying boy, then my place is in Tir Amindel."

Ithariel gave him back the regard a player might hold for a chess piece. "The life that wanted saving was your own."

"Mine!" Korendir's exclamation rang loudly in the close room. "Take care how you meddle, enchantress. However unjust the circumstances, my fate at the hands of my employer is no concern of yours."

Ithariel returned a gesture of pity and contempt. "But the duke has cited your measure. You bear no lawful surname, Korendir of Whitestorm. You descend from no recognized father, and so can claim no true honor. Should your life be forfeit for an overlord's greed and a concept that doesn't exist? I say your services are better spent on another contract for me."

Hers were the scents of lilacs and rainwashed leaves. Pooled with reflected candleflame, her eyes were mist over ocean, blue gray wells of promise deep enough to drown a man; and yet the mercenary escaped her. Some indefinable nuance had pushed him just fractionally too far. Stirred by fury near to madness, Korendir waited, silent.

At last, even as Anthei before her, Ithariel was forced to concede his victory.

But unlike an earth witch, a White Circle enchantress possessed other means to manage a recalcitrant mortal. "I know you," Ithariel said. "Even to the past you never speak of. I can describe the Mhurgai who despoiled your inheritance, particularly one with a scarlet sash who—"

Korendir's chin jerked up; both hands flinched into fists. "Enough!" His bleak shout defeated her words and still he did not succumb. His frame quivered but did not explode into violence. Winded as if he had been running, and glistening all over with sweat, he spoke past whitened lips. "Whatever sordid details your sight has raked up from Shan Rannok cannot force my cooperation."

"You are a mercenary," Ithariel stated. "You'll work for a price."

She stepped around the candlestand. As if he were a caged animal, she appraised his person at a glance. "You are dressed meanly. You have lost the sword newly forged by your companion, and your horse was slain by wereleopards."

Left no expedient except false denial, Korendir followed her with his eyes. She had touched a nerve in her reference to his past; he dared not answer thoughtlessly for fear his voice might betray him.

Ithariel reached out; her slim-fingered hand spun the candlestand, and the chamber whirled with starred spokes of shadow. "Accept my bidding, and the following are yours: first, a cloak, hose and surcoat that befit your reputation."

Korendir loosed a ragged laugh. "The last witch who offered that lies dead."

"Fine clothing is least of my gifts." The candles turned above fingers that no longer seemed to move. "You shall have mail crafted by the dwarf armorers of Emarrcek. The sword and the helm forged to match shall be wrought of blacksteel, and enspelled beyond strength of mortal weapons. Thirdly, from the horse lords of High Kelair, I offer a stallion fleet enough to keep pace with a wereleopard."

Korendir's sarcasm cut through a kaleidoscopic whirl of shadows. "No horse alive can match a wereleopard."

"You doubt me?" Ithariel tossed her head, the motion like spilled ink and moonlight behind streaming tails of candleflame. "You shall rue that mistake most sorely, prideful man."

The candlestand spun faster, and yet faster still, until the chamber seemed drowned in a revolving blur. Korendir felt his eyesight wrested out of focus; hangings, walls, and enchantress dissolved like a scene distorted through shallows. Plunged headlong into giddiness, he groped for a table, a chair back, any solid object he might grab to steady himself. Yet the fingers he closed over wood passed through with less resistance than fog.

He blinked to shake off confusion. When his eyes snapped open, he stood alone.

No chamber with tapestries and candles surrounded him. His feet trod a floor transformed to the chalk-pale sands of Ardmark. The plain cloak and tunic on his shoulders stood replaced by a glittering weight of chain mail and a black and gold surcoat fit for royalty. The scabbard at his side held a sword, dark as ancient iron, and set with a topaz at the junction of quillon and grip. The fingers that had reached for the table were fisted round the reins of a gray stallion whose tail and mane blew like combed brass in the wind.

Korendir dared not pause to marvel over wonders. Magic had cast him into Ardmark with all the terror of a nightmare. Gusts snapped at his cloak hem. Overhead, the sky brewed a witch's cauldron of clouds; a storm threatened with intensity enough to drive every wereleopard in the waste out to stalk for the savage thrill of slaughter.

Korendir took to the saddle, every nerve end alive to danger. If he could reach the escarpments to the east, he would survive, as wereleopards held no tolerance for mountain altitudes.

The stallion sidled restively, then broke to a spirited trot. Korendir knotted the reins. He guided the beast with his knees and drew the black sword from its scabbard. Surely as rain, he would be attacked; around him, the first drops struck with small explosions into the dust.

The horse shied. His breath ripped through widened nostrils, and his eyes rolled rim-white with fear. Yet he did not bolt.

"Good man," Korendir crooned. He steadied his mount with a touch and sought after whatever threat the stud had sensed before him.

The wereleopard shot from a cover of briar. Its diamond-spotted pelt gleamed like gilt; green eyes turned in its tufted face and fixed on horse and vulnerable rider.

Korendir leveled the sword. Startled by a balance that seemed at one with the sinews of his hand, he revised his initial defense and decided to impale the fey killer as it sprang. But the stallion curvetted sideways. Muscle bunched under Korendir's thighs; the stud's quarters thrust like a battering ram and catapulted into a gallop.

The wereleopard swerved and matched pace. It charged at the stallion's shoulder, its fangs dripping venom.

Korendir attempted a cut. The leopard twisted sinuously aside and lost ground with a snarl.

Rain fell harder.

They raced, rider and horse in the lead, and one stride behind, the hunter coursing with narrowed eyes and a tail that streamed through clods gouged up by flying hooves.

Korendir let his mount choose direction. He gripped the
sword with his breath grown tight in his chest, and his
concentration fixed on the killer that skimmed on his
trail.

A gully yawned underfoot. The horse broke stride to
gather its hocks and jump. Given warning, the wereleopard negotiated the obstacle more smoothly. The grace of
its leap closed the gap, and immediately on landing it
sprang.

Korendir raised the sword and rammed the point down
the gaping mouth. Teeth clicked on steel and venom
sprayed droplets in the wind. Claws raked the mail-clad
wrist behind the quillons, and sound became swallowed
by the wereleopard's near-human scream. The beast fell
back, cleared the obsidian length of the blade, and tumbled in spasms upon the ground, spotted fur dulled by
clinging dirt. Blood soaked into thirsty soil until only
stains remained.

Korendir soothed his mount to a trot. He did not circle
back, but waited with his blade angled for the inevitable
retaliation that must come from the slain killer's mate.

The sky opened. Rain streamed down in torrents that
filled his eyes and drenched him. The storm closed down
in opaque curtains that interwove and shifted, and then
spun to a texture that more resembled the flickering of
candleflames.

Without warning Korendir found himself gone from
the gray's soaked saddle. Restored to the enchantress's
chamber, he shivered and realized the waxlights no
longer whirled in circles. As their flames steaded and
lengthened, he made out the form of Ithariel standing
still by the candlestand, her eyes all secretive shadows.

Yet not everything remained as before. Korendir still
wore the dwarf-mail, and a cloak that shed rainwater in
pools onto polished agate. His grip stayed glued to a
black hilted sword by runnels of his own hot blood; between the twining of realities, the wereleopard's dewclaw
had carved a gash in his wrist.

"Your experience in the wastes was quite genuine,"
Ithariel ventured across silence. "Give me your service,
and the fine things you sampled shall be yours."

Korendir's head jerked up. His look went flat as
drenched slate and his manner radiated fury. "I've al-

ready refused. Did you think if you toyed with me I'd submit?"

Ithariel sighed. She spun precipitously away, and something about her seemed to shrink. At first Korendir assumed she wrought another spell; but when she looked back to him, she showed a face very human with chagrin. Immediately he realized she had dispensed with the glamour that made her irresistible.

Small things became visible that the potency of magic had obscured. She was small, fine-boned to the edge of fragility. Her chin had a dimple. The hair folded into its braid gleamed russet, too heavy for the constraint of jewelled pins; and the skin like perfect pearls was rosy now, as if touched to a blush by wind. Korendir stared, lost in admiration that no amount of spellcraft could achieve. Ithariel in her natural state was stunningly, immediately real, and he found himself challenged on a front he had no resource left to guard.

His breath bound up in his throat. Desperation warred with longing, and his mind tangled in a morass of ancient fears.

Yet the enchantress failed to detect his turmoil. Caught up in embarrassment of her own, she said, "Regretfully, I seem to have misjudged. By the accounts, I would have thought the reputation matched the man." She ended with a glance that searched in a manner quite terrifying for its mildness.

Korendir blocked her by turning aside. Prepared to lash back in self-defense, he was set off balance by the presence of a being who perhaps might consent to be reasoned with. Afraid to expose his vulnerability, he sought the ordinary and raised his arm to sheath his weapon.

Ithariel noticed his bleeding. "Oh, Neth, what a nuisance, you seem to have gotten yourself hurt." She crossed to his side, confidently prepared to have a look.

Korendir's uncertainty coalesced to immediate reflex. The black sword whipped up to fend her off.

Ithariel stopped. She went very suddenly white and her brows gathered into a frown. "Put that up, foolish man. Do it fast, or I'll be forced to consign a very treasured artifact to oblivion."

Korendir turned the hand that held the sword. His

eyes mirrored the reflections that skittered like sparks
down the blade. "Does that matter, since I've refused
your offer?"

The enchantress repressed an obvious impulse to
stamp her foot. "It matters," she said, and then qualified. "You seem more particular than most, but find the
right price, and all men can be bought."

"After I've finished my contract with the duke,"
Korendir snapped. "Then, only then, we'll talk price."

"Your contract with the duke will kill you." Daunted
by what seemed blind obstinacy, Ithariel showed exasperation. "The blade is yours for blood debt, if you like.
But only if you care for that gash."

To a swordless man who harbored an extreme aversion
for being touched, the offer meant safety. Korendir
stepped back. He perched upon the far cushion of the
divan, propped the weapon at his elbow, and tried to
peel back the mail. The cuff proved too snug and the
setback left him strained. He needed to strip off the
armor, and that could not be accomplished without stain-
ing a surcoat that at all costs must be returned.

The surly glance he directed toward Ithariel made her
laugh in genuine delight. She might have restored his
worn tunic, yet chose not to on feminine principle. If he
wished to stand on pride, let him continue on penalty of
extreme inconvenience. While Korendir slipped the cloak
fastenings and wrestled one-handed with laces, she seated
herself on his far side, the sword like a warning between.

Her bribe of fine velvets presently lay discarded on
the floor. Shimmering dwarf-mail joined them, jingling
unceremoniously in a heap that left the fabric crushed
flat with wet. Korendir wormed free of the linen gambe-
son beneath, then shredded the quilted sleeve to use for
bandaging. Seeing he would wrap his hurt in damp rags
without doctoring, Ithariel fetched him the ewer of water
and an herb paste from her chest for a poultice.

Korendir fought back apprehension as she resumed her
place beyond the sword. Stripped to the waist, with the
brand and the whip marks from the Mhurgai and all of
the wounds from past forays written in scars on his flesh,
he felt the enchantress's scrutiny like an unwanted physical caress.

"You've led a harsh existence," she observed critically.

Korendir knotted the linen with a savagery held back from his speech. "If you're sorry, don't burden me further."

Absorbed and edgy, his bronze hair left sleeked by the rain, Korendir finished his field bandage. While his attention was marred by the discomfort of his wound, Ithariel stole the interval for study. Her findings startled her. Absent was the reckless ego of the mercenary adventurer she had pictured. In their place, the enchantress read intelligence, sensitivity, and yearning overlaid by desperate control. Though his flesh told a history of strife, nothing else about the man who named himself Whitestorm confirmed the destruction and death that shaped his trade.

As if he sensed her probe, Korendir looked up. He caught her moment of unschooled surprise, then the sharp calculation which followed. Plainly she would set her next snare to find what in the spectrum of human desires might move him.

That above everything he must keep from her. The survival of his integrity depended upon it.

A smile like a twist of bitter iron touched his lips. He owned no defense against magic; trapped without recourse, he resorted to viciousness and tried an unthinkable countermove. When her enchantments reached to pry out his inner secrets, Korendir abandoned resistance.

Ithariel attacked with every power at her disposal sharpened for a fight that never happened.

His barriers against her parted with little else but irony for warning. Backed by full measure of her White Circle powers, her consciousness flung downward into Korendir's mind far deeper than she intended. The spell that should have framed his surface thoughts to reveal what motivated his stubbornness turned like a snare against her.

Instead the conflicts which comprised the man closed like a shackle around her.

Lost beyond all self-awareness, Ithariel plunged into emotional mazes for which magic held no remedy. Lost beyond escape, she cried out; and her scream became that of a boy hammered down by the flat of a blood-crusted cutlass. . . .

*   *   *

Smoke scorched his nostrils; helplessly he struggled and kicked, but the hands of his enemies dragged him upright. Yapping, guttural victory cries rang in his ears as Mhurgai raiders shoved him between the shoulderblades. He skidded, weeping curses, and sprawled on a carpet sodden scarlet from the slaughter of Shan Rannok's men at arms.

The same hands that had butchered them tied him there, with silken cords torn from the draperies.

"That one's the son, yes?" snapped a swarthy man with slit eyes. He wore diamond earrings, and a robe sewn with peacock's plumes and belted with a crimson sash.

Korendir choked as a kick slammed his belly. Retching, half-killed with misery, he spat bile and found his voice. "Don't listen to what they say. I'm not. Her heir is buried behind the orchard." Another blow smashed his mouth. Through split lips he continued. "Read the stone. Says husband's firstborn. Son."

The man in the sash scowled sourly. "Listen to him, thou!"

But the raider captain was not cowed. He pressed his boot on the boy's face to crush back the words that discredited him before his overlord. "This is the heir, Lord Exalted. A bastard, to the widow's shame. We tortured a serving maid to find out."

The boy wrenched his head to one side. He coughed blood. "Della lies."

"Not with her belly slit open and the first marshal raping her silly, she would not." The Mhurga captain grinned. "She screamed plenty, and she talked, while he spilled her soft guts round her thighs."

"She did not speak truth," said a clear woman's voice from one corner. An aged lady sat there, with straight features and a straighter back, and eyes that stared only ahead. She was blind. "The boy you abuse is no bastard of mine, but a fosterling."

Korendir groaned. He tried weakly to push to his feet, but the seamen who had beaten him pinioned his wrists.

The man with the crimson sash regarded the lady and smiled. "Bastard or not, pretty grandmother, we're going to make him watch. Thine heir must learn what thy husband would not: Mhurgai never fail to exact reprisal for attacks upon our homeland."

Korendir screamed in animal rage and tried to rise from the floor. His captors called more men to hold him, and though he closed his eyes and threw up and bit the fingers which forced his bleeding head straight, still he failed to escape.

The sounds of shredding cloth and the screams of the widow who had raised him tore into his ears and brought madness. . . .

Madness which had no ending, only memories like doors that opened on unmitigated horror.

Korendir's intent had been that the violence in his past would repulse the enchantress's invasion of his mind. For that he had yielded to insanity, and for that purpose only had he unleashed his recall of the obliterating defeat at Shan Rannok. But the effort backlashed, frighteningly; the event served only to wrench Ithariel's spellcraft from control. Overwhelmed, unable to separate herself from her victim's awareness, she became helplessly entangled in memories that savaged her like nightmares. . . .

Korendir was ten. He punched a rough boy who called the lady street names, and claimed that a stablehand was her lover, *his father*, and his birth a shame that a lady's charitable ways could never absolve. The brute said this of the widow, faded to gentleness by her sorrows, who grew flowers in a hothouse for the grave of her departed husband; the same lord who left to fight Mhurgai and returned to Shan Rannok within a sack, in pieces.

While Korendir and his tormentor pummelled each other with brute determination, the enspelled spark of consciousness that was Ithariel twisted this way and that, blind as a fish in a net. She lashed out and evaded the episode but did not recover herself.

Instead she reeled on to another place of black leaves and moonlight; felt *his* hand on a knife, while hot blood coursed in a gush that meant death over *his* knuckles that must not shake. The victim beneath the blade was a gut-wounded farmer whose family would not see him home from the woods. Three daughters named Mallie, Nessie, and Tesh; and Korendir's tearing anguish and

awe of a dead man's courage that humbled him helplessly
to tears. *He* could not do as Vwern, not ever in life risk
his safety with pretty young children dependent. . . .

And yet he killed; fast and ugly, mostly, because he
could not endure to witness pain.

The Mhurgai had scarred him that way: *the widow who
had raised him, tormented to her death in old age, forced
by an evil sea raider to partner an act shared only in love
with her husband. And then that same act repeated, with
the blade of a Mhurga knife.* Her screams and her agony,
and the flames and the screams of ten thousand warriors
tortured Korendir's days, unrelenting. Because suffering
itself was unthinkable; thumbless, tongueless slaves and
babies feeding vultures on battlements were unthinkable,
*and so the Datha burned. Perhaps the widows who sur-
vived after conquest might raise sons who would never
again inflict atrocities upon others.*

The sequence of memories seemed unending and every
one of them lacerated.

A duke defied for the sake of an infant in peril; *another, a tavern girl with large hands he had left, because
she had tempted him with sweet innocence and a trust that
made him sick with the resurgence of fear.* Terror founded
the worst of his faults, made him flee to fight wereleopards. Because death by fey killers alone in the dark was
easier, *easier,* than loving a girl without any wall to defend her.

There were no safe havens, no crannies of conscience
that did not sting. Carralin died in his bed, in his absence, her hopes ripped out with her throat. Korendir
had survived the brother's vengeance in the caves of Ellgol, because in pitting his sword against wereleopards,
he did not have to think; each cat slain meant one more
frightened girl might be spared.

Ithariel sampled the bitterness, the futile grief, and
every step made in purest terror. She shared Korendir's
split knuckles as he dressed gray granite into blocks for
the bastions at Whitestorm. She lived his dreams, and
could not endure them. Left no awareness beyond an
agonized instinct to flee, she doubled back to seek harbor
in the eddyless oblivion of the womb.

There, tucked like a frightened rabbit in the heart of
a half-formed fetus, she remembered her one true name.

Control returned to her scourged and battered spirit. Her magic was blunted with weariness, and drained spells clung like cobwebs over her innermind. Yet before she engaged the sequence that would key her back to consciousness, her detached enchantress's intuition uncovered a thing unknown to the man himself.

She saw a forgotten place from his infancy, bleak with smoke and battle and the shadowed, hideous shapes of creatures never born upon Aerith. There a man in bleeding armor handed an infant wrapped in blankets to a servant poised by a postern.

"Take him, and swear to me, *swear!* Never tell anyone who his parents are. If you do, that knowledge will bring his death."

The servant reached out, weeping as though his heart would break. And as the father handed over the bundle that wrapped his son, his face showed briefly by lantern light. Gray eyes, he had, and russet hair; Ithariel saw the device on his surcoat, and recognized at once who he was.

Then the man stepped back into darkness. "Go," he said gruffly to the servant. "Keep faith, and may the blessing of my gratitude reward you for as long as our lives may last."

XVII. Majaxin's Revenge

Ithariel fought through exhaustion and found the spark of conscious will needed to disperse her misfired spell. She opened her eyes to the chamber she had always known as home, but which would never again seem the same.

Her eyes streamed tears. The pins had somehow slipped from her hair, and the russet length of her braid unwound itself over her back. She had sought the key to a man's will, and instead, become heir to suffering which shattered peace. Comfort did not exist to ease the scars of such experience; the memory could only be abided.

She wondered whether she would scream, as Korendir continually feared he might, when the nightmares broke her dreams as she slept.

Her shoulders shook with emotions she could not escape. Never until now had she guessed how perfectly suited this adventurer was for the task she had chosen him to undertake. The irony cut that she might have spared herself pain and asked openly, and won his willing assistance. Now simplicity became complicated by the haunted turn of mind that made him stubborn; also, though he could not know, by the stolen secret of his paternity.

Ithariel of the White Circle wept, having tasted his measure of despair.

That moment, she noticed the hands that steadied her; their warmth cradled her back and one pearl-draped, silk-clad shoulder. At some point, the black sword had gone; he had set it aside to rise and stand by her. She looked up into eyes that mirrored all the horrors of hell, and in them found a compassion that against all credibility still endured.

The shock of discovery undid her; in all the Kingdoms

of Aerith, he alone could count her sorrows, both those newly inherited, and ones of her past she had summoned him in hope to absolve. Ithariel bent her head and collapsed, tear-blind against the hollow of his throat. "Cruel man, what have you done?"

His arms moved, folded her into an embrace that promised the patience of ages. "Compounded an error of judgment, it would seem." He worked a twist from her braid and smoothed down the loosened ends. "I intended no worse than to keep your spells from my mind."

Not to have forced her to share every waking horror he had meticulously kept hidden from every man, Ithariel knew too well. She had seen behind his reserve; his present calm was possible only because he had nothing in him left to hide. She had sounded his depths and partaken of the sick fear that drove him repeatedly into risk. Limp against him, her cheek pressed to scars left by swordcuts and slave whips, she listened to the beat of his heart. Korendir's hands on her back were steadier by far than his nerves.

For all that, he was first to ask his will of her. "Ithariel, return me to the duke."

His resumption of a principle that could only end by killing him bespoke something deeper than obstinacy. Disrupted from pursuit of understanding by a surprising sting of resentment, Ithariel pulled back from his touch. "Did you think I called you without purpose?"

He sat back on his heels, hands draped lightly over his thighs. The motive behind his insistence by now lay hidden as he said, "Whatever it is, I must refuse."

Ithariel rose. Hair fell dark as poured wine over her collarbones as she stepped on light feet to the candlestand. There, with her hands braced on cold iron and the eyes he could not see closed to dam a desperate flood of tears, she spoke. "Would you go without hearing my terms?" And she named them, though to do so was cruelest betrayal.

"Korendir of Whitestorm, undertake a single task for me, and I will grant the capstone of tallix crystal you desire to complete your stronghold. The ward imprinted within shall hold your granite firm through battle, quake, flood, and fire, even should the sea rise up, or the sun

change course from west to east. That is the prize for
my contract. Will you accept?"

Ithariel sensed movement, but dared not look around.
His boots clicked deliberately on stone floor, one step,
two; then she heard nothing at all. She need not see his
face to know the intense, ungovernable longing her offer
had loosed in his heart. The capstone he had dreamed
of could only be obtained through an appeal to the White
Circle; a boon for which no coin might bargain. Now the
vision he had labored, killed, and nearly lost his mind to
achieve was being offered in reward for a single service.

The silence stretched on. The musty wool smell of tapestries hung on the eddyless air. "What do you ask of
me?" Korendir's voice sounded lifeless, resigned to inevitable surrender.

Ithariel tightened her grip until wrought-iron ridged
her palms and every knuckle went white. She took a
breath. Candleflame shimmered in reflection over the
pearls at her neck as she said, "Destroy Tir Amindel and
the ward crystal you desire is yours."

Without warning his hard fingers caught her. He broke
her hold and spun her around in a whirl of fallen hair.
She glimpsed ice in his eyes before her last loop of
braid slipped free and veiled her vision. But his rage
remained evident in his speech, threatening as steel
across whetstone.

"Am I a child, to be coaxed with a promise of bright
stones? Destroy Tir Amindel! Gut the fairest work of
architecture in all of Aerith in trade for the immortality
of my miserable refuge? Lady, I have a price, but none
great enough to buy that feat. Return me to the duke.
Better I die for his wretched pride than perpetuate the
brutality that burned Shan Rannok."

Ithariel did not answer; could not, for the measure of
his sacrifice ceded to her the most deeply dishonorable
choice.

The man she had outraged could not know this. He
shook her, not gently, and her hair flung back to reveal
tears that had nothing to do with the pain in him. She
understood, to a fine point, precisely what she had asked;
she also had her reason. "Who was the builder of Tir
Amindel?" she demanded with sudden sharpness.

Taken aback, Korendir regarded her. "The sorcerer,

Majaxin, if the King of Faen Hallir's archives say truly."
His hands bit a shade less harshly into her flesh. "But
the transgressions of major enchanters are not the concerns of a man. Let the White Circle attend to their
own."

The rage in him remained; his eyes stayed guarded and
his mouth turned down like a cleft chiseled into rock.
He would see his dream die before he changed his mind,
Ithariel understood. She had no avenue left except to
appeal to his integrity, and that was going to cost.

"White Circle enchanters are the only powers on Aerith who are incapable," she said on a note of regret. She
moved against the pressure of his hold and this time he
let her go. "Have you ever heard of the Six Great
Banes?"

Korendir backed off. He set his shoulders against the
wall in a gap between paired tapestries. On his left, an
armored knight addressed a lady veiled in sorrow; to his
right, a hunter pursued a wounded stag. If he played the
part of the deer, Ithariel reflected, the images were apt;
his nature was his weakness. At some point, he had recovered the black sword. It rested in the sheath at his
hip, and his hand traced the grip as if each passing minute
abraded his nerves, but he was listening. "You'd better
explain."

The fate of the moment was upon her; too late the
enchantress wished she could back away. "What I'm
about to relate is unknown beyond the White Circle."

Ithariel paced to the opposite side of the chamber,
opened a drape, and stared beyond at the night sky and
stars. Her voice resumed, deadened by the hangings.
"You're a well-read man, but the Banes of the mages
are not written out in any archive. They are spoken by
rote only, and they name the perils that enchanters cannot encounter without ruin. Three reside within Aerith,
and three within the otherworld of Alhaerie."

Here another adventurer might have questioned, or
raised protest that a thing accursed to wizards might offer
greater risk for a man of mortal birthright. Korendir
spoke only to offer insight of his own. "The Mathcek
Demons must be one such peril."

Jolted by his chance irony, Ithariel nodded. "Since the
fall of Morien at Alathyr, yes. He was a fully invested

Archmaster, but his powers availed nothing. His Council Major perished with him. The second Bane is Querstaboli, the water elemental which lairs in the isles off Emarrcek. The last, to our sorrow, is Tir Amindel."

No move and no sound came from Korendir.

His silence lent her courage.

Fixed in her purpose as the stars beyond the casement, Ithariel told of Majaxin, whose obsession for beautiful things had led him to infamy and exile. Most powerful of wizards, his last vengeance against the White Circle which disowned him was the abduction of the Archmaster's daughter, then sixteen, and her father's dearest pride. Majaxin had imprisoned her in a cave on the edge of Sithmark, and ward over her was the greatest tallix crystal ever mined.

Here Ithariel caught an edge of the curtain and worried it between her hands. "Eriel bore Majaxin a son and a daughter. She died two years later from sorrow and abuse, and though her fate was kept secret for close to a decade, the White Circle enchanters heard. They moved against her murderer. Majaxin was betrayed into capture by the designs of his own son." Velvet crushed and smoothed and crushed again between the enchantress's fingers. "Although the boy's actions were just, he was never so brave. He took his own life in remorse. Majaxin stood trial, and was fairly sentenced to death."

Ithariel released the crumpled curtain, aware that if she continued her voice would break. As she strove to restore her composure, the set of her back must have alerted Korendir. She did not hear his approach, but started slightly as warm hands closed over her shoulders.

Gently he turned her around. He saw the tears that ran down perfect cheekbones, to splash and scatter droplets through her pearls. He spoke no word, but cradled her head against his chest until she steadied enough to continue.

Ithariel told of the code of redemption, which lawfully allowed the condemned a final act of good will to temper his history of crime. Majaxin built Tir Amindel. The city was offered as a home for all he had wronged, but in the inspired genius of its beauty, he wove a bleak geas of bane. Any White Circle enchanter to enter there became trapped, never to leave, never to die.

Cold in the circle of Korendir's embrace, Ithariel ended her tale. "A crystal laid in the cellars of the ducal palace compels their lives to felicity. You have walked the streets of Tir Amindel. You'll recall a people without grief, or anger, or peace. Laughter and smiles were the only expressions you observed, though tragedy or offense might ache the heart. You must also have guessed the worst, that although the original inhabitants live on to a weariness of days, their offspring do not. They bear and die as mortals do, but deprived of natural emotions."

Ithariel straightened in Korendir's arms. Her face had lost its control. "Majaxin was my father," she said, knowing understanding would tear through the mercenary like a knife.

The enchantress slipped clear of his hands. He allowed her, attuned to her need for private grief; what he had no means to guess was the disastrous potential for risk that she invoked by involving him.

Yet without his singular talents, hope died. No other in Aerith could aid her. Ithariel raised her head, stared at stars, and stated her final plea. "If the tallix crystal is shattered, the city will fall. Even now, the duchess and her husband laugh hysterically over the corpse of a little boy. They suffer most cruelly without tears. Tir Amindel is the last and greatest of my father's sins. I beg you to bring it down, to break Majaxin's banespell and set the inhabitants free."

Sunlight shone kindly over the city of Tir Amindel; it glanced in starred rays off crystal-tipped spires, and burnished stone bastions against a backdrop of glowering cloud. Korendir of Whitestorm adjusted with a sailor's ease to the heave of the ferry that battled the chop on Kelharrou Lake. A windblown figure in black, he studied the city skyline. Where another man might be reluctant to believe that hostility could motivate such artistry, the mercenary chose without regret. Tir Amindel would fall, swiftly and cleanly as a blossom razed by the scythe.

Ithariel had warned that the tallix which guarded the city's geas might unleash perils upon any who interfered with it; beyond that she could not qualify. All Korendir possessed against the sorceries of Majaxin was a sliver of spell-crystal imbued with every protection in Ithariel's power; the jewel hung from his neck on a length of braided chain. Against the wrath of the duke, she left him the mail from Emarrcek, and the stallion that had matched a wereleopard's speed. The bright surcoat Korendir had refused, out of preference for his threadbare black.

Clouds veiled the sun and smothered the rainbow refractions atop Tir Amindel's bright towers. Gusts from the east blew heavy with rain, and whitecaps smacked the ferry at the waterline, threading fingers of foam across her decks.

"Mean looking squall," observed a gaudily dressed merchant who parked his bulk against the rail. Mistaking the mercenary for a courier, he added, "If you're looking to keep dry in comfort, there's a tavern on the harness maker's street that serves a decent stew."

Korendir returned a taciturn shake of his head. His hand strayed an unfriendly inch closer to his sword hilt, and taking the hint, the merchant edged away. "Must have a message that won't wait," he remarked to the master at the helm.

The boatman spat into the wake. "That one don't carry dispatches. An' storms from the east hold off for no man's comfort."

His gloomy assessment proved true. The sky opened up as the barge reached the landing; icy, whipping torrents chased across the dock as the crew warped the craft to the bollards. The mercenary minded the storm not at all, though water trickled down his neck and wrists and soaked him instantly to the skin. Guards hunched in discomfort on the battlements would be less than watchful, and folk would not linger in the streets. Korendir's second arrival at Tir Amindel would be noticed not at all, which suited his purpose. He paid his fare and left the barge, the boom of shod hooves as his stallion crossed the pier mingled with thunder from the sky.

Korendir mounted and rode beneath the filigree that framed the north keep arch. Spires that had patterned the sunlight with such elegance now sang harmonic intervals as the wind played across them, shifting pitch when caught by an occasional gust from the north. Water cascaded into downspouts and spewed from the mouths of gargoyles. The streams crossed and re-crossed, caught

into arcs by gravity and genius for as long as the downpour might linger. Tir Amindel under cloudburst sur-
passed the renowned court of fountains engineered for
the King of Faen Hallir. Fighting the rein astride his
restive stallion, the mercenary sworn to destroy the city's
banespell found urgency impossible.

Since Majaxin had set his crystal in the deepest chamber of the duke's palace, an official would have to be
bribed or coerced to reveal the way to the lower dungeons. Korendir carried gold and weapons in readiness
for either expedient.

He passed through a tunnel between two warehouses.
Deafened by rain and the clang of steel-shod hooves,
Korendir almost missed the child.

A flare of lightning revealed her, crouched with her
arms around her knees. Wet hair clung in tangles to raggedly clothed shoulders. Though shivering from the cold,
her body remained convulsed in a fit of hysterical laughter. She was scarcely nine years of age.

Without a second's thought, Korendir reined in the
gray. He dismounted, slipped off his cloak, and tucked
it around the shaking child. "Are you lost?"

The girl raised tearless eyes. "No."

As his vision adjusted to the gloom, Korendir saw she
was a street child, most likely a pickpocket and a market
thief; but her hunger and her suffering were no less real
for that. He pressed a gold piece into her fingers and
promised her another if she could tell him of an unguarded access to the duke's palace.

The child flipped the weight of the gold, jammed it
down the cuff of her filthy shift, and returned a description of a grating beneath the west wing archway. The
iron was rusted, and with a bit of effort the palace cellars
might be entered from there.

The cloak had begun to warm her; the girl's limbs shivered less wretchedly, and a little color flushed her
cheeks. Korendir straightened up and flicked the reins
over the gray's crested neck. "Watch my horse till I return," he said kindly. "I promise you then that I'll find
us a tavern with a fire that sells hot soup."

The girl accepted with eagerness. That her enthusiasm
might not be honest caused Korendir little concern. The
stallion was the gift of an enchantress; by nature such

things tended to look after themselves. Mostly, he wished to keep the child occupied lest she become tempted to sell knowledge of his intent to the duke's men-at-arms before his entry to the cellars was accomplished.

From a lamplit alcove in her tower, Ithariel of the White Circle watched Korendir's progress through a seeing crystal in a polished oval frame. Her hair was caught back with pins like stars, and her eyes were still raw from weeping. She noted Korendir's fixed frown as he ducked beyond sight of a merchant who braved the storm on an errand. The fact that the mercenary achieved that scowl inside the city walls was significant.

A comment of Orame's had first led her to suspect that the Master of Whitestorm's rare coloring arose from an inheritance of enchanter's blood. But since the man believed himself to be mortal, Majaxin's curse found no foothold. As the audience with the duke had established, Korendir's unschooled powers did not hear the siren spells that made Tir Amindel ruinous to the mageborn.

Korendir was half-bred, Ithariel had presumed, until a moment forgotten from childhood had shown the truth. Now, her conscience ached for an action unforgivably wrong. Knowing, she had sent him through Tir Amindel's gates a second time, into peril more dire than he possibly understood. She had witnessed the hidden proof within his past: the nameless mercenary from Whitestorm descended from a line as pure as her own.

He was White Circle, and legitimate, and if his talents were presently smothered behind ignorance, his immunity to Tir Amindel's geas would be lost in the instant he moved against the crystal. The wards engendered in the tallix that ruled the Sixth Bane would recognize his birth, and exact immediate retribution.

A mortal would die in simple agony. Korendir, untrained, would call down upon himself the wrath of a condemned wizard's vengeance. The nature of his torment could not be guessed, but in all Aerith, he was perhaps the only being who owned enough resilience to cope. He alone stood a chance to unmake a prison that otherwise might endure throughout eternity.

Ithariel cupped her scrying crystal closer as the swordsman moved through the rain and took cover beneath the archway described by the beggar child. Flesh would not forget the gentleness of his touch; branded in mind and memory was the understanding that had backed his resolve as he accepted her burden of care.

The words spoken then still haunted. *Lady, be at peace. If a man can break Majaxin's crystal, the feat will be done by sundown on the day I pass the gates.*

But quietude had gone before the hoofbeats of the stallion had faded from the glen. Too late, in distressing regret, Ithariel of the White Circle wondered if the value of the man by himself did not outweigh final end to her father's atrocities.

While the step of a sentry passed beyond sight of his niche, Korendir knelt before a grille-covered window set into the palace foundation. Improper drainage had rusted the bottom palings nearly through. Korendir unfastened his swordbelt. He hung the straps from his shoulder, lowered himself into the aperture opposite the fitting, and with his back braced and his fingers clenched to the weapon across his chest, kicked the damaged iron with both feet. Flakes of corroded metal pattered downward into darkness; a second blow broke the grate through, and a slither and a twist of black-clad shoulders saw Korendir through the gap.

He hung by his hands from the sill and tried to assess his surroundings. The air was dusty and still; the storm-silvered light from the archway proved too weak to illuminate the depth of the space beneath dangling feet. The step of an approaching guardsman cancelled any chance to experiment by dropping pebbles.

Korendir could only escape by letting go. As his stomach turned with the plunge, he hoped the cellar underneath did not house an armory, with a racked sheaf of javelins waiting upright to impale him.

Korendir's fall ended with a slam and a grunt on a pyramid of stored barrels. The stack parted with a grinding, throaty boom as wine tuns cascaded to either side. Jostled like a twist of cloth in a log jam, Korendir was delivered to the floor, while the duke's casks of claret, brandy, and table wines rolled on to wreak havoc. Stores of fine spirits were milled to slivers. The crack and splinter of wood, and an unending tinkle of glass, heralded destruction until the bass rumble of the last rolling tun thudded to a tangle of snapped staves.

Korendir shouldered clear of an unbroached cask. He stood upright, reproached on all quarters by the gurgle and drip of spilled wealth. Unwilling to see how the racket set loose by rolling barrels would be received by the sentry above the grate, he refastened his baldric, then set out through darkness to find the door.

The air smelled of spirits and dust. Glass slivers grated beneath Korendir's boots. Smashed shelves made incautious movement unwise. After several false starts and minutes of blind fumbling, the mercenary located a portal. He considered searching the wreckage for a nail to pick the lock, when a flicker of illumination through the keyhole warned him back.

Someone with a lantern paused in the corridor outside.

Korendir grinned in the darkness. Soldier or steward, someone had arrived to check the disturbance in the wine stores.

Metal clanked and the door opened. The wedge-shaped flare from the lantern picked out a burst barrel, sparkles of shattered glass, and split shelving marinated everywhere with spirits.

"Neth's everlasting martyrs!" swore the arrival, a steward who stalked across the threshold with the raddled gait of a shore bird.

A sentry followed on his heels, redolent of sweat and soaked wool surcoat, and armed with a rain-wet halberd.

Korendir timed his rush. He struck with the butt of his knife and the sentry buckled, incapacitated. The mercenary caught the man's polearm before its dropped blade clanged warning against the lintel.

The steward flung backward, too late to avoid the studded haft of the halberd that hammered the backs of his knees. He collapsed, his cry of surprise cut off as hands caught him and a chilly line of steel constricted his larynx. Too terrified to swallow, he gagged and shrank against his assailant to escape the kiss of the knife.

Korendir spun his catch out of the corridor and yanked him back to his feet.

"I suppose you're the man proclaimed renegade by the duke," the steward gasped. Although the lantern trembled in his grasp, he had not lost his wits and dropped it. He cleared his throat. "However much you threaten, I cannot help you escape. My lord has halberdiers flanking every door and window in the palace. They know your description. If you kill me, you'll die. If you release me, you'll be equally dead. Give some thought to the subtleties, for my sake, desperate sir, and I promise I won't tell where I saw you for an hour."

Korendir held his blade to the servant's sweating flesh. "If the sentry I knocked down told his captain where he went, an hour of grace is no bargain."

"He mistook you for a thief," shrilled the steward. "A misfortune, now that you've killed him. His captain will call for a search."

Korendir shoved his knuckles into his captive's windpipe. "Shutter the lantern and be quiet."

The sentry regrettably was not dead; only stunned, and if he did not drown himself by inhaling spilled wine, he would waken in time and raise the garrison. As the servant groped and the lantern went dark, Korendir searched the man's livery. He removed the one penknife he found, shoved the fallen halberdier aside, and maneuvered his victim into the corridor. "Lock up," he instructed curtly. "Then guide me down to the dungeon."

The steward fumbled to sort keys and in the process burned his knuckles on the lantern. Korendir smothered his cry with ruthless fingers. Unable to move, even to lick his seared skin, the servant's plaintive nature got the better of him. He whined the instant he recovered liberty enough to breathe. "Neth, man, why the dungeons? There are rats down there, and not a cranny that'll do for escape."

Korendir's blade jerked and nicked flesh.

The proper key was procured with a jangle, and the steward moaned, "Go left."

With his captive locked in the crook of his elbow, the mercenary marked footprints in claret the length of the duke's lower service corridor.

He moved soundlessly, which disappointed the steward, who hoped a disturbance might call down a rescue. Korendir cracked the lantern only to make certain his charge did not guide him in false circles. At last, after descent of a spiral stair, the pair arrived in the deserted passage that joined the inquisitor's torture chamber with the cells reserved for condemned prisoners. There the air hung dank, stale with the odors of urine and moldy straw.

Encouraged that he had not yet been murdered, the steward twisted against his pinioned neck. "I've served in good faith," he pointed out.

Korendir said nothing. Aware of a throb of heat in the jewel beneath his shirt, he had already surmised that truth. His knife hand lifted and moved. The servant found himself released as the mercenary took the lantern from him and gently slipped back the shutters.

Flamelight revealed a five-sided nook with only one doorway. The walls were bare granite. But a looping figure carved in the floor held a great, cloudy crystal set flush at the center. Its heart glistened like scarlet veined fire as a thousand underlying facets caught the light.

"Your reason for coming here puzzles me," the steward confessed. "This is the traitor's cell. A man held for any length of time in this place loses his sanity. Though that point is likely a moot one, in your case."

Korendir volunteered nothing. The pattern indeed had a presence, one that was creepingly unpleasant. As he stared at the spell-shot tallix, he felt as if insects too tiny to see clawed for entry through the pores of his skin. Absorbed, even thoughtful, the mercenary set down the lantern.

In the moment while he seemed preoccupied, his erstwhile captive seized advantage. The steward fled through the doorway, spun, and in ungainly haste jerked a grille from a slot to one side. The steel rattled closed. A bar clanged down and trapped Korendir within.

The duke's servant heaved a sigh of overweening relief, then asked, "What possessed you to ask for the traitor's cell? My lord will see you screaming before you die."

XVIII. Trial and Judgment

If the spoken threat of torture left an impression on Korendir's awareness, he showed no reaction. Neither did the prospect of captivity appear to trouble him. The tallix within the traitor's cell absorbed him totally as he exchanged the knife in his hand for another, uglier blade, all pitted and stained with age. Left curious by his detachment, the wine steward lingered in the corridor.

Korendir shifted grip on his dagger, then knelt at the pattern's center. Ruddy light touched his face; not caused by lantern flame, but by some refracted brilliance cast back from the crystal beneath. Magic lurked there, a coiling malevolence that flurried the mind with doubt. With tentative care, the mercenary touched his steel to the axis of Tir Amindel's wardstone. A tingle of energy surged up his arm. Hair prickled at his nape, and the protective pendant from Ithariel heated on its chain until contact with the stone burned flesh. Korendir repressed a shudder. Each passing moment undermined his will with a reluctance that radiated through the tallix itself. He knew he must smash the crystal instantly, else forfeit the attempt.

Again he set his knife to the jewel's starred eye. He held the weapon upright without flinching; then, oblivious to his onlooker's curiosity, Korendir raised the lantern. He hammered the weighted base downward toward the dagger held poised against the tallix.

The motion engaged every latent defense Majaxin had enspelled in the stone.

Ithariel's protection failed to compensate; ward energies burst and her sliver of tallix heated like a meteor and shattered. Splinters raked Korendir's neck and chest, then spun like flying sparks across the cell. The steward

at the doorway gasped and flung back, and lost his moment to flee.

The lamp struck. Impact against the dagger haft jarred
bone and muscle and nerve to the junction of Korendir's
shoulder. A snap whined on the air; the great tallix which
enspelled Tir Amindel split like a fissure in ice. Sorcerous
ruby light rinsed the traitor's cell, then flickered out. For
an instant the crystal's crazed facets turned depthless and
black. Then the lantern snuffed out. The stone glimmered, woke to redoubled power with a sultry flare of
orange. Up from its faulted surface boiled a cloud of
caustic smoke. Enveloped by a shining mist that burned
and painfully blinded, Korendir of Whitestorm cried out.

The surge of Majaxin's spellwork sheared through his
flesh and recognized his hand as the one that had sun-
dered the tallix. His vision cleared. Surrounded by a
whirlpool nexus of sorcery, he looked, and saw his fist
still clenched to the knife he had only one instant in the
past set point-first against the crystal in the floor. Now,
most horribly, the tallix had redirected the weapon's original thrust.

Korendir's fingers glistened with new blood. Although,
beyond question, he remained in the cell, the impossible
confronted him: his blade was sunk to the hilt in the eye
of the little beggar girl charged to watch over his horse.

His recoil yanked the steel clear. Revulsion overset his
control and brought up the contents of his stomach. He
staggered upright, miserably retching, and the spark-shot
cloud of magecraft moved with him. His thoughts reeled
with agony. The knife he would rather have sheathed in
his own flesh; except now its spell-worked edge was a
melted lump with no trace left of temper. Korendir cast
the steel away. Struck to the heart by remorse, he fought
through the sparkle of sorceries toward the corridor.

The grillwork had blasted away from the door; riven
metal embraced the dripping remains of the steward.
Korendir stumbled. Bent double by a second bout of
nausea, he fled into the corridor beyond. The orange
smoke streamed after him, vengeance-bent as a swarm
of hornets. Destruction followed in its wake.

Cracks ripped up the stonework, and pillars groaned
and canted.

Korendir ran while the ceiling crumbled. He did not

move to save himself, though chips of masonry silted his hair, and the floor under his boots heaved and buckled. Columns crashed around him and archways toppled at his heels, but his eyes remained blind to peril. Lost to all memory but the blood-wet corpse of a child, and his hand on the knife that had butchered her, he forced his legs to bear weight. To the limit of his strength, he sprinted, whipped onward by revulsion that dismembered thought and condemned him past forgiveness as the killer Haldeth had reviled.

The staircase wound upward in jumbled disarray. Between the landing and a fallen riser was a wadded rag that once had been a sentry. Korendir leaped over the remains. Buffeted beyond reason by the writhing mist that hunted him, he scaled the piled masonry on hands and feet like a beast.

He kept no count of which turnings he missed or took; by reflex and instinct, he gained the upper levels only to lurch onward, to slip over blood-smeared bodies that littered his path at each stride. Members of the duke's household perished before his eyes, here a servant pulped between buckled floor beams, and there an aged noble who stumbled through masonry that bounced and rolled like devil's dice and dashed in his balding head. Korendir ran past unscathed, while the bane unleashed from Tir Amindel's tallix remorselessly pursued.

He escaped the palace through a gap in tumbled walls. The courtyard beyond was a graveyard of jumbled stone. The dead, the dying, and the mangled by now were too numerous to count. The squall had not abated. Rain sheeted down in torrents, rinsed streaks across shattered paving, and spilled into red-tinged puddles. Korendir heaved air into a chest too tight for breath. His body spasmed with dry heaves. The force aroused when he broke the tallix was not abating, but levelling Tir Amindel stone by carven stone; his fault, the suffering, and his burden, the shattered lives and hopes and dreams. His act magnified the malice of Majaxin and left nothing. The inhabitants of the city were smashed haplessly as pebbles before tide in a posthumous passion of spite. He, who should have been first to die, was the only soul left untouched.

Korendir remembered nothing of his purpose. He forgot Ithariel's tears, and the pitiless beauty that had lured generations of enchanters to entrapment. The centuries they had suffered within spell-wrought walls held less meaning than the wind-driven spatter of rainfall. Korendir fled and wished for oblivion. Lashed by the storm, goaded on by orange sparks, he split his knuckles scrabbling over walls; like a harried dog, he tore his way across rose gardens, shouldered through locked doors, and kicked down wicket gates. In time, his mindless run carried him to the archway where he had earlier taken shelter. His horse waited still, reins pinned by a tumble of broken marble. Crumpled nearby lay the cloak he had left to comfort the street child; one of the corners streamed red. The face it half covered lay tipped at the sky; one eye was open to the rain, and the other inhumanly savaged by the blade of a spell-turned knife.

Korendir succumbed again to sickness. Bile stung his throat and his breath labored. The spasms brought no relief; his stomach had emptied long since. He fumbled like an old man, grasped the gray's saddle with wet fingers. The stallion sidled, then stood with its ears flicking backward and forward in unease as its rider found the stirrup. Korendir pulled himself astride. Hunched over with cramps, he jerked the dirk from his wrist sheath, leaned forward, and slashed both reins at the bit rings.

The stallion surged in recovered freedom. He flung into a half-rear, while Korendir jabbed heels into streaming flanks and howled in mindless pain.

The horse from High Kelair bolted through streets transformed by catastrophe. Through screaming crowds and chaos he galloped, his eyes white rings of terror, and the breath from his distended nostrils flaring in snorts of condensation. Muscles coiled like whip-leather in shoulder and haunch and gaskin; legs cabled with tendon folded and straightened, driving a powerful stride. The horse poured its heart into running, over cobbles and flagstones and polished marble courtyards that rang with the clatter of its flight.

But the sorceries of the dead wizard gave chase with a tenacity more constant than flesh. The shining, unnatural mist streamed after Korendir like the wraith of a thing damned.

The mercenary clung to the stallion's back. He made

no effort to guide or choose direction, but rode with closed eyes and tucked head, hands locked in the whipping golden mane. No surcease existed to block sound. The grinding crash of stonework flanked the stallion's course. Spired towers toppled and fell, accompanied by screams from men and women and children, battered down in the course of their escape. The revenge of Majaxin spared no life and no edifice the walls of his city had encompassed.

Except for a racing gray stallion and a rider too tortured to care.

The horse cleared the tangle of the east wall portal with a jump that would have lamed a common mount. As his hooves touched ground, cracks like forked lightning jagged across the gate turrets. Weakened granite thundered down and swallowed a mother and grandmother who struggled with a bundle of wailing babies.

The stallion flattened its ears in a spurt of fear-charged rage. He galloped while stonework tumbled and rolled an avalanche of rubble at his heels; but the rider never moved. His mind was lost to thought, and his flesh knew only pain. The ruin of Tir Amindel might fall behind, yet Korendir still heard the shrieks of its murdered inhabitants. Their screams blended with other screams from his past until his skin felt needled by knife cuts, as if each cry from massacred thousands held physical power to torment.

The stallion lengthened stride as his burden shivered and flinched. All nerves and jangled panic, he swerved off the road. The nimbus of orange trailed after, a banner of crackling sparks. Majaxin's sorceries did not disperse as the horse gouged a track through the meadows beside Kelharrou Lake and crashed through the thornbrakes beyond. The scrub that surrounded tilled fields gave way at length to unbroken forest.

Thick growth compelled the horse to slacken pace. Branches raked furrows in his lathered coat, and the crack of hooves on dry ground became deadened in drifts of old leaves.

Korendir slumped with his cheek against the stallion's neck, limp wrists crossed on the crest; his feet slipped clear of the stirrups, and the irons clanked against his ankles in rhythm with the animal's stride. He made no

effort to ease his brave mount. Neither did he concede
to his own needs. Harrowed past self-preservation, he
recognized no hunger or thirst, but only wretchedness
and a gut-tearing chain of horrors set off by a beggar
child's death.

The gray picked a path through moss-scabbed trees,
and the orange smoke closed like an aureole around the
rider's head.

Korendir shot straight with a cry that sheared echoes
through the trees. He belted his heels against the stallion's sides. The animal lunged with a violence that
nearly unseated him and iron-rimmed hooves left a swath
of lacerated stems as the pair sprang again into flight.

Time passed unheeded. The rain ceased and the sky
cleared. Sunset glowed briefly through the forest's mantle of leaves. Then dusk faded into gloom, and the sorcerous mist bronzed the bark of the passing trees. The
stud lapsed back to a walk. He plowed on through a
white water ford as if knowing where he wished to go.

Through the night, the sorcery leached Korendir's
strength with horrors that damned, and wrapped all his
nerve ends in fire. Over and over he saw his blade strike
through a beggar child's eye. He felt the spurt of hot
fluids and the jarring scrape of bone and the shudder
that racked her small body as the steel cleaved on,
through skull and butter-soft brain. Consciousness became defined by suffering for which the mind held no
release.

Dawn lightened the haze to silver; the air rang with
birdsong and the reddish rays of first sunlight dappled
the boughs overhead. Korendir did not rouse. Slumped
with glazed eyes in his saddle, he did not stir when the
stallion shouldered through a last stand of saplings and
carried him into a glen beside a lake. A tower arose by
the shoreline, in lines and style reminiscent of Tir Amindel's fallen grace, but on a scale less grand, and without
the adornment of marble and stained glass.

An aged man mantled in power awaited on the sand
before the portal. He wore dyed boots and a cloak of
ocean gray, and his brows were gathered in a frown. He
made no move; but as though called in by a beacon, the
gray quickened its exhausted stride and halted quivering
before him.

Enfolded yet in an angry glimmer of orange, Korendir sprawled face downward across the tangled mane of his mount. His eyes were sightless and wide, and his fingers were locked against his teeth in the effort to contain an unending need to scream.

The old man caught the stallion's bridle. His autocratic touch reflected small affinity for beasts, yet the gray settled as if it knew him; its terrible trembling eased as fingers gentled by spells stroked the muzzle between lather-rimmed nostrils. They continued up the hard neck, then explored with critical care down shoulder and flank, and each mud-splashed, sweat-marked leg. The tendons were cool, which surprised the elderly wizard. He straightened from his examination and fixed his piqued gaze on the horse.

The word he spoke was not in the language of mortals, but the stud understood. His ears swept back, and his head jerked; the rider in his saddle stayed astride.

"So then, he did not abuse thee," concluded the enchanter. He shrugged back his hood and scowled at the black-clad, bronze-haired mortal who remained mounted by the sole volition of the gray.

"Fool and daughter of foolishness," the old one snapped. He stepped to the stallion's shoulder and laid his palm on Korendir's damp forehead. As the breeze off the lake stirred through his beard, the ancient tilted his head back and raised his voice in song.

The fog which mantled the mercenary's form hissed protest. Song and spell-wrought sorceries collided in dissonance, and raised a sound like water-splashed embers. The glimmer of energies flared bright, and Korendir stiffened. His limbs flinched and shuddered, and he gasped like a tear in cloth.

The old man's chant did not falter. He raised his other hand and cradled the mercenary's brow. With his wrists half-buried in bronze hair, he finished each phrase of melody in a voice that stayed crisp and well-pitched. The notes resonated through the morning stillness and slowly, finally, wrought change. Evil leached out of the mist that bound Korendir. Faded and insubstantial as smoke, Majaxin's curse of vengeance wisped away and dispersed in the sunlight.

The enchanter sang one line more, and Korendir fell

slack as a gutted fish. Sure hands caught his fall as he spilled from the stallion's saddle.

"Fire and earth, I'm too old for this," the wizard grunted. He shouldered the mercenary's weight so that half of him rested on the horse and called out a guttural name.

The tower gate cracked open. An eye appeared behind, all wrinkles and merriness, and black as an unplanted seed. "He's alive, that one?" a raspy voice called back.

"Neth." The ancient returned a nettled glance. "Would I bother supporting a corpse? Get your short bones over here before I drop him altogether."

The door gaped wider. A stocky dwarf in a red cap and jerkin bounced out and rushed to assist.

Small the fellow might have been, but the muscles under his gathered sleeves were gnarled like the trunk of an oak. He bore Korendir up with an ease much belied by his colorful string of curses. After an anxious glance at the horse, the dwarf stumped with the man back across the glen toward the tower.

The wizard watched the mercenary's trailing heels carve grooves in the sand by the entry. Unsmiling, he twitched his sleeves straight on his wrists. Although he disdained a groom's chores, he loosened the stallion's girths. He removed both saddle and bridle, then slapped a palm on sweat-sleeked hide. "Go, you," he murmured to the horse's back-turned ear. "Roll in damp grass all you wish, for you at least are blameless. Your part in this unpleasantness was well and bravely done."

The dwarf untangled his grip from a sweated mat of bronze hair, tripped the latch, and kicked open the last of three iron-bound doors. Still huffing from his ascent of steep stairs, he said, "Your man has arrived."

Within a shadowed alcove, Ithariel stirred, but did not look around. Recently changed to a leather tunic and hose cross-gartered for riding, she twisted her hands through the strands of pearls which girdled her waist. "Is he alive?"

"If he wasn't I wouldn't be packing him, would I?" The dwarf shuffled in and dumped the torso of his burden with a thump on Ithariel's best divan. As an afterthought, he lifted the man's ankles and arranged the long legs on the cushions. The boots were rain-wet, and the leather smelled pungently of horse.

The dwarf reviewed his handiwork with his head cocked to one side. Then, as if scratched and bleeding men on his mistress's brocades were commonplace as gardening, he straightened his cap over his black hair and added, "Archmaster's madder than Neth was on the day the dark spoiled His creation."

Ithariel fumbled, and pearls spilled with a clatter through her fingers. "Now whose fault is that, Nix?" She chose a nickname, since the one given by the dwarf's mother was ridiculously difficult to pronounce. "I sent no word to Dethmark."

The dwarf shrugged, his cheeks puffed out like autumn apples. "You think he's deaf, Lady? I know better, I do indeed. When the whole of Tir Amindel gets razed by sorceries, and the Archmaster doesn't hear, then Neth almighty'd better worry. The breaking of Majaxin's tallix disrupted continuity clear through to Alhaerie."

"Oh, you should earn your keep by telling tales in the taverns!" Ithariel snapped in exasperation. "Now will you leave, or must I throw you head first through the casement?"

The dwarf considered her with acute and guileful eyes. "I see," he observed quietly. He poked a stubby finger into his cheek. "One half-dead mortal means so much to you, does he?" And he spun through the doorway as Ithariel pitched a vase at him.

The crystal smashed harmlessly into panels of fast-closing oak. "Lady," admonished the dwarf from the far side, "like it or not, you have company."

The portal reopened immediately. The Archmaster of the White Circle stepped briskly across the threshold, his expression bleak as a thundercloud. He took in broken fragments and the spray of strewn flowers, and then Ithariel's white face. He gave both their correct interpretation. An anger of chilling proportions settled over his features, and he shoved the door to with a thud that rattled the hinges.

"You learned nothing, I think, in the years you spent as my ward."

Ithariel raised her chin. "I learned the extent of my father's evil."

"Your present folly matches that." The Archmaster's eyes turned pitiless as the shadowed side of a snowdrift. "What misguided instinct gave you the right to meddle with a problem too great for your seniormost peers? And was Tir Amindel's utter destruction not enough that you must risk entangling your life with that of a mortal man?"

"He is Korendir of Whitestorm," Ithariel said. "And far less mortal than he seems."

She crossed the chamber and knelt by the divan where her mercenary lay. The vibrant inner tension she remembered was absent, stilled now by enchanted sleep. Shallow gashes marred his face and hands. At his throat, the tarnished length of chain that once held her jewel of protection had seared a line of blisters across his collarbone.

The Archmaster moved to stand at the shoulder of his ward; he, too, studied Korendir, but with less sympathy. "You repeat the failings of your father, Ithariel," he cautioned. "You reach for what you want without any thought for consequences. When you called this man into service, did you think what penalty he might pay?"

Ithariel stroked the limp fingers, felt sword scars and calluses from the bridle rein. "He was brought up on suffering. Never has it proven his master."

"The scourge of Majaxin's crystal might be abided, true enough, but at what cost?" The archmaster shook his head in sudden sorrow. "The mind I just set under spell has ranged so far from reason that only the immortal maker might call it back."

Ithariel closed her hands around Korendir's sinewed wrist. "Neth and his angels won't be necessary. This man is one of ours, the lost heir of High Morien. As a baby he was spirited away before the demons overran Alathir. The servant who bore him later sickened and died of a fever, but the infant survived. He was found in the forest, half starved, by the widow of Shan Rannok's huntsman."

"And you risked his life in Tir Amindel, *knowing this?*" The Archmaster's ire intensified. "Girl, I saw perfectly well whom I dragged off the back of Nixdaxdimo's prize stallion! Orame informed me that Morien's son had not died, years back. But this boy's life cannot be sheltered by any grace of inheritance. Think, child! If Korendir discovers his bloodline, how long do you think he will last? The Mathcek Demons lurk yet in Alathir's ruins. As Morien's heir, they would hunt and destroy him, and not a ward the White Circle could devise might keep him safe."

"Are you saying he should have finished his days as a mortal?" Ithariel stood up heatedly.

"Oh yes, Ithariel. Just that!" The Archmaster spun away with a swirl of sea-colored robes. "Morien's son should have been left to find happiness and marriage as others do."

"Just what sort of life do you think he led?" Sure of her ground now, Ithariel shouted back. "Did you, or Orame, ever take time to know him?"

The Archmaster paused by the doorway. He heard the pain in her outburst, but his manner stayed critical as flint. "That point is moot, foster daughter. Now hear what your actions will bring. Korendir of Whitestorm shall live out his natural days within the wardspell I have set. You will care for him as he sleeps. He will not be wakened into suffering, and if you think to spare him by granting him knowledge of his origins, the Council Major will be forced to cast judgment. Do not meddle with this man further, Lady. Or on my authority as Archmaster, I will sentence you to the same fate as your father."

Ithariel went white to the lips. Auburn hair spilled in coils over her jerkin as she sank back and laid her cheek against Korendir. Her thoughts circled in turmoil, and she barely heard the door swing closed as the Archmaster left her presence.

The dwarf Nixdaxdimo found her still by the mercenary's side when he returned from grooming the gray. He paused on the threshold, scraped his knuckles through a beard like tangled wire, then shut the door and sat with his back against the lintel. For a very long while he watched the tears trace down his mistress's cheeks and soak soundlessly into black wool.

Finally he said, "Ach, lady, you should never have mixed your heart into this."

Ithariel did not answer.

The dwarf propped his chin on his fist and tried again. "It's my fault, too, remember? I was the one who gave

the sword and the stallion to tempt yon man into
service."

Her fingers tightened in the cloth of Korendir's tunic;
beyond that, she might not have heard.

Nixdaxdimo's virtues did not encompass patience. He
raised bushy eyebrows and stamped back onto his feet.
"Gives me the sorrows, just looking at you. When you've
had your fill of moaning over him, I'll come back."

Ithariel raised her head and said something too low to
hear.

The dwarf folded muscled forearms and scowled. "Say
that louder."

"Get out," Ithariel repeated more succinctly, and with
a grunt of disgust, the dwarf did.

Left to herself, the enchantress looked down upon a
face unrecognizable in tranquillity. The almost ferocious
reserve that pervaded the man's conscious presence was
banished completely in sleep; that more than anything
reminded of violated trust. Korendir had never owned
such peace in life. The irony wounded, that the wardstone she had promised, that he had earned at such annihilating cost, might itself bring the key to his inner calm.
Granted his most cherished desire, the Korendir who had
ceded his past to her would have struggled to reconcile
the conflicting passions that drove him. Allowed protection for his stronghold at Whitestorm, he would surely
take his chance to win recovery.

A lock of his hair had fallen and tangled in eyelashes
that showed not a flicker of reflex; Ithariel smoothed the
strands back. Only warm skin, and the steady strength
of his heartbeat, established the assurance that he lived.
The enchantress tried to imagine the future, as bright
bronze hair slowly grayed. Scars and calluses and tan
would fade away, while the face with its stern planes and
angles would sag into characterless old age.

Insanity would have been easier to endure.

In its place, the passive sleep imposed by the Archmaster offered a penalty too severe for acceptance. That
final, dispassionate judgment drove Ithariel down an avenue of alienated thought. The discovery at the end left
her shaking. When Korendir's mind had been stilled,
something irreplaceable had been lost. A thing was reft

from her that years and grief could not forgive, nor any amount of pity console.

Who else upon Aerith understood those most terrible personal memories he had bequeathed her?

Ithariel cradled a hand that would never touch back. She kissed lips unequivocally deprived of feeling, and something inside her gave way.

"There's another means to recall a mind from madness," she said aloud.

That moment the door banged open. Intrusive as a plague of stinging insects, Nixdaxdimo burst in. "Almighty powers of creation, I was afraid you'd think of that!"

Ithariel shot up straight as if slapped. "You interfering little pest! What are you talking about?"

The dwarf advanced on bandy legs and stopped beyond reach of his mistress. "If—" he said succinctly. He paused, took a deep breath, then mastered the rest in a rush. "If I thought you'd ever get soft-headed enough to take a mate, I'd never have asked Megga to marry me."

Ithariel returned a dubious frown. "Let Megga hear that, and you'll walk in the same boots you stand in."

Nix solemnly regarded his feet, whose footgear wanted mending. "Well then, I'll thank you not to tell the old battle axe." Still staring at his toes he added, "All the same, you'd better not bond with that carrot-headed madman on your divan."

Ithariel raised her brows in a manner not at all to the dwarf's liking. He hopped from one foot to the other and pulled his beard with both hands. "I knew it! You're serious. Oh Neth, but I knew it! Lady, on that score the Archmaster was very clear. You're making a terrible mistake."

Now the enchantress returned a glare. "You rotten little pest. How dare you discuss my affairs, particularly ones that this moment are purest conjecture?"

"Conjecture!" Nix ripped his hat off and threw it on the floor. "I like that! Lady, the Archmaster himself broached the subject. He saw the same stupid look on your face that I did. If you mistook him for deaf this morning, he sure wasn't blind this afternoon."

Ithariel raked her fingers through her hair. Her gut was twisted into cramps, and her back ached from hours of sitting without a chair. "If I choose to mate, not even the council at Dethmark can forbid me."

Nix wilted. He sat down heavily on the crown of his feathered hat and said, "No. But you're making a ridiculous choice." When Ithariel failed to respond, he set his elbows on the floor and rested his chin in his palms. "All hells. Telvallind Archmaster himself admitted you have the right. He just hoped you'd have better sense. Since you don't, he said to tell you that if the man Whitestorm will have you, and if you both survive, the White Circle has no choice but to disown you. And if the mortal refuses you, if he lives or dies insane, the council will pass judgment against you."

Ithariel leaned her head against Korendir's black-clad shoulder. All of her fury drained away, and her eyes went soft with distance.

"Oh, weep for an early frost," said Nix, disconsolate. "Megga and I shall end up housekeeping an empty tower, and without any regular exercise that stallion will make shreds of the garden."

"Maybe," Ithariel returned. Very quietly she added, "Maybe you and Megga will do your sweeping and cooking in the hall at Whitestorm castle, and the stallion will be muscled fit to kill."

Nixdaxdemo raised two fingers and bent his ears down. "Surely not." His words rang pessimistically glum. "Hates the sea, anyway, Megga does. Says salt winds bring her headaches."

"Liar," Ithariel said faintly. After that, she did not move for what seemed an eternity of time.

XIX. Whitestorm's Lady

The dwarf Nixdaxdimo moped throughout the morning. As Ithariel fussed over elaborate preparations, she tripped over him twice, he hung so closely underfoot. Irked by the insults she received concerning clumsiness, the lady sent the dwarf out to bridle the gray for an errand in the ruins of Tir Amindel.

"Go and recover the fragments of Majaxin's tallix," she instructed her surly servant. "And be careful of that horse, he's no longer yours."

Nix perched astride a saddle whose flaps and assorted trappings chafed his ankles. His diminutive proportions made any use of stirrups impossible, and after much grousing, he removed the irons and thrust his feet through the empty leathers; he stayed astride by dint of two fists clenched tight in the blond mane. He might have bred and raised the mount he had provided Ithariel's mercenary, but like most dwarves, his admiration for horseflesh was aesthetic and did not extend to riding. Anything higher than a pony made him dizzy. "Be careful of my head, you mean." Nix returned a scowl. "A fall would smash all my bones."

Ithariel turned the stud and smacked it into a trot toward the forest. "Be gone, you silly dwarf. You've tumbled off your bench drunk with ale too many times for me to think that any part of you is breakable."

Nix howled a curse at her. He hauled without success on the gray's reins and vanished precipitously into the forest. Only his voice drifted back: "Bother and hell's demons, why didn't I choose to breed fish?"

Alone in the glen before her tower, Ithariel felt the smile fade from her face. The ritual she had decided to attempt was never a step taken lightly. She knew apprehension, and fear, and self-doubt, but not regret. Each hour that passed confirmed that her choice had been foregone conclusion from the first. The man who lay sleeping in her tower was entangled in her life course; the absence of his conscious presence haunted her in a manner that had nothing at all to do with debt. For a White Circle initiate, that state of affairs offered few alternatives.

Either she chose to bond, to twine her being with his in a manner irreversibly final, or she lived out her days with the knowledge she was only half alive.

The Archmaster's warning was a just one; the joining of two living spirits should never be consummated in duty. This was no moment for uncertainties, and yet Ithariel's thoughts were torn with them. Korendir of Whitestorm might reject her. He might succumb to his madness, or he might sicken and die; in all cases, without redress, her fate would be tied to his own.

Preoccupied with worries, Ithariel took no joy from the spring that quickened the forest, but returned to her tower and exchanged her girdle of pearls for a knotted leather belt. Then she fetched a basket from the kitchen, went out, and launched her painted boat upon the lake. She paddled to the meadows on the far shoreline and spent the day gathering roots, rare flowers, and herbs. When the swallows swooped down and chattered questions at her, she did not answer back; their aerial acrobatics for once failed to delight her. The lake sprite did not surface to share her berries and bread, nor did she eddy the water into ripples around the painted boat's keel when Ithariel ferried the laden basket homeward.

Only one being within the enchantress's circle of influence remained impervious to her mood. The dwarf wife Megga awaited her mistress on the path before the front door. She had red cheeks and round fat arms, and hair like straw tied back under a polka dot shawl. "You left all the sausage I made, foolish girl. What man will have you if you're falling down hungry, and skinny as well?"

Ithariel stopped. She switched her basket from her left hand to her right. "I'm not the only one who's distraught. Have you forgotten? Megga, I never eat sausage."

The dwarf woman slapped her ample thighs. "Ach. So ye don't. But that's no excuse." She strutted back into the tower with a comical, rolling gait, her head turned sidewards in annoyance. "Sausage was for Nixdax, and he's off his feed because of you."

"Well, I'm guilty then, and there's an end of it." Ithariel laughed; she could not help herself. The dwarves always messed up her priorities; nothing she tried ever stopped them. She flicked pollen out of the trailing ends of her hair and followed Megga inside.

"That swordsman might be hungry when he's roused," Megga added hopefully.

The thought of Korendir wakened inspired only dread; Ithariel firmly kept to practicality. With a tact acquired through years of dwarvish service, she seized upon her opening. "Then you'll help me get him moved."

Megga shot a black look over her shoulder. "What's the hurry, mistress? His boots have already spoiled your best cushions."

"Nix's doing, and proud he was of the feat, at the time." Ithariel dodged as the dwarf wife sailed into a jibe in the passage. The enchantress caught the plump finger which jabbed scoldingly at her middle and thrust it more usefully through the handle of the herb basket. "Let be, Megga. If I'm going to bond with a mercenary, I doubt velvet cushions will very long stay a priority."

Sundown splashed mottled light through the forest surrounding Ithariel's tower by the hour Nixdaxdimo returned. He had not hurried on his errand. The gray he turned loose to graze showed a coat unmarred by sweat, but the same could not be said of his rider. Weary, pale, and lacking his habitual ebullience, he dragged his way up the stair. Ithariel's living quarters stood empty; unsurprised, but disappointed nonetheless, the dwarf jammed his cap more firmly over his ears and tackled the next flight of steps.

His mistress was busy in the topmost chamber, the one she used for magic. Megga attended her; reluctantly, as Nix could see by the set of his wife's lower lip. Given another reason to wish he had not come home, the dwarf sat heavily on the threshold.

Ithariel no longer wore her leather doublet and riding boots. Barefoot, robed in shimmering green samite, she traced runes in sand upon the floor with a small wooden paddle and a cone with a hole in one end. Nix took stock of the patterns already configured on black stone; the braziers with their bundles of aromatic herbs set up, but unlit, at the major and minor points of the compass. Centered in the circle lay the mercenary from Whitestorm, his clothing replaced by a pearlescent veiling of silk. Nixdaxdimo looked at the combed bronze hair, the closed eyes, and the spell-wrought stillness of the man's features. Then the dwarf stuffed his knuckles into his mouth and shivered in outright apprehension. No good could come of this. No good at all.

That moment Ithariel looked up, and eyes as clear as sheet silver caught sight of him. "Nix. Did you bring the thing I asked for?"

The dwarf stopped chewing his fingers. He pulled off his cap, which was weighted inside with something heavy, and lowered it with a clink to the floor. "Here." He met his mistress's gaze with visible unhappiness. "Lady, the Archmaster was not wrong. Let the Master of Whitestorm bide his days in sleep."

Ithariel frowned. "Nix, don't make things difficult. I can't do that." She rose with a slither of robes, detoured around her spell patterns and knelt before her troubled servant. "Did something in Tir Amindel frighten you?"

Miserably the dwarf shook his head. Words could not encompass the ruins he had crossed: the fallen, shattered towers, with attendant tangles of wadded cloth and broken flesh now picked at by scavengers. The aftermath of the cataclysm unleashed by Majaxin's tallix was a sight to wrack the mind with nightmares. That the man responsible had not whipped a certain stallion bloody through his frenzy of tortured flight defied credibility. Newly appreciative of the mercenary he had dumped on Ithariel's best divan, Nixdaxdimo forced courage and spoke.

"If you have any pity at all, you'll leave Korendir his peace." The dwarf finished off with a look bleak enough to curdle milk.

Ithariel returned pure exasperation. "You too! Nix, you faithless scoundrel, I'm going to let Megga have her way. She'll march you downstairs to eat sausage and then scold the ears off your head."

The dwarf declined to retort, which was unusual. He reached out, hooked two workmanlike fingers and upended his scarlet cap. Three shards of crystal slithered

out, black as the pits of hell, and faceted on those sides
not crazed with fractures. One was the size of a doubled
fist, and polished flat on the top. "On your head lie the
consequences, then, Lady of the Forest."

Nix rose, snapped for Megga to follow, and stamped
off down the stair.

"He's worried for you, that's what!" The dwarf wife
admonished as she passed her mistress. "And he's right,
if I may say so. Lady, why won't you listen?"

Ithariel glanced aside at a face that reposed in a frame
of dark bronze hair, at stilled hands that were made for
life and action, and much too fine for the sword. "That's
why, little mother. Now leave me."

Megga rustled off, grumbling imprecations. By herself
in a chamber gone gloomy with twilight, Ithariel buried
her face in her hands and sighed. The dwarves were wise
in their way, and loyal to the bottom of their cantanker-
ous little hearts. They knew, even better than she did:
the Archmaster's chosen course was merciful, and founded
upon centuries of experience. And yet she could not
abide. Terrible as the penalty would be if she failed,
still, she could not look upon the sleeping man without a
burning wild urge to rebel.

Madness, even death, was surely preferable to the passive oblivion of forgetfulness.

The enchantress's hands shook as she reached down
and examined the crystals recovered from Tir Amindel.
No cloudy lights stirred in their depths, and no trace of
power lingered to spark at her touch; the darkness in the
stones was complete. Majaxin's evil wards had drained
away and left these tallix stilled as pools under starlight.

No gain would come by waiting. Ithariel selected the
largest of the fragments. She carried it to the window,
and seated herself with the stone a cold weight between
her knees.

She began with the things she most loved. As evening
deepened about her, she gathered the peace of her forest
into a core of bright force, then sang that essence as a
note. The sound struck the tallix and generated answering resonance. Ithariel felt a brief vibration sting her
skin. Then the crystal sheared; one fragment cleaved
away and left a clean and shining facet on the jaggedly
broken edge.

Ithariel drew breath and encompassed the tranquillity of birdsongs at daybreak. She shaped a second note, and another chip spun away; she sang of the watersprite's laughter, and the dip of nesting swallows, and the smell of meadow flowers at summer noon. She added the abiding strength of rock, and the patience of oaks, and the warmth of her fires during snowstorms. Each spellsong chiseled a new facet, and slowly the light rekindled in the tallix stone's shady depths.

Below, ruddied by lantern flame in the tower's snug kitchen, Megga and Nix heard the notes which would repulse armies, and the notes which would quiet ocean gales. They knew what their mistress sang into being was a wardstone for the holdfast at Whitestorm, and their eyes met in aggrieved consternation over a plate of untouched sausage.

"I should never have given her the stallion," Nix said with recrimination. "Nor forged that black sword either."

Megga untied her shawl and twisted its length between her fingers. "You're a fool to think that made any difference. She's headstrong, our mistress, and ruled by contrary passions. If that carrot-headed swordsman has the sense Neth gave to a chicken, he'll choose insanity before he takes her to wife."

Nix did not answer, but brooded as his thoughts turned upon a single fact: the gray stud had borne no mark of abuse beyond exhaustion when he returned with Ithariel's rider. Crazed the man might become, but he would never abjure compassion. That one quality would bind him to life; and that one flaw would kill him.

Night deepened. The calls of a wakeful mockingbird rang over the waters of the lake. In the top chamber of the tower, Ithariel of the White Circle stilled her final note. She opened her eyes to starlight, and a crystal that now was a perfect jewel, round and shining with wardspells. The surface was faceted more precisely than any gemcutter's art; and the magic it contained lay beyond any natural force in Aerith to rend asunder.

One moment the enchantress allowed herself to appreciate the results of her labors. The tallix Korendir had dreamed for at last stood complete in her hands. All that remained was to waken the man and plead for a place at his side.

Ithariel rose to her feet. She wrapped the crystal in the trailing folds of her sleeve. The tremble in her knees had little to do with weariness as she crossed the chamber and ignited the first of the braziers, the north one, since the pull of greatest earth force originated there. She stepped sunward around the circle, and sparks like lit pearls leaped from her fingertips into the bundles of tied leaves. The flames caught without mishap. Smoke drifted across her eyes, and the sweet scents of burning herbs mingled with the smells of forest night that wafted in through the casements. Ithariel lit the south fire, and the west, and then the lesser points between. With the circle closed about her, she knelt by the man at the center.

Illumination from the braziers fell kindly across him. Scars became softened by shadow; the tranquility imposed upon his flesh lent the beauty of a masterwork in marble. Ithariel poised by Korendir's head. She touched the yielding line of his mouth, and for a heartbeat knew tearing remorse. Then she closed her eyes, damped her emotions, and set herself to break the Archmaster's edict of sleep.

Enchanters fashion energies into spells through many channels; Telvallind of Dethmark preferred his work in song, and he had laid the groundwork of Ithariel's training. Familiar with his methods, and blessed with a true voice, she began with random tones. Now and again, her pitch would coincide with an element that comprised the spell. An answering line of energy would flicker to life in the air, thin drawn as wire, a radiant of force in cold light. As Ithariel proceeded, more lines appeared to interlock and build on the pattern; in time she could guess at the spell's configuration, and select her notes with more method. Patient, entirely in opposition to the hurried beat of her heart, she continued until the nets of force that constrained Korendir's mind lay visible above his body.

The Archmaster had wrought with exhaustive thoroughness. His spells were convoluted and guarded, difficult in the extreme to unravel without penalty. Ithariel blotted sweating palms against her sleeves. The thought occurred, that the bindings might directly reflect the savagery of the suffering they contained. Majaxin had been clever and criminal; his hatred of his prosecutors had survived beyond the grave. The Archmaster's multiple defenses might in fact have been called for, not only to deter interference, but to ensure that Korendir never roused to torment through chance attrition.

Ithariel sat with her fingers locked to still their shaking. The complexity of the spell taxed her resolve more than words or warnings. Now would be the moment, could she bring herself to turn back. She regarded the face of the man in the spill of flamelight and spells. No help awaited her there. Only the promise of pain, whichever course she should take. At the last, the very imperviability of the Archmaster's spellwork became her inspiration to act; love could not contemplate safeguards of that magnitude and turn away. She must seek the resolution of victory, or absolute final defeat.

"Forgive me," Ithariel whispered into ears that could not hear.

She reached out, touched the vulnerable hollow of Korendir's throat. Then she raised her voice in unison with the first note of the spell. The line she matched pulsed brighter; meticulous in her control, she raised her pitch to dissonance. The spell brightened, flared red, then frayed without warning into sparks. A wisp of smoke dispersed upon the air, the first piece of the pattern unbound. Ithariel drew breath. She closed her eyes and inhaled the scents of the burning herbs to anchor her concentration. Then she shaped a second note, and cancelled another coil of energy into darkness. She worked without break through an intricate maze of ward-spells that would kill if she slipped even once. The coals in the braziers dulled to red, and the night waned at her back. Note upon note she sang while gray dawn silvered the casements, unnoticed.

Birdsong pealed through forest stillness. Ithariel began to unravel the grand ward, and exhaustion roughened her voice. She cupped her ears beneath her palms and forced her mind to track the minutest fluctuations in pitch. The centermost defenses extinguished with a whine like snapped harp strings, and disbanded energies left a stinging scent of cordite on the air. Ithariel's brows furrowed into a frown of supreme effort. Against her knee, under her hands, everywhere her skin touched Korendir's, she felt signs of returning awareness. His body twitched fitfully in dreams.

Ithariel completed the last sequence. Her note shivered the last of the spell-lines to oblivion, and her song subsided into silence.

The enchantress opened her eyes. Exhausted by fear, she watched the final vestige of the Archmaster's peace dissolve. Korendir's features spasmed. Agonized by the impact of returned memory, every sinew in his body jerked tight.

Her peril was upon her.

Ithariel caught his wrists and struggled to subdue the surge that drove him into movement. Whatever the cost, he must not break through the ward circles scribed in sand on the floor. He fought her, thrashed to rise, and his eyes reflected vistas that words lacked the bleakness to describe. She could not match his strength. Reflexes trained for the sword were too fast for her to counter, and in desperation, she reached for his mind.

"Korendir!" Ithariel's call was shaped in sound and magic. "Korendir, do you know me?"

He did not answer. His lips shaped a snarl of repudiation and he flung her off. The silken covering tore from his body as he battered his way to his knees. Beyond dignity, the enchantress threw herself against his middle and knocked him sprawling.

Shaken breathless, Ithariel recovered her grip. Korendir moved anyway, dragged her with him in a driving frenzy of pain. As his fingers grazed the rim of the first circle, she forced a thread of awareness between the turbulence that harrowed his thoughts. Again she called: "Korendir! Do you still wish a wardstone for Whitestorm?"

This time he managed a mangled reply. "Yes."

But the cry betrayed broken sincerity. Through the hurt in him, Ithariel glimpsed the image that defeated: a small girl wrapped in a black cloak, with a knife thrust home through her eye.

Resolve faltered. Ithariel recoiled in horror; and the fierce self-condemnation that burned Korendir to wildness ripped her contact clean away. His hand scattered sand grains across granite. The first ward was breached. Only two more remained, and even as the enchantress

rallied, the man crossed the line of the next. The ash in
the braziers started up in blue flame, and on two levels,
protective magic fled.

Korendir screamed as the cutting edge of memory
sliced deeper.

Frightened witless, Ithariel tackled him. The drag of
her overrobe encumbered them both. The delay lasted
barely a heartbeat, but an instant was enough: the savagery of Korendir's resistance itself inspired invention.
Before he could breach the last barrier, she fumbled and
recovered the tallix fashioned throughout the night before. Without hesitation, she hurled the stone at his face.

He fielded the crystal before it struck entirely by animal reflex. Sunlight through the casement caught upon
myriad facets, and the spells so exactingly patterned
blazed to a brilliance of glory. Some aspect of the ward's
protection must have pierced Korendir's distress, for he
stopped and crouched, his fists interlocked over the dia-
mond-clear surface of the tallix. A sob ripped from his
throat. "Too late," he whispered. "Much too late."

"Never." Ithariel flung back. She clutched to that one
thread of reason and desperately offered reinforcement.
"Never too late, but I need your trust and consent."

Deliberately she chose not to elaborate. Against de-
rangement and loss, she pitted the known qualities of a
mind that would pursue options to the final spark of life.
Korendir of Whitestorm had never been afraid to die;
his terror lay in finding himself helpless as cruelties were
inflicted on others.

He assumed risks because he did not care; and because
he cared too deeply.

The irony was fitting for a son of a former Archmaster,
but the mystery of Korendir's parentage must never be
revealed, even to spare him from ruin. While his hands
gripped the new wardstone, and his thoughts wrestled to
fathom the riddle the enchantress had cast to his discre-
tion, Ithariel engaged her powers. She sampled the essence of the banespell, and at last comprehended the
nightmare that lurked behind the memory of a slaughtered child.

The perfect and absolute ruthlessness of Majaxin's
final vengeance all but stopped his daughter's heart.

The sorcerer had laid his snare *knowingly*: only a man

of compassion would have conviction enough to break his tallix. In evil-hearted malice, the wardspells had arrayed from this assumption. *Tir Amindel's people had died, not because their lives were linked to the curse that afflicted the city, but because the man who interceded had acted out of pity for their plight.*

Had Korendir been impartial to suffering, every man, woman, and child would have survived to celebrate freedom.

But he was who he was; not the atrocities of the Mhurgai nor the slaughter of Datha's armies had been enough to unmake his nature. For this, the folk of Tir Amindel had perished: in precise and exacting proportion to the value which Korendir assigned to life.

Ithariel reeled, stunned by reflections of his guilt. Had she known, the blood of seven thousand innocents might never have flowed in the streets. And so the trap had closed. Because she, or any other White Circle initiate could never pass the city gates to discern that final peril, the one who intervened of necessity had been an outsider, untrained and insensitive to magic.

The result kindled outrage in Ithariel that no amount of risk could assuage. The Archmaster had been careless, even negligent, to set sleep over mortal pain without first seeking rudimentary understanding. Nix and Megga had been wrong to presume this mercenary's talents should go wasted. And lastly, the enchantress herself acknowledged folly, for sending into jeopardy the one man she should have cherished beyond life.

No one had consulted Korendir himself. Belatedly, in words that came with difficulty, Ithariel made the attempt.

Still within bounds of the outer circle, the man shivered in the glitter of his wardstone. He answered in a voice undone by remorse; his madness was recognition, that his best and bravest intentions had consigned a whole city to slaughter. And yet, even as he had once forborn to whip a stallion, the tatters of courtesy remained. "What do you ask of me, lady?"

Ithariel looked up with all of her feelings exposed. "I ask a home at your hearthstone, a place at your side, and permission to share your life fully."

Something flared in his expression that was outside of

insanity or hurt. Ithariel watched his fingers tighten over the wardstone until they quivered. He recovered a surprised breath. Then anguish returned, and over that a look of unmitigated determination. He was going to say no; she saw, and knew why, and the reason cut her to the heart.

He would reject her because he realized he could love her. The discovery was not new. He had recognized the attraction prior to his return to Tir Amindel; acknowledged its existence and laid it aside, for though she knew him, he had determined to spare her from sharing the wretchedness which haunted every aspect of his life.

She cried out before he managed speech. "Oh, you idiot of a man, *must I beg?*"

In that moment her distress matched his own. Her pain he understood, she saw as much through the chink she had opened in his armor. Despite the betrayal his care had brought Tir Amindel, he still could not forsake compassion. Ithariel saw him glance down. A queer expression of vulnerability crossed features too long denied emotion. His reply emerged quietly, almost an admission of surrender. "Don't beg. Never you. Not for that."

Ithariel could not pause to savor joy, or even to acknowledge her victory. She flung herself headlong into his mind, sought the wellspring of untapped awareness that Alathir's heir must own. She found his source, and entered, and mingled her mystery with another of such depth that the pairing left her awestruck. The potential owned by Morien's son was more than a criminal loss; it was tragedy of the first order. But the threat posed by the Mathcek Demons disallowed any hope for enlightenment. Ithariel kept her silence. Bonded to the mortal she had chosen, she embraced him with the peace of her presence.

"Korendir, Master of Whitestorm, beloved, you're no longer alone." The words reached his ears, and the core of his being; and the vision of a knife-slaughtered child lost further power to harm.

Ithariel recovered a measure of awareness, then. Bone weary, but wholly content, she discovered her newly sworn husband had moved. The wardstone no longer occupied his hands. His arms enclosed her shoulders, and the silk that once veiled his nakedness had fallen entirely away. His touch was gentle as she remembered, but this time not so steady. His breathing was ragged and hot, and his words were typically analytical. "Is it true, my only pearl, that enchantresses who marry must die the same day as their mates?"

She shifted slightly, saw through a strand of her own auburn hair that his eyes were watching and serious. "You'll just have to stop taking risks," she said gently, then laughed as he enfolded her into his warmth.

Morning flooded sunlight over the forest and flecked Ithariel's tower in spatters of leaf-filtered gold. A motewarmed fly buzzed circles through the window and lighted on a plate piled with sausage left uneaten from the night before. Megga shooed the insect away, and fixed a bead-bright eye on her spouse. "The singing stopped a long time ago. I think we'd better go up."

Nixdaxdemo started awake where he snored across the tabletop, and scraped his nose on a fork. "Huh?"

"Oh ye deaf lout, why not listen when I say something the first time!" Snappishly, Megga snatched the cutlery out of harm's way.

"I heard, you nag of a wife." Nix rubbed at his scratch and sleepily reached for his cap. "Go up we will, but I won't be opening yon door."

"Well, carry the bucket for your laziness, then," Megga retorted. "Otherwise I can't reach the latch." She shook out wrinkled skirts, rummaged in a closet, and salvaged an oaken tub from the clutter of brooms and utensils. Nothing rested on hooks, mainly because the dwarf wife hated to reach any higher than her shoulders. The rest of her kitchen stayed neat as a parade ground, even if pans and spoons were racked at the height of the average man's knees.

Amiably grousing, the dwarf couple ascended the stairs. Nix carried the bucket in front of his chest, his short arms clasped round the staves. After he stubbed his toes once, he changed grip; the container then trailed at his heels, bouncing and clattering from the tether of its rope-twist handle.

Megga cast a sour eye on the commotion. "Ye'll raise ugly spirits with your noise."

Nixdaxdimo shrugged. "Ugly spirits, or my big toe,

something has to suffer. And I rather hoped to wake up the man. If he's alive, and with our mistress just now, I don't think he wants to be disturbed."

Megga snorted her contempt. "You males think of nothing else, ever."

"For which you should be glad, woman." Nix gained the top of the landing and dumped his bucket face-down beneath the latch. At once he forgot his injunction against doors, and stepped up to peer through the keyhole.

Megga shrieked in affront and kicked her husband's ankle out from under him. The bucket tipped over. Nix crashed in a heap with a grunt that promised retaliation, while the washtub rolled on and bounced down three flights of stone stairwell.

"You worthless clod of a galliwag!" Megga hopped with injured agitation. "What did you see?"

Nix did not answer, but sprawled prone upon the floor. When he failed to move further, Megga cursed and got down on her knees. She found, to her rage, that he was not holding still out of pain, but staring rapt through the crack at the bottom of the door.

Megga wanted to shout insults, but decided on impulse to save them. She plumped down across her husband's back, thrust her chin past his shoulder, and aligned one dark eye with the doorsill.

Across an expanse of scattered sand, within one ward circle still untouched, stood a nest of cast off samite. Within its emerald folds lay the mistress of the tower, naked as the day of her birth. Entangled in her hair and her arms rested a bronze-haired man marked with scars, but sleeping now in the first contentment he had known since childhood.

"Ach, it'll be Whitestorm, then," Nix concluded in disgust. He displaced his wife and sat up. "Archmaster's going to be furious."

Megga took longer to respond, bemused as she was by the tableau in the tower's upper chamber. "A curse and boils for the Archmaster. Now my old age will be ruined with picking the bones out of fish."

"Old age?" Nix made a rude noise. "With that one for master, you think we'll *have* an old age?"

Now Megga sat up with a howl of irritation. "You'd better hope so, Nixdax. Because if not, I'll break up yon carrot-head's bones for my stewpot."

XX. Debt to Shan Rannok

A wedding took place in Fairhaven during the mild twilight of early summer. Although the event became the talk of every sailor, and the feasting lasted a week, news of the celebration passed the fortress at Whitestorm by. Trader ships did not stop there, except by request, and the first Haldeth knew of the affair was the echo of enthusiastic bickering in the shaft that gave access to the beachhead.

At the time, sunrise barely brightened the mist which mantled the holdfast on White Rock Head; the tide lay at full ebb. The smith set aside the axe he had used to chop wood for his breakfast fire. Belatedly he recalled that the gates to the landing were left open, and had been for nearly a fortnight.

Through Korendir's extended absence, Haldeth had ceased to feel the need for such tireless and diligent security.

The smith made his way toward the bailey with more curiosity than urgency. Whatever party of invaders plied the entry to Whitestorm, they assuredly lacked interest in stealth. Curses rang through the morning stillness, cut short by what sounded like a slap. Haldeth arrived at the upper gate in time to see a dwarf wife emerge from the passageway, her skirts lifted high, and a frizzle of straw-blond hair flying in disarray underneath the strings of her cap.

She paid the smith no notice, but whirled around, set huge fists on her hips, and screeched back down the stairwell, "Let that horse dribble on me one more time, and I'll grind up the both of you for compost!"

A reply floated querulously from the passage. "Compost, you say? There's gratitude. Who was it packed yer butt from the forests to Fairhaven, while the master's lady walked?"

This logic was followed by two pricked ears, a wide eye, then the dappled gray neck of a stallion with a sodden gold mane. Caught like a bug in the tangle was a black-haired dwarf, still waving his fist and shouting. The rest of the horse clattered out with a prance of steel-shod hooves. Once on level footing, it flicked its tail at the droplets tickling its belly. Water flew; and in reflex it shook like a dog. The dwarf astride its barrel all but fell off, and the one on the ground howled outrage.

Haldeth covered his ears in self defense. Bemused, he waited for the clamor to subside, and almost missed the laughter that issued from the passage after the stallion's magnificent tail.

"You will both be quiet," called a female voice from below. "Or I can promise the master will seal you in a barrel and hurl you altogether over the cliff face."

Haldeth's hands dropped to his sides. His brows rose. The prospect of a woman at Whitestorm left him surprised to incapacity. Unshaven, clad in the same shirt he had worn for a week, he stared openmouthed as another figure emerged from the entryway. This last was a swordsman, clothed all in black; but the face beneath familiar bronze hair showed an uncharacteristic grin. Still laughing, a woman in pearls and blue velvet rested in the circle of his arms.

"Take that brute of a stallion off and find a stable for him," she called to the scowling combatants.

As the stallion's ringing stride and the dwarf couple's grousing retreated, Korendir gained the bailey. He set his burden down and the velvets fell away to reveal russet hair and a face of breathtaking symmetry. The rest of the lady was no less magnificent, though her grooming had suffered from the sea. Still gawking, the smith forgot to breathe.

"Haldeth?" Korendir stepped forward and extended the lady's hand, which rested still inside his own. "Come welcome Ithariel of Whitestorm home."

Haldeth shut his teeth, bit his tongue, and recovered his wind with a grunt. Stupidly he said, "I thought you swore not to marry until you secured a wardstone for the watchtower?"

"But he didn't," Ithariel protested. Amused, she reached for a pouch at her girdle and removed a crystal that glittered with a thousand points of light. The mist that clung over the headlands seemed suddenly thinner, less damp, and some other color than gray.

Haldeth blinked several times and raked back uncombed hair. "Neth," he said. His voice shook. "You're White Circle?"

Ithariel nodded sweetly. The Archmaster's threat of disinheritance had apparently been bluster; thus far, Telvallind had done little but rail and shout, inform that Korendir's presence would be unwelcome in Dethmark, and obstinately refuse attendance at the wedding.

Haldeth reached out and tentatively touched the jewel that shimmered in the lady's outstretched hand. The surface tingled like a tonic against his skin. Convinced he was not dreaming, he looked at Korendir, whose face was all strange with a smile of unguarded happiness. The smith scratched his head. "The contract in Tir Amindel brought you other than gold, I see. Now what in the Mhurga's hells will you do with the coins you've got heaped in your hall?"

The Master of Whitestorm seemed surprised. "I expect Ithariel will buy hangings, furniture, and chickens with them. Or do you think the widows of Heddenton need blankets?"

"Widows of Heddenton, my backside!" Haldeth's embarrassment changed to irritation. "We need blankets, the ones we have are moth-chewed, and how in the devil can I provide enough bread and meat to satisfy the appetites of two dwarves?"

"They are gluttons," Ithariel admitted. She veiled the wardstone and looked up with an appeal that had left broken hearts by the dozen back at the docks at Fairhaven. "But on my word, Megga's a cook, and if Nix works one whit less than his worth, I'll send him back to where I found him."

Haldeth accepted the hand she offered and returned a delighted grin. "They peel onions?" he asked hopefully.

"They will." Korendir closed his fingers over his lady's and gave a gentle squeeze. "Or else a certain slave dealer who sells to the mines will find himself cursed with bad stock."

*   *   *

The dwarves made their presence felt at Whitestorm like an infestation of rats. Wherever a man turned, he tripped over them. Accustomed to solitude, and silence, and an indolent preference for clutter, Haldeth took the change in poor stride.

Megga had a tongue like a shrew, and the first thing she did was rearrange every pot, pan, and spoon in the kitchen. Haldeth came to breakfast one morning and found his favorite sitting nook jammed to capacity with buckets, candle molds, and brooms. His protest earned him a scolding so fierce that he left without tasting the sweet rolls. That mistake spoiled the rest of the day, since Nix took it upon himself to eat for two, and the raisins in the batter griped his stomach.

"You don't want Megga to think her cooking's been slighted," he confided, heroically aggrieved; the pains had reached the point where he parked in the bailey to moan and roll his eyes. "She learned how to nag from the devil's unwed sister, and her pride's just prickly as sea urchins."

"I'll try to remember." One moment of pity gained Haldeth a half-hour lecture on the feeding and virtues of the High Kelair gray, never mind that the stallion kicked its stall doors to pieces and bit everyone except Ithariel, the dwarves, and Korendir.

Haldeth retired to his forge, where he spent the morning hammering out horseshoes with rounded edges and no studs. As always, the fire and the tang of heated steel eased his pique. In time, he began to whistle, and when the sound of Ithariel's singing drifted down from the lord's chambers in the north tower, the smith reflected that life might have turned for the better.

Other things at Whitestorm altered beside the kitchens. The main hall acquired furnishings and hangings, and Megga took in an orphaned wolf pup, which chewed boots and chair legs without discrimination. Ithariel got tired of teeth marks in abalone inlay; she banished the beast to the stables, where it developed an unnatural attachment to the gray. But the most profound changes occured in Whitestorm's master.

He still preferred black tunics, and despite Megga's wizardry in the larder, he gained not an ounce of soft weight. But where once he had been nerve-edged, rest-less, and too silent, he now showed the grace of his up-bringing. He read, discussed every subject from medicine to philosophy, and never wore weapons indoors. Startled by his laughter, an unsuspected and easygoing humor, and a forthright affection for his lady, Haldeth still watched with wary eyes.

Risk and danger had ruled Korendir's character for as long as the smith could remember. The addiction to challenge might be dormant, even lulled temporarily to quiescence. But one day the drive must resurface; the mercenary who had decimated the Dathei even now dis-trusted peace. Sorcery guarded his watchtower and his gates stayed meticulously locked.

And yet the summer passed without incident. Korendir and Nixdaxdimo cut a path through Thornforest to con-nect Whitestorm with the post road to Heddenton. After that, Megga took regular wagon rides to town, bearing gold for the village poor, and shopping lists for supplies. Korendir hired in a shipwright, and set about building a boat to replace the lean, uncomfortable *Carcadonn*. He and his wife went fishing, or just sailing to enjoy the wind.

The worst shock came when Megga returned from a trip for provisions with two young boys behind the buck-board. They wore rough clothing, and were aged maybe eight and ten years. As they passed beneath the gates into Whitestorm, Haldeth caught sight of them, two mops of identical dark hair wedged between the ale bar-rels and freshly ground flour.

He hastened from the gatehouse the instant the port-cullis rattled closed and flagged the cart down in the bai-ley. "Megga, you can't. Boys are different than stray cubs. Send these back where you found them, or there'll be trouble, I promise."

The youngsters regarded this exchange with fearful and liquid brown eyes; and Megga's temper lit.

"Strays? Not these, you maggot-headed windbag!" She shook a fist under Haldeth's nose. "The master said bring you an apprentice. He meant one, true enough, but these were orphans, and brothers. They'll do much better together."

Haldeth felt his hair rise in precise and definable dread. "*Korendir* said bring children to Whitestorm?"

"Well?" Megga withdrew her threatening forearm. "What do you think, they have fleas or something?" She summed up her disgust with a grunt, then bounded down off the wagon and set the team prancing as she scuttled under their legs to reach their bridles. "Stupid man, you think I'm deaf? Fetch Haldeth an apprentice, the master said. If you don't remember manners and take these horses off to Nix, your boys are going to stay in my scullery for pot washers."

Most incredibly, her story proved true. Korendir had indeed asked for children to take residence in the loft above the forge; he went further, and did not summon a joiner, but constructed their bunks and their clothes chests himself.

The boys learned to ride, to groom the cart team, and to maintain the wood for the forge fire. Only Nix was too fussy to make use of their services, and after watching him perform inexplicable feats with perfectly ordinary tools, Haldeth understood why dwarf-wrought steel held a mystery.

The fall brought a messenger in the royal livery of Faen Hallir, to deliver a request that Korendir return to mercenary service. The contract was declined, and sailors carried word back to Fairhaven: the Master of Whitestorm was no longer available for hire.

Haldeth settled into complacency. When the snow fell thick at midwinter, he grew used to clean clothing and large breakfasts, and to breaking up fisticuffs between the apprentices. Megga's scolding and Nixdaxdimo's irrational flights of temper became first on his list of hazards, with the teeth of the slate gray stallion just behind.

A year passed. The arrival of a fishing boat when the leaves turned seemed nothing untoward at the time. The shoals off White Rock Head offered excellent harvest, and the sun-bronzed crews who plied nets there occasionally traded herring in exchange for ham and fresh bread. But as Haldeth took in the view from atop the battlements, he noticed that the paintwork on the boat was not plain, after the custom of Dunharra, but patterned in rows of checkered symbols. This craft sailed out of

Illantyr. The purpose which called her this far from local waters would not be any scarcity of bacon.

A pang of familiar dread made Haldeth draw in his breath. He spun away from a sight that seemed suddenly less friendly and headed for the master's chambers in the north keep.

Before he could knock at the door, Ithariel's voice rang down the stairwell.

"Such massacre can only be the work of those demons that mortals name Mathcek. Their powers of desecration are documented. The wizards at Alathir all died screaming. Since then not a White Circle enchanter will dare the straits north of Illantyr, and with sound reason. The powers of the demons are beyond them."

Haldeth froze, his hand half raised at the door panel as Korendir's reply came fast and flat as a whipcrack.

"But I'm no wizard. The Lady of Shan Rannok reared me. The farmers of her domain filled my belly until the Mhurgai killed the overlord who protected them. By blood debt, I am obligated. Whatever slaughter these demons may threaten, the islanders have the right to ask my service."

Light footsteps crossed the carpet beyond the door. "Nix and the Archmaster warned against my becoming your wife." Ithariel's words sounded unforced, even fond. "I wouldn't listen to them then, and I won't regret now. But I must point out that my spirit is bound to yours, even past the ending of life. If you're determined to die fighting an enemy that can't be conquered, I sail to Illantyr at your side."

Haldeth stepped back until his spine jarred into the newel post. He had relied on the woman to temper her husband's nature, not to abet his recklessness; worse, she was minded to accompany him on this insane and riskiest of ventures. The ballads from Alathir were recitals of unalloyed tragedy. Against the Mathcek Demons, Morien and his Council Major had perished in agony; and they were no mortals, but wizards born and trained.

Korendir cared not a wit for past failures. He spoke in a tone that Haldeth interpreted as unholy and arrogant pride. "Lady of my heart, I will sail to Illantyr to fight. But I've no intention of dying, and you're needed here to secure the holdfast."

At this, Haldeth took umbrage. He laid his hands
against the door latch, jerked it free, and barged uninvited into the breech.

The fisherman who had brought in the trouble stood
unobtrusively to one side, the cuffs of his smock half
crushed under twine-scarred hands. His presence had
been forgotten, and his expression revealed an unswerv-
ing wish to slink out of sight behind the tapestries.

Korendir commandeered the center of the floor, taut
as wound cable and frowning. His hands were braced on
the shoulders of his lady, and she, in her velvets, glowered back.

Haldeth dared fate and interrupted. "She's not to be
gainsaid, you half-witted madman."

At this attack, three heads turned with expressions of
astonishment. Haldeth found himself the focus of a demanding stare from the fisherman, and rapacious study
by matching pairs of gray eyes. Their intensity daunted.

The smith sweated, and shrugged, and looked down at
the floor. "Orame told me the Demons of Mathcek arose
from Alhaerie," he persisted with lame determination.
"Against the powers of the otherworld, you'll need an
enchanter's knowledge. Let the Lady Ithariel go, and
save my boys the backbreaking labor of digging graves."

The enchantress regarded her husband. She touched
his cheek with a gentleness entirely at odds with her expression, then softened his mouth with a kiss. "Sail with
the fisherman," she murmured in challenge. "And stop
me from coming if you can."

For an instant Korendir was torn between rage and a
fierce compulsion to laugh. Then his seriousness won
out. "You understand me," he marvelled, his voice too
quiet to be overheard. Then he did smile, teasingly.
"You know you'll have to put a sleep spell on the
dwarves."

"Or they'll follow us, howling, I know," Ithariel nodded toward the fisherman who fidgeted to one side.
"We'll be ready to sail with the tide."

The enchantress turned in the circle of her husband's
arms, her last instructions for Haldeth. "Fetch Korendir's
black sword from the armory. Steel will be very little use
against demons, but if his Lordship of Whitestorm

crosses the sea without a dwarf-wrought blade, Nix will most cheerfully break my neck."

Mantled in pre-dawn gloom, the fishing boat bound for Illantyr hauled anchor and unfurled lateen rigged canvas. The folk who crewed her did not sing as their sturdy craft heeled with the wind. Mist overhung White Rock Head and blotted the fast-fading stars; the water under the keel swirled black, scribed with reflections from the tallix that glimmered through fog above the fortress. But Korendir of Whitestorm did not linger at the stern rail to watch his home shoreline recede. Instead he leaned against the head stay, his eyes trained intently to the west. Beyond the horizon lay the isle whose shores held the fire-charred stones of the holdfast where he had been raised. Now, in murk only feebly cut by the flame of the deck lantern, the terrors of that past and the murder of the widow who had mothered him seemed vividly close.

Ithariel joined her man on the foredeck. She saw his tense stance, and did not touch, but settled instead on a bight of rope coiled behind his heels. Muffled to the chin in blue wool, she waited without impatience for him to break his silence.

He spoke finally in tones pitched for her ears alone. "I never meant to go back."

She heard the words, but sensed a more difficult concept behind; indirectly he tried to impart that her presence at Whitestorm had been enough. Ithariel spared him the need to apologize. "You've been your own master since the day you won free of the Mhurgai." After a pause, she qualified with the tough part. "Love by itself does not cancel obligation."

Korendir turned his head from the sea and looked at her. "If I had a coinweight of sense, you wouldn't be here."

Ithariel smiled exactly as she did when Megga tried her nerves. "If *I* had a coinweight of sense, I'd agree with you." Her eyes seemed very bright. Beyond her, the streaming mists lightened with the advent of sunrise.

Korendir watched the wind play through her coils of dark hair. "We could go back."

But the core of hardness had not left him and the enchantress was not fooled. "Go back?" She laughed

gently. "To bed, I should think, and when you had loved
me to distraction, you'd steal away while I slept?"

He recoiled slightly, fingers tightened against the head-
stay. "Witch. I should never have married a woman of
spells."

"But you did." Ithariel leaned her warmth against his
shins. "For us, there can be no turning back."

"No." Korendir looked at her intently, and shared an
insight of a depth even she found surprising. "When I
took contract for the Duke of Tir Amindel, I had already
passed the edge. That little boy's life had become my last
anchor for sanity. When I found the child could not be
saved, nothing remained that held meaning." Here he
paused and drew breath. "Lady, you should know. Majaxin's vengeance notwithstanding, my sole reprieve from
madness was through your intervention."

Unwilling to face the implications of why he should
seek to free her conscience, and doubly aware of how
near his losses at Shan Rannok threaded the surface of
his thoughts, Ithariel resumed in dogged steadiness. She
described what she knew of High Morien's towers,
though little enough was recorded in the archives at
Dethmark. The disaster had been started by a careless
apprentice who opened a wizard's gate without safeguards. His meddling went awry, tore open the fabric of
reality between Aerith and Alhaerie. Morien's council
had heroically sealed the breach, but not in time. Entities
from the otherworld had slipped through, ones with an
insatiable bent for destruction. Defeat for the defenders
at Alathir had been swift and utterly final, while the enemies which had annihilated them lived on unvanquished.

Ithariel listed the demons' attributes, those that were
documented, and although the sun struck gold through
the mist when she finished, shadow seemed to linger on
the decks. The boat that plowed through the new morning only hastened toward misadventure; for if the fish-
ermens' tales were true, the Mathcek Demons had
ranged south from Alathir's ruins and desecrated the outlying villages of Shan Rannok. No power in Aerith was
great enough to stop them; only a foolish few farmers
and three dozen hired guardsmen stood ground to contest
their advance.

Ithariel regarded the husband who stood still as a

carven figurehead upon the bow. He sailed out of duty to the widow who had fostered him, but the foe he opposed was far older. The Mathcek Demons were second of the Six Great Banes. They would recognize High Morien's heir; unwitting last survivor of Alathir, Korendir would be mercilessly hunted from the moment he offered challenge. But Ithariel knew the futility of trying to deter him with the certainty he was fated to fail. Knowledge of his father's doom would but commit him to action more firmly. By her oath to Telvallind Archmaster, Ithariel kept that secret unbroached.

Five days later, lit by the sickle of a fading quarter moon, Korendir regarded the land which bulked black against a misted, predawn horizon. The fishing boat rolled at her anchorage, a cove on Illantyr's eastern shore sheltered from the westerlies by the ridge which thrust from the isle's central plain. The fishermen slept in hammocks slung from the rigging on deck, while Ithariel occupied the stern cabin. Soft lights burned within, and scrawled pearly reflections on the wavelets beneath the counter; the enchantress used her arts to scry out the danger before their planned landing in daylight.

Korendir scanned the decks. Nothing stirred but one fisherman who snored and twitched in a dream. The boy who shared anchor watch sat beneath the deck lantern, whittling toys for his nephew. He glanced off the stern from time to time and studied the wave crests guardedly, unconsoled by Ithariel's insistence that demons never crossed water. The thought did not occur that the mercenary from Whitestorm might wish to.

Despite the chill, Korendir had not worn boots. He shed his cloak and sword belt with a predator's stealth, then pulled off the tunic beneath. Clad in leggings and shirt, he re-buckled his baldric across his shoulder. The scabbard and crossguard he secured with a length of twine filched from a net float. Lastly, cat-silent, he cleated an end of the jibsheet to a belaying pin and lowered himself over the rail.

A wavelet slapped his ankles. Korendir repressed a shiver and let the line burn through his fingers. He slipped without splash into the icy embrace of the sea. The swim to the shores of Illantyr was close to half a league; Ithariel had insisted they anchor well out, to avoid risking notice by demons. Korendir floated quietly until the current carried him beyond earshot, and the flicker of spells in the stern windows diminished to a dull spark of light. Then he struck off with overhand strokes for the shadowy shoreline to the west.

Daybreak found him stretched full length on sands packed firm by breakers. He rested long enough to catch his breath, and to ponder the dangers ahead. The enemies he proposed to challenge were nothing like wereleopards, which had been loosed by a meddling wizard who crossbred desert wildcats with creatures from Alhaerie. The demons which victimized Illantyr were directly transported from the otherworld. More than shapechangers, they could take any form, or none; on the effort of a single thought they could alter the landscape into any appearance they chose.

"Humans are endowed with like powers beyond the wizard's gates," Ithariel had explained during the crossing from Whitestorm. "To imagine a thing is to create it, fully formed from the void. A portion of Alhaerie's existence unravels to supply mass and energy. And so it is with outworld beings who trespass Aerith. They can shape into form whatever dream they desire, but our flora and fauna and soil sustain untold damage in consequence."

Korendir flexed tired muscles and rose from his hollow on the beach. He dusted sand from his skin. Shivering in his salt-spangled shirt, he drew his dirk and cut the lashings on his sword. Sunrise bronzed the ocean at his back as he struck off, barefoot, for the hills.

High Morien had met demons with spell-craft, and lost; it remained to be seen what a mortal without magic could accomplish.

Just past full daylight, Ithariel stepped from the stern cabin clad in a man's boots and tunic. The clothing was unbleached linen, but cut to her size, and bordered with leaves and birds in rust thread. Her eyes were reddened, result of a night spent scrying, and her braids were pinned back in a fashion more practical than pretty. The frown that leveled her brows was one men cared not to cross. She inquired after Korendir from the boy who whittled by the sternsheets, went forward, and discovered the decks empty; except for a tunic and cloak in a discarded heap by the rail.

Fishermen from Illantyr never wore black on shipboard; the color begged Neth for a funeral, they claimed, and only the daft tempted fate.

But Korendir remained as impervious to superstition as to his current rejection of plain sense. Ithariel's shout brought the ship's company bounding up the companionway from the galley.

These included three brothers, captained by a sprytongued grandfather who was creased like old leather from seafaring. He had seen two sons die of foolishness; the significance of Korendir's empty clothing registered in less than a breath.

He regarded the outraged enchantress with keenly considering eyes. "You'll be going after him, then." He did not wait for reply, but ordered his grandsons to unlash and lower the jolly boat.

Ithariel clenched her hands on the rail and stared toward the land which bulked to starboard. The horizon above the hills rolled black under dense blooms of smoke. Whether a village or some farmer's field was ablaze hardly mattered; her scrying showed demonsign everywhere.

"We'll find him," the old man assured her. "I and my grandsons will help."

Ithariel picked a stray thread from her cuff. As if the captain had not spoken, she said, "I should have suspected all along when he failed to try me with arguments." A stitch gave under the persistence of her worry, and a wisp of embroidery unravelled; one of the little birds was left wingless. "Damn." The enchantress clamped her hands on her forearms just as a clamor arose from amidships.

"Neth, will you look," shouted the youngest boy to his grandfather. "Block 'n' tackle's been got at, and the line's fouled."

"Oh damn him!" Ithariel hammered her fists on her sleeves. "Of course! He would have laid plans to delay us." She turned bleak eyes to the captain. "Old man, forgive my stupidity and inspect your ship. For as I know my husband, we've seen just the first of our troubles."

The fisherman glanced back in bright anger. "We'll see about that." He nodded to his eldest, who whirled at once to comply.

Ithariel joined the search, and almost immediately snagged her frayed seam on the dagger sheathed at her belt. Wholly impatient with trivia, she ripped free, drew the offending blade, and hacked off her shirt cuff, fine embroidery notwithstanding. Then, fighting tears, she bent to inspect the ship's rudder. All the pins but one had been neatly removed from their seatings.

Her man was nothing if not thorough; even should the fishing boat sail with intent to run aground on the beachhead, little could be accomplished in a westerly without steerage except a downwind run back to Whitestorm.

"I'll break your ugly clever head myself," Ithariel threatened to the empty air. She choked back a cry of frustration.

The diligent boys and their grandfather disclosed the rest of Korendir's sabotage inside a quarter of an hour. The list was impressive, from sprung planks in the jolly boat, to a weakened splice in a halyard concealed near the top of the mast. This not being enough, the mercenary had purloined the jollyboat's rowlocks, and cut all the hanks from the headsails. None of the damage was permanent. But the ship and her single tender were dependably crippled through a day or more of repairs.

Ithariel loosed an oath of aggravation. "Is there anything my curse for a husband failed to think of?"

There was not; the youngest of the grandsons wormed out from beneath the tender and announced two missing pairs of oars.

No one bothered to check on the spares stored in the aft locker. Korendir would have seen those the past morning when he fetched out the buckets to swab the decks.

Ithariel glared landward at the forests where her man had ventured without leave. "I can still swim," she whispered in defiance. Oblivious to the stares of captain and crew, or the heated blush of the youngest, she began to strip off her tunic.

Beneath her bustle of action, her heart knew a crushing end of hope. She could not possibly make landfall before noon. By then, her arrival would be too late. Her man had gone ahead of her, into dangers he lacked training to comprehend. The only protection he carried was his marriage ring, a band with a cut tallix setting. The wardspell laid into the crystal was nothing more than a token, a charm to heal cuts and abrasions, and a luckbane against broken bones.

Ithariel wound her arms around her shoulders as if racked by a terrible chill. In trying to spare her from risk, Korendir accomplished nothing more than certain doom for them both. No comfort could be wrung from his courage. Even had she broken her vow and revealed the perils of his parentage, Korendir's thrice-cursed honor would remain. His absolute disregard for danger would have dictated his behavior to the end.

XXI. Mathcek Demons

"Lady, no." The oldest of the brothers reached out and tried to catch her wrist; too late. The enchantress shucked her shirt without pause to acknowledge, and his fingers collided with bare flesh. She wore no other undergarment. Her skin in the morning light shone pale and translucent as abalone, and the form it described was breathtaking.

The brother snatched back as if burned. Scarlet as his sibling, he doggedly resorted to speech. "We can have that jollyboat patched within an hour."

Ithariel never glanced at him, but reached down to unlace her hose. "What'll you row it with, spoons?"

Her tone was shrewish, but concern drove her too hard to care. The higher the sun rose, the greater her peril; if she was going to die because Korendir went before her, she would rather the end overtook her alone in open water. The fishermen would never understand.

The older boy watched her tear at her points, and his throat tightened uselessly. Only the elderly captain regarded her beauty with impunity, and that because he had seen naked women by the dozens in whorehouses through the years he had sailed out of Fairhaven. With less fuss than he employed to unhook a flipping mackerel, he caught the enchantress's wrist and spun her around to face him.

"Daft as your man, you're being!" The anger in his eyes, or maybe the overpowering smell of fish on him forced her to take notice and listen. "That launch can be rigged to sail in less time than you might think. You'll reach the beach safely that way, and be rested enough to continue. If you go now, I promise, you'll throw your last chance to the winds. Tide's turned, can't you see?

Current's in flood and pulling north at five knots faster than you can swim."

The old man paused in his tirade. He glanced aside at his boys and sent them to work with a barked command.

Then he released the enchantress with a fatherly pat on the shoulder and left her to retrieve her shirt, which fluttered across the deck on the verge of being snatched by the breeze.

"May not be such a fool, your man," the captain concluded. He fixed faded, squint-wrinkled eyes on the ripples which scoured past the counter. "Sure picked his moment, and rudder pins? What a right bitch of an embarrassment! I packed spares. Neth, in these waters, all us south coasters do. But damned if your bronze-headed gallant didn't ask which locker, one watch a ways back 'midst the straits. Claimed a pin was fixing to crack, when I knew myself they'd been replaced the last time this bucket got careened."

Ithariel's reply came muffled through linen as she dragged her shirt over her face. "Cleverness won't save him from demons, more's the pity."

Her tousled auburn head emerged from the collar, expectant; but if the captain agreed, he kept silence.

The jollyboat was prepared in less than the promised interval, but her design was not so easily compromised. Never intended to carry sail, she lacked keel, and her improvised rig made her clumsy. Worse, the prevailing westerlies had picked up. Harried by current, and forced to tack, the craft made marginal headway. Caught between views of a landmass that promised doom, or the wake which curved behind and displayed their disastrous set to leeward, Ithariel crouched with her forehead braced on frustrated, white-knuckled fists as the sun climbed inexorably higher.

The grandfather seemed sublimely unconcerned. He and his relations worked their boat with their accustomed sarcastic banter all the way to the shore.

The jarring impact of landing threw Ithariel bodily from her seat. One brother caught her as the craft rolled in the waves, while the others freed sheets and leaped the thwarts to steady against the pull of the surf.

Helped ashore by the old man, Ithariel murmured

thanks and stepped out onto blinding white sand. The blot of shade beneath her feet was alarmingly small. Caught by immeasurable dread, she squinted toward the captain. "I'll need you, and one of your crew that's unmarried."

"Oleg." The grandfather hailed the brother whose hair was bound with a twist of red wool.

He was not the oldest, nor even the one of middle years. Ithariel regarded the boy's cheerful features with no end of trepidation. "I'm sorry," she said, touched by misgivings that echoed the captain's. "Trust me, I'll skin my husband the mercenary, if we ever recover him alive."

The wind carried a smoky taint over the fragrant resin of pines. Worn with nerves, and guilty for the dangers she must impose upon a kindly old man and young boy, the enchantress made her way inland at a pace that promised blisters. The grandson followed at her heels, while his elder delayed briefly to shout orders for the brothers who remained.

"Ye brought the axe? Good. Then find some decent driftwood and hew us two brace of oars. Bind them in net twine for rowlocks, then dismantle that limping excuse for a mast."

As the brothers' oaths of irritation fell behind, Ithariel felt gratitude for the grandfather's undying good sense; if they survived to recover Korendir, a hasty departure could save them. When the boy at her side asked a question, the enchantress found grace from somewhere to explain that over soil and rock she could follow Korendir's path without any need for spells. There were advantages to tracking a spell-bonded mate; but as she passed the dunes and plunged into brush and thick forest she sorely cursed the necessity. Twigs clawed her hair and fallen leaves mired her step. A persistent ache started at the base of her skull, warning that at last, Korendir of Whitestorm had encountered the trouble inevitable from the start.

The enchantress's discomfort intensified as she and her companions made headway into Illantyr's wooded hills. The smell of smoke and burning grew stronger. Then the forest thinned, and they crossed a village byway, where corpses rotted in a ditch by the roadside. One was a woman, with the beetle-crawling remains of an infant wrapped in her shawl. Scavengers had gnawed away her abdomen.

The boy doubled over and got sick, and with pity in his eyes, the grandfather steadied him to his feet. "Bear up, lad. You'll see much worse if we're delayed."

The boy peeled his bandanna from his brow and dabbed at his fouled mouth. His fingers shook. "Do you think Mama—"

The grandfather answered with stony lack of sympathy. "Her, and us, and yer brothers, too, if we don't find that mercenary quickly." He nodded after Ithariel, who waited with anxious impatience. "Get on and follow her, and belay the whining complaints."

The boy raised his chin. He stumbled ahead while his eyes spilled a flood of soundless tears. Behind him, the grandfather's weathered face showed sadness.

Beyond the roadway, the trees stood bare; clouds massed the sky ahead, but the going became easier, the terrain cut by woodsmen's footpaths. They crossed the clearing of a charcoal burner's hut, but his kilns were cold, and his family departed. Squirrels had nested in the tree overhanging the chimney, sure sign that desertion was not recent. Sun spilled through stripped branches and scattered bars of shadow across the ground. Through a headache that steadily worsened, Ithariel realized the light lanced straight down; noon had come, and with it, the peak of the demons' powers.

Any minute would reveal Korendir to enemies as the get of Morien Archmaster. Once that fact was uncovered, the tallix ring with its token spell of blessing was not going to spare him from dismemberment.

The trees ended soon after; ahead the ground stretched gray, an expanse of wind-sifted ash winnowed into patterns like desert sand. Shivering from pains that now laced like fire along her nerves, Ithariel paused to lay spells. Her skin wept clammy sweat and her hands shook worse than the boy's as she fought to trace symbols in the earth.

For the vista of wasteland established without doubt that they had reached the leading edge of demon territory.

At Alathir, Morien had raised magic to challenge and defy this same advance; his defense had been wrought of earth forces, and these the demons had unbound like a snag in a fisherman's knit. Yet where Korendir's father had sought to destroy, his wife wished only to conceal. She tapped the forces of Alhaerie itself to weave a glamour around her companions. Just as a man from Aerith would take no notice of pebbles, or sticks, or roots, so the demons might overlook the moiling, chaotic trace energies transmuted from their native environment.

Enchantments of this nature were a perilous undertaking in any place; elaborate safeguards must be taken to avoid an imbalance, and caution warred with the pressing need for urgency. Ithariel worked against certainty that time was now ruinously short. Halfway through setting the wards, she shuddered and cried out. Her face went gray and she flung back her head while above her, outlined against sky, the faces of frightened companions watched helplessly.

"He's not dead," she said hoarsely. "Not yet." And she forced her spells to completion, ringing her fishermen in crackling eddies that snapped and then faded to invisibility.

Ithariel arose, hunched in pain like an old woman. "If we can keep our advance quiet, we have hope. At the moment the demons are diverted with Korendir. They would make sport with him before he dies. As long as he stays alive, our presence stands a chance of being overlooked."

She did not add that they tortured him; or that like an echo, his suffering harrowed her. Instead she said he was close by, and as she staggered forward, she felt the arms of the old man and the boy reach out to steady her steps.

They progressed over ground blasted to the desolation of a volcanic plain. Burned rock and blackened cinders heated unpleasantly through layers of boot leather and hose. The air smelled scorched, and though elsewhere the land was sunlit, the sky here hung gloomy with overcast. Loose hair stuck to Ithariel's temples. Her breath ripped in gasps from her chest and her eyes watered. She blinked away tears, stared upslope to the ridge. Smoke billowed in drifts against the summit. Her stinging eyes could just make out the limbs of what might have been thorn trees at Whitestorm.

"Up there," she grated, and began the ascent over coarse rocks that gouged at her shins and palms.

The climb was relentlessly steep, and the grandfather began to wheeze. A simple man, content with his life of toil with bait and nets, he had no experience with enchanters or demons; but danger was a thing he knew well, and he understood the management of men. He held his position with a determination learned from weathering gales and acted as if he had moved through circles of spell-craft since youth.

"Look you, Oleg, see these stones?" he said to divert the boy who moved in stiff fear on Ithariel's other side. "They're sharp, full of holes like the lava rocks from the Mathcek Isles to the north. Bad shores for ships, those. They say the demons escaped to Aerith from there."

Ithariel had no breath left to correct that misapprehension, which nonetheless had given rise to the demons' name. The point became moot five paces later when a scream drowned out the old man's chatter. The cry was human agony distilled, then magnified and shattered to a thousand echoes by the riven, lifeless landscape. Ithariel shuddered again. The boy beside her balked on the mindless edge of panic. Though the grandfather had no more bravery left in him, he went through the motions and tried to speak words of encouragement.

Ithariel fought for grip on the confusion which divided her mind. Aware through the pull of Korendir's torment that around her companions were faltering, she snagged the grandfather's attention with a look and said, "My Lord of Whitestorm is alive." She qualified in a racked and scraping croak, "He's fighting for survival, and that of your loved ones, never doubt. What we hear is certain proof."

Another scream sheared the air. Ithariel felt the hair rise along her spine. She worked her fingers free of her shirt cuffs, the right one now shredded to match the other in the unthinking clench of her hands. "You must not run," she finished finally. "No matter what you see, I'll need you both to help carry him." She did not add that if she succeeded in reaching her man, the odds lay against getting him out.

They labored to climb the rugged slope. Smoke swirled around them, wind-eddied into shapes like departed spirits. The rocks rose raw-edged and dark against a sky forbidding with storm. Though elsewhere the hill was scoured clean of vegetation, they came at length upon a hollow that sheltered a stand of living trees. Their branches were cruelly barbed. The crowns which tossed in the wind were green-black, each leaf the mirrored replica of the forest which clothed the cliffs above White Rock Head. The sultry inland air carried an incongruous tang of ocean.

Stung by the manifestation of Korendir's vulnerability, Ithariel understood how the trap had been sprung. She guessed in advance what must wait beyond the last crest. As if to intensify her dread an ominous silence fell. She and her companions hurried the last steps and breasted the lip of the rise.

The outcrop fell away beneath, but not as randomly jumbled stone. Here rose battlements of blue granite, dressed, shaped, and corniced into a structure immediately familiar. The valley amidst the wasteland held a perfect recreation of Whitestorm's inner holdfast. Every detail was accurate, from Haldeth's craftmark on the gate winches, to the patterns of the cobbles in the bailey; and so they would be, since their shape had been torn intact from Korendir's mind. Yet in this place wrought by demons, the aura of the tallix in the watchtower washed a scene of living hell.

Shackles had been set into rings in the paving. Pinned spreadeagled in black iron, the Master of Whitestorm struggled with his muscles knotted and his head thrown violently back. The fetters of the demons held him fast; against their powers he never had a chance. Above his staring, wild eyes towered a post set with a hook like a butcher's stall. There a figure of delicate proportions sagged naked and half unconscious from a rope twist. Auburn hair clung damply around her face, and shoulders the color of new pearl were striped and running with blood.

Ithariel gasped in shock. She had expected to look upon horrors, but no nightmare apprehension could prepare for the vision of herself being flogged until her flesh split by a perfect replication of Haldeth.

The lash fell with a crack. The demon-formed Ithariel whimpered. Drops of shed blood pattered down on the man who flinched and thrashed and quivered against his chains. For the Master of Whitestorm, pain and death were no match for the crueler agony of helplessness. His protest pealed out like a war cry, but the fury in the sound could not last. Inevitably, his strength would spend itself in useless struggle. Logic could not distinguish the creation of demons from truth, for the chains were genuine iron, and the woman under torture was real. The heart must eventually burst before what was no dream, but the uttermost ruin of hope.

The whip fell again, wielded by an arm toughened by the drive of a blacksmith's hammer. On the ridgetop, the boy made a sound and slapped his palms over his mouth. Pale as death, the old man knelt to intercede as his grandson crumpled over in dry heaves. He supported the traumatized boy and glanced in appeal to Ithariel.

"Demons," she gasped. "They deform the nature of Aerith to shape Korendir's worst fear." Wrenched with sickness herself, the enchantress averted her face and strove to rally her nerve. She must not pity her double, but only the plight of the man. "This has to be stopped."

"How?" The grandfather squinted through a drift of blown smoke. "Where are the demons?"

"All about you." Ithariel raked back sweaty hair. "Look for ripples, something like heat waves in dry air."

The old man turned a shade whiter. He had noticed such disturbances, patches that seemed to shimmer across his vision, but he had presumed the distortion to be a natural effect born of smoke. "How can you fight a creature which lacks form?"

Ithariel shook her head. "Impossible, as Morien proved at Alathir." She qualified as much to focus her own thoughts. "The demons are beings from Alhaerie. While the stuff of our Aerith is malleable to their will, our forms are likewise their chaos. Rocks and stones and clouds lie beyond their understanding." She gestured at the recreated fortress walls. "Our emotions alone lend these meaning."

She flinched as the next scream harrowed the air. "I'm going to attempt a counter illusion. Better you don't try to watch. But if you must, understand this. Not all you see will be fashioned in malice by demons. Some of the work will be mine. Wait here. I'll return with the man. If not, when darkness falls you must flee for your lives and sail. Stop for nothing, even the rescue of your loved ones, for all of this isle will be doomed."

The grandfather grimaced as if he thought to protest; instead, he bent to check the boy who huddled unmoving under his hands. "We should help. Or do you have a way to cut chains and drag a grown man up sheer battlements?"

A ripple shivered the air; the grandfather's query received no answer at all. Except for himself and the boy, the hillside stood empty, as if the enchantress had been less solid than the lies wrought of earth by the demons.

The grandfather strove to find stability amid chaos. "She's fey, Oleg," he said to the boy at his feet. "How is a man to understand the ways of enchanters? We must be strong and bide here until she returns with her lord."

The smoke thickened. Clouds lowered, and the wind blew, strong gusts that buffeted the heights. The towers of the fortress gained a sickly violet halo. Though the whip still struck with a fiendish and unbroken rhythm, and the woman's cries cut the air, Korendir lay slack in his chains. His eyes stayed anguished and open, while blood more cherished than his own striped like tears down his cheeks. No sign appeared of the enchantress who embarked upon his salvation.

Minutes passed without change. Then a ripple passed over his form. Momentarily, Korendir seemed bathed by a lightless tongue of flame. He recoiled as if stabbed, and his chains clanged hard against their fastenings.

Listening until his ears ached over the ceaseless moan of wind, the old man heard. Despite Ithariel's warnings, he dared a look down from the walls.

He saw no dramatic rescue. Korendir's head sagged to one side, expressionless against blood-slicked cobbles. Shimmers that may have been demons whirled round his form on all sides. Only the fists dragged hard against his fetters revealed any life remained in him.

The smoke coiled thicker. Something seemed to flutter, half-veiled, on the wind. Then a billow like refraction passed over the object, and the grandfather's sight became obscured behind curtains of mist.

The lash fell and the screams continued, and the fisherman understood the White Circle enchantress had failed.

He sat in despair on cold stone. "She must be in trouble, Oleg. If not, she'd be back by now."

A brown wren appeared out of nowhere. Perhaps blown off course by the winds, it arrowed through the fog, wings stretched and closing in beat after beat of frantic flight. The leaf of a thorn tree fluttered in its beak. The weather harried it, bent its feathers at odd angles, and thrashed its tiny bones and frail sinews. It struggled, pumped harder, and clawed to reach a landing on the ridge.

The gusts were too strong for it.

Moved by a sailor's sympathy for storm-driven birds, the grandfather arose and stripped off his smock. As the wind howled and the little wren pitched sideways, he cast his garment like a net and scooped the struggling body in its folds.

An unexpected and totally unnatural weight dragged at his wrists. He staggered, caught his foot, and pitched to his knees on sharp rock. The smock and its contents tore from his grasp and unfurled; and the wren tumbled out in a tangle of light and blurred feathers. Its legs kicked once. It tossed aside the twig, and the next instant its form expanded with a lash of spell-heated air into the body of an enchantress, now naked; beside her lay no bit of greenery, but a blood-splashed, unconscious Korendir.

The enchantress panted as if her lungs might burst. She could not speak her thanks. Unmindful of the open-mouthed boy, she struggled to rise, and managed, with the help of the old man. She leaned on him, shaking, while he bundled his fishy-smelling garment over her shoulders.

Speech remained beyond her, but her eyes beseeched haste. The grandfather spoke sharply to Oleg, who scrambled up in dazed amazement and drew Ithariel's arm over his back. The enchantress stumbled forward in his childishly awkward embrace, while the elder attended to the man. He lifted Korendir as he had slung countless barrels of baitfish, then hurried downslope toward the forest.

Dangerously burdened, the party fled over terrain that could kill if a mistep caused a fall. Turbulence laced the air on all sides, distorting the eyesight, and shedding an odor like burned sawdust. Now mindful that these perturbations masked demons, the old man trembled with fear.

Ithariel began slowly to recover. Mindful of the grandfather's dread, she whispered hoarsely through her gasps, "To the enemy we appear as falling pebbles. Keep on, for the wardspells I set will not last. Our sole hope of safety is the sea."

Yet speed proved impossible to maintain. Though strong, the old man had limited stamina. Long before they reached the forest, he had to pause and share his burden with the boy. Of necessity, Ithariel struggled on alone. Taxed to exhaustion by her enchantments, she reeled forward, the smock trailed haphazardly across her shoulders. Her bare soles tore on the stones. She could not stop to wrap them, for the demons pressed close on all sides.

The land at last leveled off. Gray and tired, the old man pressed ahead with bowed shoulders; he no longer spoke to his grandson. Korendir showed no sign of returning life, but hung slack in the grasp of his rescuers as the party labored to take cover in the wood.

The shimmers followed. Inside the treeline, Ithariel paused with a whimper of dismay, then gritted her teeth and shifted magic. The effort cost her sorely. She spent the dregs of her powers to turn her protective illusion from pebbles to the form of blown leaves. Weary, unsteady as drunks, the four wove their way through forest silence. Though the clouds that had hemmed them on the heights gave way in time to bright sunlight, the encouragement came too late. All were too tired to take notice, and Korendir was yet beyond feeling. Concerned that he showed no trace of recovery, Ithariel contemplated a restorative, then put the thought firmly aside. Only if their straits became desperate would she tap the ward in his marriage ring. The powers it contained were likely too small to offer much merit anyway.

They plowed on, through brush that endlessly hampered movement, and roots and hollows that treacherously tripped the feet.

At the charcoal burner's cabin, they delayed for precious minutes to steal a blanket and poles and make a litter. Korendir never felt the hands that bundled his body inside. Slack as a gutted trout, he remained dead weight as the boy and the old man raised the poles to aching shoulders. Forward they pressed, while the louring energies of demons flanked and wove along their course.

They crossed the lane, and this time the boy passed the corpses with blindly indifferent eyes.

Ithariel moved now on reflex. Her braids had torn loose, and the ends curled damp with sweat. She strove to mind spells that burned and lacerated concentration; at any moment, her control was going to fail. Wards would unravel like shadows before light, and the demons would know her for the enemy.

Better than the rest, the enchantress understood her progress so far had been possible through surprise. Morien had defended Alathir with all the bright force of a White Circle Council Major; she, by herself, had sought only to mask and conceal. The linchpin of her plan had been the false image of the man left behind in chains upon the ridge; to spirit the real flesh away she had needed to wait until Korendir had exhausted himself to stillness. That necessity by itself had sapped her. Now, clothed in the thinnest of spell-craft, she shadowed them all in forms unobtrusively common. That the horrors which had desecrated Alathir so far did not question the semblance of a sparrow, or small stones, or a rustling drift of dry leaves offered scant margin for safety. The demons' continued pursuit indicated suspicion; once they chose to react, no last-ditch tactic would avail. Ithariel clung to spells that tattered under her mastery; she lagged behind, fighting, while the final wellspring of reserves burned to emptiness within her. The ruse she had spun to protect could hold not a minute longer.

Sea wind whispered through pine trees. Beyond flashed the white foam of breakers. A dozen steps completed in racking weariness, and the spongy blanket of shed needles gave way to dune grass and sand. The shimmery blots that were demons spun doubtfully, then lingered at the edge of the beach. They sensed the presence of water and natural caution made them hesitate.

There, with respite most cruelly in sight, Ithariel's failing wardspell sputtered out.

"Run!" Her shout split to hoarseness with fear, but the grandfather and youngest son heard. They struggled

to bear up the litter and cross the last yards to the sea.
Dry sand mired their strides. Their burden swayed dangerously, and Korendir came near to spilling out.

"Run!" screamed Ithariel a second time. If she could
overtake them, there remained the chip of crystal in the
marriage ring. But her legs trembled beneath her, each
stride more labored than the last.

The roils of churned air arrowed out from the forest's
edge. Demons converged in a rush toward three fleeing
humans and what they now perceived as the bronze-
haired son of the enchanter they had trapped to torment
to his death.

The burned smell intensified upon the breeze. It stung
the throats and lungs of Ithariel and her companions,
and seared their eyes blurry with tears. The boy and the
grandfather sprinted ahead with no thought except to
reach the sea. There, outlined against shining water, a
boat waited already launched. Steadfast and ready for
action, two brothers stood braced at her thwarts.

The demons closed. Barely a yard from the ruffled
edge of the surf, a canyon opened in the sand. The old
man gallantly jumped with the litter poles still on his
shoulders. Behind him, the boy wailed in panic. He
threw off his burden and leaped after, and Korendir tumbled outward into air.

Ithariel hurled her body over the brink. While the
earth ripped in twain underneath her, she collided with
her husband. Entangled in his unconscious limbs, she
tumbled in a sickening fall. Sand grains pattered her
clothing, then bounced off and vanished into dark. Light
and shimmers laced her flesh, and her overtaxed lungs
choked on fumes. The demons encompassed her presence, exulting in the recapture of her mercenary. Down
from the sunlit world above filtered shouts, growing rapidly fainter.

Enveloped by demons, all but lost, Ithariel thrashed
against wind and gravity and caught her husband's hand.
Still on his finger was the marriage ring with its contained
glimmer of wards. Ithariel cupped her palm over the tallix setting. She tapped the energy within, borrowed
strength, and spun spells.

Magelight ripped out like lightning, wove a net to ar-
rest their plunge. But the virtues of the ward were lim-

ited. She might preserve and defend for a short while, but the ring had not been endowed with the power for aggressive attack.

Spent past all effort at guile, Ithariel clung to her husband. Their chance was forfeit, even had she been fresh, for the demons were aware. The moment she tapped magic in their presence, her antagonists recognized her for an enchantress, an enemy like other ones vanquished in fury at Alathir. Helpless, plunging in a rush of dark down a cleft toward the depths of the earth, Ithariel could do nothing but scream in frustration as the entities which had annihilated High Morien closed in a ring of disturbed air.

Her cry echoed up from the pit as the boy and his grandfather splashed through shallows. Waves rushed sparkling to meet them and kicked rooster tails of foam around the their knees. They reached the longboat. White-faced with terror, and tried to the limits of endurance, they tumbled inside while the brothers immediately shoved off.

Behind, through air that seemed tortured by heat waves, they left the black chasm where Korendir and Ithariel had fallen. Surf that had not been close enough to save lapped now at the sandy rim.

While the longboat cleaved her way seaward, the grandfather covered his face. At his knee, curled in defeat, the youngest of his grandsons cried for shame.

"Neth, it was I who killed them!" The boy choked on sobs, while spray dashed over the bow and drenched the bowed crown of his head.

"Nay, lad." The grandfather extended a hand and ruffled the boy's dripping hair. "It was let go, or fall yourself, and dying along with the mercenary would not have saved yer ma."

The boat rocked, slewed by the currents of flooding tide. Waist deep in the waves, the elder brothers clung grimly as an undulating swell larger than the rest advanced toward them. The wave peaked and crested like an avalanche off the bow. As one, the brothers signalled agreement and clambered over the thwarts. Water spattered from their smocks as they seized their crude oars and threaded the handles through twine looped through the fittings for rowlocks. The wave kicked the prow, licked amidships, and left the boat unsupported to the mid-ribs. The craft poised, dipped, then plunged with a hard-bellied smack into the depths of the trough. For a moment the land lay eclipsed.

Then the waters roared by, and the boat heaved into recovery.

"Give those demons a wetting," muttered the eldest brother as he clawed for balance and sat. He leaned into the oars, joined at next stroke by his brother.

The wave washed astern with a roar. Whitewater rampaged up the beach, then surged in a sluice of dirty foam over the lip of the crevice. Demons roiled clear with a ripple like noxious fumes, and the grandfather screamed, "Go back!"

"What? Are ye daft?" The elder brother pulled all the harder on his looms, and his sibling followed suit.

But the old man stubbornly shook his head. "Water. The lady said that demons couldn't tolerate the sea. Bless the tide that rises, there just might be a chance."

"Get us all killed," the brother groused, but he lifted his oars in obedience. As another swell curled beneath the keel, he tensed his shoulders to swing the bow.

The next wave crashed and broke. A churning maelstrom of spray doused the rift in the sands. Something within unravelled like spilled light, and a crack echoed across the sea. Sound slammed the hills like thunder, though puffs of harmless cumulus sailed a fair weather sky. The brothers at the oars trembled in open-mouthed dread.

They searched through fright for one thing that was ordinary to restore faith in a world gone strange.

No sign appeared except a tern that shot up from the shore, half glimpsed through a dazzle of sunlight. She might have been scavenging at the tideline and started up as the water rose. Something glisteningly fishy dangled from her beak. The boy Oleg raised his head to watch her flight in a rush of renewed hope.

The morsel in her bill weighed her down out of all proportion to its size. Certain now, and revitalized by excitement, the boy called out to his brothers. "Bend your backs and follow that bird."

"Ye're daft as gramps," accused the oarsman to starboard. Slow to understand, he watched without reaction as the tern sheared down toward the swells.

She struck just beyond the line of combers, and kicked up a startling splash.

"Neth 'n' devils, that's no bird," exclaimed the eldest brother. He squinted over the handles of his looms, while the air above the beachhead swarmed and burned with a mirage-like moil of starved energies. Demons recognized their prey. They yearned toward the place where the tern had fallen, but dared not cross the encroaching flood of the tide.

Just then two heads broke the surface, shining with wet, and human. Korendir lay cradled in the naked arms of his lady. The ring's small wards were played out. She had no strength left to swim, but tumbled in the roll of green waters toward a shoreline still swarming with enemies.

"Row, or I'll keelhaul the lot o' ye," snapped the grandfather; and in just respect for his wrath, the brothers quit bickering and pulled oars.

XXII. Heir to Alathir

Sunlight slanted through the fishing boat's hatch and scribed light like a brand on worn decking. Ithariel sat on a sea chest in the gloom to one side, robed in loose cotton, but no pearls. Her hair had not yet dried, but spilled in combed ribbons down her back. Her hands lay slack in her lap. The sight of her, waiting, was the first thing Korendir noticed when he opened his eyes after his mishap in Illantyr.

He sprawled on the berth in the stern cabin, wrapped in nothing but a blanket ingrained with the aroma of cod. Late afternoon sky caught on the wavelets beneath the counter and threw reflections like ribbon on the beams above his head. He ached in every muscle and joint, and when he spoke, his voice was brokenly harsh.

"The demons. They revealed a thing about my paternity." Accusation colored his tone.

Ithariel stroked his knuckles. "All true. You're son to High Morien who once was Archmaster at Alathir. But were the White Circle to tell you, they would have sealed your doom. I could never have recovered you alive had the demons not paused to make sport with you. They will hate you the more fiercely, knowing you exist. Now, should they regain access to Alhaerie, Whitestorm itself might be attacked. My wardstone there could not stay them."

Korendir refused the implications. He trapped her small hand between his own and rolled onto his side. A glimpse of his eyes caused Ithariel to abandon her hope of sailing. She might wish one ordeal would convince her husband that his quest to save Illantyr was futile; most typically, his expression showed otherwise.

Abovedecks, one of the brothers sang a chantey while he cut up fish for the supper pot.

The uncomplicated sweetness of the moment cut like pain. Aware of what must come, and desperate to avert the inevitable, Ithariel changed the subject. "Where did you hide the jolly boat's oars?

Korendir looked at her, blinked, then rubbed at the wrappings which bound the abrasions left by shackles. "I tied them to the anchor line," he admitted hoarsely. The simplest speech came with effort. "They'll come in water-logged, but undamaged, unless they're discovered by crabs. Then the leathers might want mending."

He shifted restlessly. Ithariel recognized purpose in his frown. Every sensible part of her shrank from his decision, and she tried to withdraw her hand. His fingers tightened. "Ithariel, listen to me. The Mathcek Demons must be destroyed."

That statement, so soon, was too much. Ithariel surged to her feet. "I spared you from torture and death, and now you ask for Morien's fate?"

Korendir lay back, his head propped awkwardly against a bulkhead. "You're magnificent, did I tell you that?" He chose his next words with care, mostly because his throat pained him. "There is a way. The demons them-selves showed me how."

In labored phrases, he explained; and as the anger roused by his flattery cooled, Ithariel reconsidered. He had not lost his wits. The plan he outlined held cunning and logic, and also danger beyond reckoning. Since the demons now posed threat to Whitestorm, she knew bet-ter than try to dissuade him. Instead she paced to the grating and paused in the light shaft beneath.

"I'll help," she said to the man who held her heart. "But only if the captain agrees to loan you this boat without crew. Never will I sail the Mathcek deeps to barter with a weather elemental if one of those grandsons remains aboard."

Korendir answered with his eyes closed. "The grand-sons may think otherwise." And in the interval Ithariel took to determine whether or not she ought to slap him, he contrived to fall soundly asleep.

Lightning seared a crack across sky. The booming re-port of thunder slammed the night and shook every tim-ber in the boat where Ithariel leaned at the rail. She could sense the black currents that stirred fathoms down beneath the keel; here lay the deepest waters upon Aerith. Mortal opinion to the contrary, demons did not arise from the canyons that seamed the sea floor between Illantyr's isle and Dunharra; but weather elementals often did, and for that reason Korendir threaded oars in the jollyboat that heaved alongside.

Gusts snapped at the lines and thrummed minor strains from the stays. Korendir's sleeves fluttered in the flame-whipped light from the lantern. Prepared to cast off, he looked up at his worried wife. "Have faith. I've done this before."

"Hardly the same circumstance." Ithariel did not trust herself to qualify; at Whitestorm, against Cyondide, Korendir had been extraordinarily lucky. Although this time he carried the reputation for destroying two of Aerith's most powerful elementals, he owned no whit more protection. His plot was still based on bluff.

"Well, delay won't help my chances." Korendir tugged gently at the rope which secured his small craft to the rail, then used his wife's tactics against her. "Now tell me the name of yon tempest and cut me loose, or must I hack free with my dirk?"

Ithariel slipped the knot with trepidation. "The elemental calls itself Tolaine." She paused, the tasseled end of the painter looped between her hands. "If you're going to dedicate yourself to recklessness, drown yourself quickly and spare me from worry and gray hair."

Lightning illuminated his expression of wide surprise. "Once Illantyr is secure from the demons, what reason on Aerith could take me from Whitestorm again?"

Ithariel flipped the line into the tender. "Neth if I know. Haldeth swears on his favorite hammer you'll invent one."

"Haldeth!" Korendir dipped oars and leaned into his stroke. "Fretting's his primary occupation. Don't you start also."

Ithariel returned a look of reproof. "Give me one day without any reason to."

Korendir's laugh tangled with another crack of thunder. "Tomorrow," he called back. On his next still-expert stroke, the boat vanished into the night.

Left no task except to tend the lanterns, Ithariel stared

out into dark. On this occasion she could not follow her beloved into danger. Since elementals by nature contested power, the potency of White Circle magic itself offered liability. Belligerent with wizards, and overtly sensitive to enchantments, they would go out of their way to offer challenge. In waters under Tolaine's sovereignty, Korendir dared not carry even the burned-out tallix of his marriage ring.

Ithariel trimmed each of the lantern wicks. She paced the decks and watched lightning spear the sea, jagged as veins in obsidian. Sometimes she saw a fleck on gray waters that might be Korendir's boat. But the moments of storm-flash were too brief, and the object too distant to identify his presence with certainty.

Midnight came and went. Alone, Ithariel waited by the mainmast pinrail. A patter of rain slashed her face. She thought upon the man she had married, and those traits in his character that infuriated her: his unshiftable penchant for black, and spare words, and a wayward tendency to switch the subject when she touched upon issues that troubled him. And yet for all her frustration, she harbored no lasting regret. His deathless compassion, and gentle hands, and contentiously uncompromising integrity had altered her life. In the space of a single afternoon he had captured her heart as nothing else in Aerith ever could.

His absence made the night seem interminable. The snores of the fishing boat's captain rasped faintly from the forward hatch. In the end, after bitterest argument, common sense had prevailed; his grandsons remained ashore to look after their widowed mother. For that the enchantress was grateful. Sooner rather than later the direst mischance would overtake them.

A gust plucked at the rigging and the waves picked up. The fishing boat tossed, hove to upon raging waters; off her bow, lightning jagged the darkness with repeated and unnatural ferocity. Spindrift crowned the wave crests like wraiths, and thunder pealed in a continuous roll that rattled every tenon in the hull.

Spray-soaked and shivering, Ithariel clung to a stay. Discomfort by itself could not force her below to fetch a cloak. Although she stood a full league removed from the vortex of the elemental's force, her peril was no less than her husband's. The escalating violence of the weather offered warning: either Tolaine displayed his powers to intimidate, or else she witnessed a wrath that could turn at any instant to murder. The jollyboat was too frail to withstand an ocean squall. Korendir might already be capsized.

And yet as the storm raged and the wind shrieked a hag's chorus around her, Ithariel sensed no mishap to his person. Will was all that sustained her as the gale peaked, and the lanterns streamed red, and the decking gleamed like hot copper under cloudburst.

Suddenly everything went still. The swells thrashed and sucked against the timbers; blocks banged and squealed in the chafe of the lines aloft, but their noise was a solo against silence. The wind winnowed away to an ominous calm. The change caused the grandfather to rise and check anchor lines; swathed in patched oilskins, he straightened on the foredeck and glanced across in perplexity at the enchantress.

"Listen," said Ithariel. She forced her teeth to stop chattering.

A shout echoed faintly over the water. Above the work of timbers and the slap of loosened halyards, words could just barely be heard. "Tolaine, by your name I offer challenge. I say your strength is insufficient to hold the sea of Tammernon to a calm like perfect glass between sunrise and sunset."

The reply boomed back in a savage gust of air. "Who speaks? Answer! Tolaine is mighty enough to girdle all Aerith in stillness for a fortnight, or a decade, or a year."

"I am Korendir, who destroyed both Cyondide and Ishone, and I say your boasts are the bluster of breezes. I did not ask a year, nor all the waters of the world, but only the Tammernon Sea, and just for the span of one day."

Tolaine ripped out a lightning bolt and parted the waters with a sizzle. "Show yourself, challenger. Where stands this wizard whose presence I cannot feel? Let us duel this instant, and prove for all time whose powers are fit to best whom."

Ithariel gripped the lateen brace and murmured aloud in despair. "Neth's grace, he's gone too far."

But her failing confidence affected Korendir's nerve

not at all. His reply floated back through the darkness, imperious enough to shame an emperor. "The Master of Whitestorm does not strive against beings of inferior ability. Let Tolaine prove his worthiness by completing the task I described."

Thunder growled in reply. "Tolaine does not suffer to wait another turning of the sun."

"Then let the calm become the contest," the mortal called back. "If Tolaine can keep the waters flat through all manner of magics and distractions, Korendir will concede the victory."

Sullen breezes chivvied the waves. Heat lightning touched the sea pewter against a darkened horizon, and clouds churned, lit to the yellows and grays of boiled sulphur; like the coiled deadness in the eye of a great gale, the elemental cogitated upon the bargain. "Tolaine accepts," the being rumbled at last. "Wizard whose presence I cannot feel, I say your defeat shall be easily gained. At sunrise, let our battle begin."

The night went black in an eyeblink. Limp and beaten as old rags, Ithariel leaned her cheek against cordage that smelled of mildew. "Do you know," she said weakly, "how close my madman of a husband came to drowning us all in a whirlwind?"

Canvas slapped, sagged flat under slackening winds. The grandfather squinted aloft, his eyes sparkling by lanternlight. "But we aren't swimming yet, my lady, and a neater spinning of deception I never saw in my life. Your marriage must be a lively one."

Ithariel allowed her legs to give way; she slid down the lines, thumped on an empty span of pinrail, then laughed in a breathless release of nerves. "Old man, you have that right."

The grandfather nodded sagely. Droplets blown from wet rigging splashed his seal-slick hair. "Go below," he suggested. "Rest up. You'll need a clear mind come the sunrise."

But weary as the enchantress was, she balked at the idea of sleep. The grandfather shrugged and offered his oilskins. Ithariel accepted without hesitation over the ingrained smell of fish. While clouds broke over the mainmast and a brave few stars pricked through, she wrapped her shoulders in the garment's humid warmth and lis-

tened intently for oar strokes in the night that would
signal her loved one's return.

Morning dawned with a quiet that rang in the ears.
The sun rose over the Tammernon Sea in perfect double
image. Not a ripple stirred; the northeast coast of Illantyr
bulked like a bruise in the early, reddened light. The
waters surrounding the shoreline stayed polished to calm
like a mirror, even when the wingbeats of passing shear-
waters tapped the surface in their flight. Tolaine kept the
terms of Korendir's challenge with diligent and awesome
precision.

Too unsettled to sit while the men ate breakfast in the
galley, Ithariel waited on deck, her fingers running over
and over a crudely notched stick of wood. She regarded
the burnished ocean with eyes left gritty from sleep-
lessness, all the while pondering her distrust.

Though stillness stretched to horizons made invisible
by reflection, only vanity bound Tolaine to compliance.
The kindling in her hands was a pitiful thing, carved with
protective runes, but not yet touched by the spark that
would activate its wards. Now the moment was upon her,
Ithariel shared none of her husband's brashness. The dic-
tates of inflexible training forestalled his knack for risk.
She courted outright disaster, and the knowing jangled
her nerves even before she embarked upon the perilous
second stage of Korendir's plan.

The resonance as she engaged spell-craft would inevitably provoke Tolaine. Like all elementals, his dislike of
wizardry was total; entirely without warning, he might
reject the restrictions set upon this feigned contest of
wills. If that happened, no power on Aerith could spare
them. The seas would rip instantaneously into storm;
smashed like so much flotsam, the boat and her mangled
crew would become pickings for crabs and fish.

Ithariel traced the rune-cut wood. The edge of her nail
caught on the sigil for Safeguard, and she bit her lip.
Were the Archmaster to guess her intentions, he would
without hesitation have condemned her to Majaxin's
fate. To the mighty of the White Circle, the survival of
Illantyr's villagers was a detail of little account. Ithariel
might have agreed, in those days when her mind was
more tied to the greater energies of Aerith. Only the

spell-bonded Lady of Whitestorm who deliberated on a fishing boat's deck was no longer entirely enchantress. Korendir's ways had changed her. His priorities had become her own, and his perils she willingly shared, but never without fear.

The cries of shore birds echoed across flat water, almost masking a light tread behind her. Aware who approached, she accused, "You should be resting."

"Not now." Korendir frowned in faint reproof. He clasped her waist from behind and kissed her neck, and she could smell the sweetness of the grandfather's rum on his breath.

She stiffened, and as always Korendir's quick wit grasped why. "Our captain insisted his brew was medicinal, and how was I to deny his better judgment? He drank the lion's share." Korendir paused; his fingers curled through the sash that bound her tunic. "You know we're certain to lose this vessel. The wreck might hurt less if the fellow's gone in his cups."

She faced him, still in the circle of his embrace. "Unless he's a mean drunk. Did you ask?" He had not; Ithariel swallowed, tried to achieve the calm she would need to manage the trials to come. "And the medicine?"

Korendir released her. He flexed blistered fingers, then tested the muscles of his shoulders, brutally used the night before as he rowed through a league of ocean gale. "Marginal. The stiffness aches less, but in exchange I think my guts have been scalded."

Ithariel regarded him critically, from damp black tunic to hose which showed rings of ingrained salt. "You'll survive," she concluded without sympathy. The moment the words left her lips, it occurred with poignant clarity that he very well might not.

The rune stick flexed between her fingers; Korendir restrained her wrists before it cracked. "There are widows and orphans weeping in Illantyr for every moment we delay."

Ithariel nodded. Beyond speech, she leaned into the comfort of his shoulder, raised her carved bit of wood, and delved inward after powers that were the heritage of White Circle bloodline schooled to remorseless focus. Resigned to bad judgment, inured to the fact that her life and Korendir's and also one drunken old fisherman's hung on untenable faith, she set potency into the first carved sigil. And like calm before direst cataclysm, the ocean held glassily still.

Tolaine did not bridle at the sorcery. But over the masts sudden clouds gathered, dense and black as woodsmoke. The sun dimmed; the sea stretched beneath, flat as puddled lead.

Ithariel drew a shaking breath. She set the protections in strictest order, as if the air did not quiver with the fullness of a too-long pent breath. Spell and counterward and safeguards, she prepared the defenses that preceded the opening of a wizard's gate in open and unstable surroundings. One mistake could invite disaster. Alathir had fallen in consequence of just such an error, and interruption by an elemental storm could cause a repeat of the same.

Ithariel sang the seals into being within the warmth of Korendir's arms. He felt fine tremors course through her flesh, and smelled her sweaty fear. He leaned his face into the hair above her ear and began very softly to speak.

His words banished other, more crippling distractions: worry, and uncertainty, and reproach for follies she knew better than to set into motion. Ithariel completed her preparations. She began the sequence which would open gate access to Alhaerie, while her husband's phrases lapped the edge of her awareness and stabilized concentration.

"Lady of my heart, they lured me with the shadows of my deepest fears. I saw a Whitestorm more vibrant than life, and a wife more real than woman. The Ithariel they spun to entrap was the essence of self and love and future. When my mind lost perception of the difference, demons set everything in jeopardy." His hands caressed her through the waterstained cloth of her tunic. "But they wrought too well, these beings who dream to deprive us of Aerith. They revealed the despair of their exile, and their resentment of Morien's courage. That showed their vulnerability, and now we shall fashion their downfall."

Ithariel slipped through his hands and knelt. She laid the carved stick on the deck between her knees. The air around her rippled and burned with ward-magic; her hands glowed faintly blue. Korendir stepped back, left her space to work her craft as she laid her palms together. All her thoughts centered on her fingertips as she lowered her arms and scribed a line which sheared through the fabric of the world.

Light shimmered where her gesture passed. A tear gaped open between Aerith and the alter-reality of Alhaerie; the oily swirl of *otherness* that churned beyond the gap splintered the vision to pain.

Korendir averted his eyes. He had no arcane knowledge, only human understanding of his wife's emotional needs. He settled as near as her conjuries would allow and kept talking. "Let the bait to lure demons befit the crime, lady of my heart. Morien's fortress was razed into ruins; in justice, let us build a memorial. Stone and keep and slate-roofed hall, the stuff of Alhaerie shall be remade to replace what the demons laid waste."

Ithariel regarded her gate-spell with critical apprehension. She found neither weakness nor fault in her work; the wards contained the contact between worlds and prevented a repeat of the breach that had ravaged Alathir. If Korendir still spoke, she did not hear him. Beyond reach of fleshly sensation, the enchantress delved into mysteries and wrought the consummation of their effort to destroy the demons.

The slice of Alhaerie visible through her gate underwent a twist and a magnification, then looped through a greater second binding.

The sea held smooth by Tolaine served yet as a giant mirror; except now the surrounding waters no longer reflected Aerith's sky. Influenced by the magics of Ithariel, natural order was replaced with the seethe and boil of incomprehensible *otherness* that was the alter-reality of Alhaerie.

Ashore on Illantyr, demons gathered in a boiling shimmer of air, drawn by the vision of the otherworld.

On the decks of a painted fishing boat, an enchantress who wrought the deception licked dry lips. The balance of complex spell-craft consumed her concentration totally. One lapse would endanger all the Eleven Kingdoms. She dared not waste concern for Tolaine, whose vain pursuit for supremacy formed the linchpin of Illantyr's salvation. She did not think of the grandfather, asleep in his stupor belowdecks; nor might she spare a word for the husband who sat by her through the moments of greatest peril. Engrossed within the discipline of her magic, Ithariel engaged the last of the sigils on the rune stick.

She touched through the gate with her thoughts, and re-shaped the stuff of Alhaerie.

Ithariel wrought with calculated malice. From the oily curl of energies through the spell-gate, she reconstructed in miniature the curtain walls and towers of Alathir where Morien Archmaster had once convened his council.

Her handiwork was accurate to the smallest detail; and in perfect and magnified illusion, the reflection of Morien's fortress spread across the flawless sea.

The effect on the demons was immediate. Presented after years of exile with an untrammeled view of their homeworld, then subjected to sight of its desecration by the hands of a White Circle enchanter, they shot in turbid arrows of distortion from the shore. Their world had no solidity, as Aerith understood; no concrete sense of up or down or gravity. The fact that Alathir's battlements speared at right angles to Illantyr's beachheads gave the demons no cause for suspicion. Lashed to outrage, duped by certainty that enemies inflicted atrocity against their universe and kind, they forgot any concept of Aerith-imposed direction. They succumbed even as Korendir had fallen prey to their earlier recreation of Whitestorm.

The Demons of Mathcek rushed in a horde to succor their violated kingdom. Too recklessly angered to organize challenge, they rippled like a wave of super-heated air and plunged to their destruction in the sea.

The elements screamed with the demons' passing like hot metal quenched into ice. Water doused their life-energies and added ragged drifts of steam to already glowering overcast. But the sea's tranquillity had broken. Ripples shattered the image of Alathir's fair towers and the stonework dissolved, kicked by gusts to a foam-sheared webwork of waves.

Startled into failure by the demons' violent demise, the elemental roused to a gale-force pitch of dismay. "Where is the wizard whose presence I cannot feel?" Tolaine boomed on a rising surge of storm. "Hear now that I reject these foolish formalities and demand a straight contest of force."

Ithariel abandoned conjury and snatched the rail just as the first gust struck. The fishing boat slammed reeling into knockdown. Above the thunder of rising wind, she screamed, "Get the grandfather!"

Korendir had already left her. He dropped in a leap through the companionway, while at his back, the enchantress expanded her spell-gate in a stopgap expenditure of power.

The discharge left her dizzied. She clung weakly while waves thudded the timbers underneath her and vibrations shivered the hull. Paintwork cracked and lines streamed loose, to snap with whipcrack reports that unlaced stout splices to tassels. With a groan of stressed wood, the boat labored to rise. Tolaine intervened. Winds slapped back and prevented even marginal recovery. The beamy old hull lay awash like the flank of a wounded whale. Her mizzen gouged the sea and she rolled beyond salvage, battered over further as her ballast clattered loose belowdecks.

Korendir clawed up the tilted companionway, his legs mired by torrents of incoming waves. The sloop was foundering rapidly. The mercenary struggled to escape her death throes, his back burdened down by the drunken grandfather whose loved ones remained safely ashore.

"Korendir!" Ithariel cried. "Hurry!"

Tolaine's wrath whipped around her. She clung like a limpet to the wreck, harried by the seething elements. Lightning laced the air. Bait barrels tumbled from their lashings and battered across the decks to wreak chaos; gear caromed off the masts, snagged in spilled nets and rigging, and splashed into spindrift-torn seas.

Korendir caught the mainmast pinrail. He struggled up a sagging mesh of halyards. Winds ripped at his hold. The decks canted further, while the slamming surge of breakers shot spray like lacework overhead. Splashed blind, Korendir flung back hair that spoiled his vision.

"Over here!" Ithariel clung from the uprights of the rail, dangling from slipping hands.

Beside her the spell-gate shimmered still, an opened

maw of force more uncontrollably deadly than any ocean storm.

Tolaine sensed the resonance of ward magic. He centered the vortex of his anger on the spot, and lightning jagged splinters from the hull.

Korendir twisted like a cat, flash blind, but unhurt. A monster wave boomed and broke. The hull stove in like the cracked shell of a nut. Planking parted with a tortured scream. Seas trampled over the fragments and dashed the maindeck into submersion. As masts, then pinrail, then decking sucked under the rending waves, the wizard's gate sank also.

Ithariel lost her hold. Pummeled by a fury of water, she kicked out to reach the glimmer of her spell. Ahead, the grandfather's bulk still in tow, Korendir attempted the same. The span of wood which anchored the safewards had long since vanished in the turmoil, every guard on the spell-gate stripped away along with it. Racked to panic by each second that brought Aerith closer to ruin, the enchantress dove for the gap.

She reached the gate. Korendir was nowhere to be seen. Poised on the bridge between realities, Ithariel sensed the energies of Alhaerie on one side, and the tumble of storm-slashed waters on the other. The latter was lethally laced with slivers of decking and ropes. Ithariel spared no moment for thought. She rallied her overtaxed reserves, expanded the gate to encompass a five-span dollop of ocean, then pushed through the other side. She emerged choking within the turbid, gravityless chaos that comprised the essence of Alhaerie.

She had acted without pause to define a circle. Vulnerable to forces that easily might kill her, she reached but found her strength spent. No resource remained to shape even basic protection. Neither could she spin spells to determine whether her gate had spared any beside herself.

Ithariel tumbled over and over in the turbid otherness of Alhaerie. Broken timbers drifted with her, along with droplets of seawater like tears. She had no margin for sorrow. Bound by vows and three decades of White Circle training, her priorities were ruthlessly clear. The gate between worlds must be closed.

She groped with her last spark of consciousness for the

key which defined the portal. At risk of losing the life of her husband, and in consequence her own as well, she touched a link across burning forces, then sang the note of unbinding.

The spell-gate flared out. In a queasy, spilled-marble whorl, Alhaerie closed over the space as if no gap ever had existed.

Sick and lost and stranded, Ithariel wept in relief. She had dissolved the circle before the sea could surge away and expose an unguarded portal to air. No beings from the otherworld could leak through, as demons once had, to harass and wreak havoc on Aerith.

The enchantress's senses blurred into dark before she could appreciate that the isle of Illantyr was saved. No more would demons range south to repeat the desecration of Alathir.

The feat was not accomplished without repercussion. Off the east shoreline, a rage-crazed elemental hammered a riven hull to matchwood. Fragments shot skyward in gouts of foam which spun and twisted into waterspouts. Tolaine unleashed lightnings and whirlwinds in an atavistic display of fury. Unstable in his wrath, he sifted the waters in search of the fleeing forms of enemies. Their presence eluded his grasp. A wizard whose aura he could not feel, an enchantress who provoked his downfall, and a grandfather whose ship was annihilated evaded his killing wrath. Defeated, even as Cyondide before him, Tolaine unravelled his awareness in a crackling discharge of lightnings.

The winds slacked. Calm returned to a jumble of confused seas. Sunlight shed gold on the gale-wet coast of Illantyr, and the ruins at Alathir where Morien's lands had so long been held hostage by enemies.

XXII. Council at Dethmark

Sunlight streamed through the vaulted windows of the Archmaster's tower and traced geometrics on a floor incised with sigils and patterns of ward; in this well-guarded chamber even dust motes did not stir without leave. Stillness reigned absolute, but the place was not deserted. Eighteen masters of the Council Major sat crosslegged around the walls, the hems of dusky robes tucked beneath their knees. Their faces were creased more by the demands of their craft than age or mortal frailty. Attuned to a force shared equally among themselves, they awaited in perfect patience for their Archmaster, who traveled the otherworld beyond Aerith.

"He returns," announced the tiny, wizened lady who was spokesman in the absence of the master.

The next instant a spatter of sparks erupted from the motionless air. The circles of power on the floor blazed to life, and light speared from the central configuration.

Only one of the eighteen was seasoned enough to interpret. As glare rinsed the chamber with a brilliance that could sear less experienced eyes to blindness, the eldest enchanter of Aerith leaned forward. "He has found them."

An instant later, the spell flare framed the outline of a wizard's gate. Rainbow fires lapped the edges of the void between realities. The phenomenon lasted barely a heartbeat, then flashed out and left the midnight-cloaked form of the Archmaster standing inside rings of inert wards. At his feet, dripping seawater, sprawled an enchantress and two mortals in plain linen.

"Telvallind, well done," cried the ancient. While the other wizards stirred and murmured, he rose from his place by the wall.

The Archmage blinked like a feather ruffled hawk. He

did not acknowledge the praise; neither did he excuse his Council Major from their hours of ritual vigil. Instead, he regarded the bodies in sopped clothing that his emergency summons had rescued. His displeased gaze lingered longest on the woman, whose auburn hair draped in tangles over torn man's attire, and the tunic of her black-clad husband. "The others were ignorant mortals, but Ithariel should have known better."

At her name, the Lady of Whitestorm sighed, stirred, and closed her fingers on Korendir's sleeve. Awareness returned and brought an overwhelming urge to scratch her nose; something in the seawater had left an itch. Ithariel opened her eyes. The carved floors where she lay were unique in Aerith, and she knew immediately where she was. As if the association cued recall of the Archmaster's reprimand, she said, "My companions may be fools, and I not one whit better, but the Mathcek Demons are destroyed. Illantyr is freed from the Third Great Bane."

Her announcement caused no stir. Deep silence fell over the Council Major; Telvallind Archmaster considered the woman who had once been his fosterling, and although she was also his granddaughter, his eyes remained unforgiving. "Except the risks you undertook to achieve such a feat were unsanctionable against any threat. You might have brought ruin to all of Aerith!"

Worn from her earlier expenditure of spells, Ithariel was caught at a loss. She had not expected rescue from Alhaerie, far less intervention by the Archmaster and his council. Relations were strained further by the fact her wits were still scattered; her wet clothes bound unpleasantly and the itch in her nose had progressed to a sting that threatened at any moment to make her sneeze. But she did not appeal to childhood ties to mend the rift with her grandfather. Instinctively she sought reassurance through Korendir; her grip tightened on his arm. A tension in his muscles indicated he was both conscious and listening. His eyes remained closed, a habit he had when waking to potential danger. No sign would he show of awareness until he had assessed the nature of his surroundings.

That moment, the drunken fisherman who shared the circle rolled over onto his back. His jaw tipped open, his

lungs discharged air, and the slackened membranes in
his throat rattled through a disruptive series of snores.
Telvallind spun away in distaste. He signalled dismissal
to his council and resumed his tirade against Ithariel.
"Just because you married outside the White Circle does
not give you leave to ignore the restrictions of your rank.
Where in Aerith did you think you gained the right to
involve a man and an untrained villager in affairs of
greater magic?"

"She did not." Korendir's voice cracked across quiet
like the sheared ring of swordmetal.

The Archmaster stiffened; a vein pulsed in his forehead, blue as the graining in fine marble. The departing
enchanters of his council glanced back, discomfited, as
the swordsman arose with the alert coordination of a
predator. His hair might be sodden like an otter's, and
his clothing be deplorably unkempt, but he still wore his
blade. The hand poised lightly on the grip showed not
the slightest unsteadiness. "The fisherman was never coerced, but acting in behalf of his village. The right to
involve him was mine, as ward of the Lady of Shan Rannok. Lands that her death ceded to my protection were
under attack. Do you question my duty to defend them?"

Tall in his gold-sewn robes of office, the Archmaster
returned a look like cold fire. "Mortal, you presume far
too much. Any documents that prove your claim would
be burned by Mhurgai with the keep."

Korendir heard this without protest, but Ithariel could
sense his sudden anger. Aware as he could not be that
insolence in this place offered peril, she rose and caught
his wrist.

But her husband shook her off. He regarded the Archmaster with a control the equal of any mage's, then
shifted slightly that his appeal might also encompass
the council members who lingered near the doorway.
"Then as Morien's surviving son, I claim blood-right
to vengeance."

A rustle like wind in dry grass stirred the mages; not
a few of them murmured behind their hands, and the
eldest one nodded sagely.

Only Telvallind did not accede. He straightened trailing sleeves with a contemptuous flick of his hands and
addressed Korendir over the fisherman's snores. "The

way of the White Circle does not acknowledge revenge. You might be born of Morien's seed, but you lack any concept of wisdom."

"Whose fault is that?" Provoked, but not to the point where he became inured to his wife's distress, Korendir stepped one pace to the side and supported her waist. His right hand remained curled on his sword hilt, the fingers now dangerously unrelaxed. "I learned my true parentage through the machinations of demons. What laws I transgressed, what risks I undertook in ignorance after that cannot matter. I refuse to be held accountable for restraints your kind never saw fit to explain. My father's killers are destroyed and Illantyr freed from great evil. There is all the justification I require."

A cloud crossed the sun beyond the window; reduced by gloom to a figure picked out in points of gold embroidery, Telvallind Archmaster removed his ring of office. Its tallix setting flashed like a teardrop as he restored the signet to a chain which hung at his neck. "Your deeds have no bearing here, mortal. It is the transgressions of your wife that are at issue. Three times she has shown her imprudence where you are concerned. Now she must face her due reckoning."

Ithariel released a small cry. Wrung to exhaustion from her contest against demons, the last bit of color fled her face.

Korendir moved, very fast, and interposed his person between the Archmaster and his wife. "The lady is my soul-bond, our fates are the same."

"You're not White Circle," Telvallind contradicted. Death-dark as a battle raven, he advanced across the floor. His hand still cradled his signet, and where he passed the sigils flared scarlet. "You are nothing other than mortal, and your presence is no more significant than that of the sot who lies behind you."

"You slight a brave man and a friend," Korendir said tautly. "I don't take that well."

Pressed to her husband's back, Ithariel battled an instinct to cower. The ward-circles themselves reflected the Archmaster's anger and consequences could be dire if restraint gave way to temper. She whispered, "My lord, you must not interfere."

Korendir flung away in white rage. *"I will!"* The sight

of his lady's distress burned him to killing fury, and he glared across the gathering of mages. "You are the Council Major of Aerith. If demons should be allowed to destroy Shan Rannok's countryside, and if I did wrong to banish them, then let us amend matters now. Show me sound reasons by granting the training due the blood heir of an archmaster."

Silence met his request. He shifted baleful eyes and his hand tightened, sliding his sword in a partial draw from the scabbard. "Or else strike me down, and my curse upon your spirits to spend eternity in the Mhurga's many hells. Kill me with spell-craft, or I'll kill with steel, before I allow hurt to my lady."

"Your threats are ridiculous," the Archmaster snapped. But like a flock that startles one by one into flight, some of the mages disagreed. Unobtrusively they filed from the chamber, while Ithariel subsided into trembling. The wards now burned hot as sunset over water.

"Threats?" Korendir cleared his blade fully, and returned sun flickered down to etch the point in sharp light. "You speak of the only recourse available to me."

At his back, Ithariel held her breath. The snores of the fisherman seemed a distant and incongruous sound, and the sigils in the floor spat white sparks. Into tension as precarious as cracked crystal, the eldest of the mages offered counsel.

"Son, bared steel in this place will harm no one, but only bring woe to yourself. As Morien's heir, and as a man who has proven his worth by defeating a perilous enemy, I say your case merits argument. But not through violence or ill feeling."

A charged moment passed.

Then the wards subsided and dimmed, leaving carvings silvered with old dust.

The Archmaster released his signet with a shrug. "I say this mortal deserves nothing. What is his life but an addiction to adventure and risk? After all he is brother to the initiate whose mistake released the demons to begin with. I suggest that recklessness runs in Morien's line."

Korendir appeared not to move, but Ithariel felt recoil shock through his body. His fingers loosened on his blade, and so softly that her ears alone could hear he murmured, "Brother?"

Ithariel whirled and faced the Archmaster. "You might have spared him that! What malice makes you turn this past sorrow against a man with no memory of his family?"

"Your husband has too much pride." The haughty old wizard inclined his head. "And you, as much folly for choosing him. You sealed your fate to his. Let that bond stand. You will leave Dethmark for Whitestorm, and never again practice spell-craft. The White Circle disowns you, now and for the remainder of your days."

"I'll miss nothing," Ithariel said through whitened lips. Knowing what must follow, she snatched at Korendir's sword arm. He twisted in wordless surprise as the air whirled and closed about them in a nexus of sudden power. The floor underfoot seemed to tilt over sideways. Entangled in the clasp of her beloved, Ithariel spilled off the solid earth and into a void of thick dark.

The spell circles in the chamber at Dethmark lay empty, except for a noisily recumbent fisherman who no longer owned a boat. The Archmage Telvallind sniffed at the odors of rum, stale fish, and sea salt. "You, send this man back to Illantyr," he commanded to his last remaining council member.

The ancient who had sworn first obedience to High Morien received the order with acerbity. "A bit hard on the lad, were you not?"

Telvallind jerked in affront. "That lad as you call him is the most dangerous mortal on Aerith, and not for the reasons told by sailors."

Though nowhere close to deaf, the elder cocked his ear; a spark of incongruous cheer lit his eyes as he shuffled lame shanks toward the circle. "Boy's most like his father, don't you think?"

The sunlight faded from the floor and reappeared; without apparent effort, the elder made a gesture and activated powers that would speed a beloved grandfather home to the house of his kin. As the enchanter's seamed fingers worked spell-craft, his spate of barbed commentary resumed. "After all, Morien was the last rightfully appointed archmaster. The mysteries of investiture died

with him, and his rank became heritable by vote only
because he died before naming a successor."

Telvallind raised brows that were peaked into tufts like
an owl's. "I'll thank you to recall I'm not senile."

The elder peered up at his overlord with a smile of
maddening tolerance. "No. But neither is the Master of
Whitestorm anything close to a fool."

Korendir and his lady landed one right after the other
with a thump in a bed of ripe cabbage. Against Ithariel's
expectation, neither one became impaled on the edge of
his unsheathed sword. Whether by instinct or unconscious reflex, her husband kept the steel point out from
his body even through the vertigo of spell-transfer. Only
a slashed head of vegetable emerged the poorer from
misadventure.

Korendir rolled on his elbows in the dust. He regarded
the spray of severed leaves with an expression of colossal
confusion. "Where in the Mhurga's hells are we?"

Ithariel surveyed the view from between two furrows
of radishes. "The Archmaster's garden." she managed.
"Outside the tower walls. By that we can presume my
exile has officially caught up with me."

The Master of Whitestorm spat out dirt and examined
his sword blade for nicks. "If pitching his adopted daughter into soil spread over with pig dung is any indication
of character, I'd say he's a bitter old man." The blade
gleamed reassuringly unharmed; Korendir sheathed the
steel and glanced tacit inquiry at his wife.

She rested her chin on muddy knuckles. "Telvallind
has reason to be difficult. Majaxin caused the death of
his only daughter, after all. I resemble my father too
much to allow anyone to forget."

"Then none of the enchanters should have fostered
you," Korendir snapped in just anger. He rolled through
a patch of late sprouts and recovered his feet, then offered his hand to his wife.

She accepted, absorbed in bitter memories; how much
more irate her husband would become if he knew the
truth. Telvallind had raised her as personal assurance
that none of her father's vices might arise to cause grief
in the future. Her every move had been watched with
critical analysis, even into adulthood. But those days

were behind her now. As exile, she dared not wield power, except in peril of her life. The scope of that loss had yet to sink in.

Recovered enough to notice details, Korendir demanded, "Where's the fisherman?" Pole beans and rhubarb grew undisturbed in rows under southland sunlight, and no sound of snoring intruded to silence the rasp of summer insects.

"He isn't here." Ithariel picked bits of loam from the tangled length of her hair. "Neth, we're a mess. The crusty old bird wouldn't think to send us on with a wash and a change of clothes. But don't worry, he'll look after the grandfather."

Korendir caught his wife's fingers and pulled her close. "I like you fine with sticks in your hair." Then the eyes that searched her face went very still. "Do you regret?"

Ithariel suddenly could not speak; she managed a shake of her head before tears threatened, and she turned her face into his already salt-damp shoulder.

Korendir stroked her neck. "I have a quarrel with the Archmage," he said abruptly. "His council might send the grandfather home, but what about gold for his fishing boat? I had no chance to tell the poor man that Whitestorm would cover the damage."

"Oh, never fret about that." Ithariel caught her breath through teeth clenched hard against sorrow. "The White Circle doesn't interfere often in the affairs of mortals, but when they choose, they manage the details most righteously."

"Well then," said Korendir with that terrible mildness that had won him the woman he had married, "if they're going to discriminate and make us walk, we'll start off by kicking a few cabbages."

An afternoon hike, followed by a three and a half month sail saw the lord and lady home to Whitestorm. By the time the trader ship that delivered them dropped anchor, night had fallen over the headlands. The tide lapped high on White Rock Head, and would not ebb until morning. Korendir stood on deck, the folds of his much-used cloak thrown over the shoulders of his wife. Together they leaned on dew-damp rigging, and regarded their fortress by starlight.

Ithariel's powers might be under interdict, but the wardstone in the watchtower shone yet with all of its former radiance.

"I could have told you that would never change," Ithariel chided as she felt a long-buried tension depart on her husband's sigh.

He did not mention that he had been terrified to ask and cause her pain. Instead, he tangled warm hands in her hair and turned her slowly to face him. "What do you think if we make some magic between us, and maybe get a daughter by the spring?"

Ithariel punched him in delight. "They cheated you badly, for not telling. White Circle blood is slow to replicate. Births among our kind are very rare."

Korendir threw back his head, and his laughter blended with the rush of surf against the cliffs where he made his home. "You pose me a challenge," he teased. "Of all the contracts I have undertaken, this one will be joyful to complete."

The ship quite suddenly was too small to contain them. With shameless lack of compunction, Korendir commandeered the longboat and bundled his wife on board. Adrift on the currents beneath Whitestorm, they talked, and loved, and somewhere between passion and sleep Korendir was made to promise that a certain black cloak would be torn up and relinquished to Megga for scrub rags.

That vow he kept, even if he did ask the tailor in Heddenton to cut a replacement before winter. The seasons passed in tranquillity but for the quarrels of the dwarf couple. Ithariel never spoke of the powers reft from her in Dethmark; Korendir was considerate of her loss in his own inimitable way. He learned to read runes, taught her archery and swordplay in return, and rode out often on the High Kelair gray. Nights under stars, or wrapped in furs against the whine of winter storms, the Lord and Lady of Whitestorm lost themselves in each other's arms; but still after a span of four years they failed to conceive any child.

Korendir's shout came again, from the direction of the master suite. *"Haldeth!"* The distress in his voice had been real.

Shocked awake, the smith cast off his coverlet. The dawn beyond the casement still seemed tenuous as a dream. Never, through pain, disaster, and near death, had he known Korendir of Whitestorm to show fear. The novelty caused Haldeth to snatch yesterday's tunic from the floor and dash in bare feet for the stair.

Korendir met him on the landing, wild with anguish. The force of emotion on a face unaccustomed to expression froze Haldeth in his tracks.

"What's amiss?"

Unconsolable, Korendir gestured across the threshold at his back. In the chamber beyond, limp as a gutted fish, the Lady Ithariel of Whitestorm lay among silk sheets with her skin the color of death.

Haldeth felt his stomach tighten. "Almighty Neth, what's wrong with her?"

The wardstone in the tower still burned, a changeless magnificence of white light; under its protective aura, no threat could gain entry from Aerith. Dazed by disbelief, Haldeth pressed past Korendir, entered the room, and lifted the lady's wrist. Her flesh was cold, and lifelessly unbreathing as a corpse.

"She's still alive." Korendir fought to recover a measure of his accustomed control. "If you're patient, you can feel her heartbeat."

Deaf to the birdsong beyond the casement, Haldeth waited. If harm had come to Ithariel by treachery, no man dared predict the outcome; Korendir had lived the last years in contented peace, but the influence that tempered him was his wife. With her safety compromised, the underlying violence of his nature could never remain under wraps.

A minute passed like the nethermost end of eternity before a pulse throbbed beneath Haldeth's finger. "What in Aerith can be wrong with her?"

Korendir had stepped to the wardrobe. Busy with boots and laces, his answer came back clipped: "I don't know." He strapped his dirk to his wrist and flicked his cuff overtop without pause to button the fastening. "I intend to find out."

Like Haldeth, he was convinced Ithariel's affliction had no natural origin. Sorcery surely held her tranced, and for that, no mortal mind held remedy.

"You'd be wise to beg help from the White Circle."
Certain his advice would be ignored, Haldeth restored
the lady's hand to the blanket; her skin was fine pearl
against fingers callused over from forge bellows and hammer. Through the years since her banishment from
Dethmark, Ithariel had done nothing to mend her es-
trangement from Aerith's most powerful enchanters.

Korendir strapped on his swordbelt. He snatched up
the black cloak that Ithariel, for all her love of color,
had never successfully weaned from him. His motion as
he spun from the wardrobe was dangerously brief, and
his eyes showed, rekindled, the old spark of insane
ferocity.

*Against his every caution, and protections that cruelly
had failed to guard, his deepest fear had become manifest.*
His voice held a ring like cold iron as he said, "The Archmaster himself will give me audience. And answer with
it, or I'll level his tower from under him."

The threat was preposterous; but Haldeth could do
nothing but sit in shaken sorrow. Too well he knew that a
sword blade would sunder any protest he might attempt.
"Fortune speed you," he offered lamely.

Korendir flicked his cloak over his shoulders. His face
was still pale, but fear and anger now lay shuttered behind a grimness that reassured not at all. "Look after my
lady."

Haldeth was moved beyond caution. As if the years
since his quest by wizard's gate to the Doriads had not
inured him to his recognized limitations, he said, "Stay
with her. I'll go myself."

Korendir hesitated. His gray eyes shifted to his wife
and lingered over blanched features and loosened auburn
hair. He leaned over the coverlet, lightly clasped the
hands that had shaped his fondest dreams. "No. I'm better off on the road."

He bent and kissed his lady's mouth. "Guard her
well."

Radiating tension that threatened at any second to escape restraint, the Master of Whitestorm strode out.

Left alone with a tragedy, Haldeth stared like a half-
wit at the incongruous sparkle left glistening on Ithariel's
cheek. He reached out, touched moisture, and was struck
by a realization that made past events frightening to con-

template. The cold-blooded decimation of the Dathei had once convinced him that Korendir was incapable of pity. But tears were the man's parting gift to the lady who lay dying at Whitestorm.

A brutal two-day ride left the gray stud and another six post horses near to ruin with exhaustion. The closest White Circle initiate lay thirty-five leagues from Whitestorm, and Korendir crossed the distance without rest. If the enchanter Orame could not lift Ithariel's affliction, her husband intended to demand passage by spell-gate to Dethmark. He would not be refused. Black as his reputation was with the wizards, Ithariel was the Archmaster's granddaughter. The entire Council Major would stir itself in her behalf, Korendir vowed, his face showing vicious determination.

He drew rein and dismounted on the sun-dappled flags of Orame's dooryard and instantly sensed something amiss. Customarily the wizard's dwelling appeared as a sheer obsidian spire, polished to mirror smoothness by arcane protection. Today, where no windows should have been visible, the Master of Whitestorm viewed rows of mullioned casements cracked open to let in the spring. Foreboding drove him stumbling to the entry. The grillework gateway was not locked and the inner panel stood open. Wind had strewn leaves through the hall, and dew beaded the wall sconces.

Korendir stopped still. His initial, creeping uneasiness swelled to driving apprehension.

His knock went unanswered. His shout settled an intruder's silence over the forest at his back as squirrels startled into hiding, and birds flew. The tower was deserted. Korendir knew even before he crossed the threshold and raced to check each separate room. Hallways echoed like a tomb to his step as he descended the central stairwell. Unresolved worry left him frantic. He must now ride on into Heddenton to shed light on the fate of Orame.

Korendir paused fretfully to latch the door against the elements. The outer gates were made to lock without benefit of a key, but even so slight a delay was inconceivable. The Master of Whitestorm spun away and caught the horse's trailing reins. Over and over he reminded himself that Ithariel still lived; that one fact could not be doubted. Joined by spell-bond marriage, her passing would call him after her across the threshold of death. While he endured, hope remained for her.

The Master of Whitestorm forced his stiffened body back into stirrup and saddle. The post horse shivered and dripped lather; Korendir stroked its neck in apology, then jerked the drooping head up, reined around, and shouted like a madman until the road became a blur under galloping hooves.

By late afternoon he clattered into Heddenton on a horse that staggered under him. The groom who took the animal looked shocked, until Korendir threw him a gold piece.

The boy's face lit with greed. He bit the coin in bright eagerness, then started as the Master of Whitestorm spun him back in a grip of bruising anger. "Tend that gelding well." Spent as the animal which had carried him, and alarmingly savage-tempered, Korendir added a healthy shake. "Nurse the horse, or put it to the sword, but see that it's spared further suffering."

"Yes, Lord." The boy cowered, as the mercenary released him and urgently strode on his way.

At the house of Heddenton's mayor, Korendir slammed without ceremony through a locked door. He ignored the steward's shout of outrage over the split and ruined latch. A parade of bothered servants trailed his swift passage through the halls, where his abrupt and unkempt appearance caused the footpage to start back in fright.

"His Lordship is at tea," the boy whimpered in protest. Korendir barged past, entered the formal sitting room, and presented a query like a whipcrack.

"Orame is dead," replied the Mayor of Heddenton. A portly man in a brocade waistcoat and robes trimmed with ermine, he paused to lick honey from his fingers. The rude appearance of the mercenary caused a flicker in his hooded eyes; out of prudence he remained polite. "The woman who sells herbs called on the wizard as she does on her journeys to Northport. She came too late. His corpse was already cold."

Korendir interrupted. "When?"

The mayor selected another pastry and tried not to

look pained. "Three days past, if I remember. Your wife, now. Can I send her a healer?"

Korendir's response rang like a threat. "What did you do with the body. *Quickly!*" If, like Ithariel, the enchanter's condition had lent him the appearance of death, the answer was of paramount concern.

The Mayor's cheeks colored like plums. Only the Master of Whitestorm's formidable reputation kept the leash on his temper. "My secretary oversaw the details," he said stiffly. Opals flashed at his collar as he ducked to cram in another bite.

"Then send for your secretary." Korendir's hand flexed on the bleak black hilt of his sword. "The grave must be opened."

"My good man!" The mayor choked and dropped his pastry. "Would you have us all laid under curse? Brings about ill fortune, it does, to cross a wizard's ghost. Forget Orame. I'll send for my personal physician."

"Tell me the name of your secretary instead," Korendir demanded.

But the mayor feared spells worse than sword steel; undone by terror, he refused. Rather than waste more time, Korendir turned sharply on his heel and departed. A coin in the servant's wing bought the name he desired; additional gold in the secretary's palm revealed that Orame had been buried in a suicide's grave at the crossroads beyond the town walls.

"If his ghost is going to walk, let it do so without disturbing the rest of the decent," the servant ended nervously. He glanced aside to see how the mercenary who waited with hairtrigger impatience might handle this flimsy excuse. But to his mortified relief, the mayor's senior secretary discovered his justifications had been delivered to an empty corridor.

XXIV. Bane of the White Circle

Spring constellations glittered icy as frost over the suicide's cairn which marked the crossroads beyond Heddenton's wall. Deep in its shadow, Korendir of Whitestorm knelt and thrust his hands into the new-turned earth of a grave. His fingers grazed cloth, the coarsely woven sort used to wrap corpses appointed a pauper's burial. In spite of braced nerves, the Master of Whitestorm shivered. He could see nothing in the pitch dark. The sweat of exertion chilled on his shoulders as he scraped away dirt and loose stones. The mayor's fears were not founded on superstition; sorcerer's bones were best left unmolested by mortal hands. But Korendir held to his conviction that Orame had not been dead at the hour of his burial.

The rented gelding chinked its bit and stamped once. It showed no alarm as Korendir raised the bundled body from the earth, drew his knife, and slashed through damp burlap.

A slack hand brushed his wrist. The Master of Whitestorm started, fist clenched on his dagger haft. Then reason caught up with his racing heart. Orame yet survived; his illness had spared him from suffocation, for a corpse three days in the earth should be bloated and beginning to putrefy.

Korendir twisted away the shroud and clasped at the wrist inside. Orame's bones were as fine as his own, but frightfully chilly to the touch. The wizard wore no rings; if his robe had been richly adorned, the one left on him for burial was mean enough to shame a beggar.

Korendir wished the torment of Mhurgai slavery on the mayor's thieving secretary. A lonely minute passed as he searched for a pulse in the flesh beneath his touch. Even so basic a lifesign took an eternity to manifest. Korendir settled back on his heels with a mildness that deceived; beneath his still demeanor surged a rage of shattering proportions, that Heddenton's pompous officials had caused Orame to be interred alive.

Stung by fresh fear for his lady, Korendir raised the enchanter clear of the shroud and carried him over to the gelding. The horse sidled as the lax body settled across its saddle. Korendir eased the beast with a word, then mounted up behind. Already the stars had faded; the east showed a lit streak of rose, heralding sunrise and the prospect of rain yet to come. By day the roads would swarm with couriers and merchants bound for Northport. The first drover who stopped behind the cairn to relieve himself would discover the wizard's plundered grave; Heddenton's populace would panic. Orame must be locked safe inside his tower before a mob of vigilantes could assemble and seek to overtake him.

Wearily, Korendir gathered the reins. No wizard's gate might speed him to Dethmark now; a thousand leagues of ocean lay between Heddenton and the Archmaster, two months' sail on a fair wind. More than one life depended upon his appeal to a council who grudged to grant favors to mortals. Korendir kicked the gelding to a canter, aware that he needed a miracle.

Sixty days later, with salt-stained boots and a deck hand's callus, and nerves that had not snapped through brute willpower, Korendir reached the western strands of Dethmark. Lowering sunlight brightened the triple spire of the Archmaster's tower; behind long shadows, the oarsmen who had delivered him ashore pulled rapidly back to their ship. Wizards were distrusted by crews who plied blue water. Although the ports were alive with rumors of towers whose inhabitants had lapsed into silence, sailors across the kingdoms interpreted the news with threat. Korendir's apprehension was no less. If White Circle enchanters across two continents were all falling tranced by sorcery, Telvallind Archmaster and his vaunted Council Major must be aware of the fact. Yet not a power among them had acted.

Korendir strode away from the beachhead. There remained only direst conjecture, and worries that harried like the tireless circling of carrion birds.

The possibility existed that no wizard remained to aid his cause at all.

The stronghold at Dethmark was built of rose quartz, and roofed by the gleam of leaded slate. The lawns grew rank between gardens plots choked over with weed. Melons rotted in the sun. The outer gatehouse proved untenanted, and spikewort thrust brown, untidy stalks through the flags of the courtyard beyond. The mercenary's solitary footsteps reverberated back from baked stone, until he seemed to walk amid a legion of marching ghosts. The door to the main tower was closed, but not barred. Defense sigils glowed on panels cross-hatched with ivy, and the gargoyle boss beneath the latch lay twined in runners like a festival maiden.

Korendir's knock went unanswered. Whatever had subdued the most powerful enchanters on Aerith might only be pursued across portals spell-warded against intrusion. A mortal's only means to test whether the tower's defenses still functioned was to challenge by crossing the threshold.

The Master of Whitestorm blotted damp palms on his tunic. Whipped on by purest pain, he drew his knife, slashed away the ivy, then thumbed the latch and pushed with both hands.

The portal swung wide to reveal an anteroom dusty with neglect. A tracery of disturbed motes winnowed inward. The boom as the panel struck the stops echoed and re-echoed, disrupting silence within a well of dank stone. Shadow hung dense past the stoop, oppressive with the miasma of something dead.

Korendir sheathed his knife. He spoke his wife's name like a talisman and stepped through.

His consciousness spun like a dowel on a lathe. A whine grazed his ears, and his skin encountered a vicious sting of heat. Then his foot met the floor inside. Dizziness and discomfort disappeared.

Korendir recovered a shaking breath. He stared in disbelief at his boots, now wreathed in whorls of stirred dust. Morien's paternity perhaps had permitted him entrance; but bloodline was all that he had, and Telvallind's tower held peril for the unenlightened mind.

*   *   *

In the topmost chamber of the stronghold, Korendir found a pentagram traced in faint light upon boards whose symbols recalled another day; but the Archmaster who had refused his inheritance in cold anger was no longer a threat to be argued with. Telvallind's remains sprawled inside the spell circle. His flesh had shrivelled to his bones; the eye sockets tipped toward the doorway gaped empty. He had been dead for quite some time. Around his corpse in its midnight and gold-sewn robes lay all of his Council Major, passive as discarded puppets, and filmed with the same fine dust that layered the furnishings.

Still winded from his tour of the living quarters, Korendir braced his shoulders against the lintel. He breathed shallowly as a man with a fever, pent nerves making him shake. Behind countless closed doors, he had found only mice and old parchments. Here, sorcery was still active, and dangerous to the unversed trespasser.

Knowledge, wisdom, and spell-craft had failed to save the enchanters from whatever had stolen their consciousness; the only weapon left was simple human force. Korendir shoved off from the doorway. He strode into a chamber that rang with magic before helplessness and resurgence of past fears could master him and annihilate rational resolve.

The pentagram crackled static as the mercenary neared the perimeter. When he crossed its glimmering border, it dealt him a jolting shock and snapped out. Shadows swelled, heavily spiked with ozone. Uneasiness prickled Korendir's spine. He advanced another step, felt his heels scrape the sigils carved into ancient floorboards. No magics flashed to restrict him. A beetle scuttled from the cuff of Telvallind's crumpled sleeve; everything else remained still.

Korendir knelt by the nearest enchanter. The body was still living, but grown grotesquely thin. Ithariel might have wasted in similar fashion. Dread crashed through self-control and raised the specter of horror, of pearl-clear skin webbed over with creases, and hands crabbed like claws by sickness. The nightmare intensified, recurred in a dozen pernicious forms, until Korendir trembled outright. He thwarted the screams that battered to escape him through a mindless frenzy of action. He made eighteen unconscious bodies comfortable, then wrapped up the corpse of the Archmaster. He interred Telvallind's remains beyond the walls. Past sundown, sweating more than physical labor should warrant, the Master of White-storm fetched wine and smoked sausage from the cellars and ensconced himself in the library.

The silence weighed oppressively there, as though the air with its scents of ink and parchments lay impossibly stiller than elsewhere. Stoneworked gryphons supported shelves of scrolls and books; most lacked titles, and the few that did not were stamped in gleaming runes. Ringed by mounting inner terrors, Korendir reminded himself that he offered his lady's only hope. He had pursued obscure knowledge all his life, and since marriage to Itha-riel, had spent his winters in study. Only those texts de-fended by spells lay outside his means to decipher. By morning, surrounded by a jumbled mass of volumes and the sockets of spent candles, he had unravelled what caused the enchanters' affliction. One of the Six Great Banes had slipped its guardian ward. The White Circle had no written name for the evil, as if to assign it identity might lend power to augment its threat. Common lan-guage held less scruple. Herb witches called the thing Valjir, intelligence spawned from the void, and given form by a composite mass of purloined souls. One of them was Ithariel.

Korendir shrank from the implications. His madness knotted back on itself like the dreams of the priest-oracles who used drugs to induce ritual insanity. Arisen from the netherspace between existence, the Valjir's re-cent thefts enabled an emergence into the otherworld of Alhaerie. White Circle enchanters were vulnerable to its call because their craft attuned and directed forces counter to Aerith's reality. Alhaerie afforded the well-spring for their powers, and established within that envi-ronment, the Valjir overcame safe-wards and the minds which shaped them with the mundane ease of a hunter trapping sparrows with birdlime.

Korendir pinched out the last candle. He stretched his cramped back and ground his knuckles into stinging eyes. Behind him lay a lifetime of survival against the most dangerous hazards on Aerith; in Alhaerie, that store of experience might make him a powerful wizard, or else a target for destruction. By every account, the untrained mind could not survive without a sorcerer to shield the awareness. Grimly, Korendir arose. He left the library knowing the fact could only be questioned by the attempt.

The Master of Whitestorm assumed position on the central array of sigils where the bones of Telvallind Archmaster had lain unattended in death. Here, a wizard's gate had once opened to rescue three lives cast adrift into Alhaerie. Prepared with no more than a phrase purloined from a spell book, Korendir prayed he could duplicate the feat. Overtop his tunic he wore the blue-black robe of an adept, filched from Telvallind's wardrobe. On a chain at his neck hung the tallix signet borrowed from the fallen wizard's hand. Denied the particulars of his heritage, the swordsman could not guess that ring and stone had once belonged to High Morien.

The sentiment would hardly have comforted.

All the achievements of his life shrank to insignificance before the deed he presently contemplated; the risk he assumed was unconscionable. But Ithariel's peril eclipsed reason. The jewel held the key to access the otherworld; the clothing, Korendir had added as bait for the Valjir, hoping to lure it with belief that one sorcerer still eluded its control. The only flaw in his masquerade was the left-hand pocket, which he had stripped of its lining to free the blade strapped beneath.

Korendir raised the ring, discarding acknowledgment of the disasters he courted by his actions. A brother he had never met had loosed demons upon Alathir through the opening of an unsanctioned wizard's gate. Korendir could only hope that the sigils beneath his feet held some residual power of warding. Not for the living peace of Aerith could he accept that Ithariel was lost beyond recovery. She was his lady; guilt for her peril whipped him steadily back toward the deep, mindless silence that had engulfed him those early years after the burning and sack of Shan Rannok. For the wife he had unforgivably failed to safeguard, Korendir spoke the phrase of opening. He raised the Archmaster's tallix and brought the ring downward through the dust-still air.

A line scribed through shadow where the crystal

passed. Then light flared from the edges and a rift became visible between. Korendir released the jewel to its tether of silver chain. He extended his fingers toward the gap, braced for pain.

Nothing met his touch. His hand encountered no sensation at all, but vanished clean to the wrist.

The wizard's gate was opened through the void. Stripped of protection, woefully short of wisdom, Korendir contemplated the scope of his handiwork. A step would send him across the nether space into the alter-reality of Alhaerie, perhaps never to return. He could become no more frightened; never again since the moment he had wakened to a spring morning, and his beloved had not.

Nothing else in Aerith held meaning for him.

Korendir framed the memory of Ithariel in his mind. For the first time since she had been stolen into thrall by the Valjir, he set fully free the emotions that harrowed his being. If by the bonds of marriage his spirit would follow hers across the barrier of death, perhaps the same attraction would guide him to the horror that imprisoned her. The thinnest smile of irony curved his lips as he made the irrevocable step through the gateway. He would find his lady, either way.

The change was like stepping from dry rock into whirlpool. Sensation became consumed. Korendir trod a spinning, incomprehensible void. His ears were needled by patternless sound, and febrile light eddied round him. The Archmaster's robe was transformed; opaque no longer, the fabric displayed its living history in a tapestry that bewildered the eyes. Summer warmed the powdered wings of silk moths, and the steam from the dyer's vats twined, warp through weft, with the tracings of tailor's chalk and the needle of a willow-thin seamstress. Korendir walked, clothed in alien power that radiated presence like a bonfire.

No White Circle initiate would have dared traverse Alhaerie without first setting spells of concealment. Korendir knew enough not to stop moving, but his unschooled mind could not sort the assault to fleshly perception. Disorientation was immediate, and virulent enough to disable. Already his temples pounded; in time that pressure would mount to a debilitating headache, followed by paralysis and dissolution.

Alhaerie resisted motion like thick syrup. Each footfall roused whorls of light which oozed and spilled like flourishes in marbling before fading slowly away. The eye had no reference to measure distance. Uncertainty harrowed Korendir's nerves, and he longed for a firm and recognizable path.

A crackle of sound answered his wish. His body felt momentarily dashed to particles; then his boot sole jarred against cobblestone. Continuity slammed back into focus, and through widened eyes, Korendir beheld a wonder: a road sprang straight as a draftsman's line across the murk of Alhaerie.

Surprise drove his hand to his sword hilt. The weapon clanged half clear of the scabbard before he understood his own mind had imposed the stonework underfoot. Though the discharge of unexpected power left him dizzied, a laugh escaped his lips. The sound was visible, in that place, as a glassy, jagged-edged ripple that fell and smashed like crystal against the paving.

Korendir paused. Ithariel had once confided that intangible things on Aerith held solid form in Alhaerie; this anomaly formed the working basis for her magic. The Master of Whitestorm bent and fingered one of the scattered fragments. It proved exceedingly sharp. On the chance that noise might prove useful as a weapon, he tried calling out his wife's name.

The syllables spun like scythe blades, carved through the oily film which passed for atmosphere, and vanished out of view. Pensively, Korendir moved onward. Underfoot, the cobbles stayed convincingly firm; the muted click of his heels scattered shards like sleet at each step, and the implications stunned.

In Alhaerie, sound was an object, and thought, an act of physical creation.

Korendir's breath stuck in his throat. Only now did he fully comprehend the capabilities of the demons he had banished from Illantyr. The White Circle feared beings from the otherworld because their power over reality beyond the gates was proportionally the converse of this; *and Aerith, stripped of its wizards, was left vulnerable as wet clay should any denizen from Alhaerie slip through the tallix gate left open at his back.* Korendir made himself run. The Valjir must be destroyed for more than

Ithariel's sake; now the continued existence of Aerith itself might be forfeit.

His boots struck like hammerblows, firing silvery crescents of sound. The whisper of his breath trailed a wake of glittering threads, but he paid such marvels no heed. His every resource concentrated upon the overwhelming need for urgency.

His hurry became wasted effort since his bond with Ithariel in the end drew the Valjir to him.

The Master of Whitestorm saw the horror first as a gossamer sphere which spanned the width of the roadway. The chaos native to Alhaerie unbound the solidity of the cobbles where the void-spawned being passed. Winded from more than exertion, Korendir checked. Sweat slid in droplets down his wrists. He wiped his palms instinctively, lest a dampened grip on his sword lend unnecessary advantage to an enemy.

Yet on sight it seemed unlikely that steel could vanquish this adversary. Insubstantial as a silk balloon, the Valjir advanced. Closer, its surface revealed an astral mosaic of heads, bodies, and limbs, lapped one against another without break. A few of the faces were familiar. Korendir jerked his eyes aside to forestall a painful search for the single one which mattered.

The records failed to describe what sort of being lurked inside that envelope of souls. Dwarfed by its drifting presence, Korendir chose not to speculate. He shouted a verse from Neth's litany of creation on the chance that whetted edges of sound might breach the Valjir's defenses.

His words shaved the atmosphere into strips that streamed like twisted ribbon. Consonants thin as razors cleft the Valjir's spirit mantle. They passed clean through and emerged from the far side without inflicting a mark. Before the Valjir swept over him, Korendir abandoned verse and dove headlong off the road.

He landed in a patch of spikeweed. Dry stalks tore his skin and snarled the Archmaster's robe with burrs. Korendir's disgruntled curse pruned away a scattering of leaves. Apparently his recitation had imposed portions of Aerith's flora into being in Alhaerie. Backlash left him queasy and a scratched lip coated his mouth with the taste of blood.

Korendir thrashed to his feet as the Valjir loomed to

confront him. It could not retaliate with the keen edge of a shout since it possessed no flesh to shape sound. That did not make it defenseless. Since its abilities were only comprehensible on an enchanter's terms, Korendir could not guess what form its attack might take.

Air whispered through a thousand stolen mouths. "Mortal, what are you called?" The Valjir's words spooled forth from row upon row of lips and snagged, fragile as frost, against the forms of weeds and man.

Korendir flicked the threads away. Pain began behind his breastbone and flared unpleasantly through his nerves as the Valjir grappled for the hold his untrained mind could not provide. He could only attempt to answer in forms an intangible being could not master.

Korendir framed thought; and Alhaerie's reverse properties transformed intent into substance with the immediacy of a thunderclap. A wall of stone rose up, steep and flint-blue as the granite that comprised the bastions at Whitestorm. Graven on the face which blocked the Valjir was an inscription shaped more for the captive souls of wizards than for demand by any being from the netherworld.

I am son to Morien of Alathir, and also husband of Lady Ithariel. For her, for Orame, for Telvallind Archmaster who was murdered, and for every enchanter you have stolen alive from Aerith, I challenge your right to exist. Korendir swayed, light-headed. Sweat sheened his body and dampened the wizard's robe. The backlash inflicted by his creation exacted a merciless toll. Half-crippled by an exhaustion that seemed to drain the marrow of his bones, the man understood that rock in Alhaerie could not protect him. The Valjir would pass through as easily as it had banished the roadway, but at least the obstacle might buy time.

That hope endured but an instant. Blue quartz unbound and tumbled like dry sand; between heartbeats the last grains eddied away, restored to the roil of wild energies that comprised the otherworld universe. A searing ache flared behind Korendir's eyes. Cast adrift into chaos, he felt his stomach turn from dizziness. With his jaw clamped against nausea he tumbled, flotsam stirred in a medium of jelly.

The Valjir advanced. "You are no sorcerer," it whispered. "You possess only mortal awareness, and worse than a fool's perception. Aerith cannot take form in Alhaerie without unbinding the soul from your flesh. Each act of transformation saps your substance, and hastens your mind to insanity."

Korendir shook off a trailing tinsel of spun sound. He ignored every screaming signal that insisted he lacked equilibrium, and fumbled one hand into his pocket. The sword slipped free of his scabbard with a scroll of metallic sound. With it came the warmth of the forge fire, and the shock of running water which had tempered the blade; Korendir drew comfort from ore-bearing bedrock, to the dwarf armorer whose expertise had smelted raw metals into steel. Their strengths lent steadiness to failing muscles, and purpose to sick confusion. Fire, water, earth, and flesh, the weapon was wholly of Aerith. Surely no being of chaos could disregard such a talisman.

Korendir swung.

The sword clove through souls like smoke and drove on unresisted into a pocket of limitless cold. Contact shocked through the blade and laced its sheen jagged with frost. The flesh of palm and knuckle froze fast to the grip in a flash of indescribable pain.

Korendir screamed.

His agony drew a bright arc of sound. His arm jerked back in recoil, and the sword followed, dragged by fingers incapable of releasing their hold.

The Valjir continued its advance, scatheless.

Korendir felt its pull against his mind even through his torment. He responded the only way possible. The enchanters had been born of Aerith. They had been stolen through their affinity for manipulating alien reality. The Master of Whitestorm dragged his sword upright in lacerated fingers, determined to remind them of their rightful existence.

He swung the blade two-handed, carved an arc through Alhaerie's unreason. Even as the Valjir moved to obliterate the cut, he braced the span with images drawn from a lifetime of travel.

Aerith unfolded into vivid existence. A meadow blossomed into spring and thousands of scattered wildflowers nodded under a sapphire sky. The sword reversed stroke. Ardmark's ridged mountains plunged sheer into the

paintbox reds and purples of desert sunset, swept aside
by the sparkle of ocean swells dashed to lace and jewels
on a reef.

Korendir's breath rasped into lungs that felt silted with
grit. The sword handled like stone in his grip; its black
weight dragged at the sinews of shoulder, elbow, and
wrist. He forced another stroke. He could not see the
Valjir at all through the raging creation of his thoughts.

Autumn flared red across Thornforest, and dawn
tipped fuchsia and gilt over the snow-bound peaks of
Illantyr. Korendir thrashed on, though his head spun;
water splashed, exotically patterned by the King of Faen
Hallir's incomparable Court of Fountains, and stars
glanced like tears through the pines of Southengard. The
sultan's vanquished city of Telssina gleamed, enamel and
filigree, against sand flats coppered with heat haze.

Images spilled from the sword edge until Korendir's
heaving mind could frame no more. Alhaerie invaded his
being and unbound the will which knit his sanity. He saw
between, into memories too terrible to contemplate; and
the sword slipped from weakened fingers and was lost.
Korendir tumbled after it. His eyesight rippled, torn by
wave upon wave of blind dark. The screams of Mhurgai
victims shivered his flesh. Worse things flapped down
and gorged on his nakedness, ravens with gobbets of
scarlet trailing from snapping beaks. He suffered reliving
of the unthinkable past, became macerated by horrors
that this time overwhelmed him. His body thrashed beyond control. Between snatches of image, and cruel fragments of nightmare, he saw the Valjir, untouched still,
and almost upon him.

"You are undone," it whispered softly.

Korendir heard without understanding. With his doom
inevitably at hand, every scrap of will he possessed was
absorbed in his final desire. The treasure he valued beyond life remained out of reach upon Aerith. At the last
he determined to master the nightmares within him,
shape his ending statement before the chaos of Alhaerie
crushed reason and the Valjir claimed his spirit in
triumph.

Korendir rolled to his knees. Shadowed by the sphere
of the Valjir, he shaped the memory of his wife.

She materialized between his spread hands exactly as

she had appeared on the morning of his departure. Dark
hair fanned like ribbon across his shoulder. He cradled
her softness against his chest, warmed beyond hurt by
the lustrous perfection of her flesh. Like the sword, and
the Archmaster's robe, Ithariel was wholly of Aerith:
lilac, pearls, and rainwashed earth; and night transformed to mystery under moonlight.

The act of creation set Korendir beyond reach of his
own handiwork. Sucked in the downward spiral toward
unconsciousness, he knelt with blind eyes, unaware that
the Valjir now battled against dissolution of its own.

One soul in its composite thousand had recovered self-
awareness. Ithariel strained against the Valjir's hold, desperate to reach the flesh recreated in the arms of her
husband. Her efforts distended the Valjir's patchwork
perimeter until the seams between spirits stretched dark
with stress. A small bead of black leaked through. The
seep was followed by a droplet which swelled to a trickle.
Like a breach in a weakened dam, the Valjir's forces
parted, and Ithariel of Whitestorm ripped free.

For a moment, the mists in Korendir's mind swirled
thinner. He beheld the form of his lady etched in light,
a solitary sparkle like a star shining through the hollow
of her hips.

Then the woman in his arms stirred with life. Her eyes
opened just as the Valjir burst asunder. The plundered
spirits of enchanters unravelled and scattered like wisps
blown in a gale.

Darkness poured forth from the space their life-force
had defined; hungry and cold, it ran like ink through the
uncolor that comprised Alhaerie.

"Fly, Korendir!" Ithariel tugged at her husband's sleeve.
"What you see is the essence of the void unleashed."

Her voice dispelled some of his stupor. Korendir
shoved to his knees, dimly aware that she had broken
the Archmaster's edict against magic; or else another sorcerer had provided a semblance of solidity to orient his
stumbling feet. On all sides, blue-edged and luminous,
the spirits of Aerith's enchanters fled the Valjir's spilled
contents.

Korendir struggled to rise, to follow Ithariel's liberated
colleagues toward safety. But his legs buckled. His silly,
useless flesh had no strength left, and tripped by his for-

gotten sword, he tumbled headlong into a fall. He thrashed, aware of his lady's entreaties to rise; but his struggles only drove him deeper into darkness. Faintly, through someone's cries of rage, he heard Ithariel call his name. . . . .

XXV. Last Summons

Korendir's next sensation was that of being caught by a pitiless force and dragged back into himself. He exclaimed in pain, then choked off the cry as he fully recovered awareness. His head hurt and his eyes stung, seared by too much brightness.

"Merciful Neth, we have him back," said a cracked and reedy voice.

The light, which proved to be common candleflame, withdrew.

Korendir discovered with some discomfort that he lay on the sigil-carved floor in the Archmaster's tower. In his weakness he was surrounded by the dust-grimed faces of a revived Council Major. Clean as a new pearl by contrast, and still clad in her nightrobe, Ithariel cradled his head between her hands. The oldest of the enchanters hovered at her shoulder, alert and bright-eyed as a fighting rooster. Orame crouched alongside, kneading salve into Korendir's palms, which were ghastly white with frostbite.

The Master of Whitestorm struggled in protest against such a surfeit of attention and managed to ease the shoulder pressed into cramps against the carvings. The moment he reliably mustered breath, he tried speech. His voice emerged as a scratched whisper that revealed, to his shame, that between his downfall and Ithariel's recovery, he had accomplished a great deal of screaming. Flushed red, he forced his words out anyway. "Orame, have you checked on your tower lately?"

The enchanter crossed his wrists across his knee and looked thoughtful. "No," he said at last. "Should I?" And his head tilted as if he listened to something far distant.

Then his dark brows peaked and his gaze sharpened

in vexation upon Korendir. "The Heddenton guard is attempting to pound in my gate with a fir log! Whatever you did, my friend, those meddling townsfolk took it badly."

Orame stood. The tin of salve fell rattling across floorboards as he vanished through a wizard's gate, presumably to defend his beleaguered tower.

An enchantress knelt to retrieve the medicine, but Korendir gave in to restlessness. He freed himself from Ithariel's hands, sat up before the nursing could continue, and stared at his lacerated palms. Behind his expressionless facade raged an anger he no longer had reason left to bridle.

Ithariel had nearly come to harm through the vulnerabilities of the White Circle that had disowned her. The Master of Whitestorm regarded eighteen impassive wizards, prepared to vent outrage should even one of them speak of risks undertaken without safewards.

Yet the council did not raise the issue of purloined crystals, or dimensional gates left unguarded; the eldest strove instead to make amends. "The White Circle owes you debt, my Lord of Whitestorm. To dare the perils of the otherworld was a consummate act of courage. Telvallind Archmaster would have been forced to show gratitude, had he survived. In his memory, past sanctions against your lady shall be reversed. I think the others will support me in offering the training due the son of High Morien."

Suddenly uncomfortable under the scrutiny of half the major wizards in Aerith, the acknowledged heir to Alathir pushed to his feet. No longer quite so guarded, he straightened a mantle left rucked with burrs like a dog's coat; if he chose, he had won the right to keep the tallix which hung at his neck.

The enchantress who still held the salve touched his shoulder in gentle encouragement. "Your accomplishment is celebrated on more than this side of the void. The gate you left open stayed unbreached because even the inhabitants of Alhaerie were driven into hiding by the Valjir. Its demise has freed both worlds, Korendir."

Yet to the surprise of every enchanter present, the Master of Whitestorm shook his head. "That's not what makes me hesitate." He drew a difficult breath.

"What will happen," he began, and broke off, defeated by a hint of unsteady laughter. He glanced at his wife and tried again. "If I accept training, who would be reckless enough to help the next time enchanters fall tranced like a bunch of corpses? I think for the future I'll be content to leave spell-craft to my wife."

The surrounding Council Major heard his refusal with smiles; even Whitestorm's lady did not spare him. Something about the quality of her joy set Korendir desperately near to the breakdown that had threatened him since Heddenton.

The eldest enchanter spoke still; at a jab in the ribs that certainly had been copied from Megga, Korendir belatedly listened.

"The solution is obvious, my friend," the spokesman for the wizards concluded. "Morien's inheritance must be awarded to the heir forthcoming to Whitestorm."

While the rest of the council voiced agreement, Korendir spun with a swordsman's poise, then spoiled all grace by staring open-mouthed at his wife. He recalled the star-like presence half-glimpsed in the interval before spirit reintegrated with flesh. "You?" he said, astonished.

Ithariel nodded, crying now with a happiness that hurt to witness. "I conceived you a son," she admitted. "But you weren't meant to hear until the night of midsummer festival."

Korendir recovered with such lack of ceremony that all in the chamber raised eyebrows. Then he threw restraint to the winds, shouted, and scooped his wife in his arms. "How did you ever bribe Megga to keep quiet?"

Ithariel hooked his chin in her palm. "Jewels, lots of them. The ones left over from South Englas. Nixdax will never in a century admit it, but a dwarf will do anything for riches."

Winter came, and Callin, heir to the fortress on White Rock head, was born during a diamond fall of snow. The King of Dunharra sent a charter officially acknowledging the domain of Whitestorm, and Nixdaxdimo celebrated by sounding his dwarf pipes from the watchtower. The music was created on a contraption of drilled horn and skins, and noisy as caterwauling beasts. Haldeth's apprentices determined the din an offense. They fetched out short bows and fired off volleys of blunted shafts, until the screeches from Nix grew obscene enough to be differentiated from his instrument. Resignedly the smith emerged to collar the boys.

Peace settled over the courtyard of Whitestorm keep, but only momentarily. Callin had lungs at least the equal of Nix's pipes, and no reservations about using them.

"Neth, he's as stubborn as his father," Ithariel murmured sleepily from the bed.

Korendir left off pacing the rug and sat down lightly on the mattress. He smoothed the blankets over his wife, then regarded the yelling infant in her arms. A mouth unaccustomed to softness melted into a smile. "You know, my promise to you is unsatisfied."

"What?" Ithariel paused in the task of loosening her bedgown.

Her husband reached across and helped with the unfastening of laces. When their son subsided to suck, he replied. "I said I'd never rest until we'd got a daughter between us."

Wind gusted outside and snowflakes rattled across the leaded window. Ithariel leaned in contentment against her husband's black-clothed side. "You have a delightful memory for details." Mischief lit her eyes. "But I'll lay you a wager. You'll sleep very little for the next six months, and not for conception of any daughter."

"One little imp will prevent that?" Korendir stroked the reddish fuzz that sprang from Callin's crown. He matched his wife's gaze with delight of his own, and capped her irresistible challenge. "I'll swap your wager for another. By autumn, I say you'll be widening the waists of your dresses."

Ithariel scowled at her newly flattened middle. "You randy goat! If I win, will you give up black tunics?"

"Assuredly." Korendir seemed taken aback. "You hate my favorite color that much?"

"Oh, get out!" laughed Ithariel. "Dark clothing makes you look like a carrion crow. Take that gray stallion for the gallop you've longed for all night, and leave me in care of my women."

"Maybe I will." Korendir bent. He kissed his wife and

young child, then rose with the killer's coordination that never entirely left him.

A draft swirled through the door as he departed. Slapped by a breath of cold, Ithariel shivered; jostled by her start, Callin lost his grip on the nipple and began to wail. His cry brought both midwife and maid to the bedside, and with coaxing his distress soon subsided.

But for some ominous and inexplicable reason, Ithariel could not think past midsummer without feeling inwardly chilled.

Yet the seasons passed over White Rock Head and brought no winds of ill fortune; the days of golden sunshine lingered. Young Callin rattled the toys his father made from shells. He pulled his mother's hair, plucked at Nixdax's nose, and gave Megga equal measure for provocation. The dwarf wife spoiled the boy without shame, then made up the lapse by increasing her slangs at Nix. The henpecked husband took refuge beneath the worktable in Haldeth's forge, and as his visits became frequent, the smith suggested building a chair there. Nix replied with curses, but showed up the next day with cushions filched from the apprentice's cots.

"They spend their nights fighting anyway," he declaimed when the boys came inquiring at dusk. Haldeth withdrew before the shouting turned into a scrap; when the boys chose to set aside differences, they were practiced at trouncing dwarves. The pillows returned to the loft with half their stuffing missing, and for weeks Haldeth could not lift a tool without batting at disturbed drifts of feathers.

Ithariel announced her second conception as the days began to shorten. No longer restricted from use of power, she admitted when pressed that the forthcoming child would be female. Korendir laughingly wore blue through the next fortnight to console her for losing their wager.

"You give me far better than I deserve," he admitted in the dark when they were alone. "A daughter's the best thing I could wish for."

But autumn came, and on the morning the ship sailed in flying the flags of a foreign envoy, Whitestorm's master reverted to his customary black.

The arrival by itself was not unusual. Couriers periodically brought offers from kings, and lords, and once a disgruntled royal nephew who disputed the succession in Dunharra. Without exception, the appeals met with refusal. Although it was known that the mercenary no longer took contracts, the most persistent petitioners came anyway.

Korendir treated the latest pair as he had each one of their predecessors. A signal arrow fired from the battlements offered them Whitestorm's hospitality, and at slack tide Haldeth went down to usher the guests to the keep.

The pair who waited on the beachhead could not have been nearer to opposites. Swarthy and clothed in royal finery, the taller was not yet twenty. He wore a fillet of jade-studded gold, silk robes, and a belt bossed with gems that was going to fascinate Nixdax. Haldeth took note of the other, who was wiry and small and much older. His leather tunic was edged with fur, and dyed in whorled patterns. Creamy fair skin bore similar tattoos, and the cap jammed aslant on salt-and-pepper hair was crested with the feathers of skyshears. Hawks with scarlet plumage were rare, their eyries only found in mountainous lands to the east.

The boy straightened haughtily in his finery. The man who had greeted him was not wearing livery, but neither did he carry badge of rank. "Salutations to the Lord of Whitestorm from my father, the King of High Kelair," the prince said noncommitally.

Haldeth returned the bow of a master craftsman. "Welcome to Whitestorm, Your Grace. Lord Korendir awaits you in his library. Kindly follow me."

The smith led the ascent of the stairs. At his back, the prince and his mountain-born escort conversed in heavily burred dialect. Haldeth caught phrases of admiration, a reference concerning a tournament, and wagers that somebody had lost. Then he stepped from the gloomy stairwell into a flood of fall sunlight.

The prince and his companion emerged blinking.

Nixdaxdimo peeped out from the forge, saw the strangers in the bailey, and slammed the door with a yelp.

The mountain born squinted in the direction of the disturbance. "You keep a dwarf servant?"

"Not a slave," Haldeth said quickly. "Nix swore free service to a White Circle enchantress, but he's a pest most always nonetheless."

The red-feathered cap bobbed agreement. "So say the foremen at the mines. Trouble dwarves are, but they don't sicken with underground labor like humans. For that, the unscrupulous continue to trap. But my clan shares no part in such cruelty."

Haldeth shrugged. "By now, Nix will be crammed so far underneath my spare bellows that no amount of coaxing will call him out. Eventually he'll get hungry. Or else his dwarf wife will fetch after him with a meat knife, and there won't be any peace for the yelling."

The Prince of High Kelair laughed with a flash of white teeth; his more taciturn companion made no comment. Chilly winds raked the bailey, and Haldeth hurried the visitors as quickly as politeness permitted into the shelter of the keep. Although the stair that led upward was unheated, the chamber above offered comforts. A log fire burned in the grate, and the table beneath walls lined with bookshelves had been laid with fine wine and food. The Master of Whitestorm arose and greeted his guests. He carried no weapons. Not so much as a dagger adorned his belt and though black, his tunic was on the courtly side of practical.

Prince Teadje accepted a chair and after him, the others chose seats. Korendir alone remained standing. As the mountain born reached for a dish, the mercenary saw, and returned a fractional shake of his head. "You're a guest. Let me." With a bow to his visiting royalty, he pointedly tasted each platter, then sampled the better of the wines. Candleflame struck sultry highlights in his hair as with enviable grace he sat down.

The mountain born coughed in apology. "Your man implied that a dwarf wife ran your kitchens."

Korendir raised his eyebrows. "Megga? Poison guests? I'd spit her before she ever dared."

Aware the quick words masked shock, Haldeth interrupted. "Nix saw tattoos on the Arrax man, and mistook him for a slave master."

The Lord of Whitestorm relaxed, but only fractionally.

His attention flicked back to his company. "Then I ask you to forgive the discourtesy. As a refugee from the mines, the poor dwarf probably had reason." Gray eyes shifted to the prince. "I regret to disappoint you further, Your Grace, but I don't any longer take contracts."

Prince Teadje hooked a slab of meat with his knife. "That is indeed regrettable." He raised eyes like unmarked brown velvet and sighed. "If we'd paid heed to the gossip of sailors, I could have avoided a tedious voyage."

Korendir filled the prince's goblet, unconcerned by the intensity with which the Arrax man studied the scars beneath his cuff. "The best I can offer is to hear your case and recommend a replacement."

Jade trappings glinted as Teadje inclined his head. "The king my father specified he would hire no other but yourself."

The Arrax man refused food, no longer on account of dwarf servants. His age was younger than first appeared, under graying hair and tattoos. His acerbity derived from hardship, and the clefts by his mouth reflected no other feeling but grief.

Korendir set aside the wine. His appetite was spare at any time, but the dishes that steamed by his hands also stayed untouched. "However dire your troubles, they cannot follow within these walls."

"Memories can," the Arrax man said bluntly.

His comment effectively stifled conversation. High Kelair was an island kingdom, not given to wars or disputes. The dispatch brought by Prince Teadje would not be the usual request to command armies, or assassinate a political enemy, or stand as bodyguard for some fearful nobleman. Firmly as Korendir insisted that his days of adventuring lay behind him, he could not look upon need without pity.

He retrieved the wine flask after a pause, then arose and stepped around the table. Personally he filled the Arrax man's goblet. "Drink," he urged firmly. "I would take it very ill if the hospitality of my house did not at least grant refreshment."

The Arrax man followed with his eyes as Korendir knelt to Prince Teadje, then lifted palms marked from all his past forays and formally asked to see the contract.

Haldeth nearly choked on his salad. Pale, almost sick with alarm, he watched the prince draw out a document crusted with seals and tied in the manner of the eastlands with cords of emerald silk. The knots were an art form, each one ritually significant, but to Haldeth they resembled nothing so much as an obscene coupling of snakes.

Korendir accepted the parchment with steady hands. He arose, selected a knife from the table, and retired to an alcove window.

Only Prince Teadje kept his appetite while the former mercenary broke the seals. Haldeth and the Arrax man watched Korendir's back as he slit the knots and read. Neither saw anything that might lend a clue to his mood; only something about his stillness caused Haldeth to feel threatened.

"Fetch Ithariel," the Master of Whitestorm said presently. His tone was inflectionless and short.

Haldeth murmured excuse to the prince and left at once to complete the errand.

The enchantress answered her husband's summons alone. Warned by Haldeth's refusal to return, she had left young Callin with a servant. The lady reached the chamber just as Korendir laid aside the parchment. His voice masked the click of the latch as he asked the Arrax man to describe the predator which terrorized the passes through the Hyadons.

"Huge," came the bitter reply. Though Korendir remained gazing outward through the window, the mountain born continued without pause. "Looks like a great dark bird, but large enough to kill cattle. The horse lords in the valleys lost foals, until they moved their herds. That's when the monster took to slaughter among the caravans bound for Arrax."

Ithariel spoke sharply from the doorway. "Is the beast feathered or scaled?"

The guests at the table both started in surprise; neither had noticed her entry. Now, the presence of Korendir's wife caused noticeable impact. In robes of gold-bordered violet, with her cheeks flushed from her hasty ascent of the stair, the Lady of Whitestorm was stunning. Caught with his mouth full of vegetables, Prince Teadje succumbed to a frankly stupefied stare; the Arrax man simply answered with a directness as dour as his manner throughout.

"The beast has feathers over wings and tail. The breast and neck are scaled with horn something like tortoise shell."

Ithariel crossed to the table. Looking troubled, she regarded the Arrax man with eyes a mistier gray than her husband's, and said, "Talons or claws?"

Her beauty at last made an impression; the mountain born reddened behind his tattoos, and his voice became defensively surly. "Talons, Lady. Ones curved as sabers and long enough to pierce a man's chest."

Korendir left off his contemplation. He encompassed his wife's arrival with an uncharacteristically savorless glance, and said, "You know of this creature, Ithariel?"

Whitestorm's lady set her hands on the back of Haldeth's vacant chair. She directed her reply to the Arrax man as well as the husband poised too tautly by the windowseat. "The killer our guest has described fits nothing else but the Corrigon of elder legend. Such a beast should not exist. Dethmark's records claim the last of them died nine centuries ago, as witnessed by Morien's forbears."

The Arrax man banged the table, causing silverware to jump. "Would I voyage the breadth of Aerith just to speak lies to strangers?"

Prince Teadje woke from admiration and at last recalled diplomacy. "Peace, man," he murmured across a glare like swords; but the offense he strove to smooth over seemed not to trouble the mercenary.

"We believe you." All light-footed edginess, Korendir retrieved the parchment from the windowseat. The ribbons and seals shimmered faintly in the tremor of a hand no longer relaxed. "My Lady, were the records specific? How did the Corrigon replicate, and how came the last one to die?"

Ithariel turned the chair. She sat down with her eyes on her husband and pushed aside Haldeth's uneaten meal. The chink of plates and cutlery half masked her initial reply. "The females laid eggs in volcanic ash. The time of gestation was not known, but warmth triggers incubation and hatching. Unless they are discovered as chicks, a Corrigon is notoriously difficult to kill. The last one listed in the records was never vanquished. Apparently it perished of old age."

"After a lifetime of slaughter and destruction?" Korendir sounded incredulous.

Still looking at him, Ithariel shook her head. "The monster hunted the wastes of Ardmark and terrorized nothing but wereleopards."

"Well, this one makes orphans," the Arrax man interjected. "It preys upon helpless people, even as we speak. Come the winter, without caravans to bring supplies through the passes, my countrymen in the Hyadons will starve."

Korendir slipped into his seat. He smoothed the elaborate parchment on the cloth by Teadje's elbow, then lifted the wine carafe and refilled the Arrax man's goblet. An expression crossed his face that Ithariel had never seen, as with incisive clarity he said, "You have my sympathy. When the tide ebbs at dawn, I'll see you off with a letter of recommendation to an adventurer who lives down the coast. He has a fast sword and a knack for the unusual. He might take your contract."

The Arrax man shoved to his feet. His eyes glittered with fury as he seized his filled goblet, spat on the rim, then deliberately emptied the contents. Wine splashed his plate and reddened fine linen like blood.

Prince Teadje skidded back to safeguard his finery.

Unmindful of the spatters which stained his leathers, the mountain man finished acidly, "I have misjudged, and will waste no more words with a coward." Ignoring Prince Teadje's shocked outcry, he spun and hurled the goblet into the hearthfire. The crash of crystal masked his step as he stalked in hunched anger through the door.

Beneath the table edge, Ithariel set her hand on her husband's thigh. The muscles beneath her touch never so much as hardened at the insults. While Teadje floundered to make apology, the Master of Whitestorm said nothing to anyone at all.

Korendir walked the wilds along the clifftop until sundown. He returned before Megga could notice and complain that his supper stood in jeopardy of getting cold. Following the meal, he spent an absorbed hour entertaining his son. Together he and Ithariel tucked Callin into bed; they read as they always did over tea, but when candles burned low and eyes tired, they did not speak of the day's events, or of the guests whose needs Haldeth attended in another wing of the keep.

"I have everything in life that I desire," Korendir said simply, when he caught Ithariel watching him over the edge of her book. "All of my happiness is here."

Then, exactly as he had on the night she had been his bride, he arose and lifted her in his arms. He carried her down a flight of steps, and up three more to their bedchamber. There he shared without words exactly how deeply she pleased him.

Ithariel roused much later to the chill of a solitary bed. That caused her awareness to sharpen instantly. Since the setting of the wardstone at Whitestorm, Korendir's nightmares had ceased, as had the nocturnal visits to the clifftops that once had been his way to stave off sleep. Alarmed, Ithariel propped herself on one elbow and shook tangled hair from her eyes.

But her husband had not wandered far. She located his silhouette, framed in the square of the casement. He had donned shirt and hose against the cold. Perfectly still, he stared over starlit ocean toward a horizon not yet gray with dawn. By his stance, she knew he was frowning.

Ithariel repressed a shiver. She curbed her impulse to call him back to bed, and instead chose her words by intuition. "You know already that Stendarr will refuse Prince Teadje's contract."

Korendir recoiled, not entirely because she startled him; at times her enchantress's perception seemed to tap his deepest thoughts. He shifted position in the window. His head turned to reveal his profile, etched in shadow against sky. "Stendarr has courage enough. He's at his best while managing armies, and good because he loves war. An appeal that concerns a monster is outside his usual experience."

Ithariel felt a shudder jar through her, the same she had known the past winter in the hour after Callin's birth. All at once the darkness no longer seemed friendly. She sat up. Her hair tumbled loose on her shoulders as she reached for candle stand and striker.

From the window Korendir added, "This has given me

a bad feeling from the first, and not through an Arrax man's insults.''

Flame bloomed under Ithariel's fingers. She set the lit candle by the bedside, her face bathed in light like a cameo. She weighed her words carefully before she spoke; in her heart she knew that no others, ever, would suffice. Her voice shook all the same. "Why hide your heart? The man I married would be asking himself why the children of Arrax should suffer and die, while his own daughter should be born in protected safety."

He moved with a speed that startled and caught her into his embrace. "Ithariel! You, and Callin, and our baby yet to come are the joy upon which my life turns."

She wept then, from cruellest certainty. "But pleasures and wants do not make the measure of a man."

He caught her shaking shoulders, slid his hands up the sides of her neck until he cupped her face in his fingers. His eyes, meeting hers, were fearfully deep and steady. "Neth in his mercy, what gives me the right to set you and our child at risk? I might be killed for those other mens' children and wives, and forfeit the joy of my family."

Ithariel covered his hands with her own. She could not face the tautness in him, and almost, she could not speak. "Could you live with yourself if you didn't?"

The answer could be read in his stillness. Ithariel laid her cheek against his chest. Too much a part of his spirit to muddle his anguish with lies, she set herself instead to console. "High Morien before you thought not. You survived him. In the end, the children must inherit."

Korendir's arms tightened over her back. He held her fiercely, for long moments incapable of speech. "I'm amazed," he choked out at last. He caught his breath, changed tack, and tried afresh. "Ithariel, beloved, you are unique among women. You understand a truth that I never grasped until now."

Something within him let go, then; Ithariel felt his softness against her. He relaxed inside as he never had since before he lost peace to the Mhurgai.

Cut by a sorrow more poignant than tears, Ithariel struggled for mastery of herself. The temptation was cruel, to renounce principle and say the one word that could keep him. At the same time aware how wide were the pitfalls, and how narrow the margin of his happiness, she fought her manner to lightness. "I knew all along that I'd married a maniac." She untied his points. "It's not dawn yet. Did you have to get dressed?"

As his hose slithered loose under her fingers, he buried his face in her hair. No word did he say but her name, and that, the way he phrased it, held meanings within meanings, but no regret. Compassion was his master, and his moment of final understanding had set all the universe in her hand.

In the hour that preceded daybreak, Prince Teadje awakened to a knock at the entrance of the guest suite. The Arrax man was dressed and already pacing the floor in his eagerness to be away from White Rock Head. It was he who minded the sleepy request of his prince, and stepped to unbar the door.

The portal opened to reveal Korendir, black-clad as always, but this time armed with sword and throwing knives, and a dagger inset with a cloudy jewel tucked in a sheath at his cuff. "The tide slacks in another hour. Your longboat has been summoned, if His Grace will arise and make ready."

The Arrax man's glower changed to critical interest. He began a remark, glanced at the mercenary's face, and chose silence. Korendir's manner held an edge that had not been evident the day before; in retrospect, instead of cowardice, the Arrax man recognized a quietude that should never in honor have been disturbed.

"Tell your prince the terms under which I take contract," instructed the Master of Whitestorm. "No coin will change hands. But for the death of the Corrigon, I demand your sovereign will set seal to an edict that abolishes slavery in the mines. There will be no more dwarves kept captive in the realm of High Kelair."

Upon sworn consent from the prince still cocooned in his blankets, the Master of Whitestorm closed the door. The final minutes before departure, he spent by himself with his son.

Autumn winds whipped the battlements of Whitestorm keep, and leaves torn from Thornforest flew scratching across crannies in the stone. Haldeth ventured out to make sure his apprentices had lighted the forge fire. A gust caught his cloak and forced a blast of chill through the fastening. The smith raised his eyes to curse the weather, and spotted the lady on the seaward embrasure with her hair unbound in the breeze.

The smith stopped short in his tracks.

Only one reason could bring the Lady Ithariel to stand lonely vigil above the sea.

Haldeth overcame disbelief and raced for the stairwell to the beachhead. Halfway down, with the breath burning in his lungs and every muscle protesting, he saw through the gap of an arrowslit that his effort came too late.

The envoy ship from High Kelair even now spread her canvas under the sky.

Nothing remained except to climb the battlements and consult with Ithariel; to try and comprehend what insane drive could lure Korendir from wife and child to his former feckless adventuring.

The lady waited until after the last sails vanished over the horizon. The ocean beneath the cliffs stretched empty and vast, and the wind held the mournful cries of gulls. Ithariel turned her head. A gust snatched back her hood, and morning sun lit her face. From the place where he waited by the postern gate, Haldeth saw her pain before she recognized his presence.

The smith never tried to stifle outrage. "Already you dread that he won't be coming back."

Ithariel started, her eyes like the mists off the beachheads in early spring. After a moment she nodded.

Haldeth clenched forge-toughened hands in bewilderment. "How could you let him go, then?"

The enchantress turned toward the sea, as if she could find answer within the rolling boom of the swells. "Sometimes a life must be given for life." When Haldeth moved to protest, she spun back and cut him short. "Don't speak of obligations. You're his friend, perhaps his only trusted one. Understand that Korendir is of High Morien's line, and White Circle enough to see his fate."

Haldeth gave vent to his bitterness. "He's a fool, and a son of a fool, if he could abandon his life here with you."

Ithariel looked back with all the coldness of her en-

chantress's heritage. "He has finally found his freedom.
Would you take that peace away from him? *Would you
dare?*"

The smith persisted in frustration. "What of the daughter you conceived in such joy, that may never know life
beyond the womb?"

Ithariel battled to stem her sudden tears. "She is only
one, Haldeth. And I knew what I chose on the day I
bonded in marriage."

The smith no longer noticed the brisk wind. Dwarfed
by the wide sky of Whitestorm, he shrugged at his own
helplessness. "Could a man be worth so much?"

The enchantress raised brimming eyes and nodded.
"That one, yes. Don't be sorry."

Too diminished to offer anything but the inadequate
comfort of his embrace, the smith extended his arms.
Ithariel gave in to grief and need. She leaned into his
chest; fine-boned and fragile as a bird, she shed the tears
she had restrained in Korendir's presence through the
length of his last night at Whitestorm. And as he held
her, Haldeth was plagued by the riddle that lingered like
an echo from his dreams; as if somewhere a truth existed
that forever escaped his grasp.

XXVI. High Kelair

Cold came early to the kingdoms in the north; frost etched jagged patterns across the windows of Prince Teadje's cabin on the morning his ship raised sail for return to High Kelair. The captain in command chose prudence over risk of winter gales. He charted a southerly course, to the undying disdain of the Arrax man, who claimed to read weather like a fisherman. Flushed beneath his tattoos, the mountain born expostulated in guttural tones of insult that blizzards would choke the passes before the ship could make port. Prince Teadje settled the dispute as the ship wore past White Rock Head and pitched to the roll of unprotected waters; His Grace turned precipitously green and retched in undignified postures over the rail. While servants rushed to escort him to his berth, the quartermaster minded his captain's barked command to maintain the chosen heading.

The Arrax man retired irritably to the maindeck; if he was galled to discover the prior presence of Korendir, his mood precluded complaint. Apparently inured to bad weather, he settled by the foremast pinrail and remained there despite the fact that his position interfered with the crew.

Tired of the mountain born's temper, the captain pretended tolerance. As the ship heeled into her beat to windward, spray flew in sheets over the bowsprit. The mettlesome man from the northpeaks became drenched and in time retired below. Only Korendir remained; quiet as shadow, he lingered at the rail long after the glimmer of Whitestorm's wardstone faded astern.

The envoy vessel reprovisioned at Fairhaven and left in driving snow. The gales closed in and whipped up whitecaps that battered at timber and sail; the calm between storms brought skies of glacial blue, and ice that jammed the running rigging. Sailors sent aloft to clear tackle borrowed the Arrax man's oaths; none of them understood mountain dialect, but guttural consonants and bitten syllables seemed suited to misery and salt water sores that chafed on stiffened canvas until every knuckle bled. By the time the ship backed sail in her home port, she showed the wear of a difficult passage. Her sails were patched, her men weary, and the pilot who boarded at the headland informed that the passes through the Hyadons were blocked by thirty-foot drifts.

Korendir absorbed this setback without reaction; except when he boarded the longboat with the Arrax man and the prince, he asked for a place at the oars. The craft crossed the bay with surprising speed. If the crewmen complained that their backs ached from matching the mercenary's stroke, his look quickly stilled their complaints.

Upon a wharf chipped clear of ice, the party was met by a herald in ceremonial colors and an escort of fifteen men at arms. The heir to the realm and his guests were marshaled through streets narrowed to tunneled alleys by piled snow. Craftsmen paused in their shovelling, and children blocked dooryards to stare as the royal cortege climbed a succession of switched back curves behind soldiers who cleared aside traffic. The captain snapped orders at their destination, and his company saluted in double columns before the gateway to the Palace of Kings.

Inside, warmed by a roaring fire, Korendir of Whitestorm paced to the casements and looked out on a town built in tiers against the hillsides. The islanders claimed that no land in High Kelair was created level, and the setting of their port affirmed the notion. Shops, temple spires, and gabled houses were built upon terraced foundations. All lay mantled under snow, looking like ornaments sugared over by the generous hand of a confectioner, except the smoke that trailed from level upon level of chimneys marred that image of charm. The Corrigon's predation had grown to trouble more than Arrax. Savaged by untimely freezing weather, the island's coastal settlements were threatened by a scarcity of wood.

Deeply morose, Prince Teadje's royal sire huddled amid cushions and toyed with a cut crystal game piece.

He was elderly. His hands shook, and the massive crown of state weighed heavily on his eggshell head. His jeweled cuffs flashed by firelight as he lamented that his summons to Korendir had been sent out too late to matter.

"Sledges with dogs could cross the passes, but not while the Corrigon flies." The sovereign tipped the chess pawn onto its side. "The last teams who tried were slaughtered. Only one driver returned to tell of their fate. He died soon after from his injuries."

The mountain born listened from a corner, expressionless behind tattooed sigils; only his eyes followed as a chancellor in embroidered robes resumed the recitation of bad news. "The town of Arrax is lost. The grain stores are nearly exhausted, and hunters who dare the wilds to set traps only become prey for the Corrigon. The creature has grown larger. It is said to fly over the rooftops by day and strike at the folk in the streets. Families have taken refuge in the mines, where they need not have fire to keep from freezing. But shelter is all the caverns can offer. The last messenger to report said that children were languishing from starvation."

"Last messenger?" Korendir never shifted from the frozen tableau through the casement. But his words cut. "How did that man win through?"

"He was no man, but a dwarf, my Lord of Whitestorm." The chancellor affected a deprecating cough. "That one reached the coast by scaling the peaks of the Hyadons. He survived a great folly. That route has no trail and no pass."

Now Korendir did turn. He bent his level gaze upon the King of High Kelair and said, "What one dwarf accomplished, determined men can equal."

The councillor looked askance at this, yet the king stroked his combed silver beard, and his mood of despondency brightened. "I could offer twenty-five men and relief supplies. But their own children are not dying, and the escarpments must be climbed upon ropes. My soldiers are willing and strong, but they have limited experience at mountaineering. What will keep them in heart when the winter peaks tax their endurance?"

"That can be solved," Korendir said promptly. "But we'll need more men to carry food."

The Arrax man had followed this exchange with rapt

intensity; now he spoke up and cut off rejoinder from the chancellor. "I can find volunteers who are willing. They could be ready to leave by afternoon."

"And who will guide this rescue mission?" The chancellor sneered his derision. "The dwarf?"

Korendir returned an expression of surprise, then coldly surveyed the official from the jewelled tips of his slippers to the fur-capped crown of his head. "Who else?"

The chancellor jutted his chin. "The mission you propose is ill favored, and to consider a dwarf as guide a worse misjudgment yet. Their kind lie. The one who came in was a branded slave. He would just as soon lead humans off the nearest vertical precipice."

"Not when he stands to gain freedom for his people," Korendir snapped back. "Your thinking's as blighted as a slave master's. The people of Arrax will be dead before spring and the Corrigon by then grown too large for any man's weapon." He spun and faced the old king, who had lifted the toppled pawn and sat turning it mindlessly between his palsied fingers. Yet Korendir framed his address as if the man were not infirm, or indecisive, or half lost in the blankness of advanced age. "Act now, or not at all, Your Grace. I came to your realm to spare lives, not to belabor the obvious."

The king set the chess piece upright upon the board. He blinked at the very still shadow framed in the brightness of the window. "Let it be now." If he was no longer young, he was still quite capable of command, for his chancellor bowed and kept silence.

Four mornings later, muffled in a jacket of sables sewn skin side out, Korendir stood at the end of the sleigh road and bent to strap snow shoes to his feet. Around him, the king's men-at-arms exchanged gripes, while a cluster of Arrax men and eight mismatched dwarves did the same, but less boisterously, and pointedly at a distance from the rest. The packs the small folk donned were at least as heavy as the humans' and in snowshoes, they waddled like ducks.

Someone noticed and cracked a jibe. The laughter that resulted was silenced by reprimand from Korendir.

That moment, in sunlight that glared off of snowdrifts and the blade-sharp peaks that divided the coast from the upland plateaus, the mountain born understood a thing. He traced the honor sigil at his forehead, while around him, his countrymen went still. They watched in disbelief as the one who had been Prince Teadje's envoy prepared to give Korendir his name.

The Arrax man stepped forward and slapped his patterned jacket with his fist. "Lord of Whitestorm, I am called Echend. Let it be said that you know me in honor." He ended in sarcasm, expectant that his gesture would meet with incomprehension.

A few kingsmen appointed to the expedition knew something of mountain ways; these paused in their preparations to stare.

Except the mercenary, who raised passionless eyes from his lacings. Without hesitation he dropped to one knee and scooped snow into his bare right hand. "Echend," he repeated clearly. "Korendir, son of Morien, accepts the honor of your name. May the gifted prove worthy of the hour, and the day, to the crossing into spirit yet to come." In acceptance of sealed pledge, he let droplets of new-melted snow trickle down his collar toward his heart.

Echend shouted in pleased surprise, for the response was the proper one, and flawlessly executed. "You are my kinsman from this day forward."

"Let it be so." Korendir recovered his glove and oversaw the final arrangements as if unaware of the eyes that watched his back. The king's soldiers regarded him with faint distrust, while the dwarf guide, Indlvarrn, whispered to his fellows that there was more to this mercenary from Whitestorm than met the casual eye. How he had known mountain tradition, and when he had memorized so obscure a ritual response, no one present could guess.

On that observation, the expedition to spare beleaguered Arrax set off across a valley of pristine drifts.

At the instant Korendir's party broke trail, a storm breaker boomed on the shores beneath Whitestorm keep. The sound rattled the window glass and shook the timbers of the gates, but the knock upon the panels outside was heard by Haldeth in the forge. He frowned, laid aside his hammer, and stepped out into windy afternoon.

The knock came again, plain over the thunder of the surf; not an illusion. The smith unbarred the side postern, and the portal swung open to reveal the enchanter, Orame.

Haldeth recoiled in astonishment.

"Is my arrival so surprising?" The wizard stepped into the bailey, as groomed as though he had just set forth from his tower. Sunshine struck autumn colored highlights in his hair, and his eyes sparkled with impatience. "Your mistress Ithariel has need of me."

Haldeth sucked a breath of frosty air and reached around the wizard to draw the bars. "And Korendir?"

Orame raised his brows. "Crossing the valley of Kashiel, which is logical, since he plans an ascent of the Hyadons by way of the Graley glacier. Now show me to your lady."

Haldeth dropped the bar with a clank that shook the braces. He had been drinking with sailors often enough to have heard of the Graley, a sparkling, near-vertical couloir whose ridge was always smothered under cloud. "Glaciers?" he said sharply. "Are the passes closed, or has the Corrigon grown so aggressive that the roads are considered unsafe?"

"Both." Orame's lips thinned with the beginnings of annoyance. Since the smith lacked the manners to desist from questions, the wizard stepped aside and sought the chambers of Ithariel on his own.

Haldeth remained standing in the gusts that raked the bailey. He should have known better than to badger a wizard. Plagued by rising uneasiness, the smith called the boys from the forge, then hastened ahead to the kitchens for the ordinary bother of Megga's scolding, and hot soup to drive off chills.

Evening came; Orame stayed on as guest of Whitestorm's lady. By night the wardstone in the watch tower burned a strange and unsettling blue. Haldeth huddled in his blankets, unable to sleep; and the dawn brought a second White Circle initiate asking admittance at the gates. At week's end, the pair became joined by others, bringing the total to five. By the hour that Korendir and his company set foot on the ice beneath the Hyadons, nine enchanters took up residence at Whitestorm. By day and night the keep rang with powers that made the sun-

light shimmer strangely, and the fires burn green in the
kitchen. Megga baked bread in the ovens undisturbed,
but Haldeth was never so complacent. He moved his cot
and blankets into the drafty forge. Waking between
nightmares in the deeps of winter dark, he swore he
would ask the wizards of their purpose. Yet mornings
came, sunlit or gray with snow, and always his courage
failed him. Whether the wizards opened gateways to Alhaerie or meddled with natural progression, dread undermined his curiosity.

The expedition to relieve Arrax labored ahead through
soft snow, and crusted over drifts that grabbed at each
stride, and glass hard, wind-scoured glacier. Gusts ripped
down from the Graley and caught up gouged ice from
the crampons strapped onto each man's boots to prevent
slipping; slivers whirled like crystal into the aquamarine
depths of the fissures. The landscape was white, gray,
and steel-blue, the sky frosty; cold bit into the bones of
the living without reprieve. Days had passed since anyone could remember being warm. High Kelair grew little
timber, and the foothills above the Kashiel valley supported no forest at all.

Each noon the company halted for a meal of biscuit
and sausage, chipped frozen from wrappings cracked to
brittleness. The dwarves sat apart; between them and the
Arrax men lay a rift no common cause might breach.
And the mountain born with their tattoos and sullen silences mingled uneasily with king's men.

Yet when the pitch of the slope forced the company
to pair up, Korendir would tolerate no dissent. The
safety of each life in the party was interdependent upon
the others; only the dwarves were permitted to form separate teams, and these only due to practicality. A man
who tumbled into a crevasse could not be saved if he
dragged his partner along with him. Though tough and
very strong, a dwarf weighed a great deal less than a
mature human. To mingle the races on a perilous traverse would be folly, not when the next step might bring
a collapse of soft snow and a sliding fall into fissures that
plunged to untold depths. A man might break limbs or
spine, or jerk his unwary companion over the brink to
lie mangled beyond reach of rescue.

The valley steepened and the glacier banked upward into a bowl of slashed clefts, capped by snowfields that bore the arrowed scars of avalanche. Worn already from fighting the drifts that mantled the foothills, the rescue party tightened crampons and checked ice axes, and cast doubtful eyes upslope.

The cloud cover had thickened. Indlvarrn the dwarf guide shook an irascible fist at the sky, his brow crinkled into a frown. "Storm moving in," he observed in his gravelly voice. "Have to be under shelter by then, and not in those first few crevasses. Full of seracs, they are, and thaw rotten ice. To bivouac there would be begging to get ourselves crushed."

"Seracs?" called one of the king's men-at-arms. "What in Neth's creation are they, that we should be frightened to shaking?"

Indlvarrn shoved his thumbs under the straps of his rucksack. "Ice peaks, are seracs. And frightened to shaking you will be." The dwarf nodded his fur capped head at the soldier. "Best get on. Storms and nightfall won't wait."

The guide opened a pouch at his belt and selected an assortment of screws forged for purchase in ice. While he issued ropes, harnesses, and other gear, Echend appeared at his side. Under orders to set aside prejudice, he worked with the dwarf, while Korendir directed redistribution of stores from drag-sleds to packs that could be hoisted in pitches through the ascent.

Few men joked through the preparations. Threat of snow set a gloom on their mood; many were sobered further by awareness that from this point forward, their lives must be trusted to a whip-scarred dwarf who had no cause to love humans.

Korendir gave slackers short shrift. The lead team departed. Headed by Indlvarrn, their task was to choose the route, and flag loose footing and hand holds that following parties might proceed with speed and safety. Crags of jutting ice soon hid the three from view. Their progress became marked by puffs of wind-borne snow, and clattering falls of ice fragments; sometimes the acoustics of the mountain returned the clang of Indlvarrn's hammer as he pounded home an ice screw, or the distinctive hiss of rope coils flaking down a precipice.

The ends were caught and used to belay the trailing members of each team. Progress was slow. Rope-length by rope-length, the less experienced climbers followed to a staging camp on an ice ledge. There, under seracs that glistened with the dangerous beauty of swordblades, the same ropes were used to hoist the supply sacks, then the follow-up team gathered in gear and what pins they could recover without undue waste of stamina. After a restorative ration of chocolate, the process was repeated again, and yet again in failing light as snow began to whirl across the Graley.

Korendir anchored the trailing teams through the last pitch. By now the dark had thickened, and wind blasted the ice face in the fury of rising storm. Each hand and foot hold became agony to maintain, as muscles shivered and cramped, and fingers raw from abrasion suffered numbness from cold as well. When failing light marred judgment, and vertigo dizzied the senses, the slope seemed relentlessly sheer. Now was the moment when the nerve which sustained the stoutest hearts at daybreak faltered and threatened to fail.

The wind gusted, demon-shrill; its force gathered until it seemed determined to rip the climbers from the Graley and dash them upon the pressure ridges below. Loosened chunks of debris rattled down and battered a man from his grip. He tumbled, screaming, jerked short as the rope slammed taut. The soldier on belay snarled with strain as his fallen companion spun, whimpering, over an abyss of dark and rushing air. Roped to a ledge to oversee progress from the midpoint, Korendir reached out and grasped jacket. He jerked the man bodily back onto the face, and yelled encouragement as trembling hands scrabbled for new purchase. The rope eased as the man recovered. Above, the teammate who had held through his narrow escape cursed in ragged relief.

"Too close," somebody exclaimed. "Keep on in these conditions, and people are going to start dying."

"Then we'll just have to make Indlvarrn's camp," Korendir called back. To descend would in fact be more dangerous, with the ascent screws removed and the snow silted deep in the hollows. The light had failed to the point where a man could not see to secure ropes.

No one argued the mercenary's decision. All were impatient to press onward, except the soldier who whimpered, paralyzed with panic against the overhang. His partner could not continue until his shaken teammate regained his wits, and ahead, no ledge offered respite for a vertical ascent of thirty yards.

Korendir's response was instantaneous. "Dalon," he called crisply. "You're on your own." His next words commanded the man above to draw steel and cut the belay rope.

That the coward now blocked the only safe retreat from Korandir's vantage point made no difference. Conditions were deteriorating rapidly; trapped between blizzard and darkness, the party could not delay without forfeiting a survival already in jeopardy.

"Move out," snapped the mercenary to the man who led the team. "Don't wait, and on peril of your life, don't turn back."

The climbers resumed their ascent. As ice chips loosened by their crampons rattled down, Dalon unabashedly started to sob. Voices and the scrape of boots became lost in the wail of the wind, and still, Dalon shivered and balked. Korendir made no attempt to cajole him, but waited, motionless in thickening drifts of snow. When the man failed to master his hysteria, he resumed his climb in grim silence, but over an outcrop Indlvarrn had avoided; no choice remained but to risk that route to regain the known upper trail. The bypass became a nightmare, unroped as Korendir was, suspended by torn gloves and determination over a chasm of storm-whipped air. The ice was unforgiving. It resisted the blows of his axe, sent the blade rebounding back against his hand. His palms chafed bloody as the shock of vibration passed down the oaken shaft. The times the blade caught firmly, Korendir hauled his weight from toe-hold to crumbling toe hold, utterly dependent on the grip of his lacerated hands. Almost, he welcomed the pain as distraction from hostile elements as he inched away from the nook where Dalon cowered.

"Soldier!" Timed between gusts, Korendir's voice cut downslope through the storm. "There's hot tea waiting topside, I promise you." –

Dalon returned no answer. With a heart that inwardly

wept, Korendir reached upward, stabbed his axe into a crevice, and abandoned the man to his fate.

In an hour, the storm had worsened; blizzard whipped the Graley with near to annihilating force. Korendir advanced by slow inches, blinded by driven snow. His gloves froze to his axe haft; the feet inside his boots numbed until they dragged at his ankles like dead wood. Slipping from a precarious hand hold, he jammed his sole in an ice ridge. A quarter hour was lost as he worked to jerk himself free. By the time he succeeded, he was shivering and spent. His fingers slid from the cleft where he clung and caught, as if by miracle, on the screw that fastened a rope.

A fixed line had been left, set out of pity by the dwarf guide when he had ordered young Dalon cut loose. Korendir clung to solid, twisted hemp and gasped in exhausted gratitude. By now, the darkness was complete; without that rope to show the way, he could never have found the bivouac. He dragged upward, aching, but feeling discomfort much less in the encouragement of renewed progress. The gusts carried fragmented sounds of voices, then a flare of yellow torchlight; at most, safety and warmth waited twenty feet above. Korendir thought very little of the soldier abandoned behind. What resource remained he focused on that last, most precarious ascent, when strength was at lowest ebb, and impatience might drive him to carelessness.

But the storm and the dark did not triumph. A cheer went up as Korendir reached the ledge. Indlvarrn and Echend caught his wrists, dragged him like a brother over the brink. He was given a place by the coal fire, and hot tea, and chocolate. No one asked about Dalon. When the uproar died down, and tired men crawled under peg-secured canvas to sleep, Korendir waited alone. Wrapped in furs by torchlight, he remained until the snow thinned and stopped. Clouds broke; the silvery light of a half-moon bathed the Graley's lofty heights. Korendir sat solitary under sky. In time his vigil was rewarded. The rope creaked on its peg. A wretched, shivering pair of hands clawed upward from the abyss, followed by a frost-bearded face.

Korendir arose, helped the half-frozen soldier to the ledge, and still without speech, poured hot tea. He stayed while Dalon drank, then offered food and shelter under blankets for rest. Of cowardice, he said no word, nor did any other man, when the camp roused at dawn, and the first to stir noticed the survivor asleep in their midst. Whatever his weakness, Dalon had found his measure by himself in the storm-torn dark. His triumph over fear had taught strength, and a humble, unfailing confidence. He was the first among the king's men to offer to relieve Indlvarrn's overtaxed lead team. Echend and another man from Arrax formed the core of the reserves that spelled the unflagging dwarves.

Days passed in wearing succession. Frostbite and torn skin became themes for rough jokes as men gained competence on the mountain. Ones with less gift for climbing attended the chores at each bivouac, checking ropes and equipment, or carefully rationing the food. The Graley taxed all to their limits. Some days were spent in huddled misery listening to the song of wind and storm; other times, in blinding sunlight, men carved steps and hand holds up cathedral towers of blue ice. Each pitch had its frustrations, its failures, its false trails, and its triumphs.

In the upper heights, the couloir narrowed. The glacier lay rucked into shards and blunt cornices, capped with spotless new drift. Clefts became traps to twist the ankles, and snow dislodged from bad footing could turn and roll, and kick loose grinding falls of ice. The climbers toiled on in the uneasy knowledge that their lives were precariously secured, and dependent upon the frailty of their companions.

The expedition crossed the cloud line and Indlvarrn advised caution. The snow pack on the summit ridge was unstable; but one team gave in to curiosity and strayed. Their footsteps carved faults in the drifts, and the bridge where they explored caved away. The storm-piled mass at the head of the couloir loosened and thundered downslope, sweeping all in its path with a roar. One man was milled under, never to resurface. The other had been roped to a belaying pin before the disaster began, and when the avalanche subsided to a clatter of scoured stone, the king's men traced the line and dragged him free.

Indlvarrn watched with his mouth pursed tight in disapproval. "Better to be rid of that fool," he concluded over the fuss as the survivor was checked for injury.

"You speak of a king's man!" an offended companion shouted back. "Would you dare to mouth insults if the one needing rescue was a dwarf?"

"I'd do better," snapped Indlvarrn. "I'd send him to his maker with my dirk, were any of my race born so stupid."

The dead man's brother bridled at this. Known for strength and quick temper, he rushed the cheeky guide with his hackles raised for a fight. His swing at the dwarf was stopped by the vise-hard grip of Korendir, whose tolerance did not extend to petty feuds; the mercenary looked angry enough to kill outright. He spoke instead, too softly for bystanders to overhear. But the brother's aggression subsided. He retired though dwarves watched his back with unfriendliness.

The king's men clustered to organize spirit rites for the departed; Indlvarrn was informed of their intent while sorting out ropes for rappel lines. He sprang to his feet in agitation, but Korendir reacted first and took on the onus of intervention. This time his words carried to all of the waiting company. No time would be allowed for sentiment. The soldiers broke up disgruntled, somehow still blaming their misfortune on the dwarves. In sullen knots, the men turned toward the valley and the ridge that remained to be crossed.

On the face behind the Graley, summits like upraised knives funneled the wind between ridges. Black banded rocks were stripped bare of snow and polished sheer by weather. Here the company unstrapped crampons and began their first abseil, dropping by stages into a valley swathed in cloud. Gusts set the lines swinging as men rappelled straight down through winter air. Hands still raw from the axe handle suffered rope burns as friction heated through gloves and wrappings and savaged the tender flesh beneath. Bared rock absorbed the sun's warmth, causing melts that glazed a sheen across the crags. Refrozen to glassy hardness, such ice at times seemed bewitched; crampons pulled hastily from rucksacks screeched and skidded. The sharpened steel teeth left score lines, but gained no purchase. Men lost their balance and cracked heads and shoulders against the cliff face. They bruised and cursed and hoped their fellows on belay were prepared for trouble when they fell. As the last team reached the bowl of the valley, the talk swelled boastful and loud. Except for the misfortune of the avalanche, no man's safety had been compromised.

The surrounding Hyadons soared upward with the magnificence of fortress spires; rocky spurs punched through mantles of sparkling ice, to rake clouds that plumed in the bitter cold of altitude. Ahead spread a snow-choked plateau and frozen lake. Vulnerable now to attack by the Corrigon, the men donned cloaks of white wool for camouflage. They clustered to listen while Indlvarrn sketched out their route with stubby, mittened hands. They must cross by night, preferably under cover of storm, when the Corrigon was likeliest to roost.

On the far shore lay boulder fields deposited by some mighty and ancient glacier. Progress there would be treacherous. Drifts masked pitfalls and warm springs glazed over by parchment thin ice. The route wound through a twisty maze of melt-streams. Even in places where winds had stripped the snow cover, dangers awaited the unwary. The largest rocks might turn and fall, and sink-holes laced the land where underground streams had leached off the sediment of moraine. Hidden fissures could swallow a booted leg like trap jaws, macerating flesh and bone beyond hope or healing.

"Misstep, and you're bait for the Corrigon," Indlvarrn warned. "This place has no pity for the injured, so I advise: use your axe spikes, and trust no ground you have not tested thoroughly. Fhingold or I will lead. Use the boot tracks of the man in front wherever you can, and still, check before you shift your weight."

But the weather which had harried their progress up the Graley perversely failed to cooperate. The nights turned diamond clear. Rather than stall and consume stores needed sorely in Arrax, the expedition pressed on. They crossed the lake, nakedly exposed and raked by winds that whistled through the northern escarpments. Tracks marked their progress like a scar. Mountain born traced their faces with luck signs, and soldiers not in the habit of praying appealed to their maker for protection until gusts erased their trail. The dwarves became simply silent; except Indlvarrn, who sat with Korendir through hours of scholarly argument.

All without exception huddled under blankets each

dawn to watch the Corrigon kite skyward from the
ridges. The monster's black-feathered, horn-scaled breast
knifed the winds like old bone. Swift as a crossbow quarrel, it soared in tireless circles and scoured the mountains
for prey. Once it dipped overhead, a yearling bullock
impaled in blood-crusted talons; the animal was still
alive. It thrashed and bawled in pitiable agony. The monster turned narrowed, bead-yellow eyes, then whipped its
head down between wing beats and crushed the beast's
brain in its beak. Men and dwarves, the company
sweated in terror as the predator arrowed away. Confronted firsthand by the monster which afflicted Arrax,
the king's men exchanged whispers, but furtively, lest
Korendir overhear their talk.

Nightfall saw the company on the move once again.
Dragging the supply sleighs, they marched over frost-
blasted tundra, shadowed by a grandeur whose desolation dwindled the soul. Restlessly urgent, Korendir exhorted the stragglers to haste, though the storms returned
and gale winds screamed like curses across the vista of
ice and rock.

The party paused on the rising ground at the far edge
of the valley. There, harried by driving snow, Indlvarrn
ordered teams to rope up for ascent up a vertical gash
in the rockface. That the fourth pitch must route them
within yards of the Corrigon's eyrie was noted by the
king's men-at-arms; several shot glances at their captain.
Korendir noticed. With keenest intuition he assigned the
ones who clustered to separate teams. Now each rope
was led off by a mountain born or a dwarf. They had
most to lose if nerves faltered, and no one needed to
name what would befall any climber who strayed from
protection in the cleft. The Corrigon's insatiable appetite
caused it to hunt during gales; snowfall might hamper its
eyesight, but not its ability to kill.

Slowly, with much trepidation, the party began the
final stage of the journey. Arrax might lie in the valley
beyond the next ridge, but dire were the hazards in between. The fissure was damp, runged with frozen cascades where springs sprang from the rock. Icicles offered
precarious footing. Patterns of freeze and thaw had set
down layers that shattered under the jab and pressure of
crampons; the slate beneath was less trustworthy still,

crumbled with erosion and frost. Indlvarrn drilled his screws well away from such watercourses, but often that precaution necessitated a pitch off the direct route up the cleft. The dwarf guide wormed up slippery overhangs, threaded past seracs riven with cracks. Forward progress stalled while he side-tracked. Men were compelled to wait for untold spans of time, while muscles stiffened, and faces burned numb from the cold. None but the leaders could see to know the reason for delay. Nerves frayed, and tempers shortened, and the strain told the worst upon Indlvarrn. His partner noticed and suggested with utmost tact that Dalon's team head the next pitch.

"What would you do if I refused?" Indlvarrn called from above. Between a blast of driven snow, Fhingold caught a merry smile that belied the attrition of fatigue.

Fhingold framed answer in the same spirit. "Say no, and I'll gnaw through your boots at the ankle. Then here you'd be, pink as a baby and wiggling your toes for the Corrigon."

Indlvarrn returned an epithet torn short by another gust; the back draft wafted a stench of putrified flesh, probably from the carcasses that rotted in the nest up above.

"Dastardly housekeeper," muttered Fhingold. "Birds usually are, Neth in His wisdom knows why."

"What d'you expect from a species born without a sphincter?" Dalon offered up from the ledge below.

Fhingold scraped an itch under his cap and searched for a stinging retort. That moment Indlvarrn shouted warning.

An overwhelming, monstrous shadow raked past. Air sang over taut feathers and overlapped scales of burnished horn. The Corrigon swooped out to hunt, and this time its flight cut too close. Indlvarrn ducked a slashing talon; his axe fell, clanging and showering ice as it tumbled. Startled to instinctive reaction, Fhingold crooked his knuckles and hugged the face of the mountain. Braced with fear, he listened as the scuffle continued above.

Indlvarrn clutched to the outcrop as his body swayed out over air. His glove caught, scraped, and snagged for a second in a cleft. He grunted. His lips pulled back from his teeth as he strained in the effort of recovery. Then

his hold ripped from the mountain. Gravel pelted downward, and Indlvarrn twisted.

"Hang onto me jewels," he gasped as he lost his last
purchase and plunged.

"You'll owe me an ale," Fhingold replied, eyes
screwed shut in anticipation of the moment when the
dwarf guide would fetch against the belay rope. Dread
spared no thought for the Corrigon, which had flown on
to Neth knew where. A safety line had been secured to
the face above Fhingold; but the rock had accepted the
drill too readily for the younger dwarf's liking. He dared
not rely on that anchor to spare the guide's life from
disaster.

His hands scrabbled desperately for purchase as the
safety line whumped taut. The screw ripped out, and the
rope yanked short a second time. Jerked cruelly against
his harness, Fhingold grunted. His feet slithered free,
and his body slammed full length into rock. The last gasp
of breath was wrung from his lungs. But his hands held.
Fhingold disregarded the ache of overtaxed wrists. With
dwarvish obstinacy he set himself to endure for as long
as his companion might require.

But the harness dug into his shoulders for barely a
second's interval. The rope sang short and sharp and then
went ominously light.

Fhingold banged both knees and hastily recovered his
footing. "Dal," he gasped painfully. "Where's Indie?
There's not any pull on the line."

The king's man called up from beneath. "Probably
caught himself. The mountain born swear he's half spider."

But a glance down the face revealed only a tassel
swinging in the wind.

Indlvarrn had gone without a sound.

Heartsore and shivering in reaction, Dalon pulled in
the trailing rope. The plies were sheared cleanly, perhaps
by ice, or more likely by the edge of an escarpment as
the dwarf swung upon impact; except that the damage
looked for all the world like a cut induced by honed
steel. And now the expedition to save Arrax was left in
the wilds without a guide.

XXVII. Corrigon

Jammed shoulder-to-shoulder on the sloping confines of a ledge, the climbers raised voices in dissent. Indlvarrn's fall had splintered a unity flawed from the first, and while dwarves might suspect the safety line had been slashed by a human's knife, men swore the Corrigon was to blame. Arguments festered.

The predator had not flown back for a second pass; if it had, Echend, from beneath, would have seen. "Indie made no outcry. Surely a man skewered by a monster would have screamed in pain or warning."

"Not if the bird snipped his head off with that great, ugly beak," called a king's man. "Remember what happened to the bull?"

The mountain born found this suggestion preposterous; they made their opinion plain by crossing to stand with the dwarves. More teams arrived. Angry men packed more tightly together, and as news of Indlvarrn's fall reached the newcomers, grudges resurfaced with freshened vigor. The king's men spoke of turning back. Whether by accident or design, the guide's death offered them excuse; the Hyadons by themselves were murderous, and the lair of the Corrigon too close. A thieving dwarf might slip by alone, but not a company of fifty men. Any fool could see that the town beyond the ridge was inaccessible.

The dwarves shook their fists. "Murderers! Slave trappers!"

Other less savory insults mingled with rejoinders from the mountain born, who scorned that the rations for starving kinfolk should be squandered by soldiers who had no better honor than to flee home to the hearths of their mothers.

The trailing teams reached the ledge just as the king's

captain took umbrage and a fight started. Fhingold
shoved forward to tear the combatants apart, and a bystander with a dagger took a slice at him. Fhingold
ducked clear, and ducked again to avoid Korendir, just
arrived, and driving through the press with bared steel.
The offender with the knife was knocked sprawling, half
paralyzed by a kick that had seemingly arisen from nowhere; Korendir had not unstrapped his crampons. Neither had he lightened his blow to compensate, but instead
swept down his sword and laid the edge to the fallen
man's throat.

The soldier gasped in his pain, but carefully; each
spasm of his windpipe drew blood against the blade that
bore steadily against his flesh. He regarded the hand of
the mercenary with his eyes ringed white with fear. The
scrap between mountain born and captain ended abruptly
of its own accord. Before the look on Korendir's pale
face, even Fhingold edged back toward the warmth of
his fellows.

The mercenary's gaze swept them all: the dwarves in
their grease-stained leathers, the tattooed features of the
mountain born, and the surly lowland soldiers whose
king had commanded them to a duty too harsh for the
asking. Lastly, he glanced at the wretch on the floor
whose bleeding leg and stifled, agonized sobs raised
plumes of condensation in the air.

"What a sorry pass we have come to," Korendir said.
The sadness behind his words did not show, only the
anger, cold as death, and as pitiless. He did not appeal
to reason, for generations of prejudice understood none;
neither did he plead for reconciliation. What rapport he
might have fostered with king's men had withered on the
Graley, when urgency had disallowed pause for a funeral
rite.

The silence stretched on and became brittle. Korendir
had no intention of inviting dissent by volunteering his
opinion. Stung to disadvantage by a command tactic he
knew all too well, the king's captain spoke in defiance.
"I say we strive for a useless cause. The people of Arrax
cannot possibly last the winter on our pitiful store of
supplies. If we survive to reach the town, what then? We
couldn't leave. Only offer ourselves up to starve, or add
to the mouths taking food from children. If, I say, this

Neth-forsaken mountain and the Corrigon don't kill us first." The captain raised his stubbled chin. "The dwarves and the Arrax born may do as they wish, but no man in my company will die of foolishness. We lost our luck on the Graley and now we have no guide. By my order, the king's men-at-arms go no further."

His determination rooted a new brand of quiet in the party gathered within the ice cleft. Argument could not reunite them, Korendir sensed at once; to speak of suffering children would just wed each side the more firmly to a course that must end in disaster. Instead, in nerveless detachment, the Master of Whitestorm sheathed his sword. The offender sprawled at his feet accepted reprieve with a whimper. He scuttled to rejoin his fellows where, pointedly solicitous, the captain helped him to his feet.

Korendir rejected the inuendo, that misdirection had brought them to impasse. "A dog team can reach the coast in five days," he contradicted crisply. "Relief could reach Arrax in a fortnight, and properly rationed, the supplies we deliver might be stretched to last for a month."

"All true," the captain allowed, but smugly. "Except for the Corrigon, of course."

Korendir returned a look like a whetted blade. He gave no sign that his patience was spent. Always more loner than leader, he announced his own style of countermeasure. "Then by dawn tomorrow, I'll give you the Corrigon's death. Failing that, you may each do as you please. Otherwise, *as a company*, you shall all press on to Arrax."

The captain gained no space for rebuttal. Korendir gathered up crossbow and quarrels, a quarter flask of ale, and an ice axe. He slipped out into the whiteness of the storm before anyone present had fully grasped the impact of his promise.

Fhingold was first to recover. "My ancestors would weep for shame, that one man should be left to go these cliffs alone. Will we stand here stunned while he tries to slay that horror by himself?"

"Won't find me stopping him," retorted the soldier whose leg stung yet from the effects of Korendir's reflexes. "If that madman from Whitestorm seeks death for the glory of Arrax, I say let him."

Fhingold disdained answer and reached for his tattered gloves. He was joined by Echend, and after a moment, by the steadfast presence of Dalon. Quietly the three assembled their gear. The eyes of the others stared elsewhere; not a man or a dwarf in their number was not diminished by Korendir's brave challenge. Families might languish in slavery, or children starve, but dread of the Corrigon shackled all but one dwarf, one Arrax man, and one soldier who held a mercenary that kept faith in higher regard than his captain.

Lights seared the dark from Ithariel's chamber each night since Orame's arrival. Rays speared like blades from the casements of the upper tower, shining and silver as moonbeams, but bright enough to blind any mortal who lingered too long in awed wonder. That nine White Circle enchanters raised their powers to generate the phenomenon brought scant comfort to Haldeth. Huddled on his cot in the forge, and muffled under blankets and counterpane, he strove to escape into dreams. Yet sleep would not come. His feet went sweaty and cold by turns, and the hours dragged without relief.

The smith rolled over yet again. He kicked at an offending fold of blanket and stubbornly forced himself still. The familiar tang of iron and woodfire failed to lull his senses to forgetfulness. When the first, creeping sensation that he was not alone pricked at the nerves along his spine, Haldeth screwed his eyes closed and concentrated upon the whine of the wind across the eaves.

He would not yield to the impulse that urged him to shove back the bed clothes and rise.

In time that early, inward suspicion became an itch; Haldeth clamped his fists between his knees. The particulars of the weather outside suddenly acquired critical importance. Focused on the moment the next gust would peak, he considered prayer, while the itch became an ache, then swelled into compulsion that stung his mind like a burn. Finally harried past conscious volition, the smith flung off the covers.

"You sleep soundly," Orame commented from the

dark. His robed form shifted like shadow against the cherry glow of the forge coals.

Hot where he had earlier been cold, Haldeth kicked clear of his bedclothes. The knife he kept to trim leather tumbled out, unsheathed, from the cranny between mattress and forearm. The pommel struck with a clang that condemned on the swept stones of the floor.

"Remarkable you should sleep at all, for a man whose distrust abides with him even in bed." The enchanter gestured disparagingly. "That lump of a crossguard looks hefty enough to put your back out."

It had in fact done exactly that, but Haldeth was too flustered to retort. That magic had made him uneasy in the first place was reason enough to be peevish. "What do you want, wizard?" The smith ducked the sorcerer's look of rebuke by raking the hair from his brow. An afterthought troubled him. "And you didn't waken me."

"Certainly not." Deceptively agreeable, Orame flicked one hand. The forge coals flared up into flame. "I wish you to dress yourself, master smith. In precisely one hour a midwife will come calling at the gate. Someone must be up to let her in."

Haldeth shot upright in his quilts and a rip in the patchwork loosed a puff of goose down in the draft. "Midwife? Who for? Ithariel's due to bear at spring equinox, not solstice. I know we've had blizzards, but hasn't your pack of conjurers bothered to look out and check the stars?"

Orame shrugged. "What does a star know? White-storm's daughter, now, she will be naming her own hour."

"Neth forsake us, not three months early." Haldeth swiped at a drifting bit of lint. He missed.

The feather shot aside in the rush of disturbed air, then angled through the space which should have been occupied by Orame. But the wizard had silently disappeared.

The smith muttered the rude phrase he should have thought of earlier; then he swung his feet from sweaty sheets and stood erect. His first step set him skidding on the haft of his forgotten knife. He escaped being skewered in a fall, but consoled himself without expletives. Shaken at last to straight thinking, Haldeth interpreted

the only possible reason for Ithariel's labor to defy
nature.

His heart missed a beat from comprehension.

When the curses came, they were each and every one
for the Master of Whitestorm, and whatever lofty folly
had sent him on a harebrained chase into the Hyadons
to slay the Corrigon.

Korendir must have forsaken the ice cleft immediately
after his departure; at least Dalon had been unable to
overtake him, or find any trace of human passing as he
set off to lead the first pitch. Behind came the grieving
Fhingold, and Echend, who had given his Name, and
intended to honor the significance of the deed whether
he died in the attempt. Snow swirled off the heights,
blindingly dense, and without any sign of abating. Visibil-
ity closed down to inches during gusts, when the white
of blown drifts added to the flakes already falling. Conditions were too severe to locate a man alone on the mountain, Dalon knew this. He shifted grip on his axe and
scrabbled under snowfall to find footholds. Pursuit of
Korendir at this point was stubborn folly, with darkness
nigh and not so much as a track to affirm their purpose.
Yet when the team of three paused in a cranny to rotate
leaders, no one suggested turning back.

"I say we climb past the Corrigon's lair, then traverse
the open slope," suggested Echend. "He'll be there, if
he hasn't fallen, and my feeling is that he won't."

"Not that one." Dalon slapped his glove in frustration.
"But after dark, how will we know the place where the
Corrigon nests?"

Fhingold snorted. "You can't smell it?" He scrubbed
his knuckles over the ice which fleeced his eyebrows, that
his frown of contempt not be wasted. Each gust since
noon had carried the stink of putrescent meat; only a
stone-headed human could miss it. But the soldier and
the mountain born could hardly be ranked among the
selfish, if they would venture up these rocks in a blizzard.
The dwarf adjusted his harness and relented. "Anyway,
Indlvarrn's notes were very clear. The ice near the Corrigon's lair will be streaked with frozen blood."

"How reassuring." Dalon glanced through falling snow

to Echend, and received an unsmiling affirmation. "Off we go, then, to yon haven of stench in the clouds."

"Not funny, soldier." Echend flicked the belay line clear of his knees and shouldered forward to lead. "Not funny at all, when by dawn all our bones might be beak fodder."

"Hell," muttered Fhingold as he jammed up his snow-crusted hood. "Better that than drink coward's broth with the rest of them."

Echend hauled himself with a chink and a grate of crampons into the teeth of the storm. "Hope you still feel that way later, dwarf."

Dalon waited while the diminutive, broad-shouldered bundle tackled the ice face ahead of him. "Just hope we're alive to feel anything at all. Damn Korendir for recklessness, I say we make him stand us to a barrel of jack cider. The night we get down off these peaks, I definitely want to get drunk."

Conversation died after that, as the climb demanded total concentration. Here the cleft was choked with icicles from melt streams, and springs which seeped from the rocks. The footing was rotten and undependable; Echend, leading, had to test and triple test the screws he set for his safety rope; the water had frozen in layers that faulted at the slightest bit of pressure. The only relief to offset the dangerous ascent was the fact that the storm began to slacken. Snowfall tapered off, and the gusts subsided to the barest whisper of a breeze. Clouds drifted clear of a sky vaulted aquamarine and citrine in the after-glow of sunset, and silence settled over the mountains. Uncanny and complete, it enfolded the climbers in comfortless isolation. Companions, warmth, and memories of family and home seemed more like a dream in the midst of waking nightmare.

The cleft narrowed. Coarse-grained slate closed until even Fhingold, who had labored in mines, cursed the confines and the dark. The climbers wedged between butting stone walls and clumsily fumbled off crampons. Here hands had to scratch to find holds, and ropes looped the ankles, or turned under bootsoles, a constant and much cursed impediment.

The chimney narrowed, showed the sky as a deepening slit of cobalt at their backs. Clothing scraped and tore on frost-split quartz, and even leather gloves sprouted holes like old socks at the fingertips. Dalon slipped and wedged his shin; minutes were lost as he tried to work free, an interval of worry made miserable by the over-powering taint of carrion that wafted down the shaft. Threaded through rotten meat came another smell, rank enough to make the stomach turn.

"Stinks like damned old gull spatters in here," muttered Echend, to whom things of the sea were thrice hated.

In process of jerking off sweat soggy gloves with his teeth, Fhingold enunciated thickly, "That has to mean we're close." The gloves ripped free. He added more clearly to Dalon, "Catch this and pass it under your knee."

A line uncoiled in the darkness and lashed the low-lands swordsman in the cheek. His voice echoed faintly up the shaft.

Gravely smiling, Fhingold waited until the blasphemies stopped. "Ready, Dal?"

A rustle issued from below. "Yes, may the frostbite shrivel your member at the roots."

Fhingold clamped the line around chapped palms and heaved something more than gently. Cloth tore, and Da-lon's jammed knee scraped free.

"Hellfire, Fhin. Ye've ripped my breeks. Want me to perish of the draft?"

The dwarf slacked the line and set after restoring his gloves. "Watch the frostbite."

Bruised and scuffed and angrily determined, Dalon bound up his ripped leggings. "Next time you want a whore, I'll buy for us both. We'll see then who lasts the night."

Fhingold stifled a bark of laughter and scrambled to continue the ascent. "Got a wife who'd outlast us both, you giant. If she ever gets free of the mines. Five years, it's been, since my woman's seen the sun."

Which reminded them both of Korendir, somewhere ahead in his solitary quest to slay the Corrigon. The fis-sure cut deeper into the mountain, became yet more nar-row and crooked. The climbers moved blind, shut off from any glimmer of sky. For what seemed hours their existence became limited by grunts of exertion, the scuff of boots over stone, and the bone-deep ache as exhausted muscles dragged the body from cranny to crevice to the skin-rasping stone of shallow ledges. Twice they blundered up shafts that ended in cul-de-sacs of blocked stone. Tortuously they doubled back, worked around, started over. Echend continued to lead because Fhingold had no space to scrape by to relieve him.

At long last the terrain opened up again. The clouds had cleared off the face. Mare's tails marked the air where the winds met the thermals off the valley, entangled with stars like sequins. Elsewhere the heavens were sapphire. Night enfolded the Hyadons and shadowed the saw-toothed cut where two stubborn men and one dwarf emerged.

The summit rose up in front of them, a serried pinnacle mantled under pristine ridges of snow.

Dalon, last out, crammed back his cap and scanned the vista with narrowed eyes. "Neth! What happened to the Corrigon's lair?"

At silence from the dwarf and the mountain born, he turned and surveyed the route mapped out by Indlvarrn. Beneath the cleft, the terrain fell steeply to form a gully, chiselled by the assaults of uncounted winters and seamed by prying frosts. The jutting shoulder of an outcrop cradled eddied snow, and also a log jam of timbers inconsistent with its setting. Like a festered scar underneath ran the cleft that had sheltered their ascent. Dalon shuddered. The shaft they had climbed in damp darkness had been no true cave at all. The crevice had been blocked, not by rock, or ice, nor even the frozen seep of spring waters, but by a jumble of horrific debris that had no place in the clean winds off the peaks.

The truth was shatteringly revealed: *Indlvarrn's route had sent them through a seam that cut directly beneath the Corrigon's nest.*

Dalon recovered a shivering breath of air. Cold clawed his lungs, made his sinuses ache, and he clenched his teeth through an interval of outraged futility. "We've overshot," he gasped in an amazement that was half compounded with fright. The thought followed that Korendir must inevitably have done the same.

"Not there." Nervelessly practical, Fhingold scanned the upper slopes and pronounced them empty. "The man

had to have known about the nest site. He probably
never entered the cleft."

Echend could not help voicing the other possibility.
"Unless he fell."

But all of them remembered crossing the chaotic vista
of the plateau; evenings, exhausted from the day's trek,
they had huddled against companions to share warmth
that perpetually seemed inadequate. Each one recalled
falling miserably asleep to the sound of voices, Korendir's and Indlvarrn's, exchanging Neth only cared what
ideas through the purpled shadows before dawn. Dwarf
guide and mercenary had debated every irrelevance from
crop growing to treatises on experimental navigation.
Echend did not read. Fhingold had been born a slave in
the mines, and Dalon was solely a swordsman; only a
fanatic or a scholar would have bothered to follow those
overheard snatches of conversation. Too late, on a desolate upper scarp in the Hyadons, two men and one dwarf
recalled that Indlvarrn Keth'sget was at heart a hunter
and forester. The deceit behind his ruse was unraveled
painfully late, that in fact he had been revealing the route
to the mercenary from White Rock Head; but the particulars had been shared with no one else.

"Our company would've balked on the Graley, else,"
Echend concluded for all of them. "Sky and storm, I'd
have let them, if I'd guessed our path would cross within
spit of a Corrigon's nest."

Only Fhingold stayed silent.

"You knew," Dalon accused suddenly. Sharp, even
hostile with suspicion, he spun on his dwarf companion.
"Your talk of blood-flecked ice was just lies. You could
have warned us where the route led, all along!"

A fatalist to the end, Fhingold shrugged his resignation. "I'd hoped Korendir didn't know, and that we'd
find him blundering about on the summit." As Echend
stiffened, lividly offended, the dwarf added, "Neth's
damnation on you, man, there was nothing at all we
could do if we tried to go topside! One sword or four
against the Corrigon quite simply adds up to suicide. For
the freedom of my kind, and the survival of your children, I hoped we'd find our mercenary above the chimney. Then we might've talked him back to scare sense
into those whining dogs below."

Echend snapped back a contradiction. "Not that one. Got a mind as set as a priest's tattoo, and never one thought of a compromise. Damn you, dwarf, we trusted you! Give us a line for rappel down to the nest, or I swear I'll draw steel and unwind your guts for the purpose."

"Too late," Fhingold said, and he pointed.

The waning moon had edged over the saddle above the Graley. Light polished the snowfields and snagged black swaths of shadow off buttressed escarpments; the wildest range of the Hyadons stood revealed in unspoiled splendor, except where oiled steel flashed reflection and vanished into dark. Guided by that anomaly, and by Fhingold's dwarvish eyesight, Dalon and Echend could just make out a figure crouched on the face. Korendir had discarded his crampons at the edge of the ice. His sable jacket blended almost invisibly with the slate which jutted beneath the monster's eyrie. Dalon drew breath to argue that they still might have time to descend when steel flashed again. Both men saw the Master of Whitestorm arch out over windless air, set his foot, and cock his crossbow.

Moonlight fell also on jumbled timbers, reeking and blackened with spills of old blood. It silvered splinters of white that were the bones of countless kills, and shone also in eyes like faceted quartz, but vicious, and deathly cruel. The Corrigon raised its head. Horny scales glimmered in crescents as, watchful, its hooked beak turned toward the glint of metal on the slope that abutted its nest.

"Almighty Neth," breathed Dalon.

Echend fumbled after the amulet he wore strapped to his wrist.

Fhingold did nothing but stare, heartbroken, for upon the frailty of one man rested the freedom of his wife and race. To watch that hope die was worse than any loss he could contemplate.

Korendir stared upward into the ice-splinter gaze of the Corrigon. If he trembled, no man was near enough to see. The wire-wrapped string of his crossbow caught on the trigger latch with a clear, metallic ping.

The Corrigon ruffled its crest feathers. It bobbed once, then unfurled black wings with a gusty rush of air. Its

terrible cry shivered over the valley as it thrust horned
legs and launched aloft. The twenty-span breadth of its
primaries raised gusts that plumed the drifts; one beat,
two, and it cleared the ridge. Korendir was lost in whipping drafts of blown snow. Clothed in a nightmare grace,
the adversary he swore to destroy soared and banked in
a tight arc, then drove direct for his position, a scythe
that carved downward to kill. The moon etched scales
and feathers with a beauty that had no mercy, as sword-
sharp talons rose to rake and impale.

That moment, Korendir notched the bolt; one had
time to recall that although he seldom smiled, he never
failed to be courteous. He endured through what seemed
the impossible by exhibiting courage that daunted, and
then most pitilessly inspired. He dealt both life and death
with a precision that repeatedly seemed inhuman, and
yet, they all knew—the mountains stripped a man to his
naked, most grasping self—Korendir did not risk for
fame. He did not belittle with his competence; he had
no pride in him at all. Only Echend had seen him in his
chosen setting, with wife and son in the home left behind
at Whitestorm; almost, the mountain born had missed
the compassion that shaped the man. Nearly too late he
had offered Name, only to have his honor forsworn by
the misdirected mercy of a dwarf.

Dalon wept, shattered to shame by recognition. The
manhood he had earned on the Graley, here in the Hyadons seemed dwindled to insignificance by the act of one
fool with a crossbow.

For the breast of the monster offered no target. No
steel-tipped quarrel ever forged could pierce those un-
godly scales. Korendir endured, perhaps hoping for
opening to fire into the softer tissue beneath the wing;
but even an accurate shot to the heart could not possibly
kill in time. The mercenary would be plucked from the
rock and skewered, and not even miracle might save him.

In the instant the Corrigon swooped, Fhingold alone
managed speech. Impelled beyond grief for kinsfolk still
shackled in slavery, he howled his abject despair. "What
are my people, and the children of Arrax, to be worth
such sacrifice as this?"

His cry rang out over snowfields, swelled by a sorrow

that shattered Neth's most perfect quiet. Distracted, the Corrigon turned its head.

Korendir squeezed his trigger. The crossbow fired with a whap and a hiss of taut cable through air. The bolt leapt out, a needle against the blue dark of the abyss.

It struck the monster in the center of its eye and stabbed on through to the brain.

The great wings clapped down in spasm. Primaries whipped and closed an arc that sheared up snow from the slope. Ice crystals whirled like smoke, and the beak clashed closed with a crack. Korendir flung himself flat. The crossbow dropped from his hand. Steel fell, turning in rhythmic flashes, lost into shadow as the Corrigon crashed against the peak.

Feathers crumpled and snapped, and scales grated shrilly over stone. The body of the monster hit with a thud of burst bones against slate, and also the vulnerable, exposed, and helpless human body that comprised the measure of its bane.

Korendir of Whitestorm took the brunt of the Corrigon's fall. Hammered into rock by the force of momentum and mass, he was smashed and then ripped from his hold. The slain beast rebounded and tumbled, a crushed mass of sable and scarlet. Like a mote, the man fell with it.

"Neth," choked Dalon. "Oh great Neth."

Numbly Echend drew his dagger and scratched a cross of shame over the tattoo on his forehead. His blood ran, fell in drops on stainless snow, while far below, a great evil and a tragic loss plunged in a shared rush of air toward the distant valley.

One had time to remember that Korendir of Whitestorm had not failed this, his final contract.

Fhingold crumpled with his cheek against ice and wept. Blind with tears, overcome with sadness and a conflicting release of joy too overpowering to deny in the same moment, he was the only one of the three who missed the searing flash. Light ripped out of nowhere and obliterated the smaller of two falling rags of black.

When the disturbance cleared, the corpse of the Corrigon tumbled alone to final impact.

*   *   *

The horrified scream of the midwife echoed over the wind-battered towers of Whitestorm. Waiting with his guts clenched in tension, Haldeth recoiled against the balustrade that headed the stair beyond the lady's chambers. Sorcery burned like a beacon from the slit beneath the door; dazzled, sweating, and harrowed by unnatural dread, Haldeth could bear ignorance no more. Knowing surely was better than this shredding, tormented strain. He unhooked the latch and flung wide the chamber door.

Chaos met him, a confusion of searing light, shot through with steam from basins that brimmed with heated water. The midwife screamed again, and someone, possibly Orame, snapped out a reprimand to quiet her. From the far side of the place where the bed should be—Haldeth strained to see through the hedging brilliance of sorceries—a child hiccoughed and wailed.

Someone arose with a bundle that squirmed amid bloodied sheets. Confused by contradictions of brightest light and bleak shadow, Haldeth hurried forward and tripped.

His fall threw him headlong into a spell-circle woven by sorcerers, just as the counterbalance to the miracle of Ithariel's early birthing flashed and achieved full fruition.

"We have him!" cried Dethmark's newmade Archmaster. He rose from the dark in one corner and raised hands that seemed rinsed with white light.

The floor flooded with illumination that swelled for a heartbeat and faded. Ordinary candleflame remained to reveal a bundle, sprawled on a carpet still traced like a battleground with runes and sigils of spent power.

Haldeth blinked. As his aching eyes adjusted, he made out a jacket of sables sewn skin side out, and sodden scarlet; then a wisp of bronze hair. Korendir. His clothes were raked into ribbons, the flesh beneath not spared; his chest was ripped through with jagged white ends of bone. His sword hand was a bruised mess of pulp, and his legs. . . . Haldeth shut his eyes against sight and his lips against an uprush of sickness.

But friendship compelled him not to run. Numbly, the smith shuddered upright. He clawed forward with intent to fetch blankets. Somebody had to veil the wretched mess on the floor from the wife still weakened from childbirth.

And yet solicitude occurred too late. Already Ithariel inquired in tired words from the bed.

"Quickly!" shouted Orame.

Someone began to sing. Her clear tones were matched by others, and enchantments arose once again. The resonant powers of the White Circle burned higher and flared through the chamber like flame.

Haldeth forced open stinging eyes. He beheld Korendir's face, still perfect and undamaged. Gray eyes matched his gaze with a look of searching clarity. The lips, very blue, struggled without breath to frame sound.

"Let them know." Korendir fought through a wilderness of pain to be understood. "Corrigon slain. For the sake of the children of Arrax. Tell Nix that his breathren—"

Haldeth squeezed the fingers of the left, the sound hand, and nodded through a wretched ache of helplessness. "They'll know," he assured. No more could he force through the pressure that closed his throat. Through a scalding rise of tears, he watched the man whose unique abilities had seen him free of slavery turn and seek the woman on the bed. Korendir's failing eyesight encompassed the form of a beloved face, then abandoned the light of the living.

"We can still save him," insisted Orame. Light shone steadily between his fingers and traced the scene dazzlingly blue. "Ithariel, call his name."

The Lady of Whitestorm responded as if in a daze. Propped in a nest of crumpled pillows, flushed yet from the exertion of childbirth, she encompassed the lacerated flesh that rested loose-limbed on her floor. One moment she looked, then averted her eyes and shook her head. "What would you be calling him back to?"

Orame regarded her, wordless. And the spells he held poised for instant action faded and flickered out between his palms. He waited a still moment, then nodded. Around him, the enchanters broke their circle of concentration and filed in silence for the door.

"No!" Haldeth's protest pealed out over resignation and set the newborn crying. Into the gathering dark, he pleaded in hoarse-voiced desperation. "His wife and two children, are they not enough?"

Ithariel regarded him sadly. Her eyes, so like crystal,

more than ever seemed to reflect those depths and mysteries the smith had never grasped. Gently, the enchantress let him down. "We were always enough, Haldeth. That's why my beloved went against the Corrigon, and why, if he returned, he would leave us when they asked for him again."

"I don't understand." Haldeth crashed a fist against his thigh. "Who in Aerith would dare ask? After this, who could ever argue he'd earned his peace?"

But the lady did not seem to hear; Orame, whose tireless work had accomplished all for this bitterest surrender, answered for her. "He would, of himself, master smith. Since Shan Rannok, Korendir has never been other than driven by his gift of compassion."

Shivering with long, incongruously fine fingers cooling between his hands, Haldeth drew breath to offer protest: life itself was justification enough, never mind the legacy due the children left a parentless inheritance at Whitestorm.

But Orame stopped the smith with a glance like winter frost. "Could you have Lindey and your two girls back, would you, if they lived knowing fate must repeat itself? They never suffered the cruelties of survival after murder. Would you teach them your fears, entangled in reaction to memories you could never forget, but only master?"

Haldeth gasped as if he had been kicked.

Unnoticed above him on the bed, he did not see the Lady of Whitestorm raise welcoming eyes toward the doorway left open at his back.

XXVIII. Epitaph

Ithariel's fingers unwound from the sheets wadded up in her hands. The ruined flesh that stained the weave of her carpet in one heartbeat ceased to have meaning. Sorrow transformed, and mourning absolved, for he awaited her in the shadow past the threshold.

Korendir still wore black. That could never change, not now; but his face was smiling in an unselfconscious bliss that had never been his throughout life. His eyes were very clear and wide. Like the open sea, or sky at summer dawn, Ithariel thought. An upwelling surge of affection made her push impatiently at blankets that suddenly seemed to burden her like shackles.

"Are you coming with me, beloved?" Korendir raised two unblemished hands. A hint of purest mischief suffused his expression as he tilted his head. "We had a wager, and you lost, I think."

Ithariel laughed. She slipped from the sheets and stepped onto a floor that was not cold, and did not run with fresh blood. She ran one step, two, and the pain of a difficult childbirth fell behind her. In the doorway she threw herself into the arms of her husband. For the first time she could remember on his return from campaign, she did not bash her hip on his sword hilt as he lifted her strongly and spun her.

"She is Shayna, after your foster mother," Ithariel whispered, naming the daughter that his love and Orame's determination had bequeathed them. Though the emptied body that remained on the bed was forgotten in the ecstasy of reunion, her words were heard by a white-haired smith and a dark, weary enchanter. These left the comfort of an orphaned newborn to the midwife. In homage they closed the woman's eyes. Then they knelt before the mangled remains of a legend and wept for grief.

The White Circle built a tower for them, of the native quartz that veined the cliffs on White Rock Head. When the structure stood completed, the wizards fused the blocks with the combined brilliance of their powers. Ithariel's wardstone they reset into a beaten gold cradle at the top, above a name plaque forged by the dwarves. The memorial faced the western sea and reflected the sun like a beacon for mariners bound for ports to the south and north. The children, Callin and Shayna, Haldeth raised at Whitestorm under the carping supervision of Megga. As adults they would choose whether they wished to claim apprenticeship with the White Circle masters at Dethmark.

But ten years after the date engraved on the capstone, on the eve when the elder of two grown apprentices celebrated marriage, it was not the children of Whitestorm that Haldeth thought of when he retired beneath the tower with a bottle of Faen Hallir's best wine. The old smith set his shoulders against the stone, which somehow on the chilliest nights never seemed to harbor cold. He listened to the repetitive boom of the breakers and regarded the stars and drank, while the young and the invited guests from Heddenton feasted and celebrated in the bailey.

Haldeth thought of the pair just married, the flush of young love and innocent anticipation of joy; as always when the wine softened his guard, he fell into recollection of his family. The anger and the grief never left him, that two daughters murdered by Mhurgai should never know feasting and marriage.

The smith snorted wryly to himself. All his days he had berated Korendir for fleeing the nightmares of the past.

Shayna and Callin remained; and a grouchy old smith who finally admitted that his obsession for quiet had bought loneliness. He had suffered Mhurgai slavery rather than die, and shunned what he called useless risk. In the end, he endured, but never recovered courage to forget. He could not even bed a whore without being haunted by the screams, two daughters and a wife butchered wholesale.

Haldeth took a pull from the bottle. The wine warmed his mouth, and settled a glow in his gut, but on this night the alcohol hoarded its magic. His maudlin mood would not lift. He wondered whether the children grown to maturity at Arrax remembered the name of the man who had saved them. For the relief expedition had gone on to cross the Hyadons and deliver their hard won supplies. Echend, for honor, had personally sailed back to Whitestorm to bring word. From his people he left a sigil stone to stand by Korendir's grave; the same slate marker that Haldeth employed for a seat, and which always seemed damp, never failing to aggravate his arthritis.

The wine was nearly gone. Haldeth wedged the bottle between his knees and sighed. Years late, he sensed the irony of Whitestorm's legacy. Too old, he suspected that Korendir had transcended the nature that had killed him; at the end the mercenary from White Rock Head had found something more lasting than walls of impregnable stone. Growing aged within the shelter of towers that would never know ruin, Haldeth wished he had argued less hotly. Had he clung less to reason, and listened better to fear, the mystery might not have escaped him.

He might have understood his closest friend.

Haldeth raised his flask and belted down the bitter dregs. "I wish I knew your secret, you stubborn lunatic," he muttered to the empty dark. "I'll die one day, and I still won't."

A step sounded on the stair which led to the tower. Haldeth started drunkenly and turned his head. "Who's there?"

A wave broke loudly on the shore, obscuring the name the man returned. He was young, clad in a cloak of scarlet wool. Haldeth did not recognize the trappings, but the odd silhouette was a giveaway. The angled bulge of the instrument beneath the visitor's arm identified the young harper who had played in celebration for the wedding.

"Wine's all gone, boy." Haldeth shrugged with unwarranted sharpness. "And sure's I'm here, there's not a young woman to kiss."

The harper took gruffness in stride and sat on the moss

that nobody had time to scrape from the merlons of the battlements. Without rancor, he said, "It's not a young woman I seek."

Haldeth spun his empty bottle away. It skittered with a rattling clink and wedged beneath the gargoyle Callin had carved on his eleventh birthday. The thing had no beak, because the wood split, and the eyes were crooked as a thief's.

The smith sighed, his mind still half in the past. "What then? I've got no ear for pretty notes."

The harper reached out and touched the sealed stone of Korendir's tomb. "You knew him," he said softly. There was reverence in his tone.

Haldeth raised his head. His untrimmed hair tousled in the breeze off the sea as he answered with rare honesty. "I didn't. I lived with him though, and often wished I hadn't." Grief seeped through his bitterness. Probably because of the wine; under his breath, Haldeth cursed the grapes of Faen Hallir.

But the harper seemed not to hear.

"I didn't come just to play for this wedding," he went on, as if Haldeth were listening and sober, and not thinking through his stupor that the boy seemed somehow familiar. The recognition both frightened and disturbed.

At the smith's continued silence, the harper shrugged with sudden diffidence. "I was born in Arrax," he admitted. "The people of the town paid my passage. They sent me to make a ballad to commemorate the life and the deeds of Korendir, Master of Whitestorm."

"You don't sound like an Arrax brat," Haldeth observed bluntly. "Every mountain born I ever saw had tattoos like women wear dresses."

The boy's fingers drummed on his harp. He grinned without embarrassment and settled back against the tomb. "My mother wasn't native. She came from the coast just north of here, where she met my blood father. I learned when my step sire got drunk once that she'd been a sailor's doxie."

"Black haired," Haldeth said quickly. "With dimples and a way with the cards. I knew one like that once." He did not add that she had left him and stolen with her one oversized cut glass ornament that once had adorned the figurehead of a Mhurgai galley. On this night, the memory was too painful.

"Tell me about Korendir," urged the harper. "I want to know his adventures before he slew the Corrigon and saved Arrax and freed the dwarf slaves from the mines."

The sea boomed and broke against the cliff base. Haldeth thought back to a time when ice floes had made a death trap of the harbor. After years of silence and a reputation for surly refusals, he decided on impulse to give in. If the children of High Kelair had not forgotten, perhaps he owed Korendir that much.

"The Mhurgai took him prisoner," Haldeth said, for he knew no other way to start. "It should begin there."

The smith was hoarse by the time he finished. Cold sober now, and chilled despite the shelter of the tomb's enchanted stone, he sat and watched the sky brighten with dawn. By his side, still maddeningly fresh, the harper picked out his first stanzas. The boy had a gift for verse. If his melodies were a bit overdone, time and imperfect memory would smooth out the pompous ornamentation; the result might be poignant enough to survive.

Haldeth shifted his stiffened frame as the sun slanted around the tower's base. He glanced aside at the harper, who was swarthy, and frowning, intent in concentration over his strings. His tired fingers missed an easy note. He cursed, and the harp shifted. Light caught and splintered scarlet in the unwieldy jewel set in the boss by the tuning pegs.

The square cut bauble was painfully, wretchedly familiar. There could never be more than two of them on this side of the ocean, not unless the Mhurgai forswore raids and stopped sailing.

Haldeth placed a palm over his belt buckle, which held a matching stone. He interrupted the spill of music before he thought to hold his silence. "Where did you find that ruby?"

The harper's hands flattened and stilled an arpeggio of plucked notes. "Ruby?" He tossed back tangled hair. Then his puzzlement lifted and he laughed. "You mean glass." His supple fingers traced the silver which cradled the stone in its setting. "Silly thing's worthless, if the robber of a dwarf who peddles gems in Arrax speaks words a man can trust. I never bought the thing. It was given to me by my mother, who won it at cards from a traveller.''

Too pale, and sweating out the throes of a particularly nasty hangover, Haldeth stared at the boy. In daylight, the resemblance that had haunted through the night seemed obscured. This harper had dark hair, like the Heddenton whore the smith had shared a winter with so many years in the past. The eyes were different, and the chin, but perhaps the hands were not. The glass gem kept its secret. Through watery eyes, Haldeth acknowledged that perhaps, as final gift from Korendir, he might look upon his own grown son.

The coincidence was too much to bear.

"Boy," Haldeth said gruffly. "I warned you I'd no ear for tunes. After too much wine, I've got less. Take your harp, and your strong voice, and move them elsewhere. Leave one sorry old man to suffer his headache in peace."

The boy raised his brows in a way that caught at the heart, so alike was the mother's expression of reproof. The harper was her child, beyond doubt. Young, unmarked as yet by life, he departed without song or words.

Alone and more comfortable for it, Haldeth watched the waves at the beach head unravel into rolling scarves of spume. The echo of his past question to Ithariel seemed repeated in the endless crash of surf. *Could a man be worth so much?*

So much that she would take him in full recognition of her loss, and still find joy before heartbreak; Haldeth thought upon the young harper, and wished he had the humility to call him back.

Now, shocked past the sting of old irony, Haldeth pondered the memory of Ithariel's reply. For the first and last moment of his life, he understood that Korendir had remained true to his nature, and died for it.

Haldeth saw too clearly that he had lost himself on the night the Mhurgai attacked his loved ones. He should have died on the swords of his enemies in the moment they laid hands on his wife. Afterward, shattered beyond reprieve by his guilt, he had never again risked the question, never tried to discover who or what he might become if he reached and sought the riddle that might redeem him. And so he survived, and cursed the shade of his departed friend.

The ballad written this morning might finish on the slopes of the Hyadons in winter; but death would not claim the last word. Endings did not happen with such clean simplicity. The future was shaped upon the moment that had preceded, back to Neth's first creation.

Callin would take up his father's sword. He had tried since the first time he was old enough to stand upright and yearn toward its peg on the wall. Quiet, enigmatic Shayna would initiate with the enchanters at Dethmark, and the legacy of Korendir and Ithariel would extend through the next generation.

Still the world's wheels would turn, and always Haldeth would weep because he was only a smith, and never enough the brash hero to forgive his past failure and call back the harper to compare dates.